THE GRAPHIC NOVEL
Charles Dickens

ORIGINAL TEXT VERSION

Script Adaptation: Seán Michael Wilson
Pencils: Mike Collins
Inks: David Roach
Coloring: James Offredi
Lettering: Terry Wiley
Associate Editor: Keith Howell
Design & Layout: Jo Wheeler & Jenny Placentino
Publishing Assistant: Joanna Watts
Additional Information: Karen Wenborn

Editor in Chief: Clive Bryant

A Christmas Carol: The Graphic Novel
Original Text Version

Charles Dickens

First US edition published: November 2008
Reprinted: April 2011, May 2013, July 2015, December 2017, November 2019, January 2022

Library bound edition published: January 2012
Reprinted: December 2017, January 2022

Published by: Classical Comics Ltd

Acknowledgments: Every effort has been made to trace copyright holders of
material reproduced in this book. Any rights not acknowledged here will be
acknowledged in subsequent editions if notice is given to Classical Comics Ltd.

All enquiries should be addressed to:
Classical Comics Ltd.
PO Box 177
LUDLOW
SY8 9DL
United Kingdom

info@classicalcomics.com
www.classicalcomics.com

Paperback ISBN: 978-1-906332-51-8
Library bound ISBN: 978-1-907127-40-3

This book is printed by Graphy Cems, Spain using environmentally safe inks, on paper
from responsible sources. This material can be disposed of by recycling,
incineration for energy recovery, composting and biodegradation.

The publishers would like to acknowledge the design assistance of
Greg Powell in the completion of this book.

The rights of Seán Michael Wilson, Keith Howell, Mike Collins, David Roach, James Offredi
and Terry Wiley to be identified as the artists of this work have been asserted in accordance with
the Copyright, Designs and Patents Act 1988 sections 77 and 78.

Contents

A Christmas Carol

Dramatis Personæ

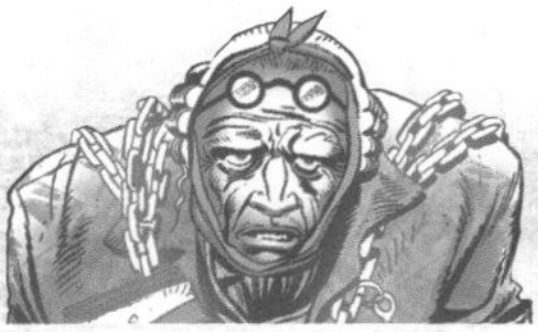
Ghost of Jacob Marley

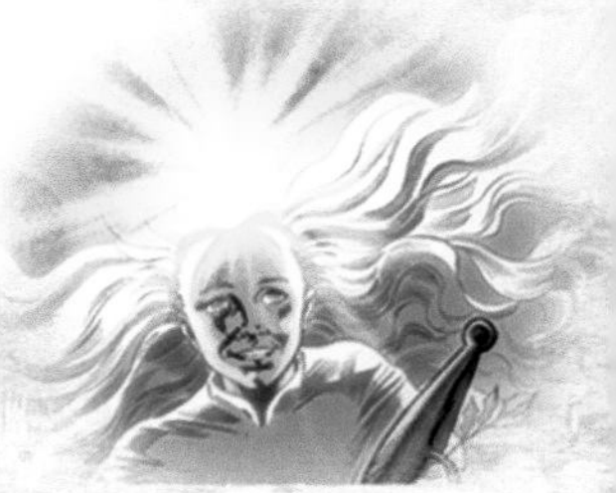
Ghost of Christmas Past

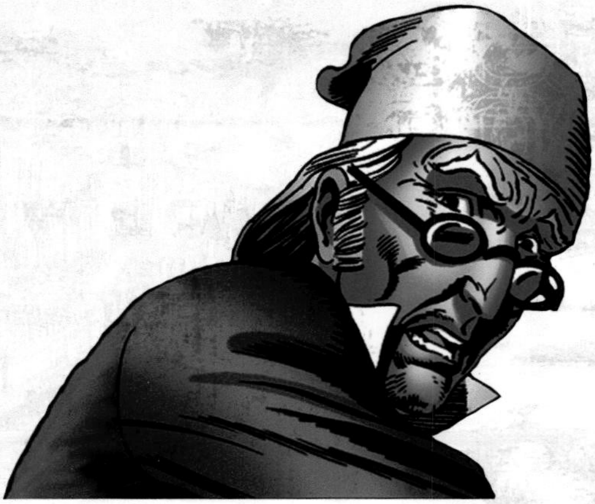
Ebenezer Scrooge

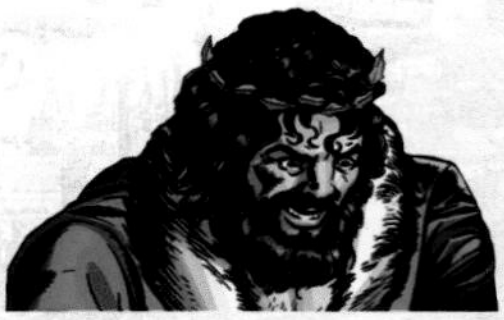
Ghost of Christmas Present

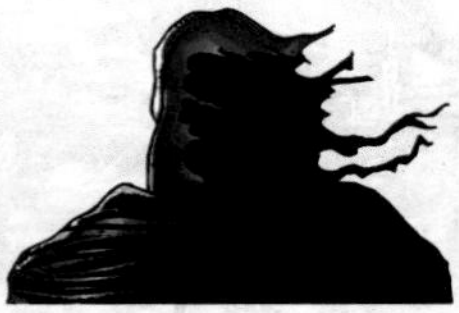
Ghost of Christmas Yet to Come

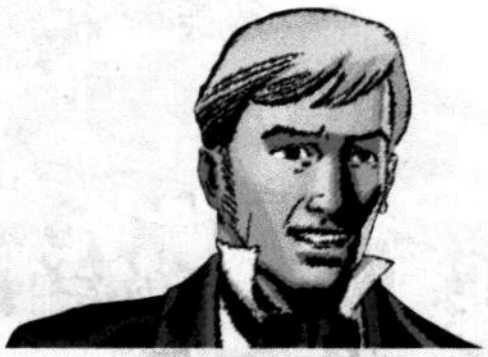
Bob Cratchit
Scrooge's clerk

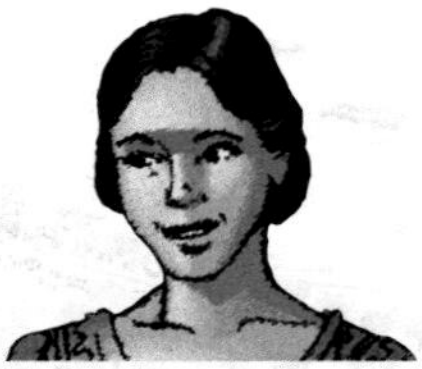
Mrs. Cratchit
Bob's wife

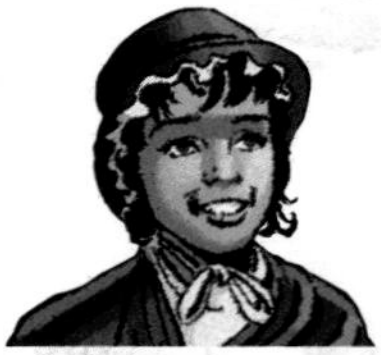
Martha Cratchit
Bob's eldest daughter

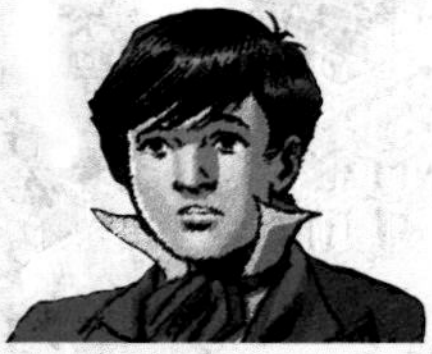
Peter Cratchit
Bob's eldest son

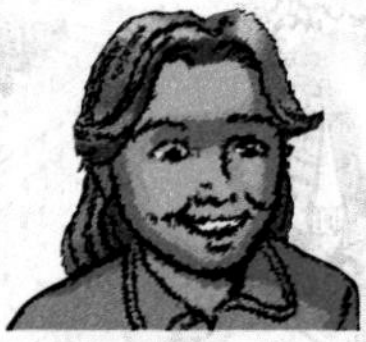
Belinda Cratchit
Bob's second daughter

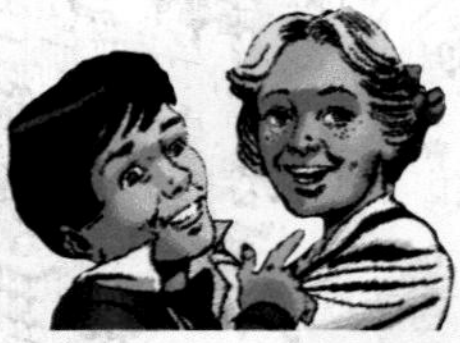
Cratchit children

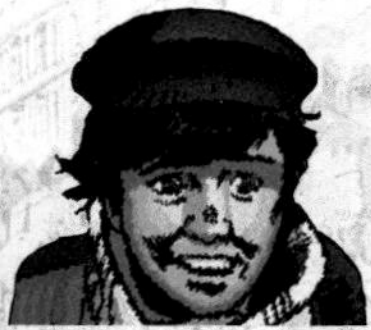
Tiny Tim Cratchit
Bob's youngest son

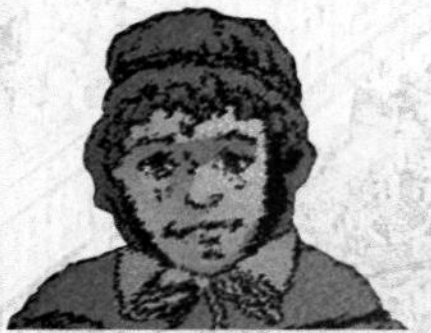
Fan
Scrooge's sister

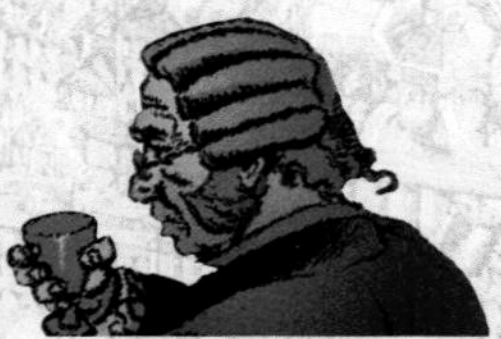
Schoolmaster

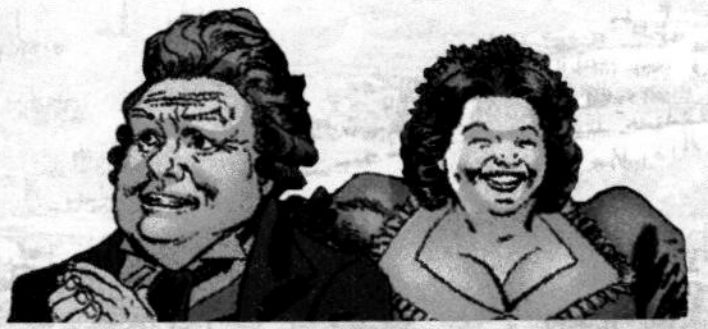

Mr. and Mrs. Fezziwig

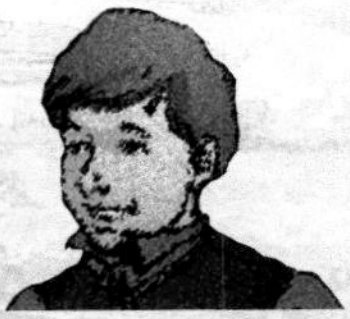

Dick Wilkins
Scrooge's fellow apprentice

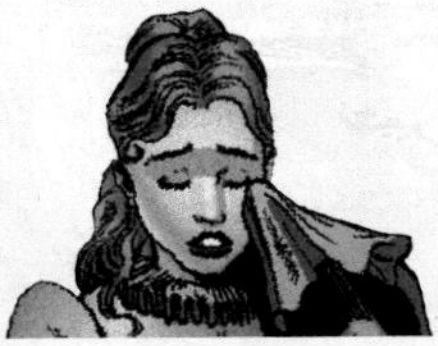

Belle
As a girl

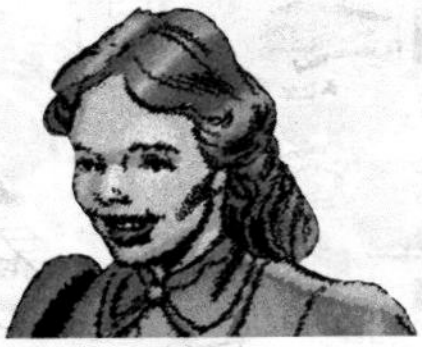

Belle
As a married woman

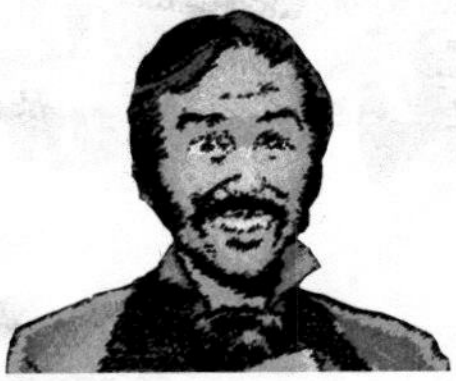

Belle's husband

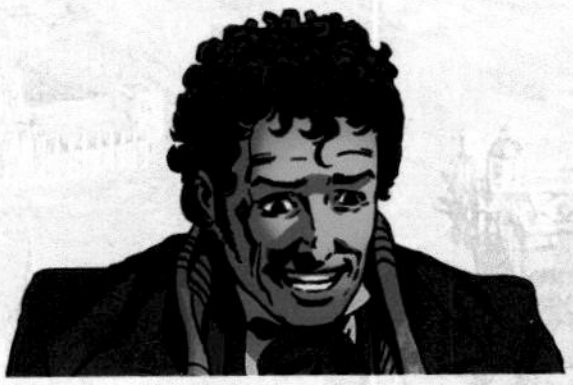

Fred
Scrooge's nephew

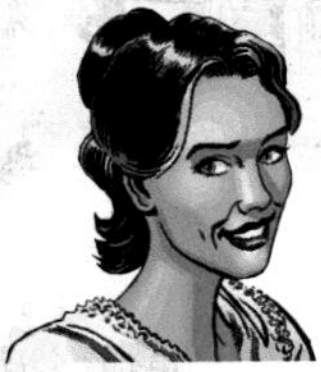

Alice
Fred's wife

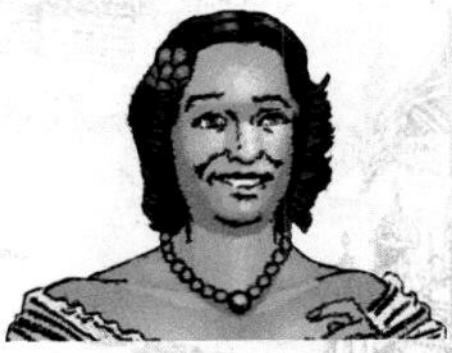

Alice's sister

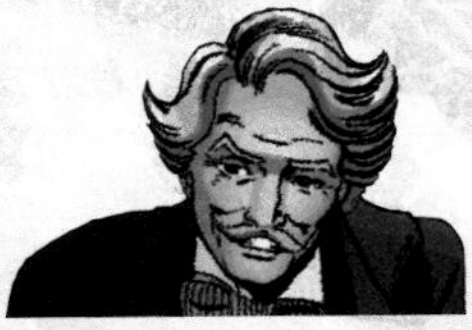

Topper
Friend of Fred

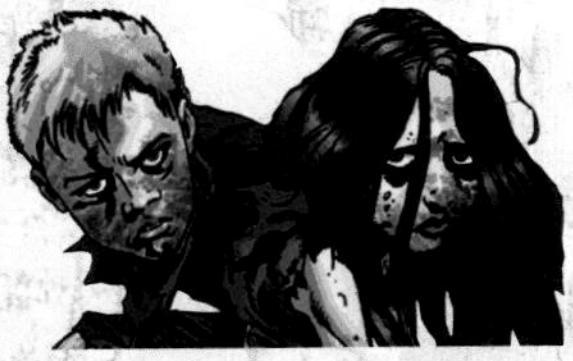

Ignorance and Want

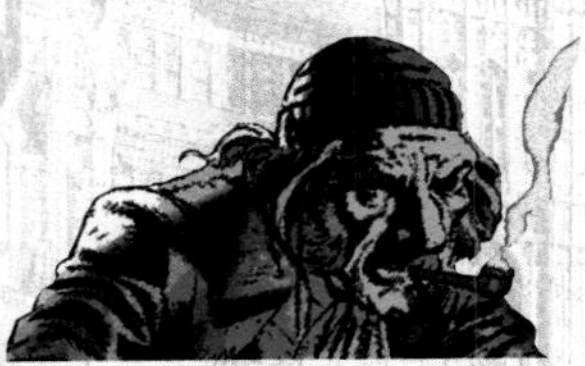

Old Joe
Pawnbroker

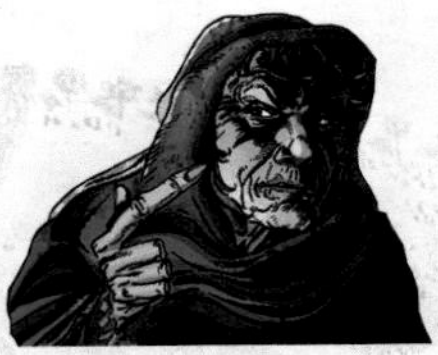

Charwoman

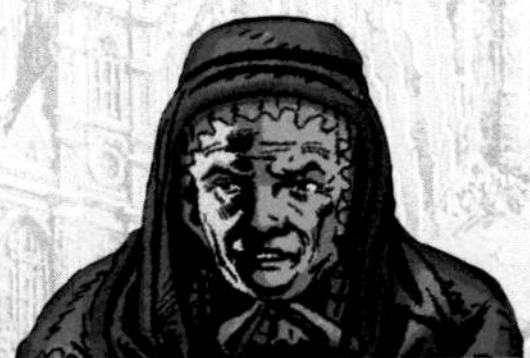

Mrs. Dilber
Laundress

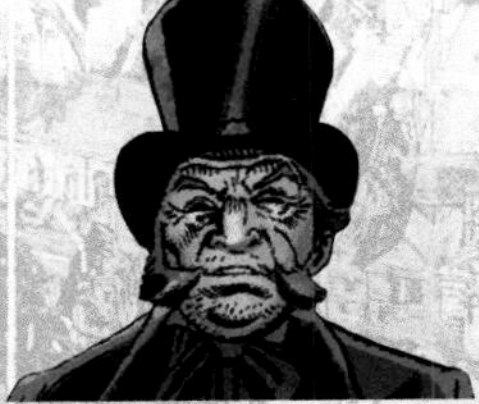

Undertaker

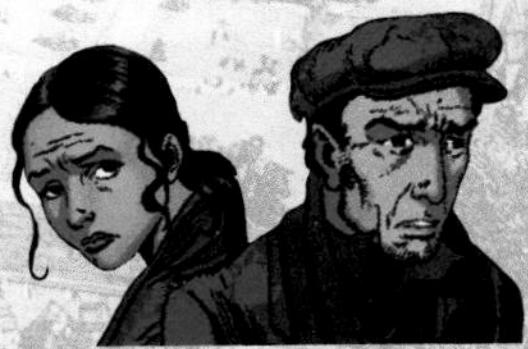

Caroline and her husband

A Christmas Carol

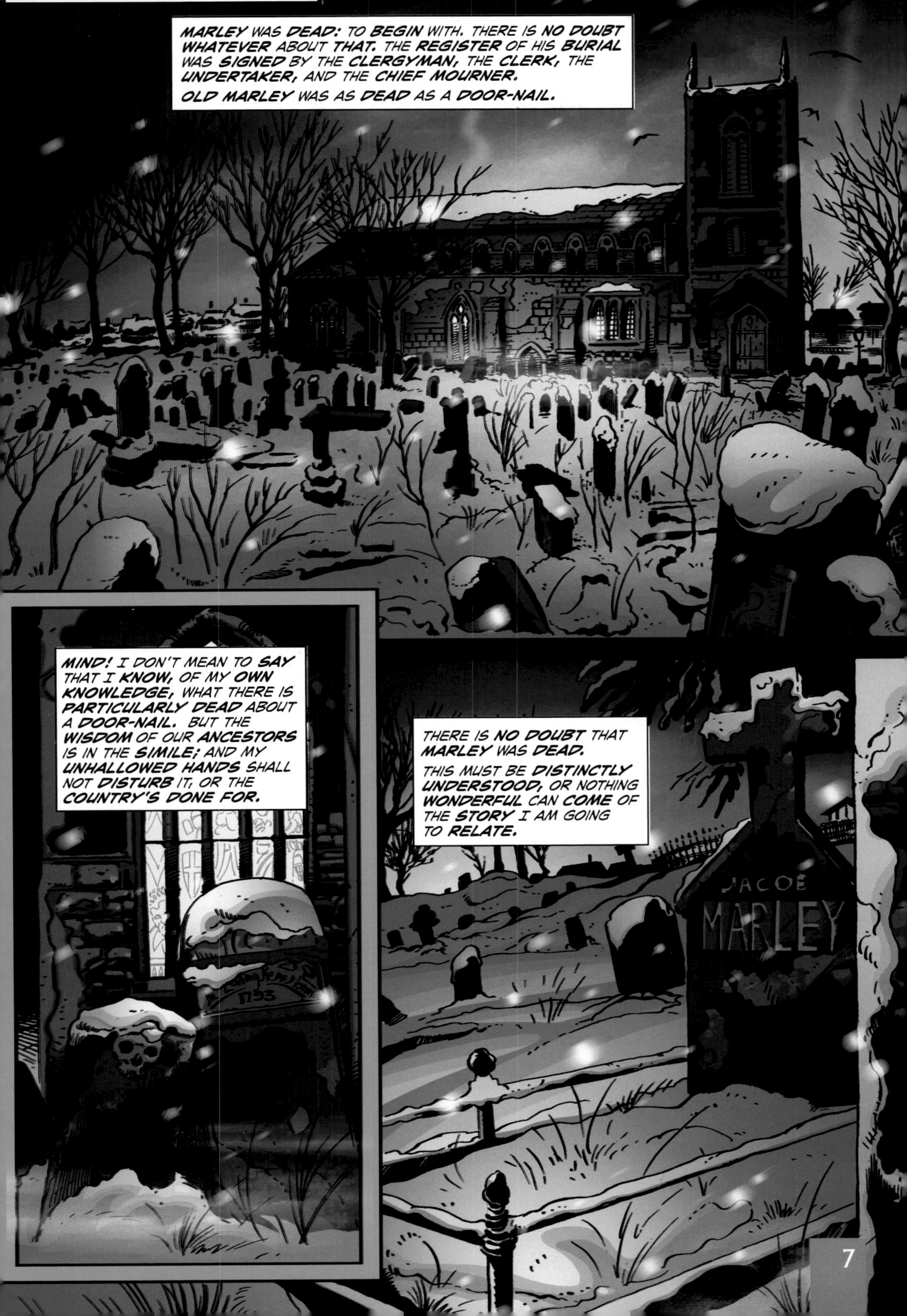
MARLEY WAS DEAD: TO BEGIN WITH. THERE IS NO DOUBT WHATEVER ABOUT THAT. THE REGISTER OF HIS BURIAL WAS SIGNED BY THE CLERGYMAN, THE CLERK, THE UNDERTAKER, AND THE CHIEF MOURNER.
OLD MARLEY WAS AS DEAD AS A DOOR-NAIL.
MIND! I DON'T MEAN TO SAY THAT I KNOW, OF MY OWN KNOWLEDGE, WHAT THERE IS PARTICULARLY DEAD ABOUT A DOOR-NAIL. BUT THE WISDOM OF OUR ANCESTORS IS IN THE SIMILE; AND MY UNHALLOWED HANDS SHALL NOT DISTURB IT, OR THE COUNTRY'S DONE FOR.
THERE IS NO DOUBT THAT MARLEY WAS DEAD.
THIS MUST BE DISTINCTLY UNDERSTOOD, OR NOTHING WONDERFUL CAN COME OF THE STORY I AM GOING TO RELATE.
JACOB
MARLEY

SCROOGE AND HE WERE **PARTNERS** FOR I DON'T KNOW **HOW** MANY YEARS.

SCROOGE WAS HIS SOLE **EXECUTOR,** HIS SOLE **ADMINISTRATOR,** HIS SOLE **ASSIGN,** HIS SOLE **RESIDUARY LEGATEE;** HIS SOLE **FRIEND,** AND SOLE **MOURNER.** AND EVEN **SCROOGE** WAS NOT SO **DREADFULLY CUT UP** BY THE **SAD EVENT,** BUT THAT HE **SOLEMNISED** IT WITH AN **UNDOUBTED BARGAIN.**

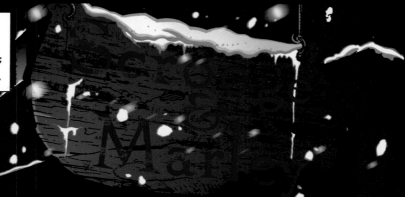

SCROOGE **NEVER PAINTED OUT** OLD MARLEY'S **NAME.**

THERE IT **STOOD,** YEARS **AFTERWARDS,** ABOVE THE **WAREHOUSE DOOR:**

OH! BUT HE WAS A **TIGHT-FISTED HAND** AT THE **GRINDSTONE, SCROOGE!**

A **SQUEEZING, WRENCHING, GRASPING, SCRAPING, CLUTCHING, COVETOUS, OLD SINNER!**

THE **COLD WITHIN** HIM **FROZE** HIS **OLD FEATURES,** NIPPED HIS **POINTED NOSE,** SHRIVELLED HIS **CHEEK,** STIFFENED HIS **GAIT;** MADE HIS **EYES RED,** HIS **THIN LIPS BLUE;** AND SPOKE OUT **SHREWDLY** IN HIS **GRATING VOICE.**

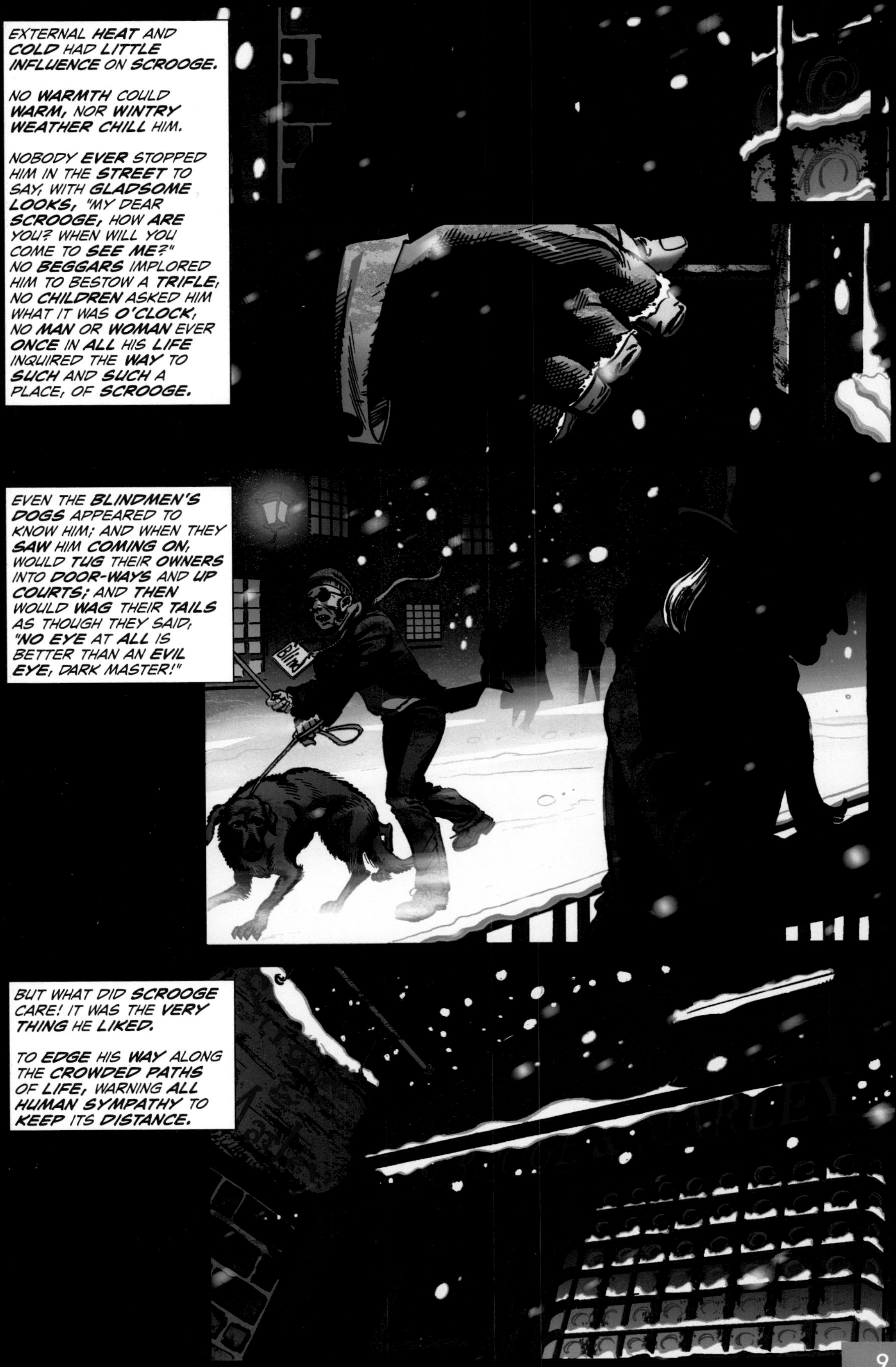
EXTERNAL HEAT AND COLD HAD LITTLE INFLUENCE ON SCROOGE.
NO WARMTH COULD WARM, NOR WINTRY WEATHER CHILL HIM.
NOBODY EVER STOPPED HIM IN THE STREET TO SAY, WITH GLADSOME LOOKS, "MY DEAR SCROOGE, HOW ARE YOU? WHEN WILL YOU COME TO SEE ME?" NO BEGGARS IMPLORED HIM TO BESTOW A TRIFLE, NO CHILDREN ASKED HIM WHAT IT WAS O'CLOCK, NO MAN OR WOMAN EVER ONCE IN ALL HIS LIFE INQUIRED THE WAY TO SUCH AND SUCH A PLACE, OF SCROOGE.
EVEN THE BLINDMEN'S DOGS APPEARED TO KNOW HIM; AND WHEN THEY SAW HIM COMING ON, WOULD TUG THEIR OWNERS INTO DOOR-WAYS AND UP COURTS; AND THEN WOULD WAG THEIR TAILS AS THOUGH THEY SAID, "NO EYE AT ALL IS BETTER THAN AN EVIL EYE, DARK MASTER!"
Blind
BUT WHAT DID SCROOGE CARE! IT WAS THE VERY THING HE LIKED.
TO EDGE HIS WAY ALONG THE CROWDED PATHS OF LIFE, WARNING ALL HUMAN SYMPATHY TO KEEP ITS DISTANCE.

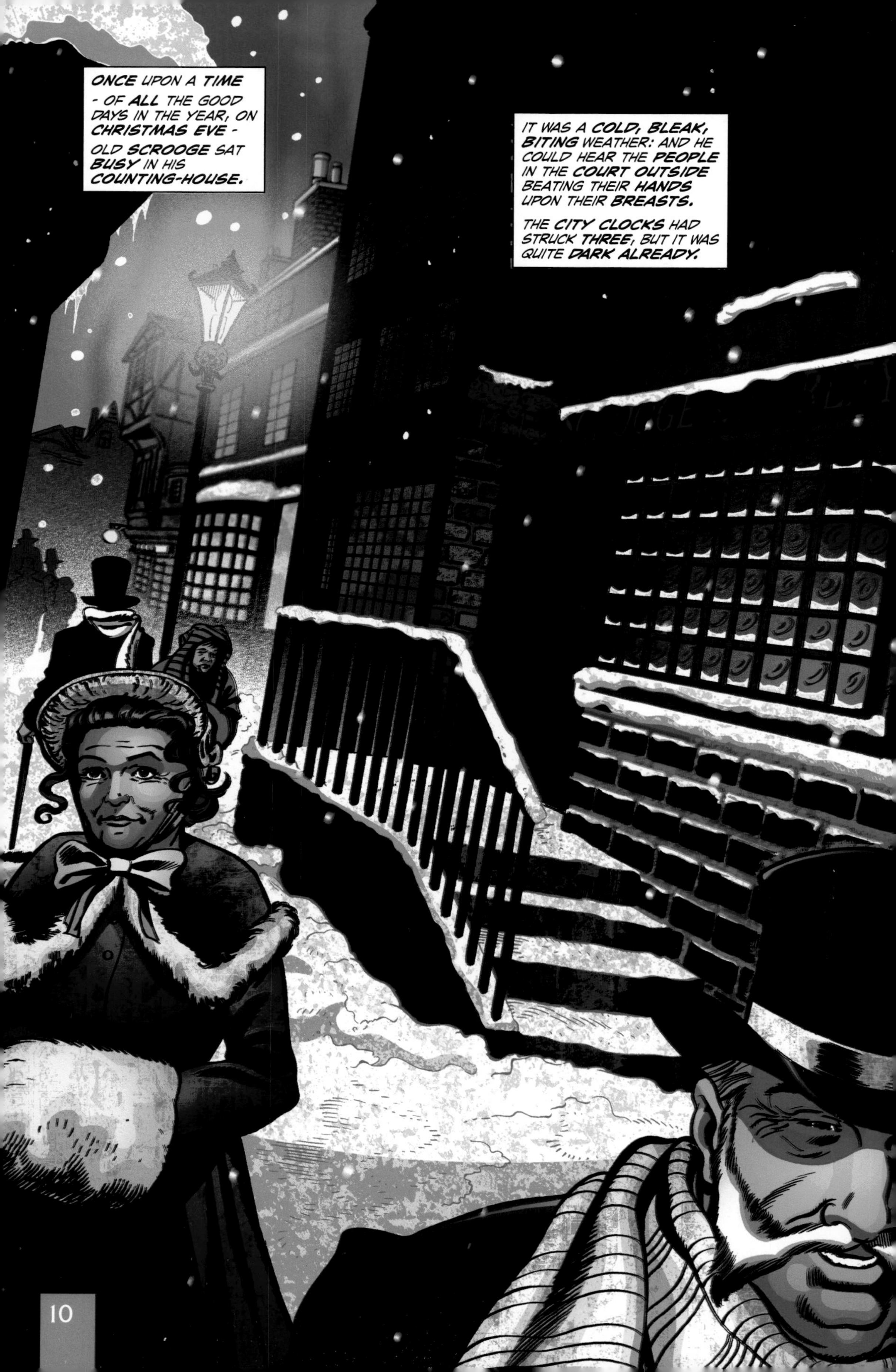
ONCE UPON A TIME - OF ALL THE GOOD DAYS IN THE YEAR, ON CHRISTMAS EVE - OLD SCROOGE SAT BUSY IN HIS COUNTING-HOUSE.
IT WAS A COLD, BLEAK, BITING WEATHER: AND HE COULD HEAR THE PEOPLE IN THE COURT OUTSIDE BEATING THEIR HANDS UPON THEIR BREASTS.
THE CITY CLOCKS HAD STRUCK THREE; BUT IT WAS QUITE DARK ALREADY.

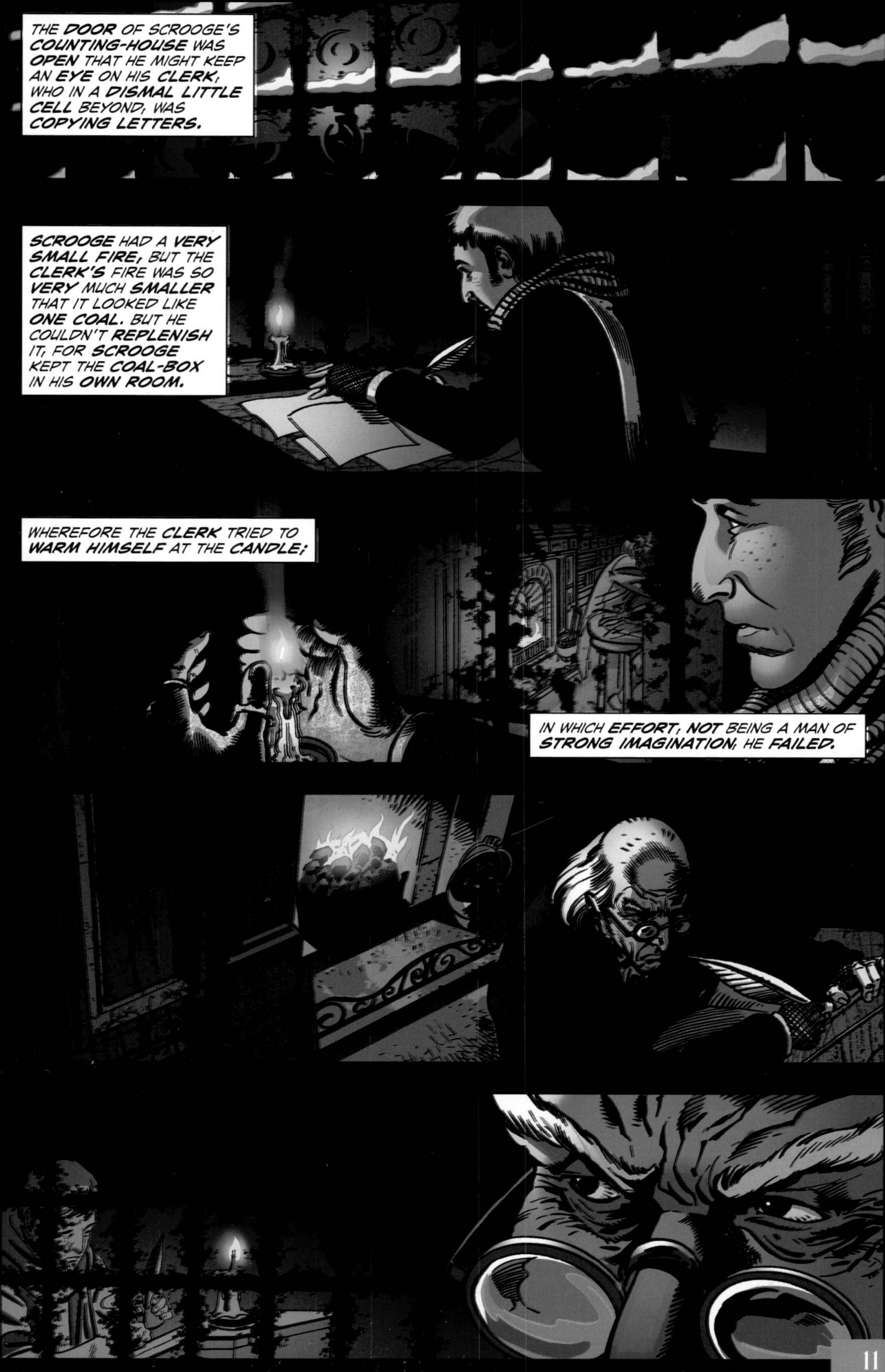
THE DOOR OF SCROOGE'S COUNTING-HOUSE WAS OPEN THAT HE MIGHT KEEP AN EYE ON HIS CLERK, WHO IN A DISMAL LITTLE CELL BEYOND, WAS COPYING LETTERS.
SCROOGE HAD A VERY SMALL FIRE, BUT THE CLERK'S FIRE WAS SO VERY MUCH SMALLER THAT IT LOOKED LIKE ONE COAL. BUT HE COULDN'T REPLENISH IT, FOR SCROOGE KEPT THE COAL-BOX IN HIS OWN ROOM.
WHEREFORE THE CLERK TRIED TO WARM HIMSELF AT THE CANDLE;
IN WHICH EFFORT, NOT BEING A MAN OF STRONG IMAGINATION, HE FAILED.

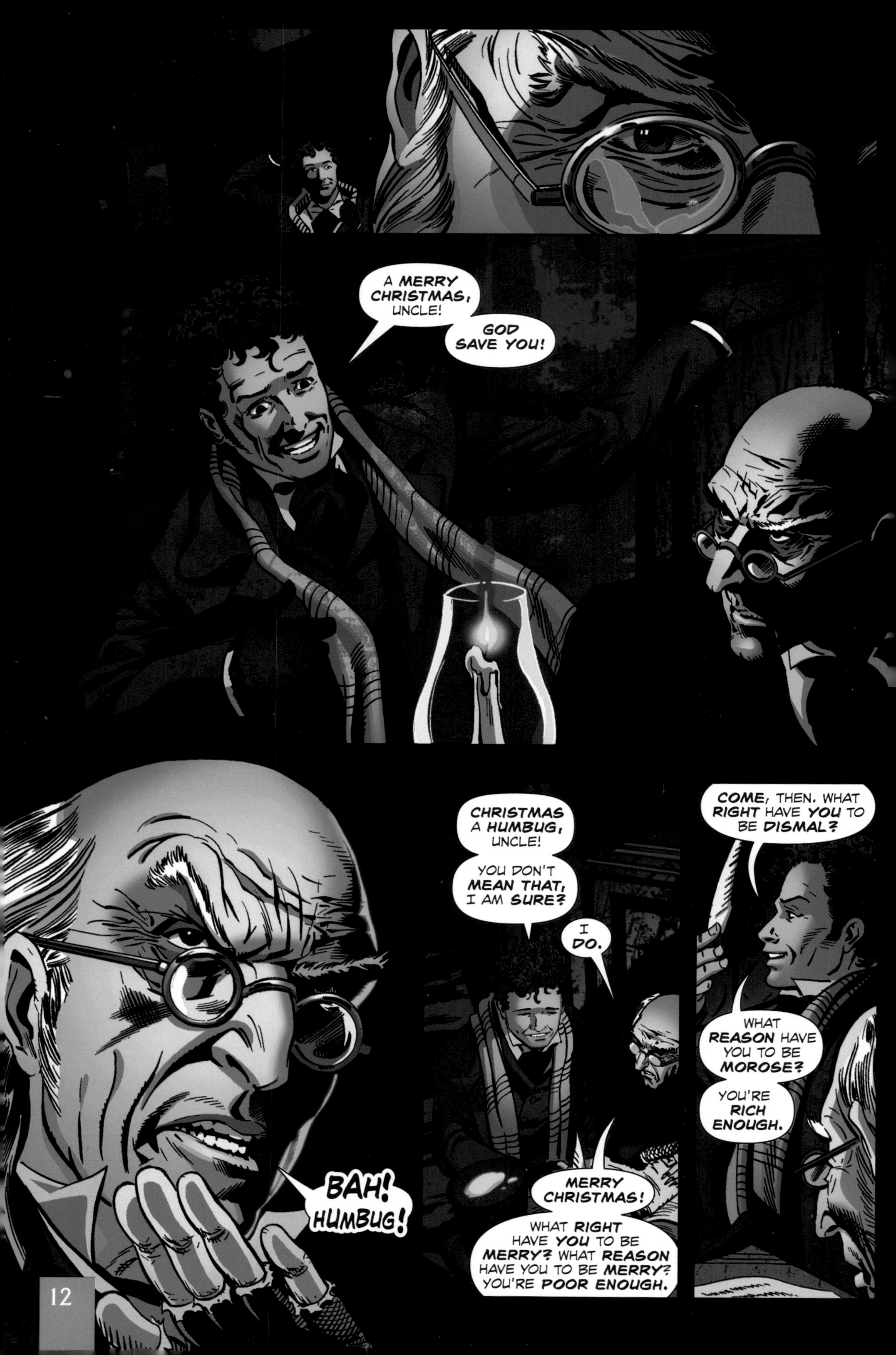
A MERRY CHRISTMAS, UNCLE!
GOD SAVE YOU!
BAH! HUMBUG!
CHRISTMAS A HUMBUG, UNCLE!
YOU DON'T MEAN THAT, I AM SURE?
I DO.
COME, THEN. WHAT RIGHT HAVE YOU TO BE DISMAL?
WHAT REASON HAVE YOU TO BE MOROSE?
YOU'RE RICH ENOUGH.
MERRY CHRISTMAS!
WHAT RIGHT HAVE YOU TO BE MERRY? WHAT REASON HAVE YOU TO BE MERRY? YOU'RE POOR ENOUGH.

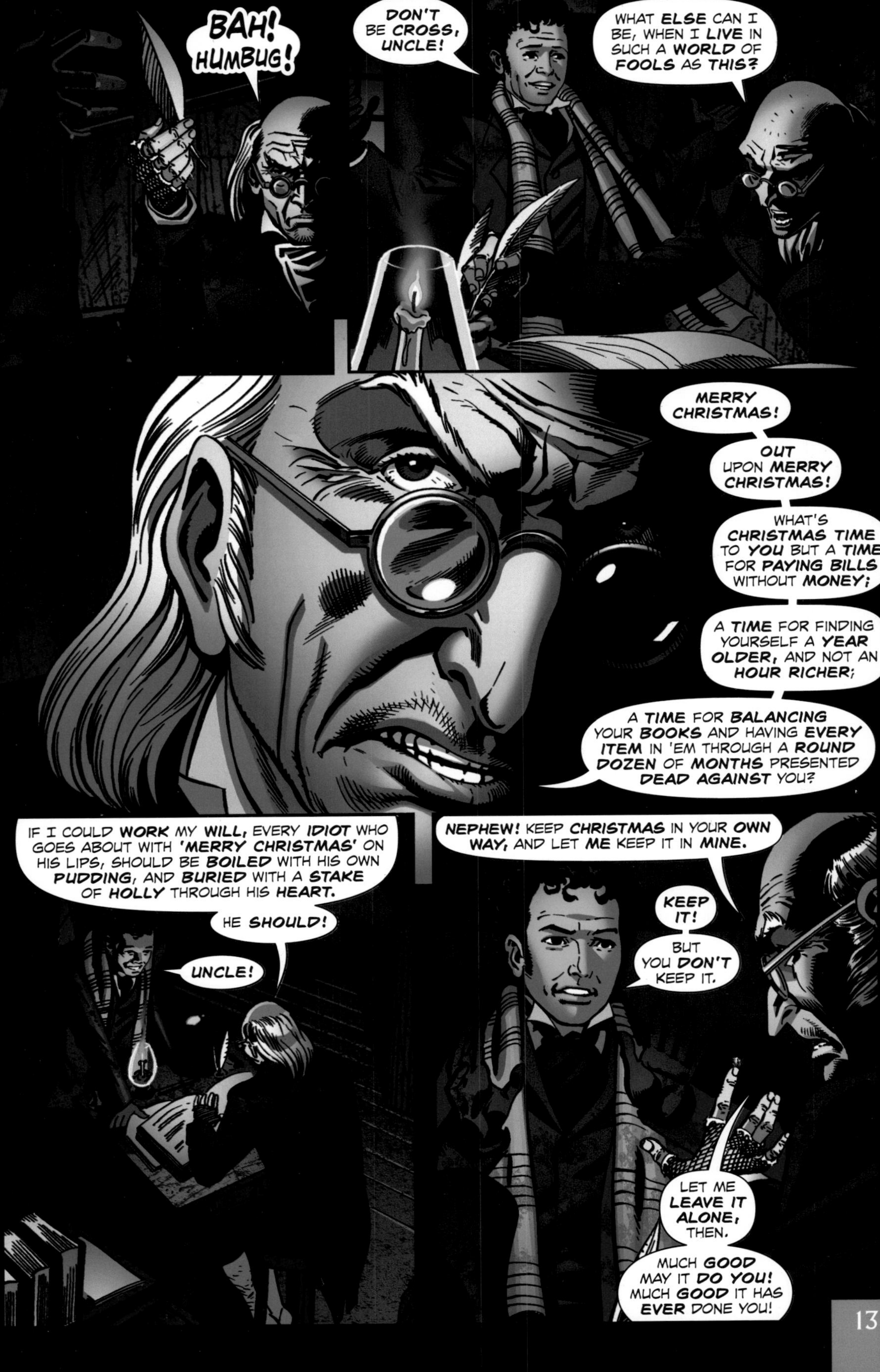
BAH! HUMBUG!
DON'T BE CROSS, UNCLE!
WHAT ELSE CAN I BE, WHEN I LIVE IN SUCH A WORLD OF FOOLS AS THIS?
MERRY CHRISTMAS!
OUT UPON MERRY CHRISTMAS!
WHAT'S CHRISTMAS TIME TO YOU BUT A TIME FOR PAYING BILLS WITHOUT MONEY;
A TIME FOR FINDING YOURSELF A YEAR OLDER, AND NOT AN HOUR RICHER;
A TIME FOR BALANCING YOUR BOOKS AND HAVING EVERY ITEM IN 'EM THROUGH A ROUND DOZEN OF MONTHS PRESENTED DEAD AGAINST YOU?
IF I COULD WORK MY WILL, EVERY IDIOT WHO GOES ABOUT WITH 'MERRY CHRISTMAS' ON HIS LIPS, SHOULD BE BOILED WITH HIS OWN PUDDING, AND BURIED WITH A STAKE OF HOLLY THROUGH HIS HEART.
HE SHOULD!
UNCLE!
NEPHEW! KEEP CHRISTMAS IN YOUR OWN WAY, AND LET ME KEEP IT IN MINE.
KEEP IT!
BUT YOU DON'T KEEP IT.
LET ME LEAVE IT ALONE, THEN.
MUCH GOOD MAY IT DO YOU! MUCH GOOD IT HAS EVER DONE YOU!

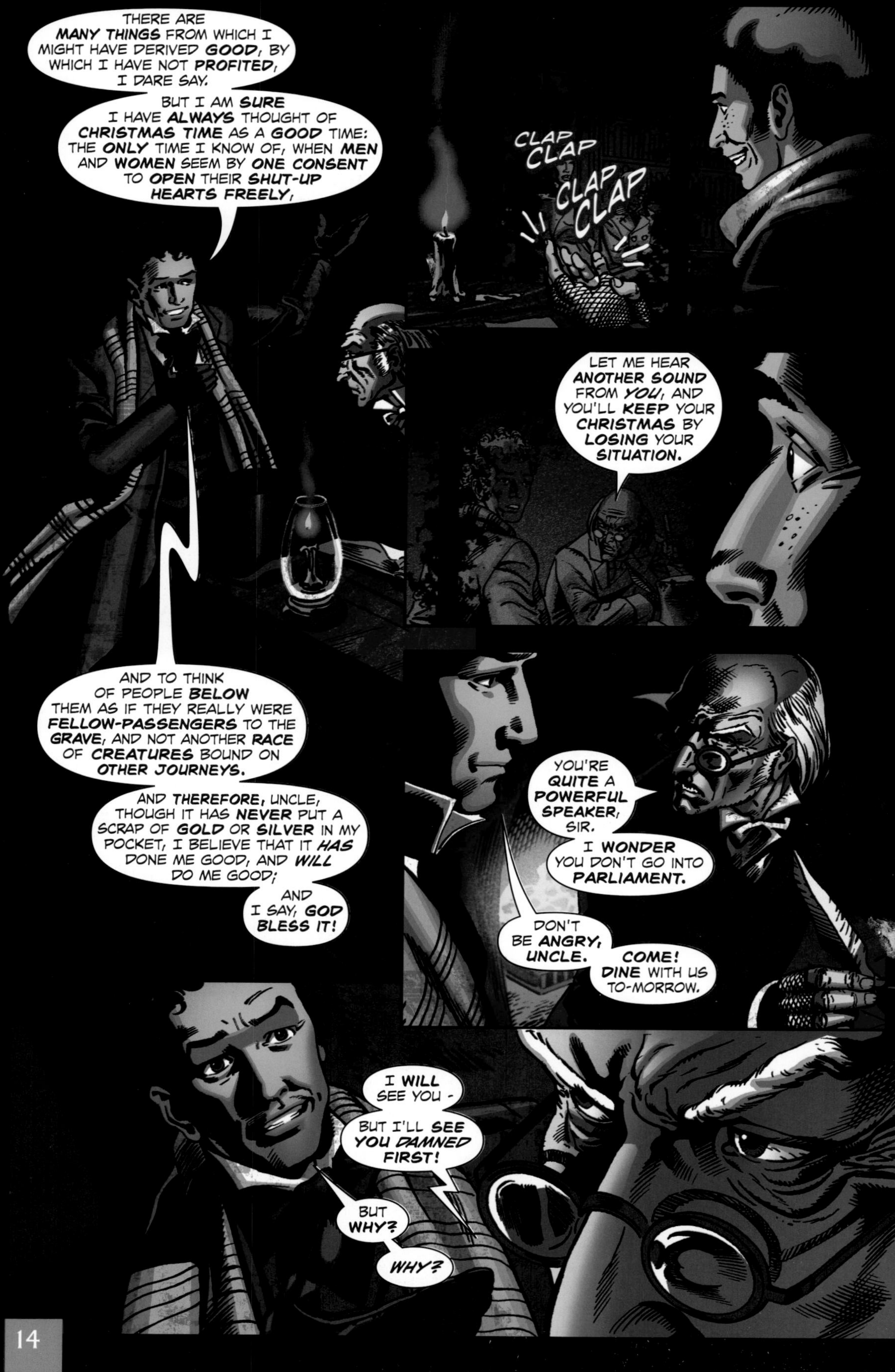
THERE ARE MANY THINGS FROM WHICH I MIGHT HAVE DERIVED GOOD, BY WHICH I HAVE NOT PROFITED, I DARE SAY.
BUT I AM SURE I HAVE ALWAYS THOUGHT OF CHRISTMAS TIME AS A GOOD TIME: THE ONLY TIME I KNOW OF, WHEN MEN AND WOMEN SEEM BY ONE CONSENT TO OPEN THEIR SHUT-UP HEARTS FREELY,
AND TO THINK OF PEOPLE BELOW THEM AS IF THEY REALLY WERE FELLOW-PASSENGERS TO THE GRAVE, AND NOT ANOTHER RACE OF CREATURES BOUND ON OTHER JOURNEYS.
AND THEREFORE, UNCLE, THOUGH IT HAS NEVER PUT A SCRAP OF GOLD OR SILVER IN MY POCKET, I BELIEVE THAT IT HAS DONE ME GOOD, AND WILL DO ME GOOD;
AND I SAY, GOD BLESS IT!
CLAP CLAP CLAP CLAP
LET ME HEAR ANOTHER SOUND FROM YOU, AND YOU'LL KEEP YOUR CHRISTMAS BY LOSING YOUR SITUATION.
YOU'RE QUITE A POWERFUL SPEAKER, SIR.
I WONDER YOU DON'T GO INTO PARLIAMENT.
DON'T BE ANGRY, UNCLE.
COME! DINE WITH US TO-MORROW.
I WILL SEE YOU -
BUT I'LL SEE YOU DAMNED FIRST!
BUT WHY?
WHY?

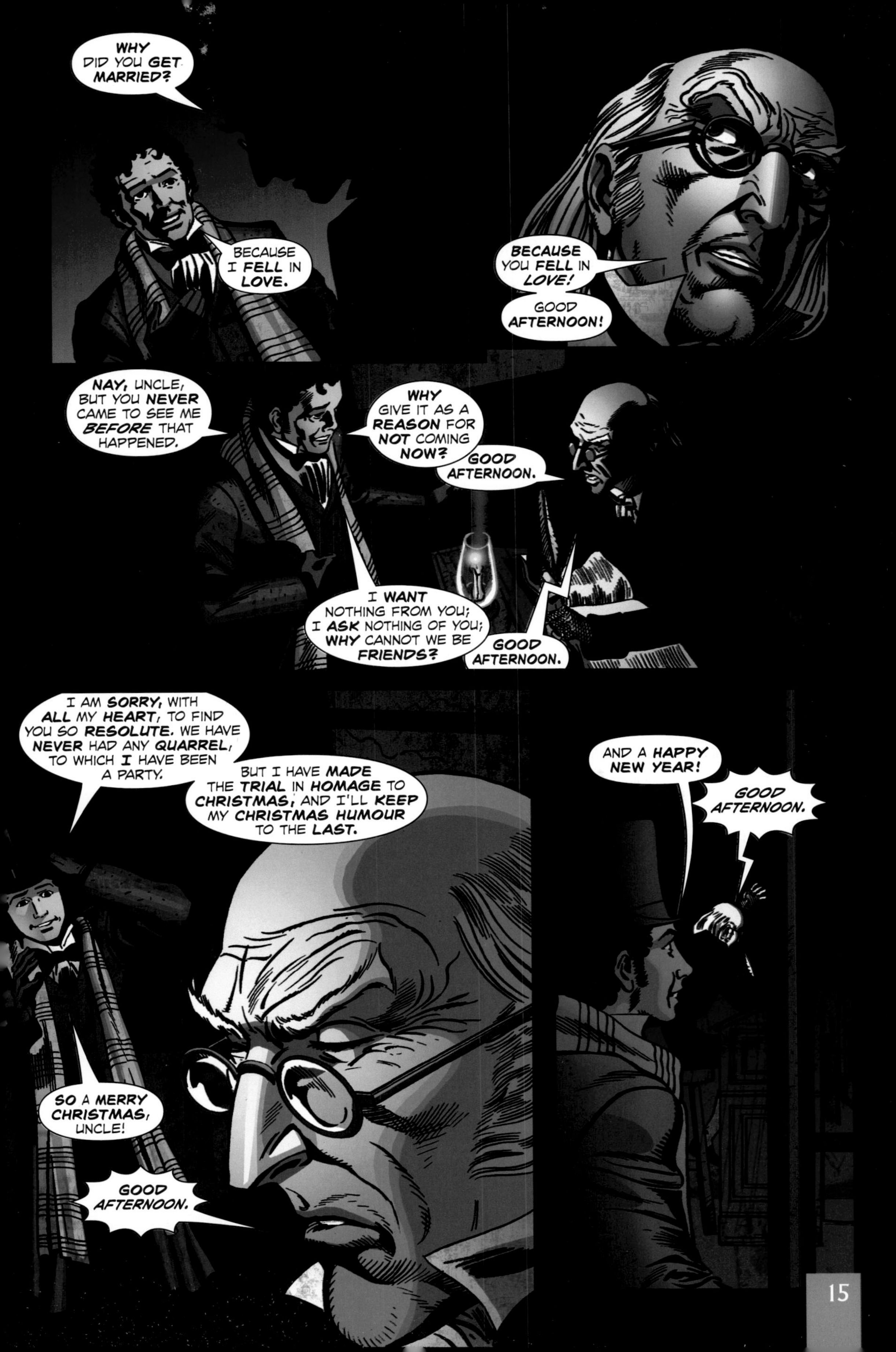
WHY DID YOU GET MARRIED?
BECAUSE I FELL IN LOVE.
BECAUSE YOU FELL IN LOVE!
GOOD AFTERNOON!
NAY, UNCLE, BUT YOU NEVER CAME TO SEE ME BEFORE THAT HAPPENED.
WHY GIVE IT AS A REASON FOR NOT COMING NOW?
GOOD AFTERNOON.
I WANT NOTHING FROM YOU; I ASK NOTHING OF YOU; WHY CANNOT WE BE FRIENDS?
GOOD AFTERNOON.
I AM SORRY, WITH ALL MY HEART, TO FIND YOU SO RESOLUTE. WE HAVE NEVER HAD ANY QUARREL, TO WHICH I HAVE BEEN A PARTY.
BUT I HAVE MADE THE TRIAL IN HOMAGE TO CHRISTMAS, AND I'LL KEEP MY CHRISTMAS HUMOUR TO THE LAST.
SO A MERRY CHRISTMAS, UNCLE!
GOOD AFTERNOON.
AND A HAPPY NEW YEAR!
GOOD AFTERNOON.

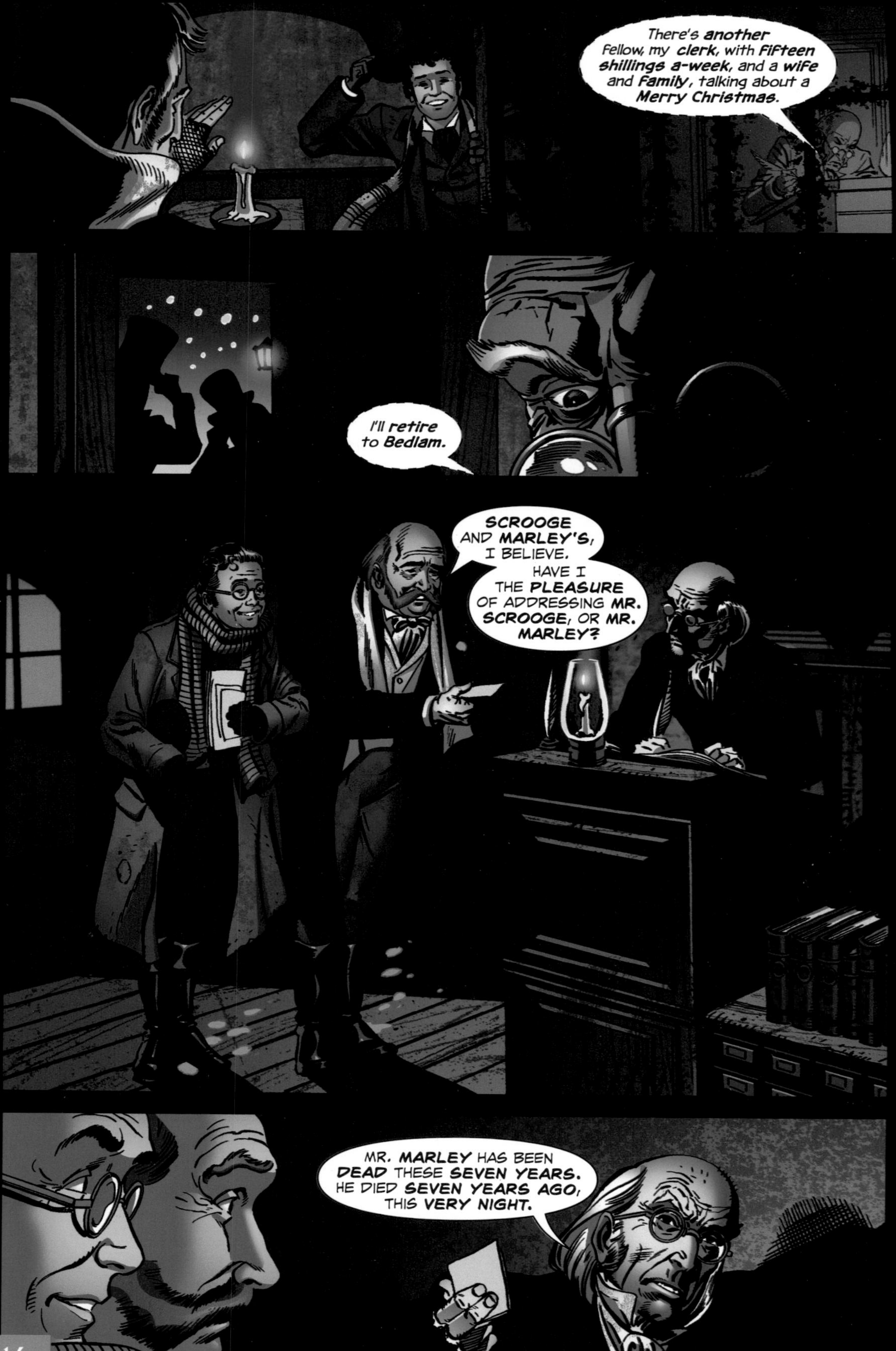
There's another Fellow, my clerk, with Fifteen shillings a-week, and a wife and family, talking about a Merry Christmas.
I'll retire to Bedlam.
SCROOGE AND MARLEY'S, I BELIEVE.
HAVE I THE PLEASURE OF ADDRESSING MR. SCROOGE, OR MR. MARLEY?
MR. MARLEY HAS BEEN DEAD THESE SEVEN YEARS. HE DIED SEVEN YEARS AGO, THIS VERY NIGHT.

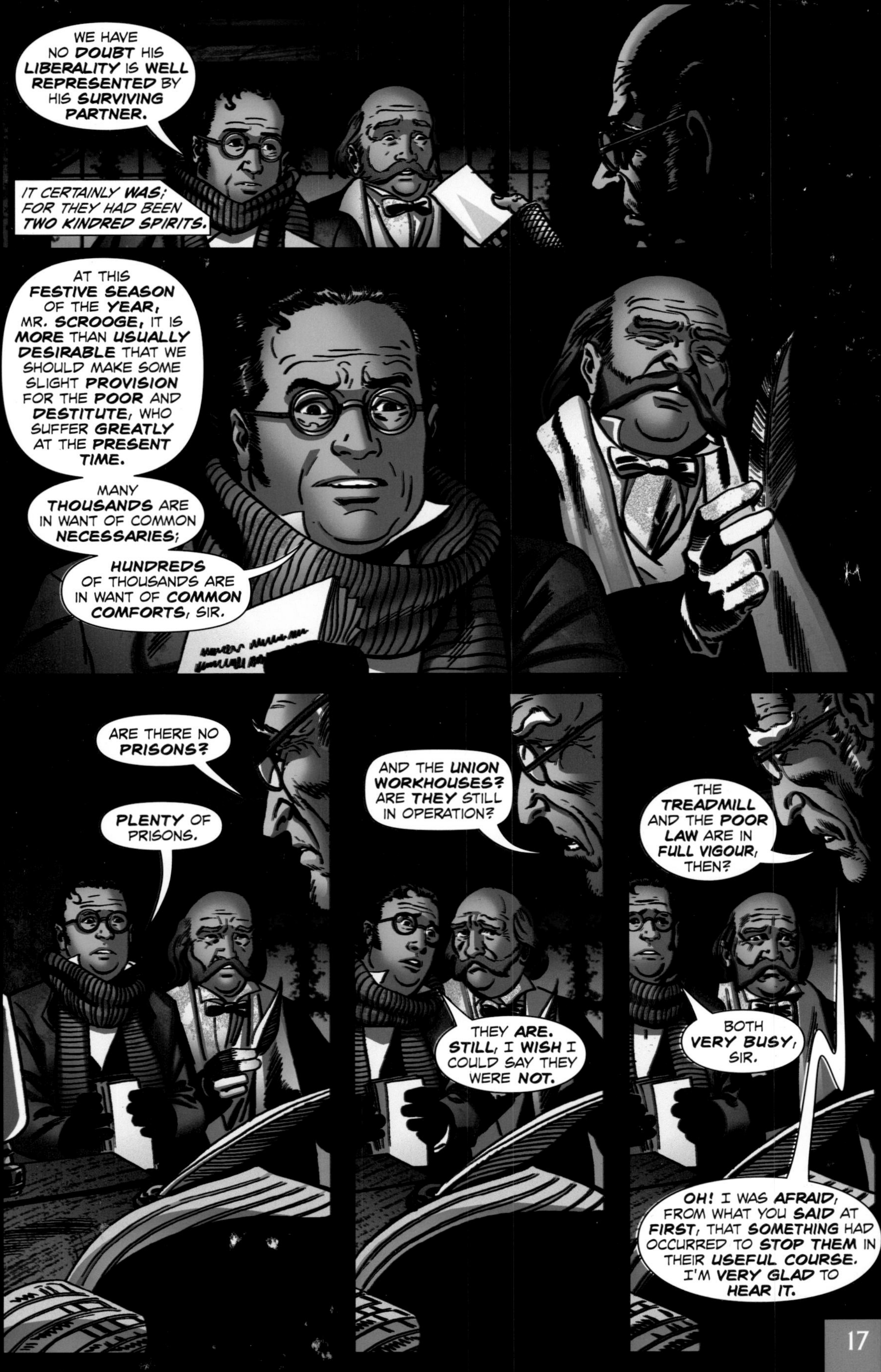
WE HAVE NO DOUBT HIS LIBERALITY IS WELL REPRESENTED BY HIS SURVIVING PARTNER.
IT CERTAINLY WAS; FOR THEY HAD BEEN TWO KINDRED SPIRITS.
AT THIS FESTIVE SEASON OF THE YEAR, MR. SCROOGE, IT IS MORE THAN USUALLY DESIRABLE THAT WE SHOULD MAKE SOME SLIGHT PROVISION FOR THE POOR AND DESTITUTE, WHO SUFFER GREATLY AT THE PRESENT TIME.
MANY THOUSANDS ARE IN WANT OF COMMON NECESSARIES;
HUNDREDS OF THOUSANDS ARE IN WANT OF COMMON COMFORTS, SIR.
ARE THERE NO PRISONS?
PLENTY OF PRISONS.
AND THE UNION WORKHOUSES? ARE THEY STILL IN OPERATION?
THEY ARE. STILL, I WISH I COULD SAY THEY WERE NOT.
THE TREADMILL AND THE POOR LAW ARE IN FULL VIGOUR, THEN?
BOTH VERY BUSY, SIR.
OH! I WAS AFRAID, FROM WHAT YOU SAID AT FIRST, THAT SOMETHING HAD OCCURRED TO STOP THEM IN THEIR USEFUL COURSE. I'M VERY GLAD TO HEAR IT.

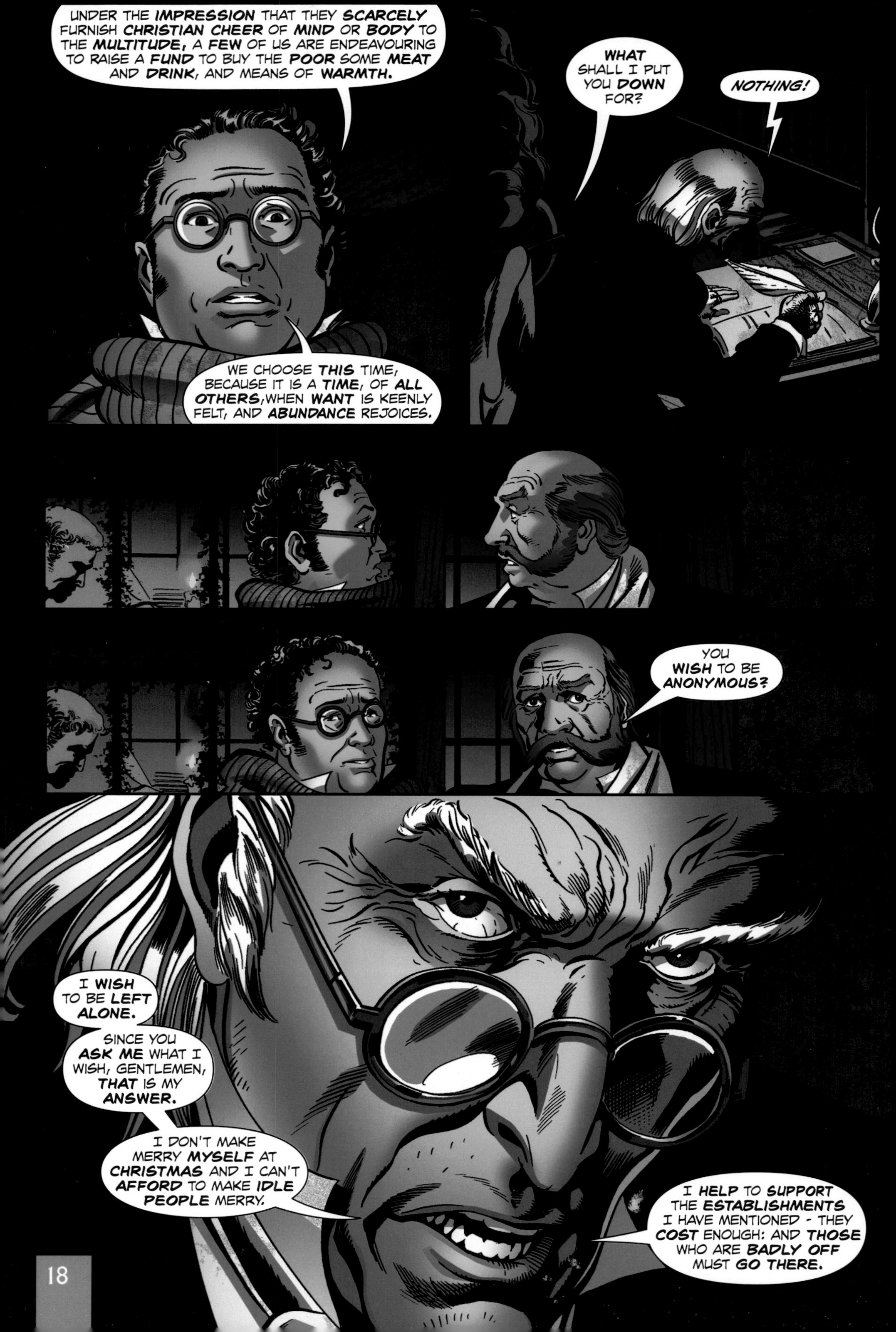
UNDER THE IMPRESSION THAT THEY SCARCELY FURNISH CHRISTIAN CHEER OF MIND OR BODY TO THE MULTITUDE, A FEW OF US ARE ENDEAVOURING TO RAISE A FUND TO BUY THE POOR SOME MEAT AND DRINK, AND MEANS OF WARMTH.
WE CHOOSE THIS TIME, BECAUSE IT IS A TIME, OF ALL OTHERS, WHEN WANT IS KEENLY FELT, AND ABUNDANCE REJOICES.
WHAT SHALL I PUT YOU DOWN FOR?
NOTHING!
YOU WISH TO BE ANONYMOUS?
I WISH TO BE LEFT ALONE.
SINCE YOU ASK ME WHAT I WISH, GENTLEMEN, THAT IS MY ANSWER.
I DON'T MAKE MERRY MYSELF AT CHRISTMAS AND I CAN'T AFFORD TO MAKE IDLE PEOPLE MERRY.
I HELP TO SUPPORT THE ESTABLISHMENTS I HAVE MENTIONED - THEY COST ENOUGH: AND THOSE WHO ARE BADLY OFF MUST GO THERE.

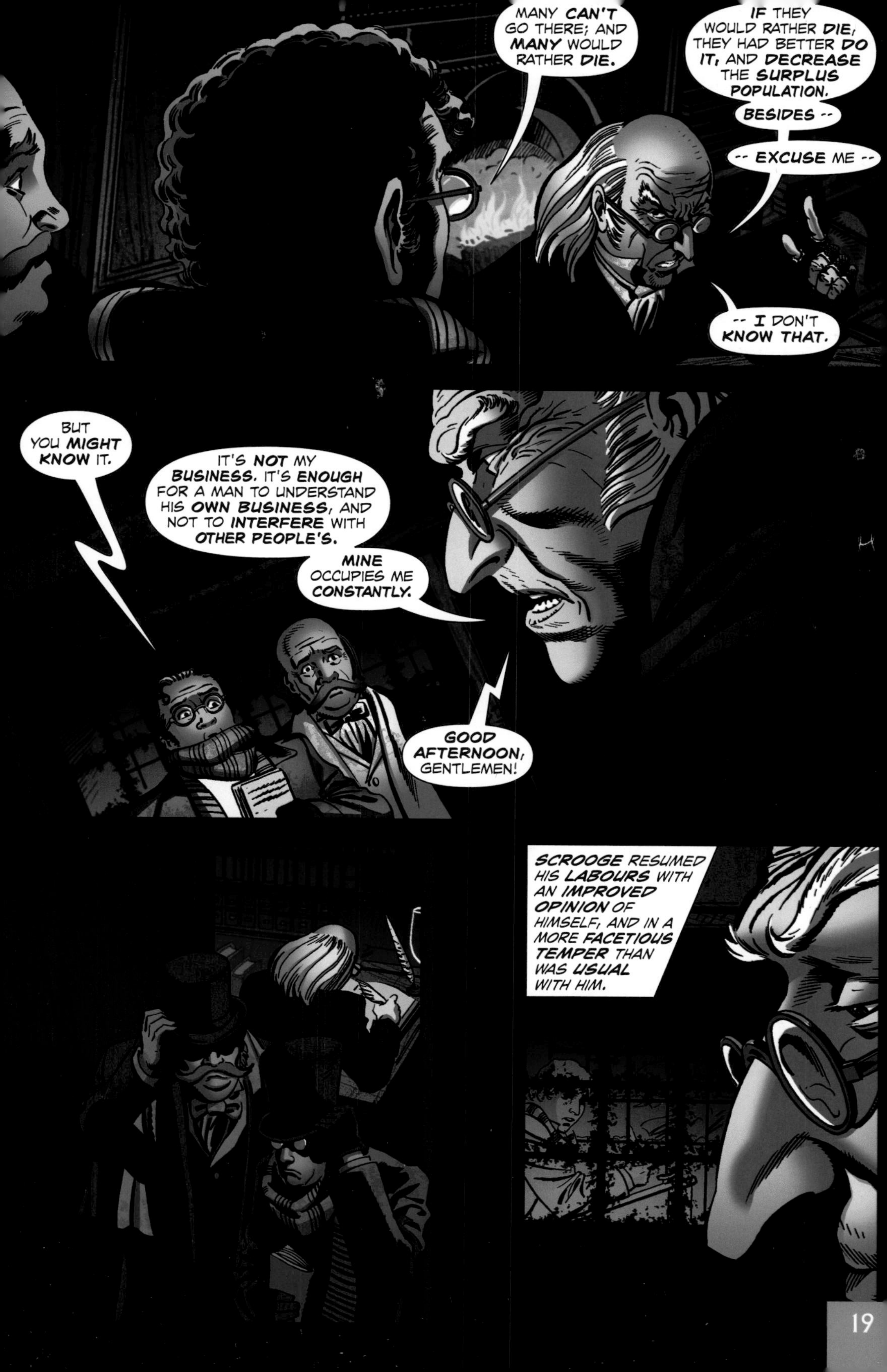

MANY CAN'T GO THERE; AND MANY WOULD RATHER DIE.
IF THEY WOULD RATHER DIE, THEY HAD BETTER DO IT, AND DECREASE THE SURPLUS POPULATION.
BESIDES --
-- EXCUSE ME --
-- I DON'T KNOW THAT.
BUT YOU MIGHT KNOW IT.
IT'S NOT MY BUSINESS. IT'S ENOUGH FOR A MAN TO UNDERSTAND HIS OWN BUSINESS, AND NOT TO INTERFERE WITH OTHER PEOPLE'S.
MINE OCCUPIES ME CONSTANTLY.
GOOD AFTERNOON, GENTLEMEN!
SCROOGE RESUMED HIS LABOURS WITH AN IMPROVED OPINION OF HIMSELF, AND IN A MORE FACETIOUS TEMPER THAN WAS USUAL WITH HIM.

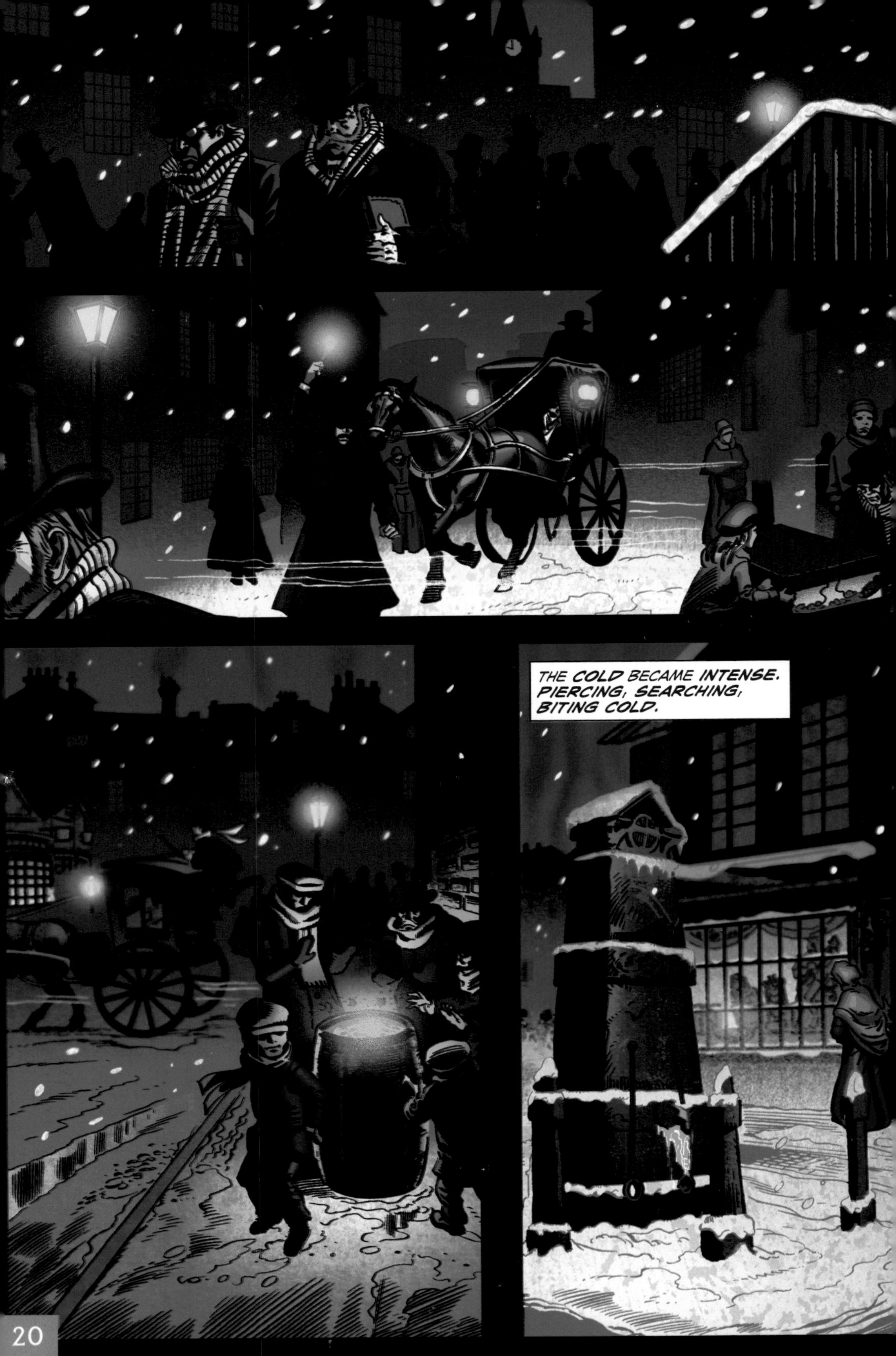
THE COLD BECAME INTENSE. PIERCING, SEARCHING, BITING COLD.

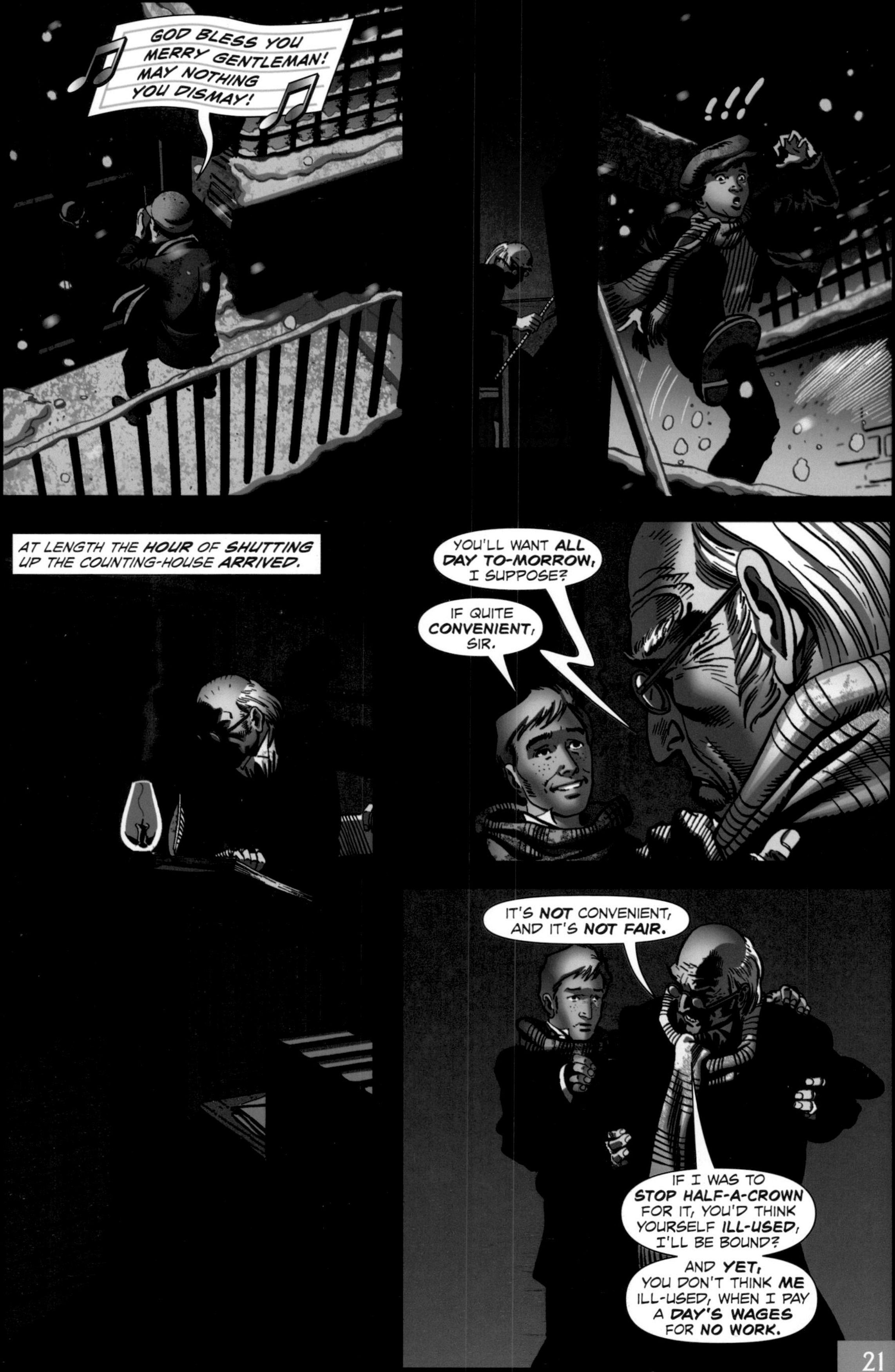
GOD BLESS YOU MERRY GENTLEMAN! MAY NOTHING YOU DISMAY!
!!!
AT LENGTH THE HOUR OF SHUTTING UP THE COUNTING-HOUSE ARRIVED.
YOU'LL WANT ALL DAY TO-MORROW, I SUPPOSE?
IF QUITE CONVENIENT, SIR.
IT'S NOT CONVENIENT, AND IT'S NOT FAIR.
IF I WAS TO STOP HALF-A-CROWN FOR IT, YOU'D THINK YOURSELF ILL-USED, I'LL BE BOUND?
AND YET, YOU DON'T THINK ME ILL-USED, WHEN I PAY A DAY'S WAGES FOR NO WORK.

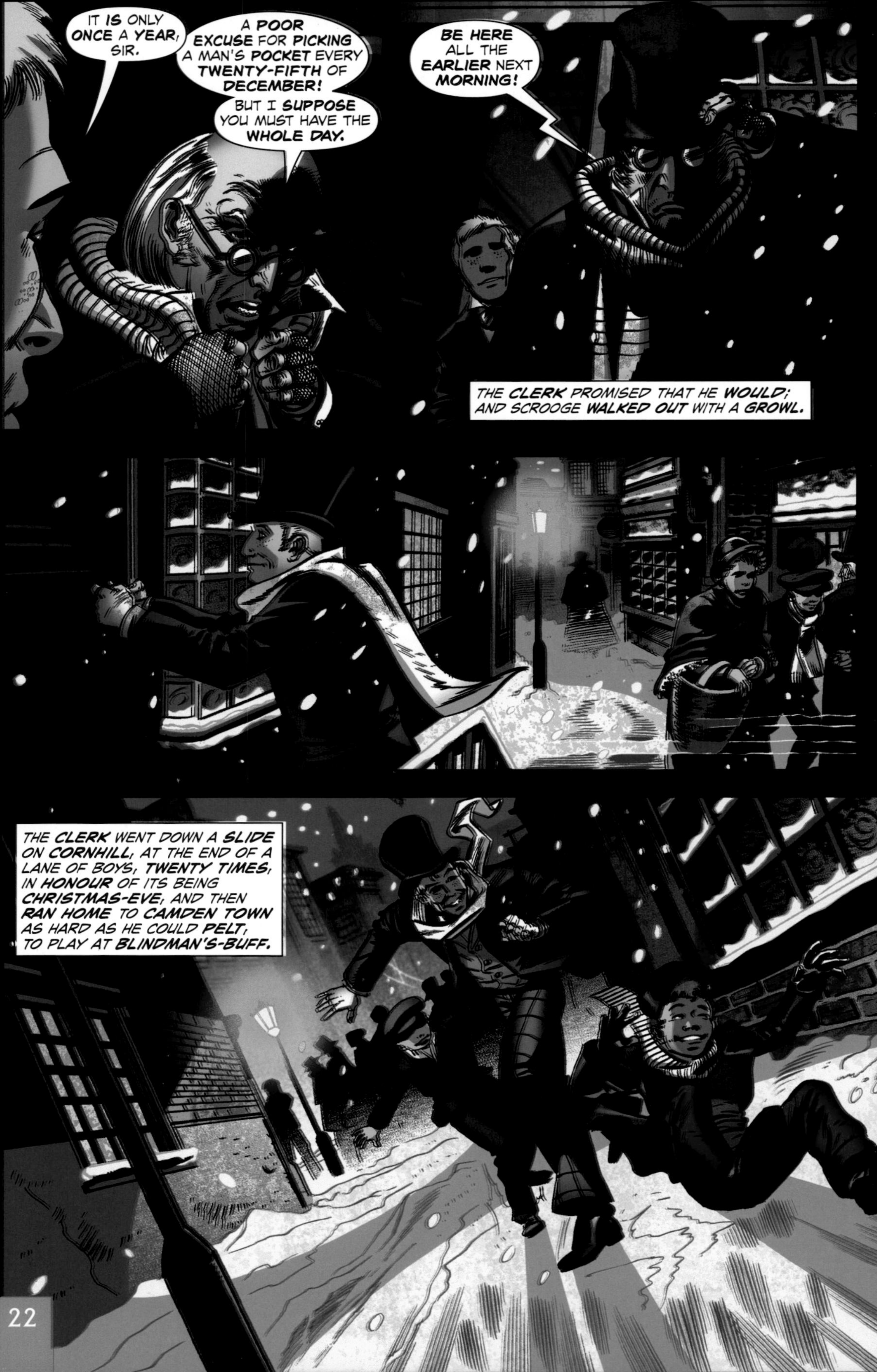
IT IS ONLY ONCE A YEAR, SIR.
A POOR EXCUSE FOR PICKING A MAN'S POCKET EVERY TWENTY-FIFTH OF DECEMBER!
BUT I SUPPOSE YOU MUST HAVE THE WHOLE DAY.
BE HERE ALL THE EARLIER NEXT MORNING!
THE CLERK PROMISED THAT HE WOULD; AND SCROOGE WALKED OUT WITH A GROWL.
THE CLERK WENT DOWN A SLIDE ON CORNHILL, AT THE END OF A LANE OF BOYS, TWENTY TIMES, IN HONOUR OF ITS BEING CHRISTMAS-EVE, AND THEN RAN HOME TO CAMDEN TOWN AS HARD AS HE COULD PELT, TO PLAY AT BLINDMAN'S-BUFF.

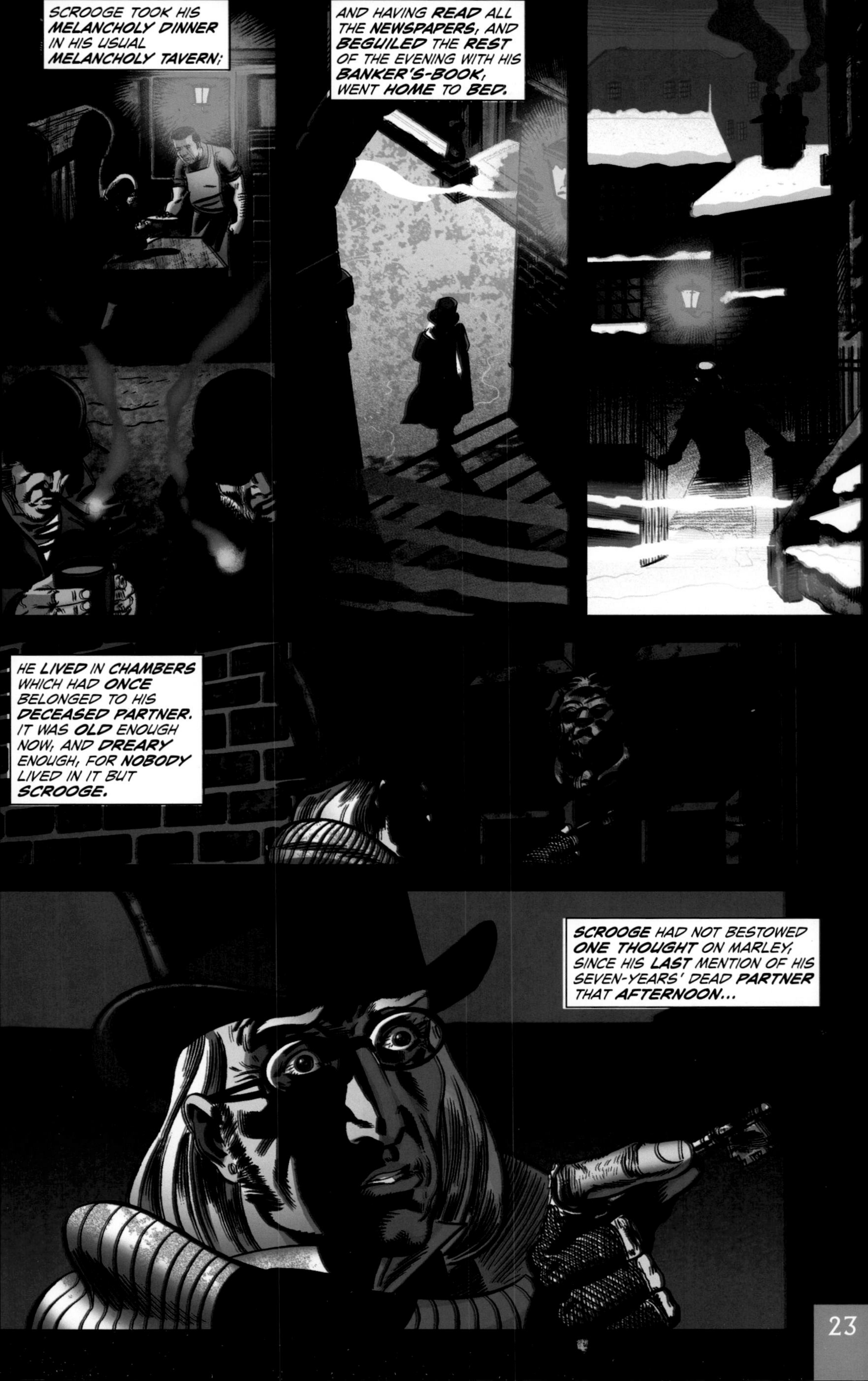
SCROOGE TOOK HIS MELANCHOLY DINNER IN HIS USUAL MELANCHOLY TAVERN;
AND HAVING READ ALL THE NEWSPAPERS, AND BEGUILED THE REST OF THE EVENING WITH HIS BANKER'S-BOOK, WENT HOME TO BED.
HE LIVED IN CHAMBERS WHICH HAD ONCE BELONGED TO HIS DECEASED PARTNER. IT WAS OLD ENOUGH NOW, AND DREARY ENOUGH, FOR NOBODY LIVED IN IT BUT SCROOGE.
SCROOGE HAD NOT BESTOWED ONE THOUGHT ON MARLEY, SINCE HIS LAST MENTION OF HIS SEVEN-YEARS' DEAD PARTNER THAT AFTERNOON...

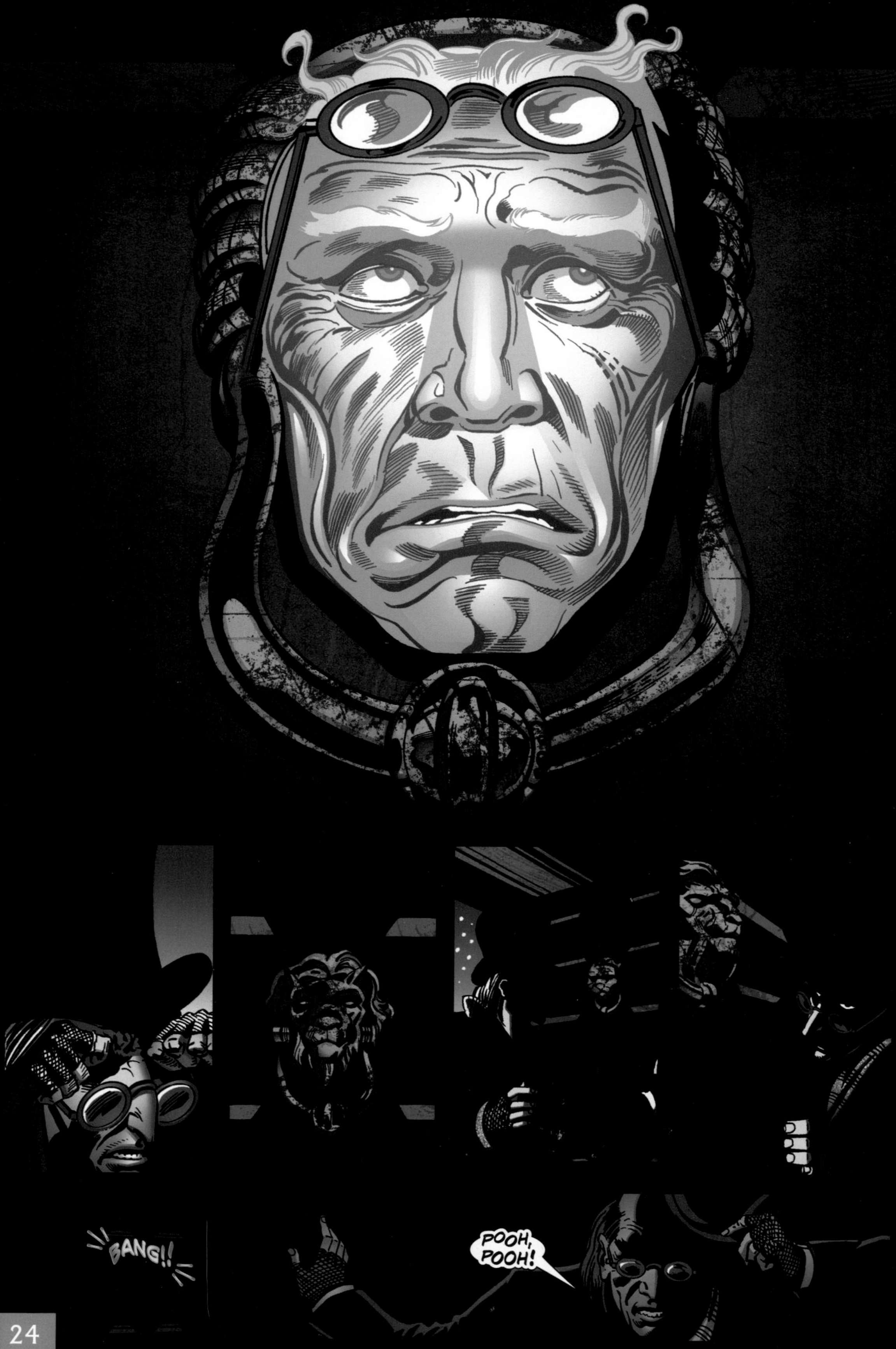
BANG!!
POOH, POOH!

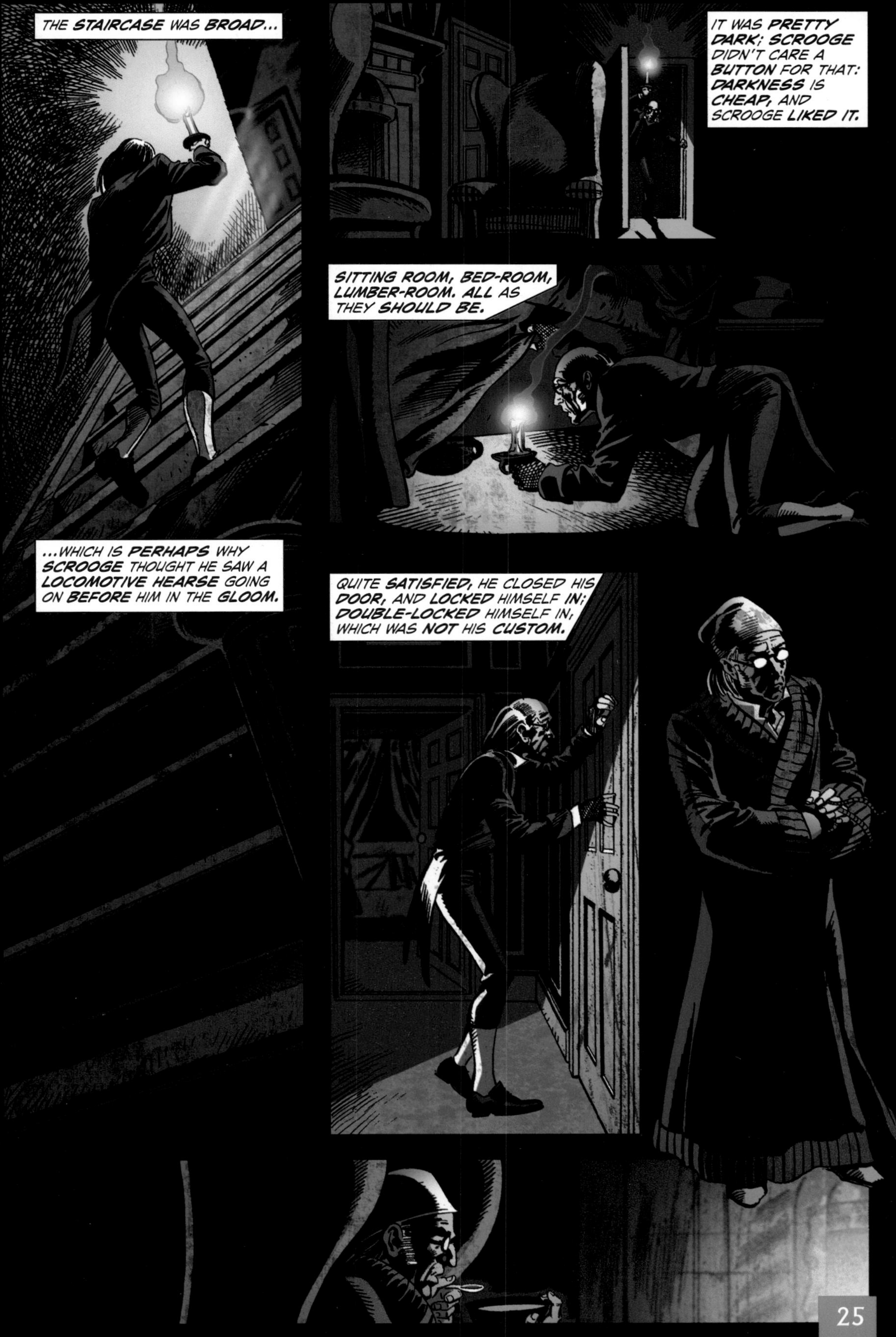
THE STAIRCASE WAS BROAD...
IT WAS PRETTY DARK; SCROOGE DIDN'T CARE A BUTTON FOR THAT: DARKNESS IS CHEAP, AND SCROOGE LIKED IT.
SITTING ROOM, BED-ROOM, LUMBER-ROOM. ALL AS THEY SHOULD BE.
...WHICH IS PERHAPS WHY SCROOGE THOUGHT HE SAW A LOCOMOTIVE HEARSE GOING ON BEFORE HIM IN THE GLOOM.
QUITE SATISFIED, HE CLOSED HIS DOOR, AND LOCKED HIMSELF IN; DOUBLE-LOCKED HIMSELF IN, WHICH WAS NOT HIS CUSTOM.

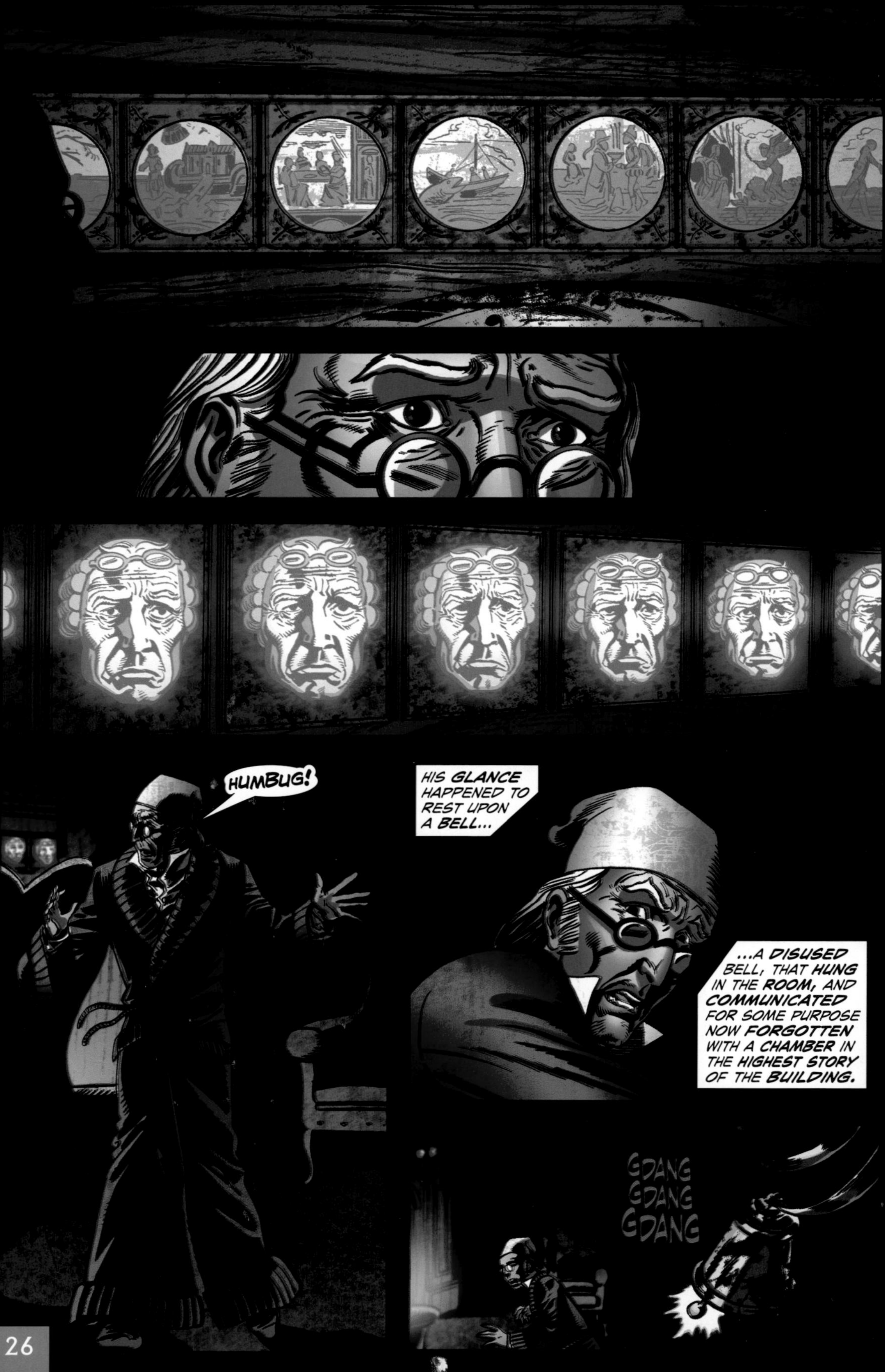
HUMBUG!
HIS GLANCE HAPPENED TO REST UPON A BELL...
...A DISUSED BELL, THAT HUNG IN THE ROOM, AND COMMUNICATED FOR SOME PURPOSE NOW FORGOTTEN WITH A CHAMBER IN THE HIGHEST STORY OF THE BUILDING.
GDANG GDANG GDANG

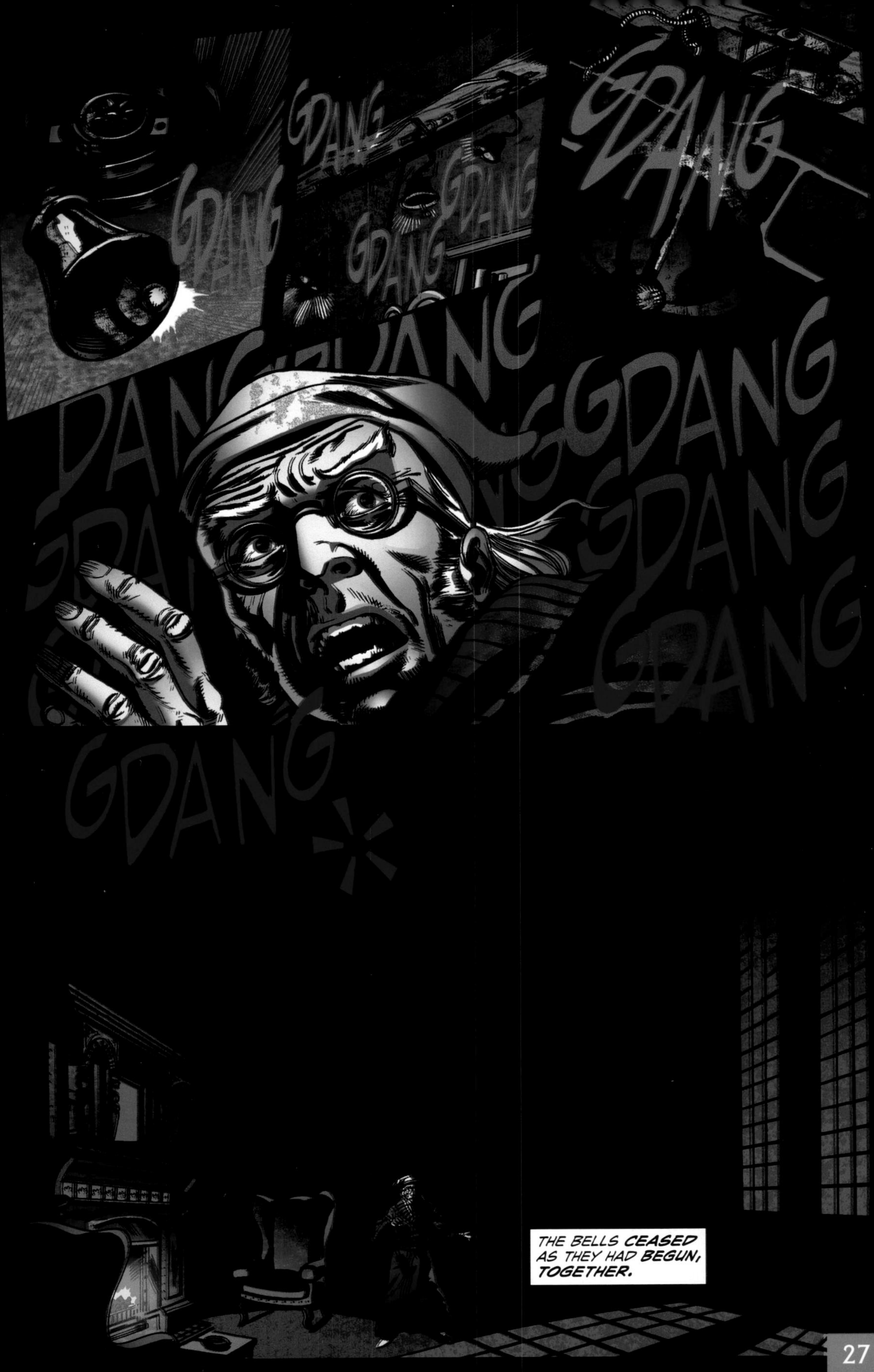
GDANG
GDANG
GDANG
GDANG
GDANG
GDANG
DANG
GDANG
GDANG
GDANG
GDANG
GDANG
THE BELLS CEASED AS THEY HAD BEGUN, TOGETHER.

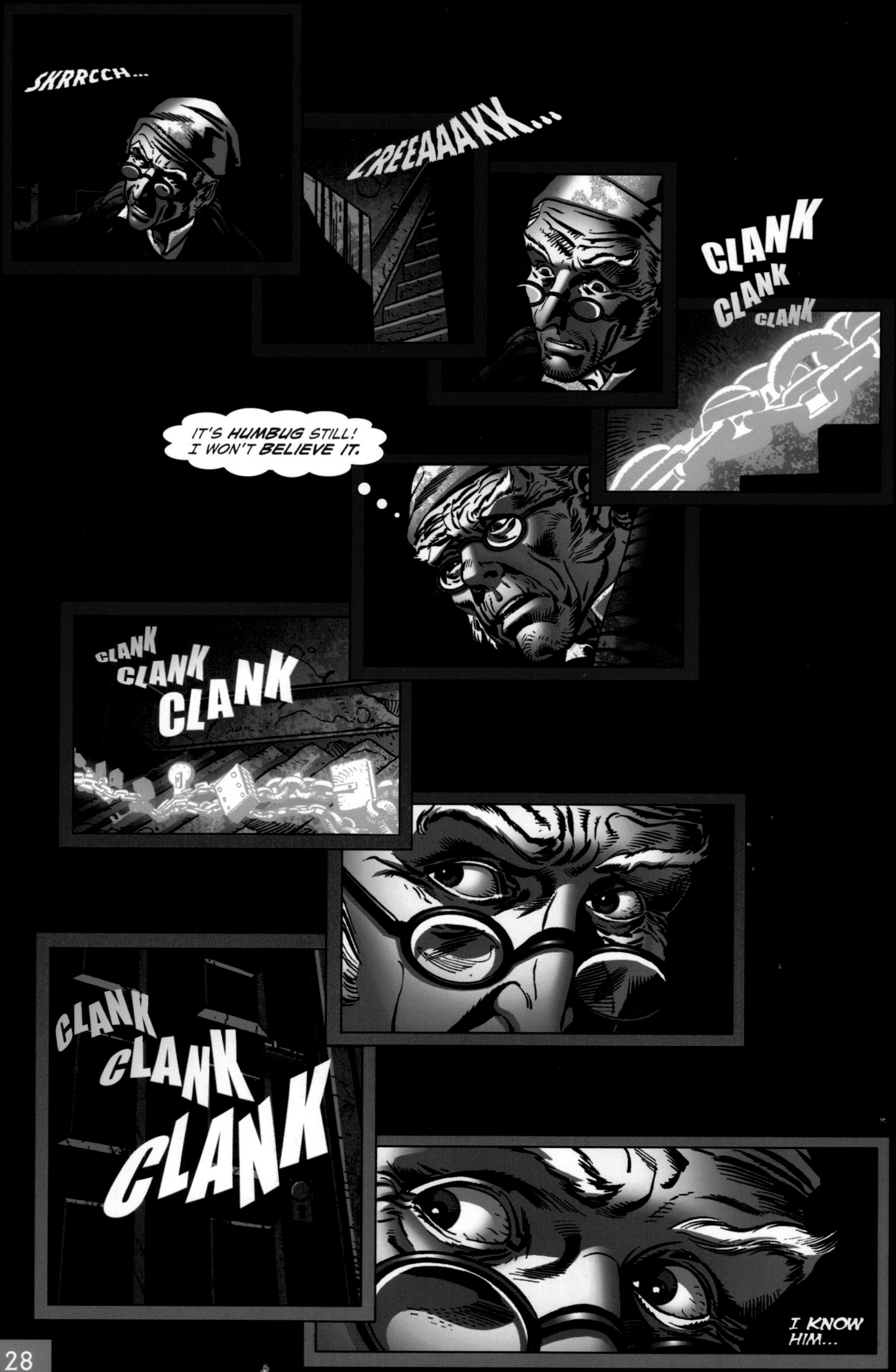
SKRRCCH...
CREEAAAKK...
CLANK
CLANK
CLANK
IT'S HUMBUG STILL! I WON'T BELIEVE IT.
CLANK
CLANK
CLANK
CLANK
CLANK
CLANK
I KNOW HIM...

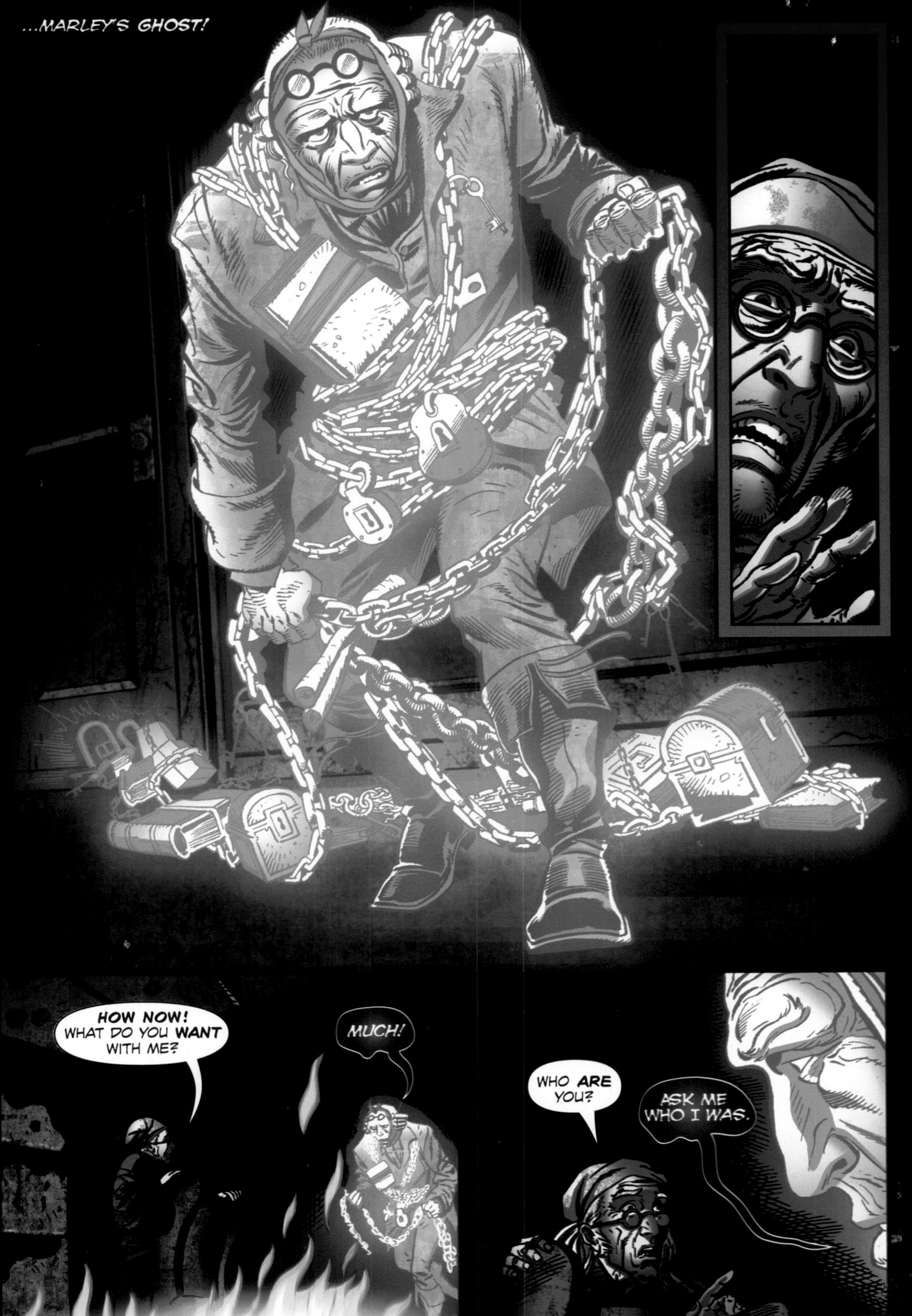
...MARLEY'S GHOST!
HOW NOW! WHAT DO YOU WANT WITH ME?
MUCH!
WHO ARE YOU?
ASK ME WHO I WAS.

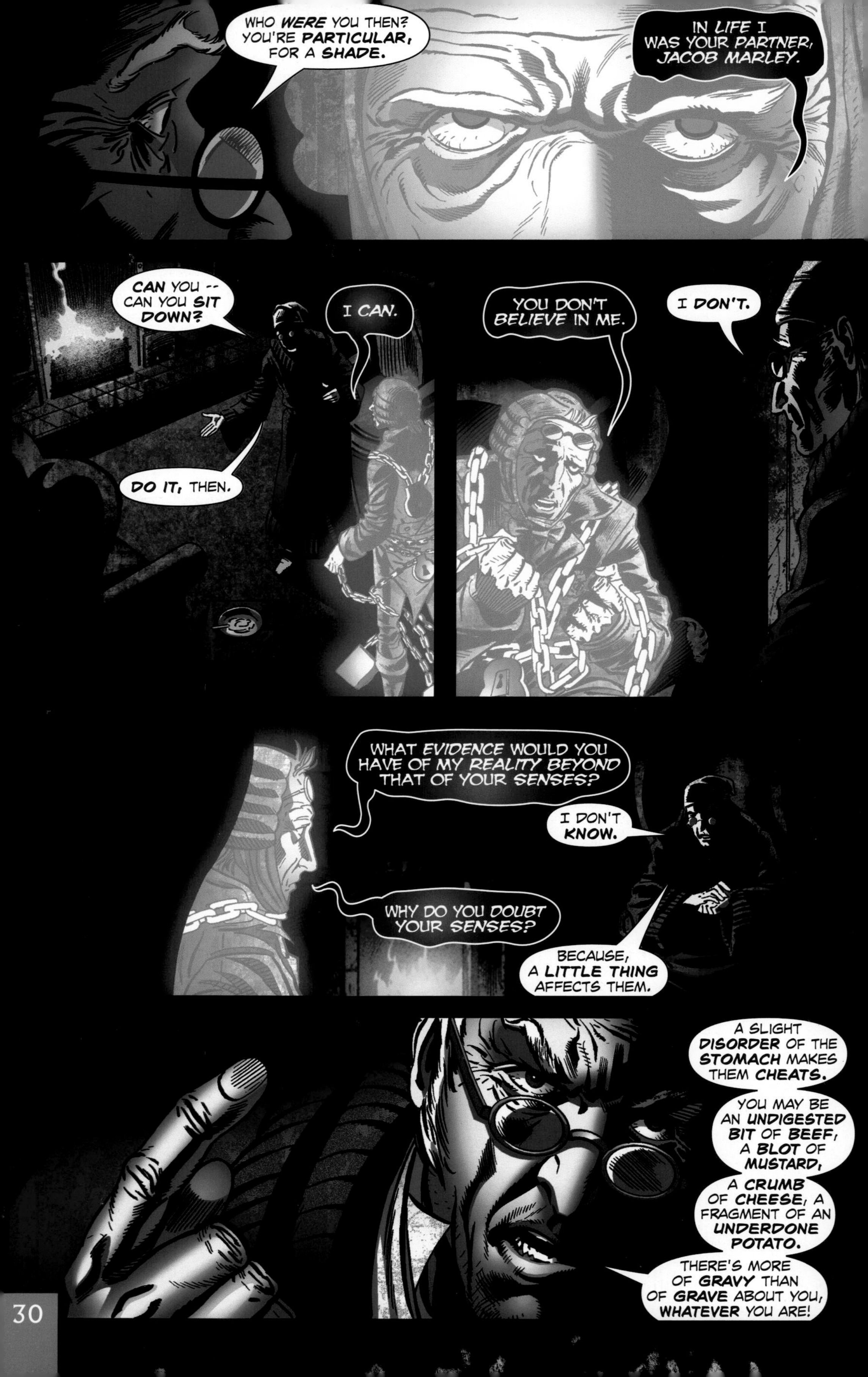
WHO WERE YOU THEN? YOU'RE PARTICULAR, FOR A SHADE.
IN LIFE I WAS YOUR PARTNER, JACOB MARLEY.
CAN YOU -- CAN YOU SIT DOWN?
I CAN.
DO IT, THEN.
YOU DON'T BELIEVE IN ME.
I DON'T.
WHAT EVIDENCE WOULD YOU HAVE OF MY REALITY BEYOND THAT OF YOUR SENSES?
I DON'T KNOW.
WHY DO YOU DOUBT YOUR SENSES?
BECAUSE, A LITTLE THING AFFECTS THEM.
A SLIGHT DISORDER OF THE STOMACH MAKES THEM CHEATS.
YOU MAY BE AN UNDIGESTED BIT OF BEEF, A BLOT OF MUSTARD,
A CRUMB OF CHEESE, A FRAGMENT OF AN UNDERDONE POTATO.
THERE'S MORE OF GRAVY THAN OF GRAVE ABOUT YOU, WHATEVER YOU ARE!

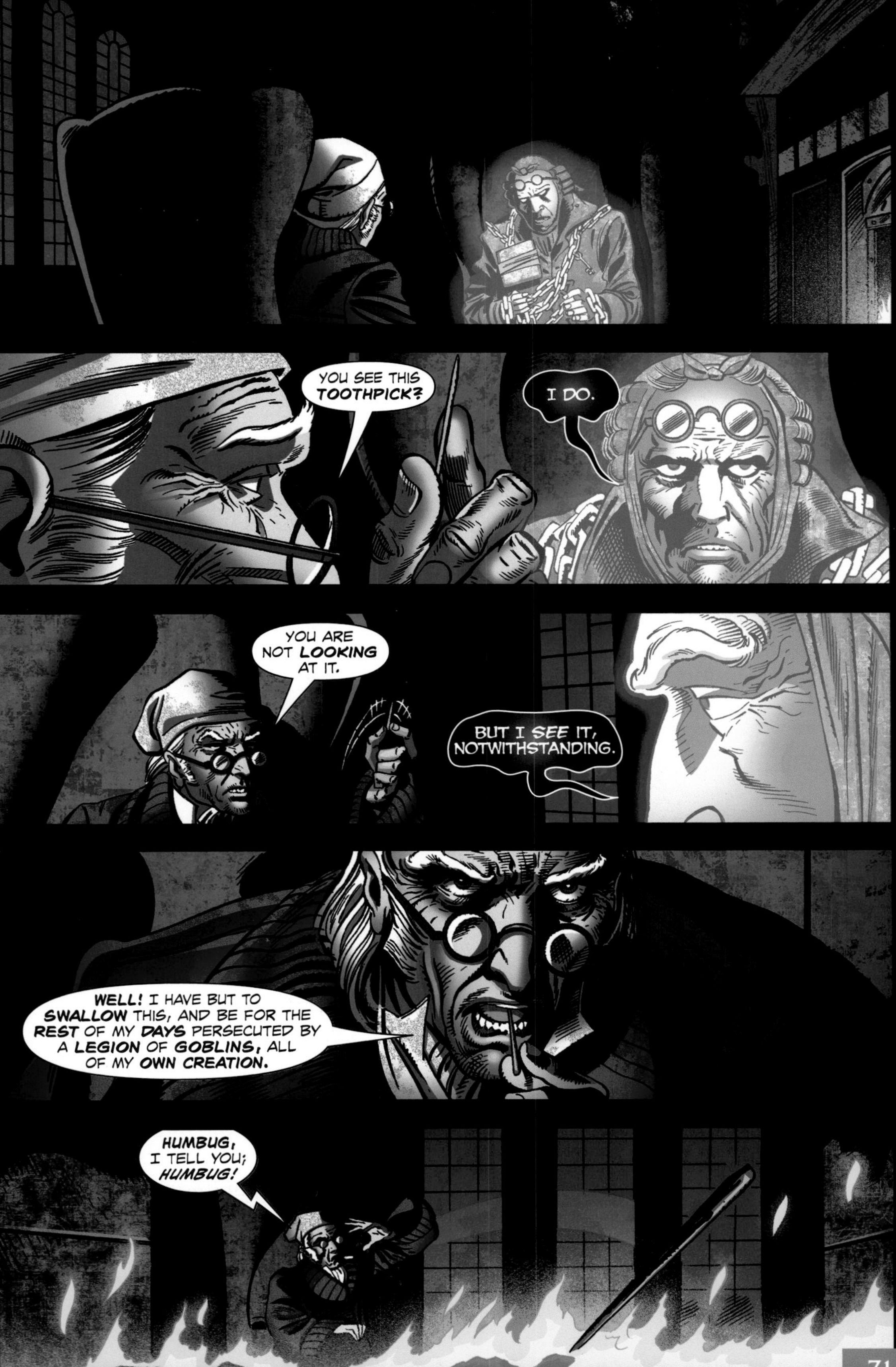
YOU SEE THIS TOOTHPICK?
I DO.
YOU ARE NOT LOOKING AT IT.
BUT I SEE IT, NOTWITHSTANDING.
WELL! I HAVE BUT TO SWALLOW THIS, AND BE FOR THE REST OF MY DAYS PERSECUTED BY A LEGION OF GOBLINS, ALL OF MY OWN CREATION.
HUMBUG, I TELL YOU; HUMBUG!

OOOOHHHHH!
AAARGHHH!
OOAARGH!
AAAAH!
CLANK
CLANK
CHINK
CHINK
RATTLE
RATTLE

MERCY! DREADFUL APPARITION, WHY DO YOU TROUBLE ME?

MAN OF THE WORLDLY MIND!

DO YOU BELIEVE IN ME OR NOT?

I DO, I MUST. BUT WHY DO SPIRITS WALK THE EARTH, AND WHY DO THEY COME TO ME?

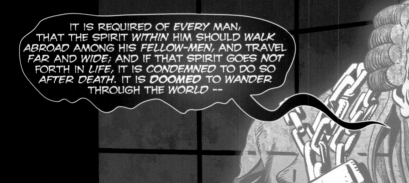

IT IS REQUIRED OF EVERY MAN, THAT THE SPIRIT WITHIN HIM SHOULD WALK ABROAD AMONG HIS FELLOW-MEN, AND TRAVEL FAR AND WIDE; AND IF THAT SPIRIT GOES NOT FORTH IN LIFE, IT IS CONDEMNED TO DO SO AFTER DEATH. IT IS DOOMED TO WANDER THROUGH THE WORLD --

-- OH, WOE IS ME! --

-- AND WITNESS WHAT IT CANNOT SHARE, BUT MIGHT HAVE SHARED ON EARTH, AND TURNED TO HAPPINESS!

OOOHHHHH AAAAHHH!

AAHHH!!

CLANK CLANK

RATTLE

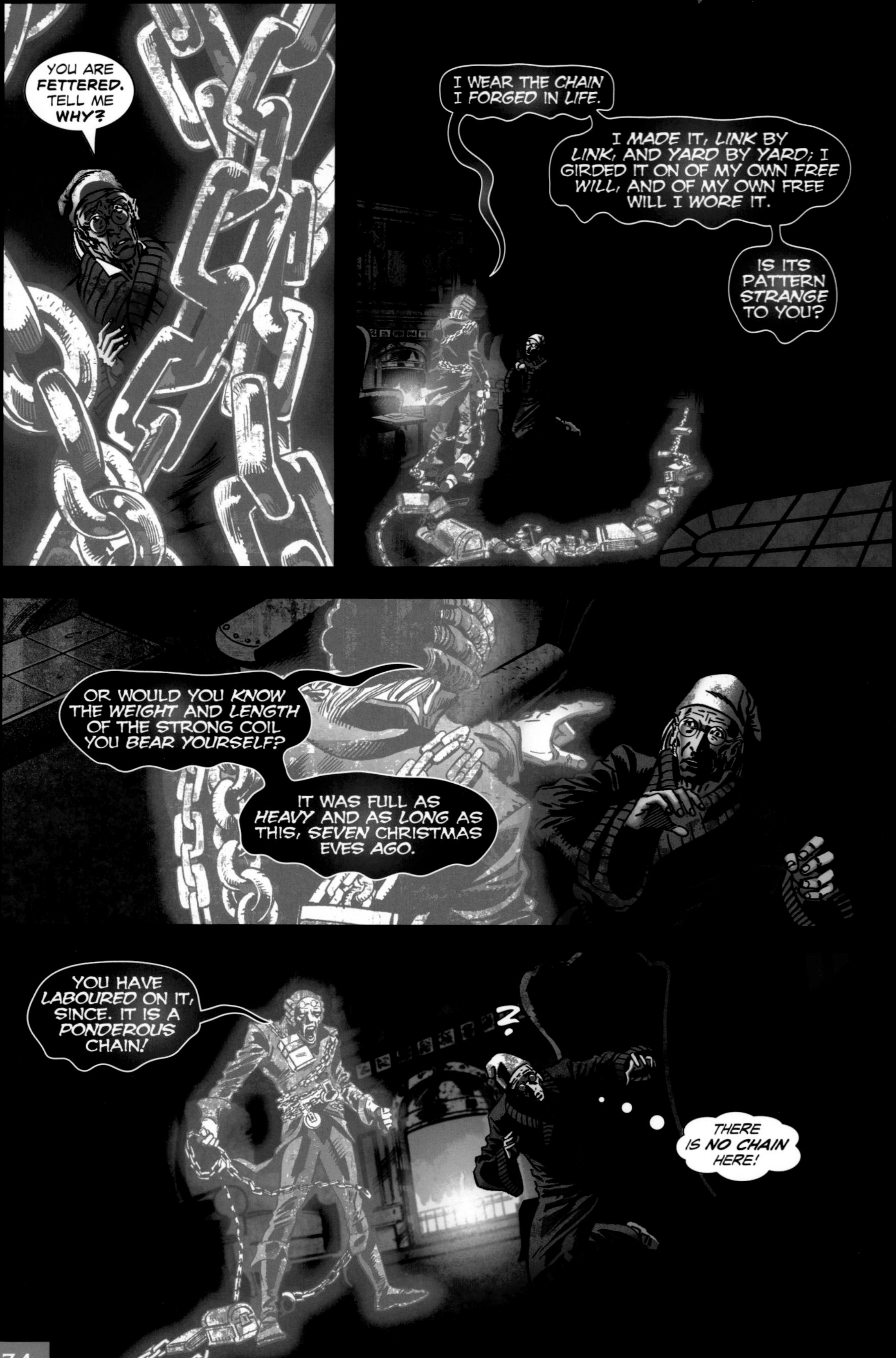
YOU ARE FETTERED. TELL ME WHY?
I WEAR THE CHAIN I FORGED IN LIFE.
I MADE IT, LINK BY LINK, AND YARD BY YARD; I GIRDED IT ON OF MY OWN FREE WILL, AND OF MY OWN FREE WILL I WORE IT.
IS ITS PATTERN STRANGE TO YOU?
OR WOULD YOU KNOW THE WEIGHT AND LENGTH OF THE STRONG COIL YOU BEAR YOURSELF?
IT WAS FULL AS HEAVY AND AS LONG AS THIS, SEVEN CHRISTMAS EVES AGO.
YOU HAVE LABOURED ON IT, SINCE. IT IS A PONDEROUS CHAIN!
?
THERE IS NO CHAIN HERE!

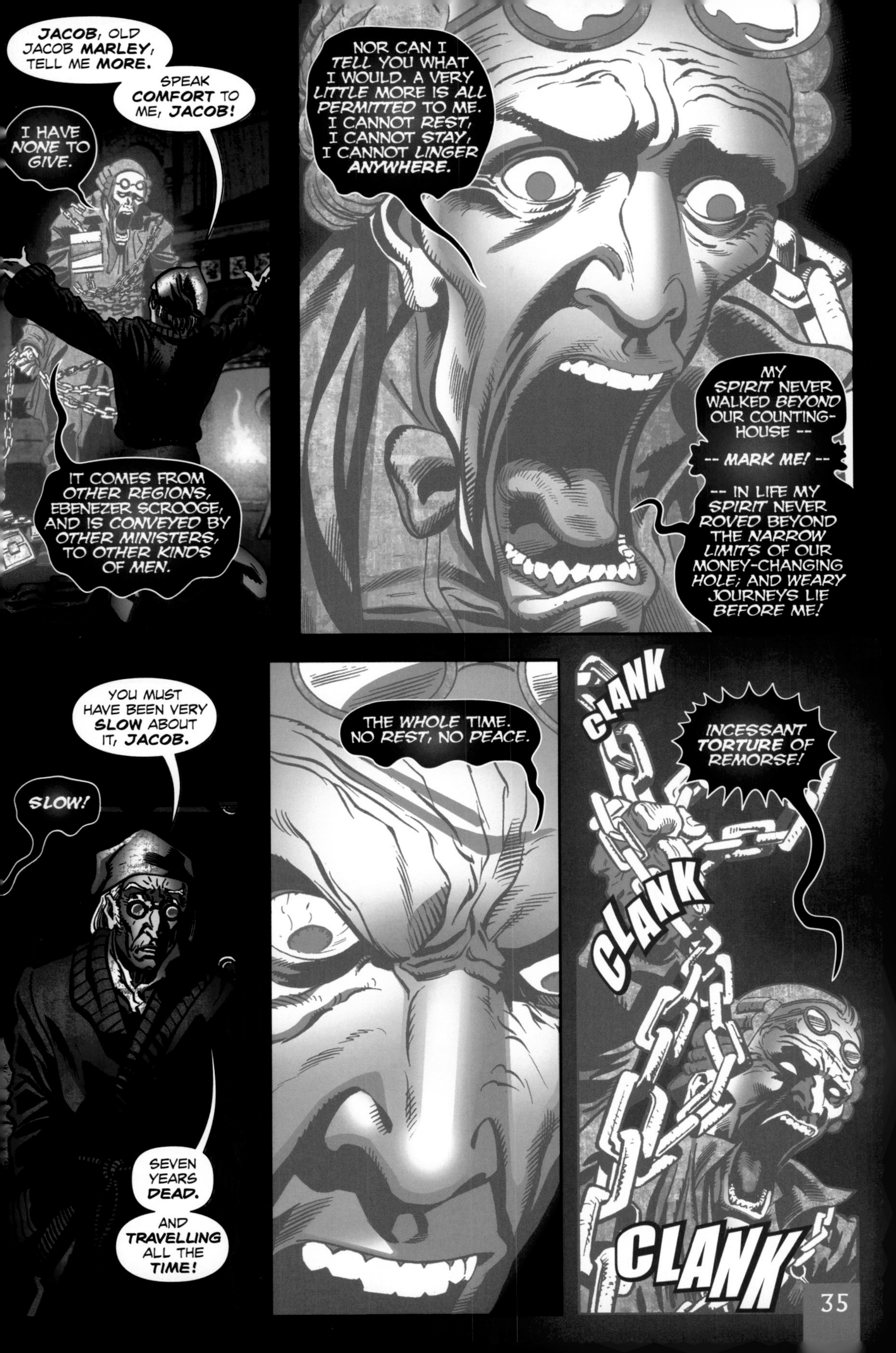
JACOB, OLD JACOB MARLEY, TELL ME MORE.
SPEAK COMFORT TO ME, JACOB!
I HAVE NONE TO GIVE.
IT COMES FROM OTHER REGIONS, EBENEZER SCROOGE, AND IS CONVEYED BY OTHER MINISTERS, TO OTHER KINDS OF MEN.
NOR CAN I TELL YOU WHAT I WOULD. A VERY LITTLE MORE IS ALL PERMITTED TO ME. I CANNOT REST, I CANNOT STAY, I CANNOT LINGER ANYWHERE.
MY SPIRIT NEVER WALKED BEYOND OUR COUNTING-HOUSE --
-- MARK ME! --
-- IN LIFE MY SPIRIT NEVER ROVED BEYOND THE NARROW LIMITS OF OUR MONEY-CHANGING HOLE; AND WEARY JOURNEYS LIE BEFORE ME!
YOU MUST HAVE BEEN VERY SLOW ABOUT IT, JACOB.
SLOW!
SEVEN YEARS DEAD.
AND TRAVELLING ALL THE TIME!
THE WHOLE TIME. NO REST, NO PEACE.
CLANK
INCESSANT TORTURE OF REMORSE!
CLANK
CLANK

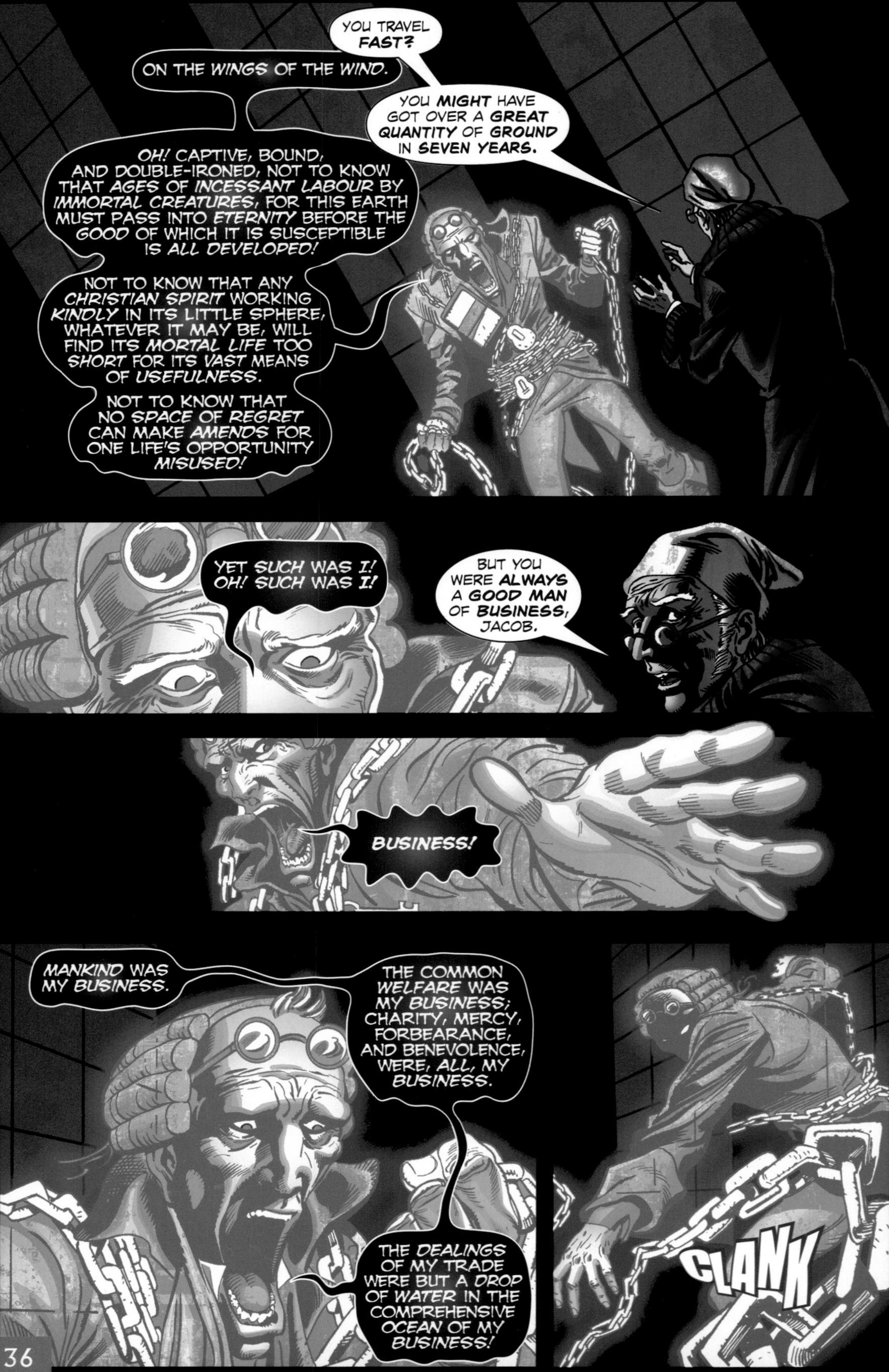

YOU TRAVEL FAST?
ON THE WINGS OF THE WIND.
YOU MIGHT HAVE GOT OVER A GREAT QUANTITY OF GROUND IN SEVEN YEARS.
OH! CAPTIVE, BOUND, AND DOUBLE-IRONED, NOT TO KNOW THAT AGES OF INCESSANT LABOUR BY IMMORTAL CREATURES, FOR THIS EARTH MUST PASS INTO ETERNITY BEFORE THE GOOD OF WHICH IT IS SUSCEPTIBLE IS ALL DEVELOPED!
NOT TO KNOW THAT ANY CHRISTIAN SPIRIT WORKING KINDLY IN ITS LITTLE SPHERE, WHATEVER IT MAY BE, WILL FIND ITS MORTAL LIFE TOO SHORT FOR ITS VAST MEANS OF USEFULNESS.
NOT TO KNOW THAT NO SPACE OF REGRET CAN MAKE AMENDS FOR ONE LIFE'S OPPORTUNITY MISUSED!
YET SUCH WAS I! OH! SUCH WAS I!
BUT YOU WERE ALWAYS A GOOD MAN OF BUSINESS, JACOB.
BUSINESS!
MANKIND WAS MY BUSINESS.
THE COMMON WELFARE WAS MY BUSINESS; CHARITY, MERCY, FORBEARANCE, AND BENEVOLENCE, WERE, ALL, MY BUSINESS.
THE DEALINGS OF MY TRADE WERE BUT A DROP OF WATER IN THE COMPREHENSIVE OCEAN OF MY BUSINESS!
CLANK

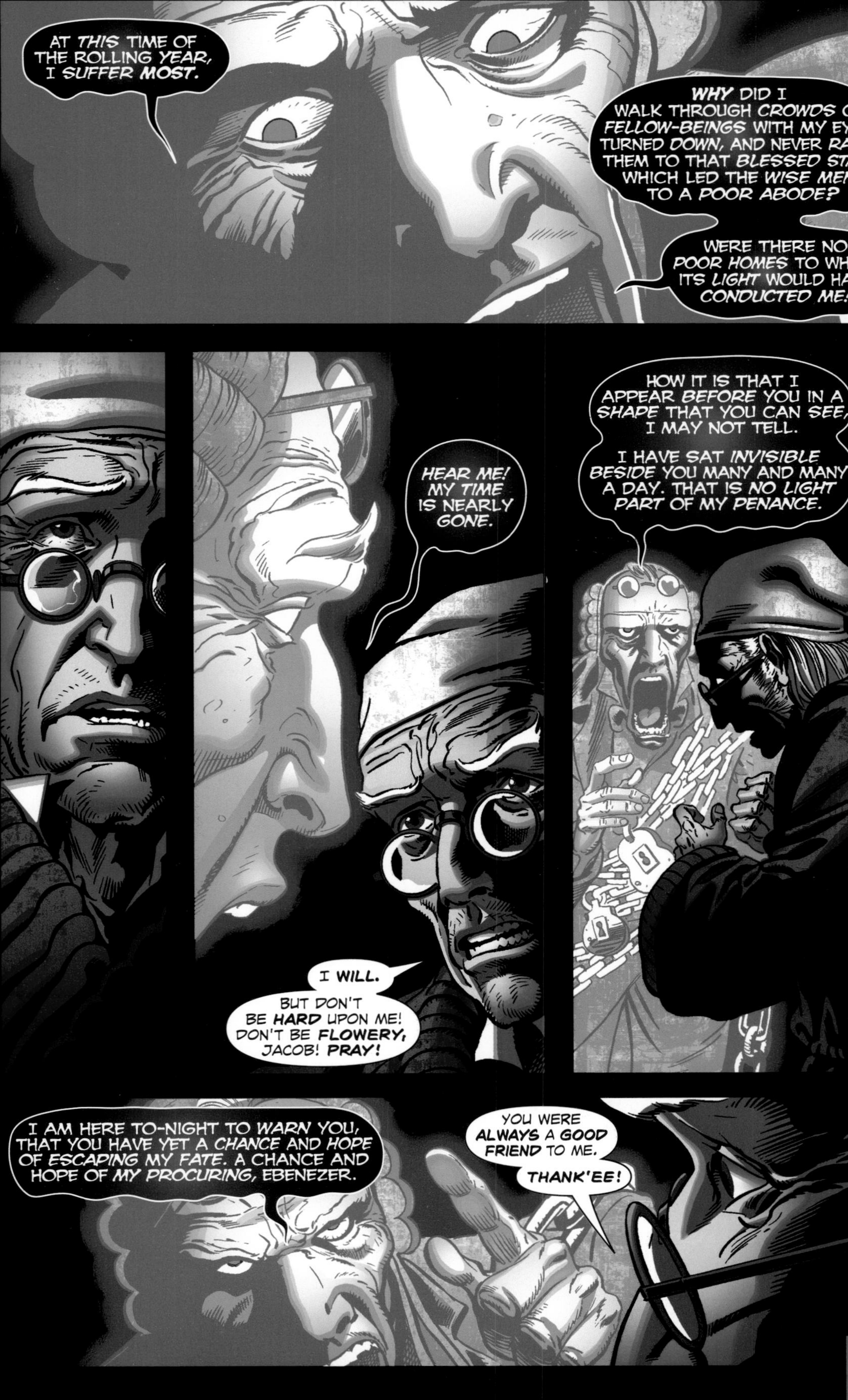
AT THIS TIME OF THE ROLLING YEAR, I SUFFER MOST.
WHY DID I WALK THROUGH CROWDS OF FELLOW-BEINGS WITH MY EYES TURNED DOWN, AND NEVER RAISE THEM TO THAT BLESSED STAR, WHICH LED THE WISE MEN TO A POOR ABODE?
WERE THERE NO POOR HOMES TO WHICH ITS LIGHT WOULD HAVE CONDUCTED ME!
HEAR ME! MY TIME IS NEARLY GONE.
I WILL.
BUT DON'T BE HARD UPON ME! DON'T BE FLOWERY, JACOB! PRAY!
HOW IT IS THAT I APPEAR BEFORE YOU IN A SHAPE THAT YOU CAN SEE, I MAY NOT TELL.
I HAVE SAT INVISIBLE BESIDE YOU MANY AND MANY A DAY. THAT IS NO LIGHT PART OF MY PENANCE.
I AM HERE TO-NIGHT TO WARN YOU, THAT YOU HAVE YET A CHANCE AND HOPE OF ESCAPING MY FATE. A CHANCE AND HOPE OF MY PROCURING, EBENEZER.
YOU WERE ALWAYS A GOOD FRIEND TO ME.
THANK'EE!

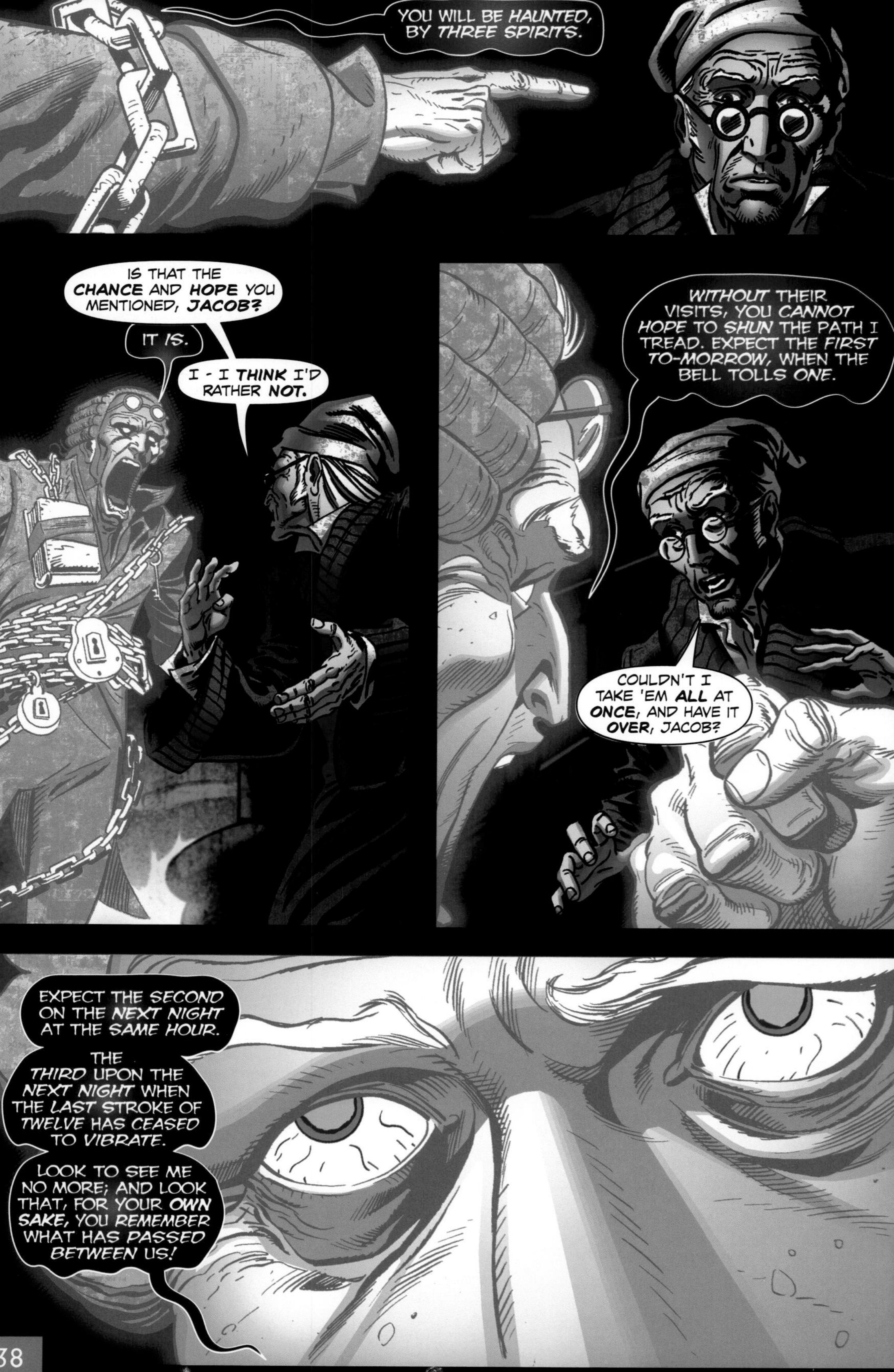
YOU WILL BE HAUNTED, BY THREE SPIRITS.
IS THAT THE CHANCE AND HOPE YOU MENTIONED, JACOB?
IT IS.
I - I THINK I'D RATHER NOT.
WITHOUT THEIR VISITS, YOU CANNOT HOPE TO SHUN THE PATH I TREAD. EXPECT THE FIRST TO-MORROW, WHEN THE BELL TOLLS ONE.
COULDN'T I TAKE 'EM ALL AT ONCE, AND HAVE IT OVER, JACOB?
EXPECT THE SECOND ON THE NEXT NIGHT AT THE SAME HOUR.
THE THIRD UPON THE NEXT NIGHT WHEN THE LAST STROKE OF TWELVE HAS CEASED TO VIBRATE.
LOOK TO SEE ME NO MORE; AND LOOK THAT, FOR YOUR OWN SAKE, YOU REMEMBER WHAT HAS PASSED BETWEEN US!

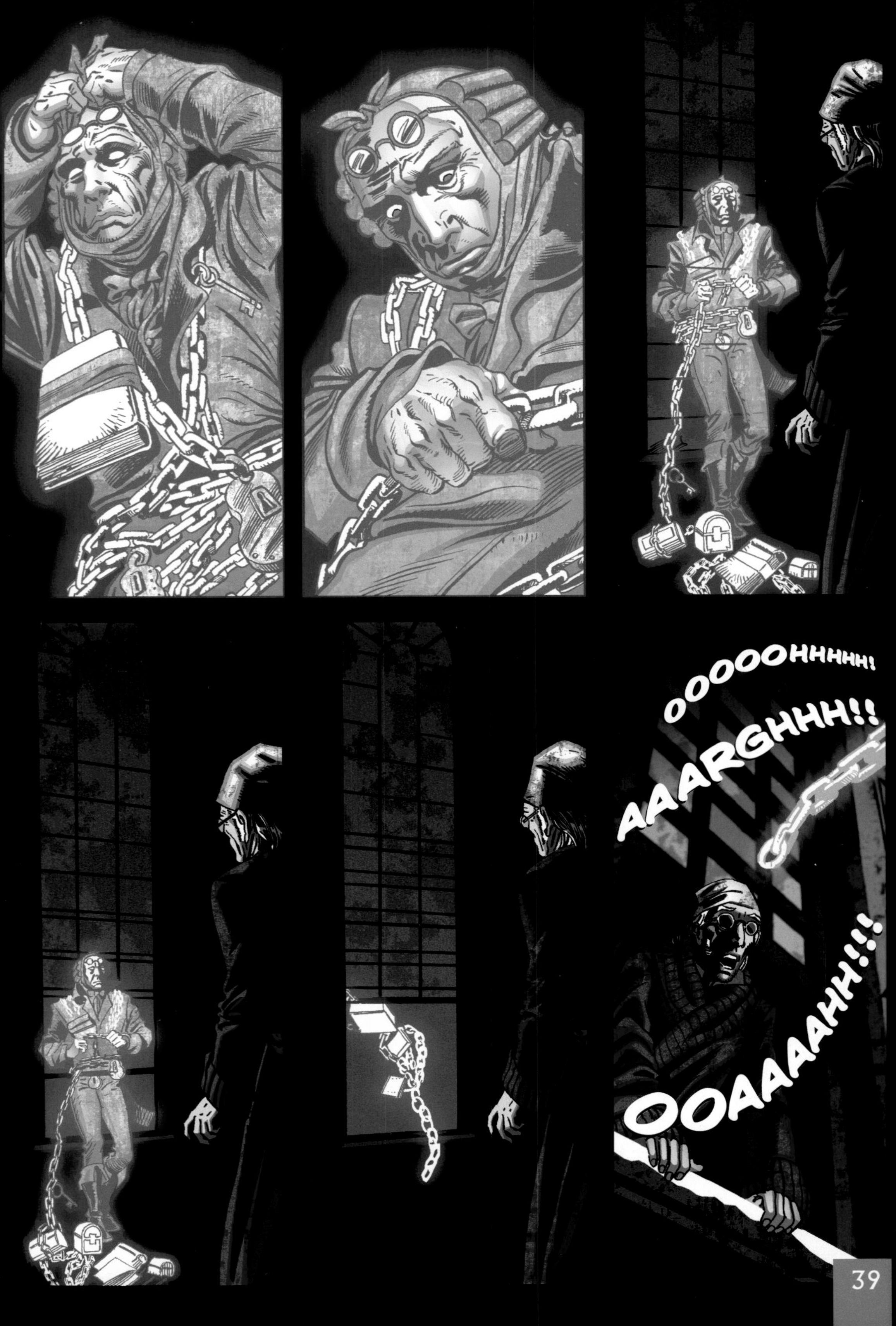
OOOOOHHHHH!
AAARGHHH!!
OOAAAAAHH!!!

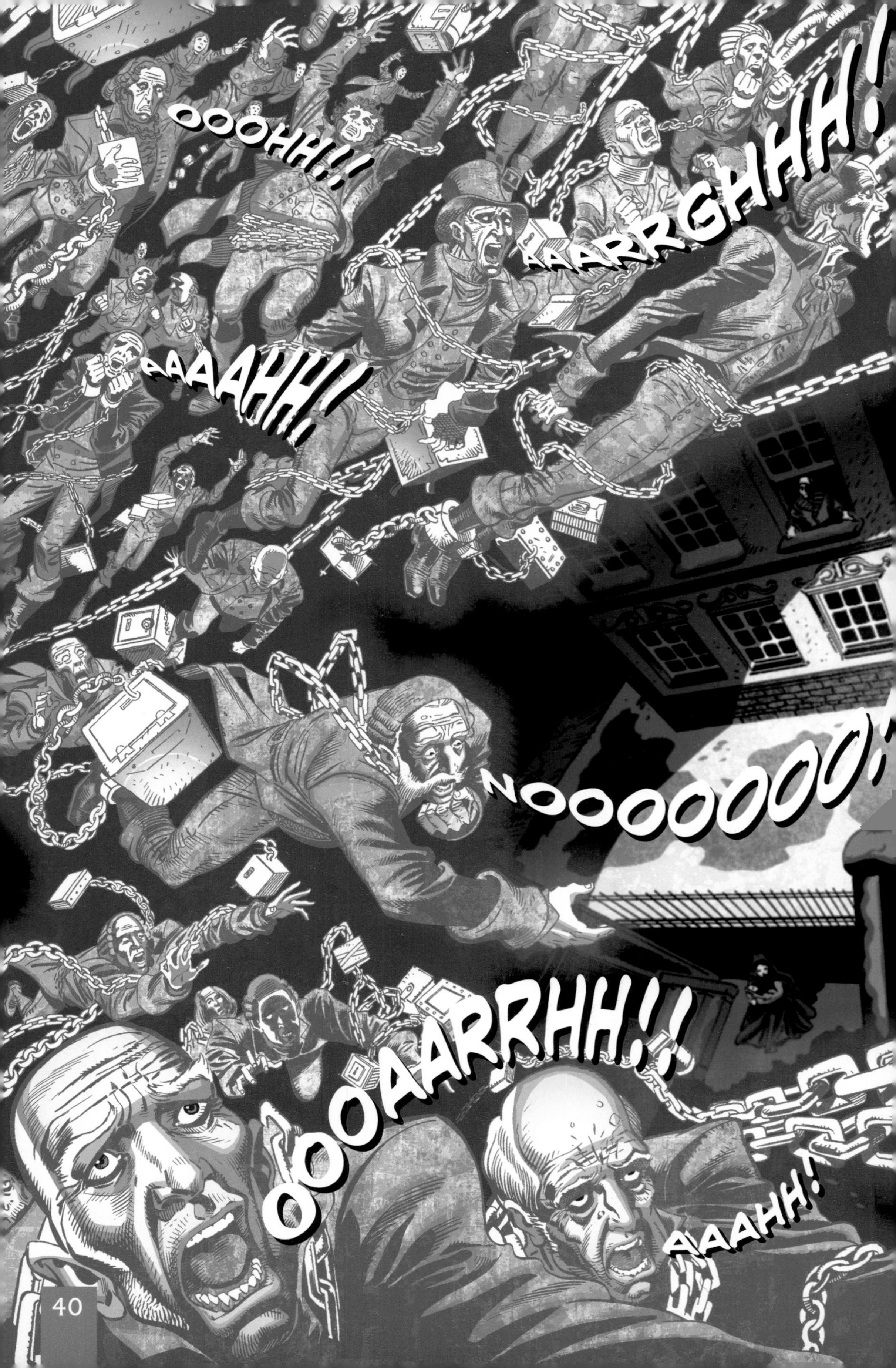
OOOHH!!
AAARRGHHH!
AAAAHH!
NOOOOOOOO!
OOOAARRHH!!
AAAHH!

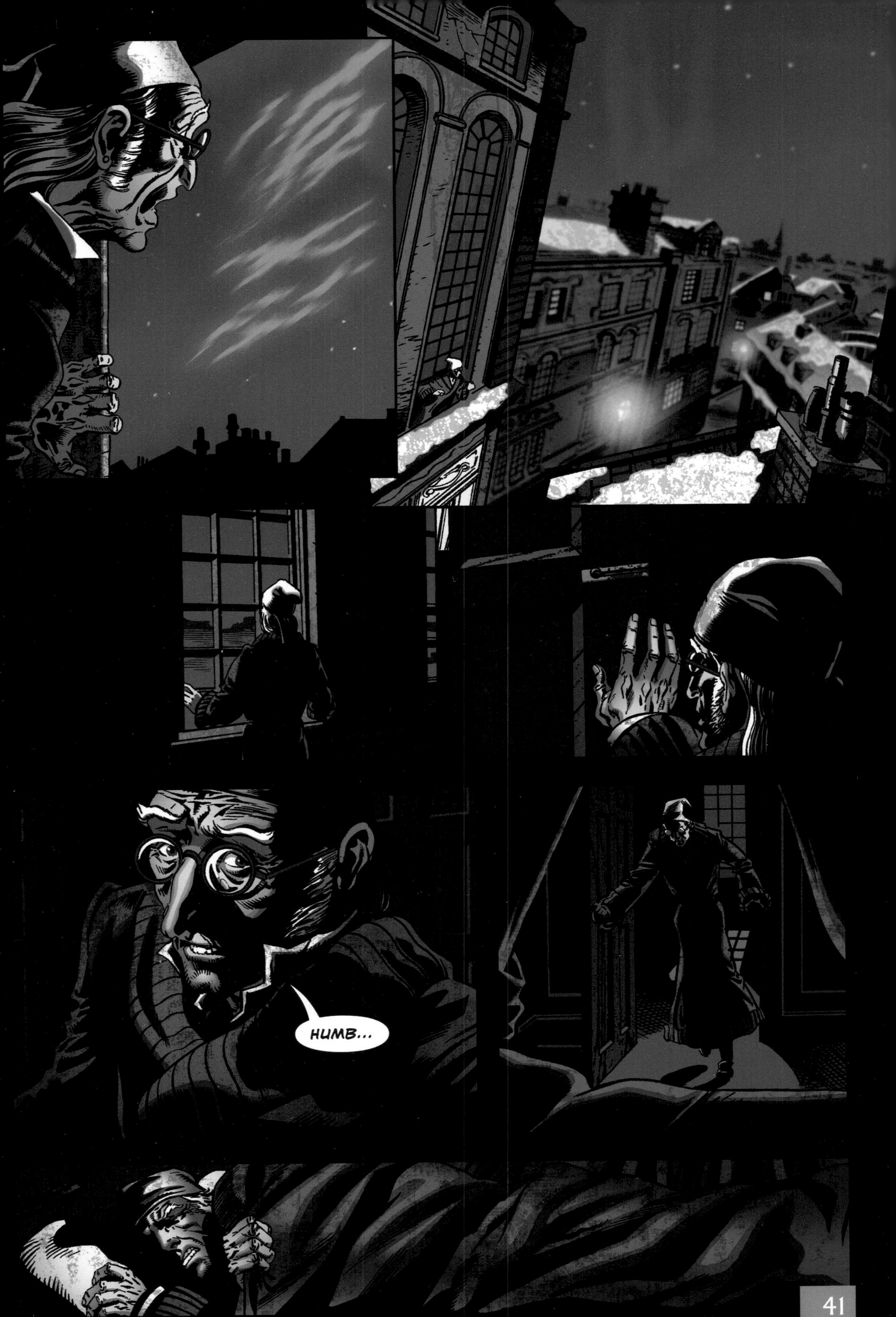
HUMB...

Stave Two: The First of the Three Spirits

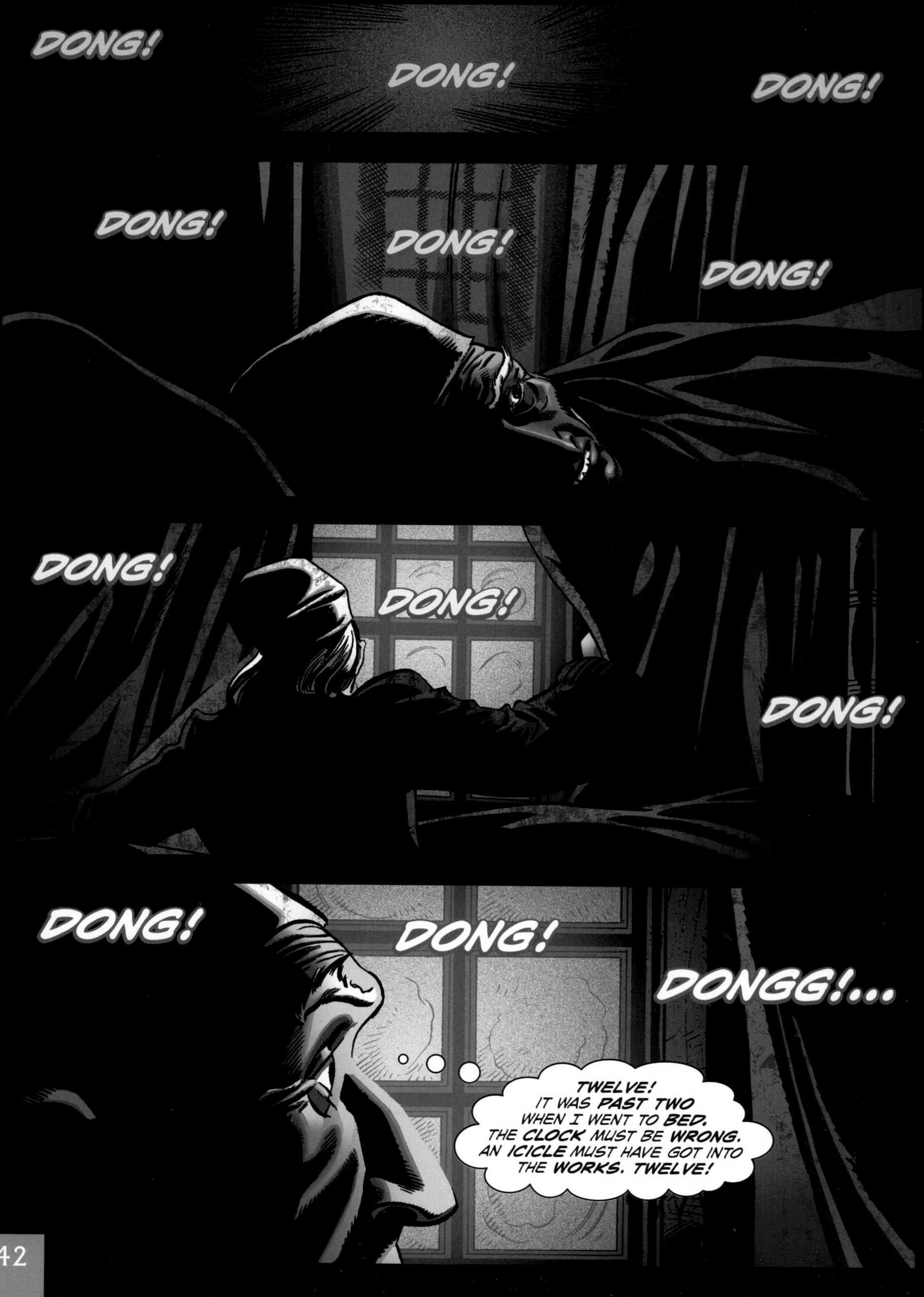
DONG!
DONG!
DONG!
DONG!
DONG!
DONG!
DONG!
DONG!
DONG!
DONG!
DONG!
DONGG!...
TWELVE! IT WAS PAST TWO WHEN I WENT TO BED. THE CLOCK MUST BE WRONG. AN ICICLE MUST HAVE GOT INTO THE WORKS. TWELVE!

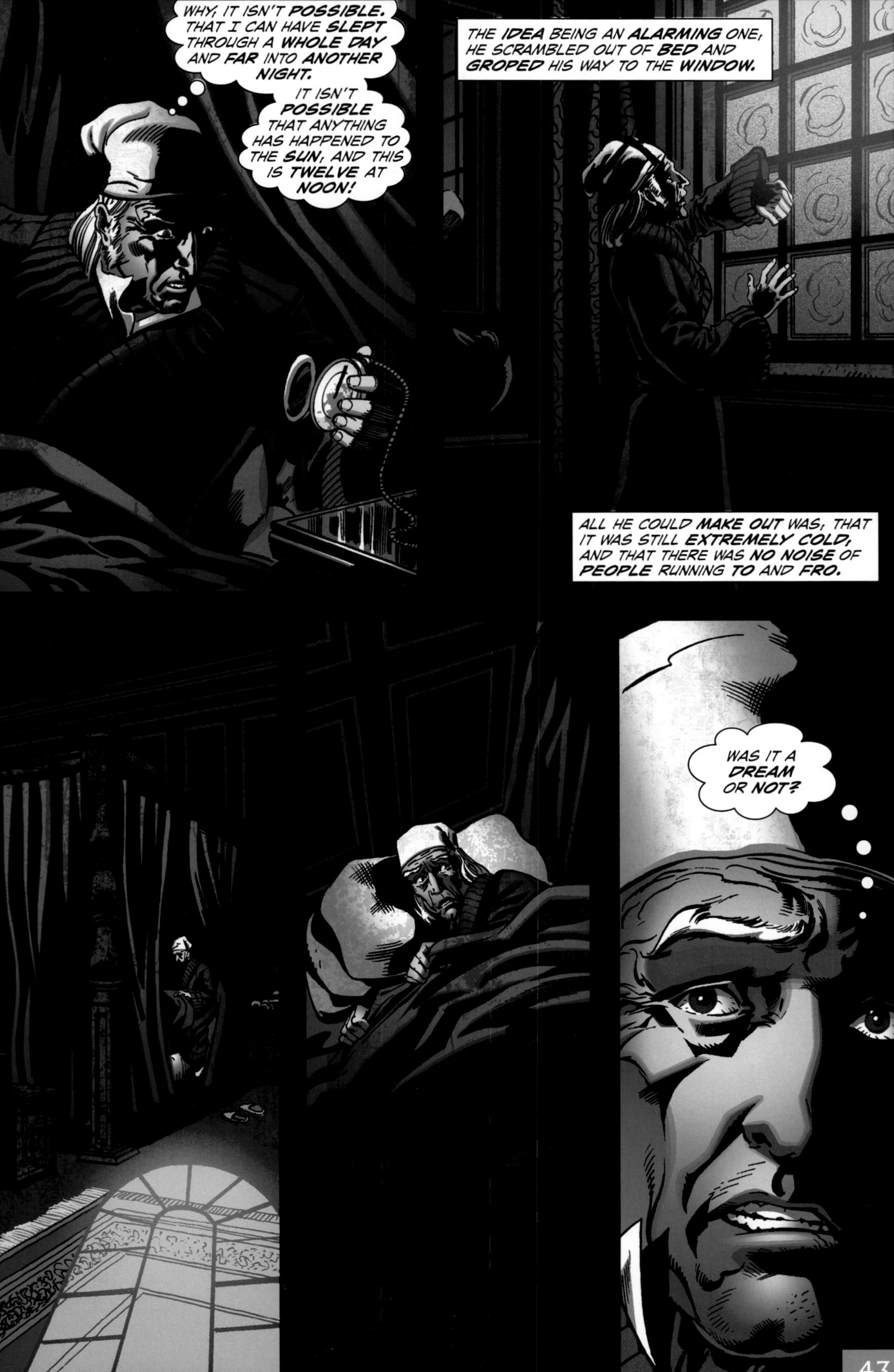
WHY, IT ISN'T POSSIBLE. THAT I CAN HAVE SLEPT THROUGH A WHOLE DAY AND FAR INTO ANOTHER NIGHT.
IT ISN'T POSSIBLE THAT ANYTHING HAS HAPPENED TO THE SUN, AND THIS IS TWELVE AT NOON!
THE IDEA BEING AN ALARMING ONE, HE SCRAMBLED OUT OF BED AND GROPED HIS WAY TO THE WINDOW.
ALL HE COULD MAKE OUT WAS, THAT IT WAS STILL EXTREMELY COLD, AND THAT THERE WAS NO NOISE OF PEOPLE RUNNING TO AND FRO.
WAS IT A DREAM OR NOT?

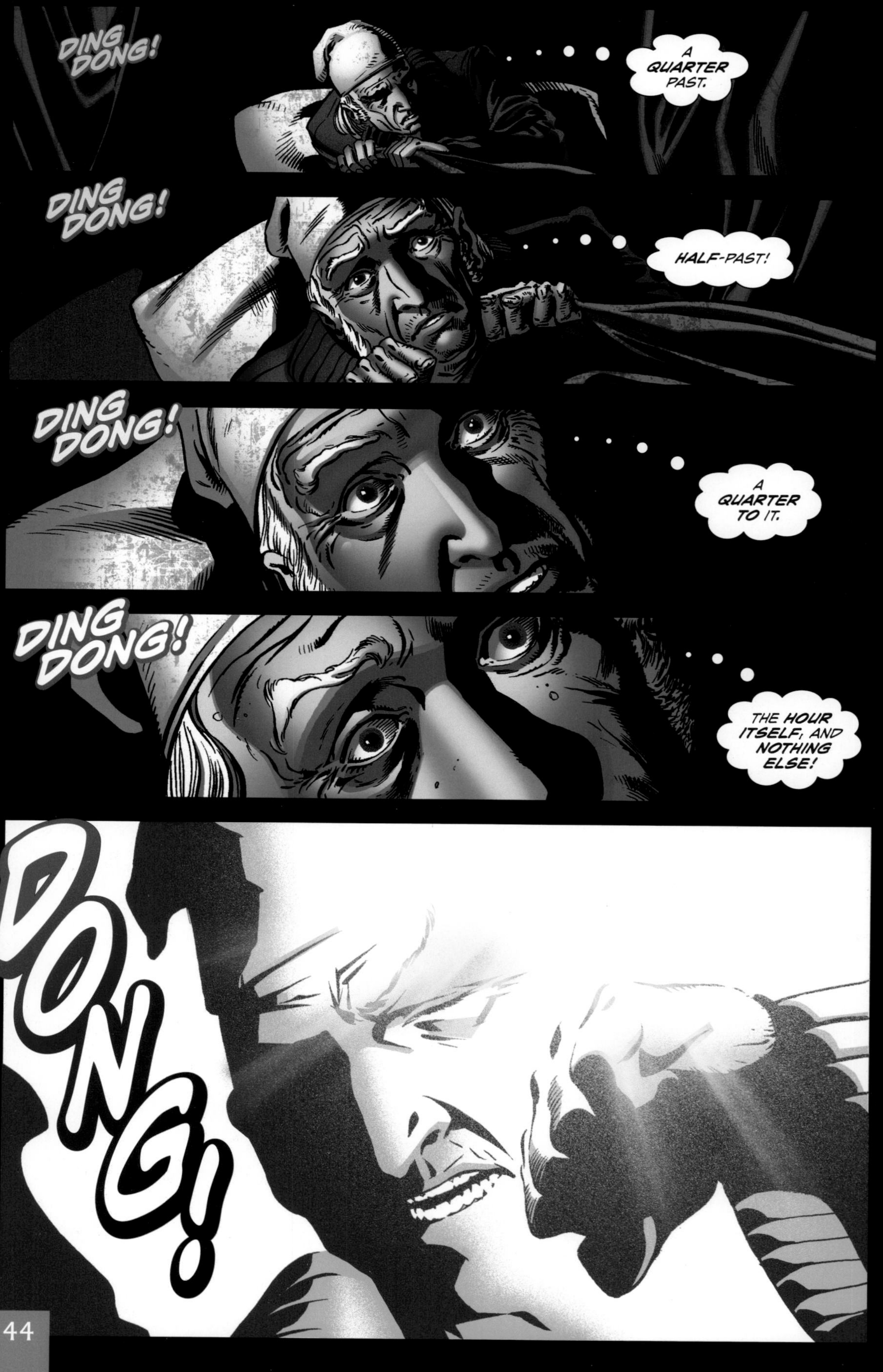
DING DONG!
A QUARTER PAST.
DING DONG!
HALF-PAST!
DING DONG!
A QUARTER TO IT.
DING DONG!
THE HOUR ITSELF, AND NOTHING ELSE!
DONG!

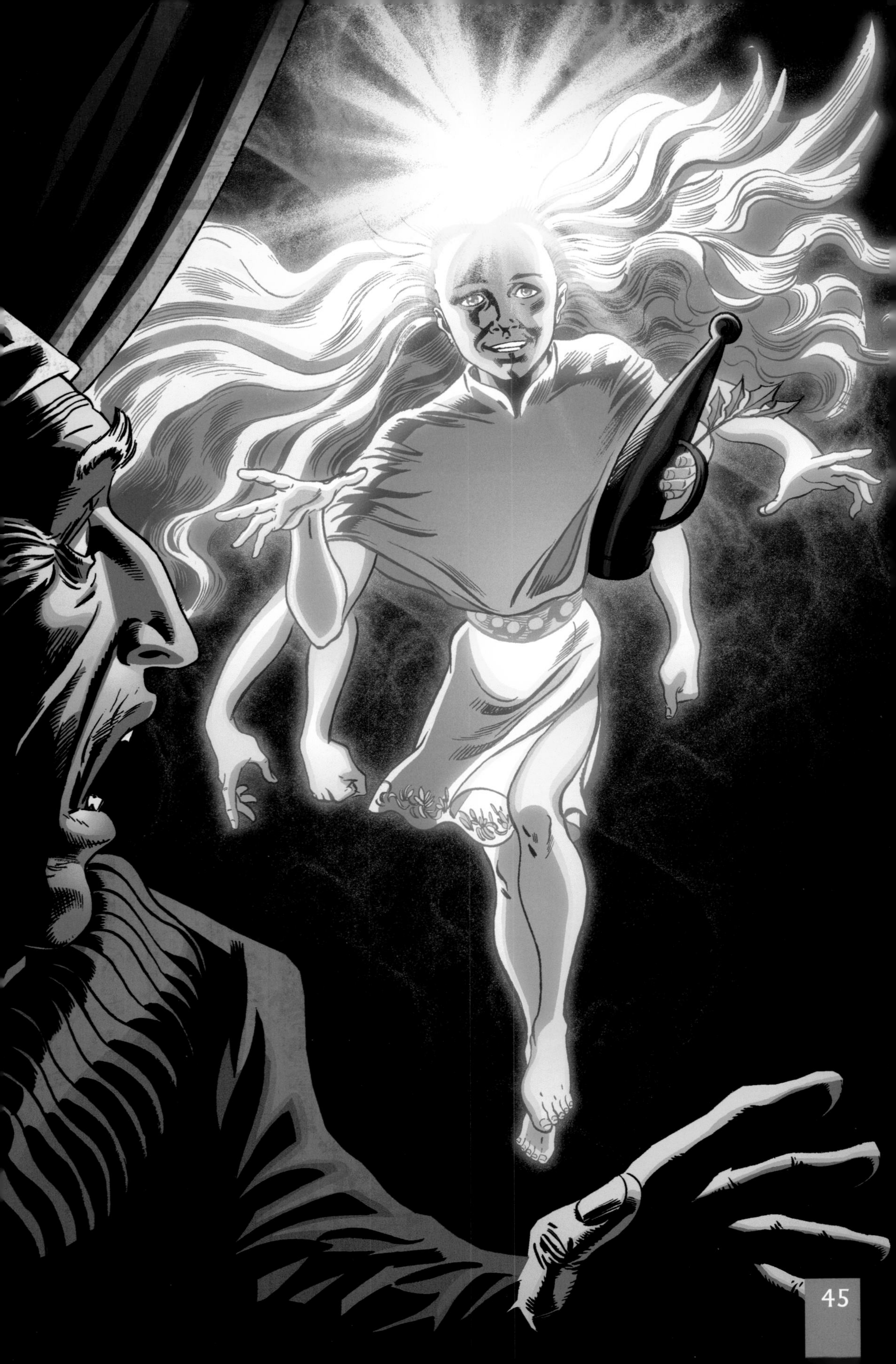

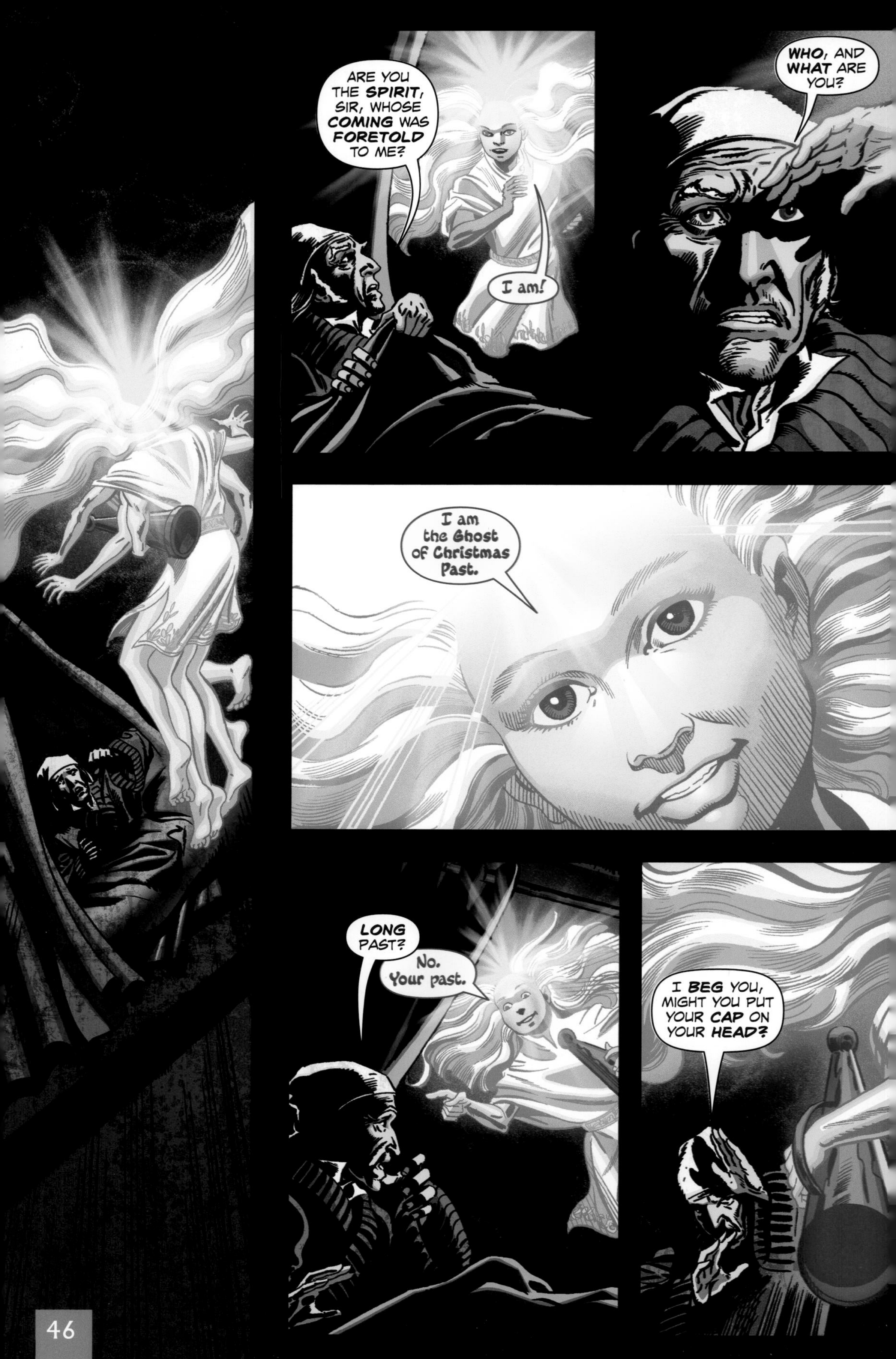
ARE YOU THE SPIRIT, SIR, WHOSE COMING WAS FORETOLD TO ME?
I am!
WHO, AND WHAT ARE YOU?
I am the Ghost of Christmas Past.
LONG PAST?
No. Your past.
I BEG YOU, MIGHT YOU PUT YOUR CAP ON YOUR HEAD?

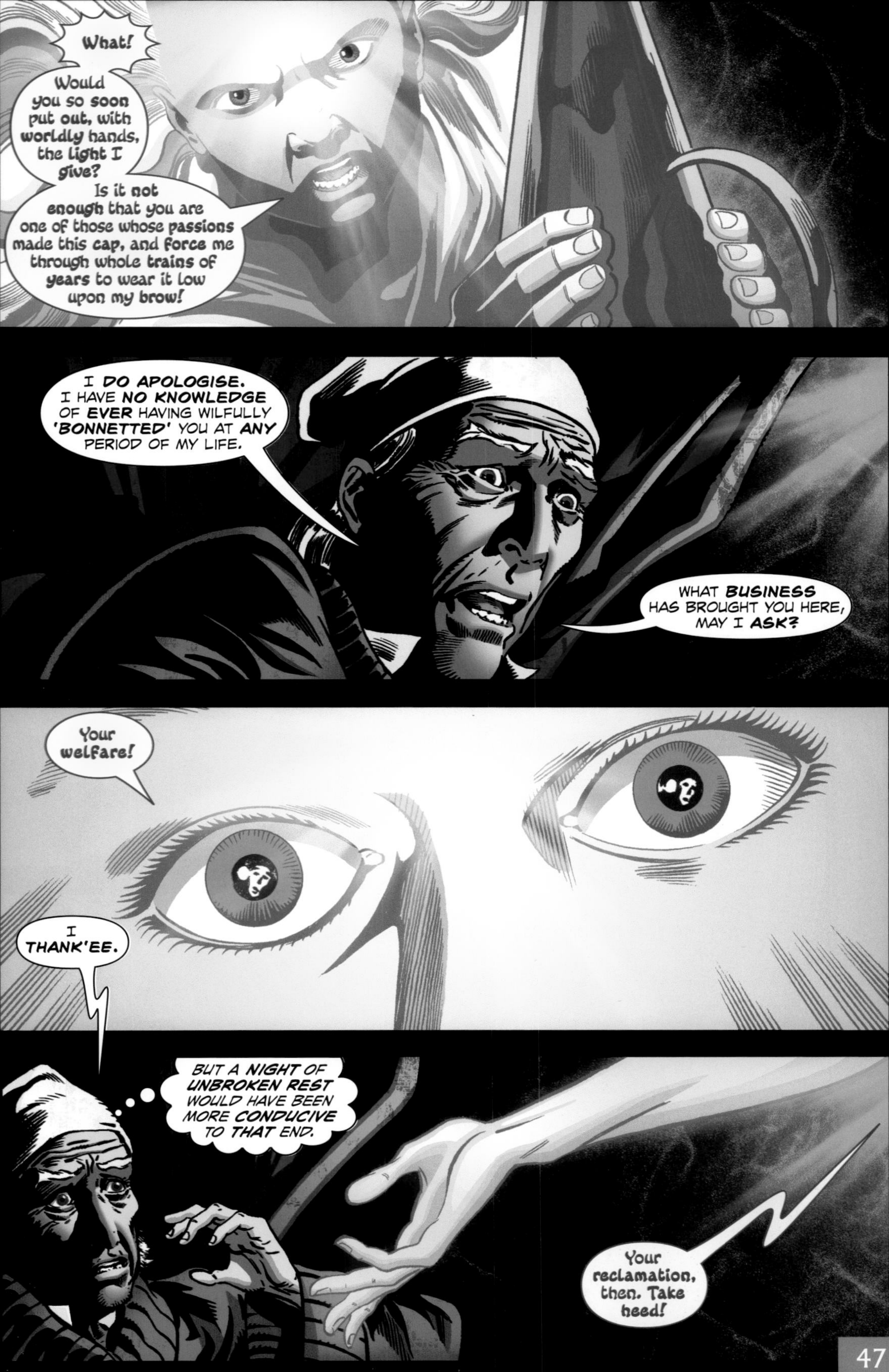
What!
Would you so soon put out, with worldly hands, the light I give?
Is it not enough that you are one of those whose passions made this cap, and force me through whole trains of years to wear it low upon my brow!
I DO APOLOGISE. I HAVE NO KNOWLEDGE OF EVER HAVING WILFULLY 'BONNETTED' YOU AT ANY PERIOD OF MY LIFE.
WHAT BUSINESS HAS BROUGHT YOU HERE, MAY I ASK?
Your welfare!
I THANK'EE.
BUT A NIGHT OF UNBROKEN REST WOULD HAVE BEEN MORE CONDUCIVE TO THAT END.
Your reclamation, then. Take heed!

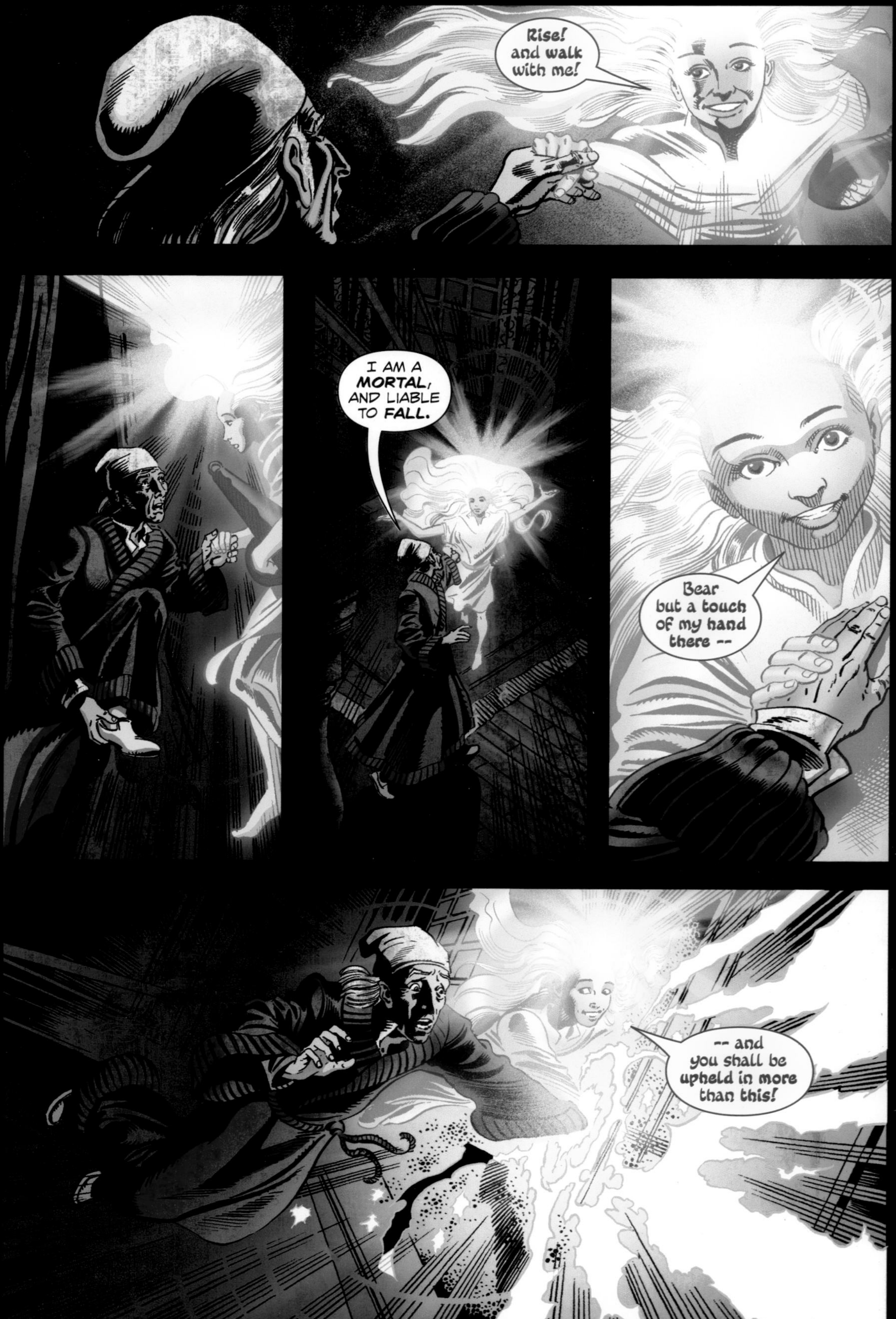
Rise! and walk with me!
I AM A MORTAL, AND LIABLE TO FALL.
Bear but a touch of my hand there --
-- and you shall be upheld in more than this!

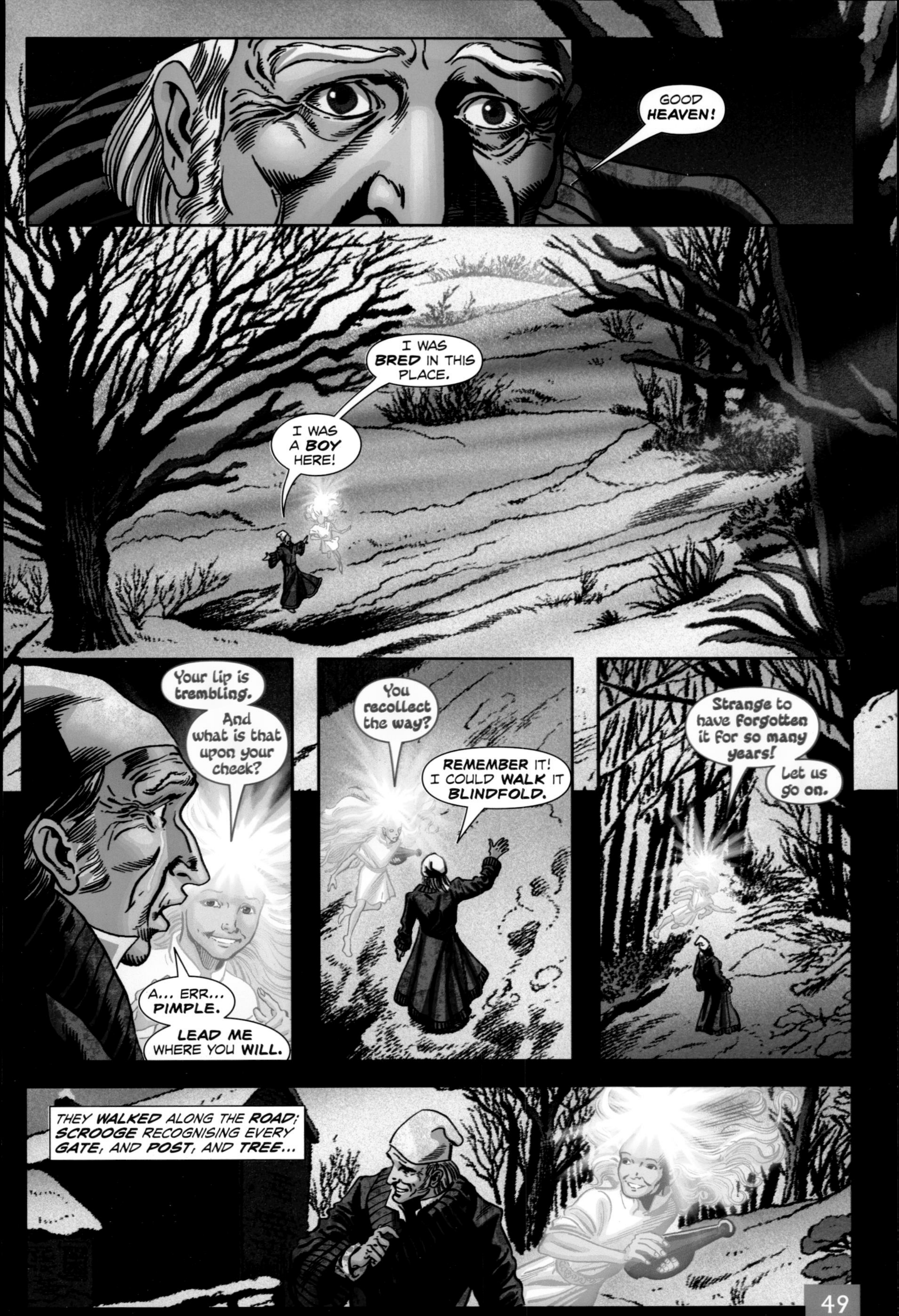
GOOD HEAVEN!
I WAS BRED IN THIS PLACE.
I WAS A BOY HERE!
Your lip is trembling.
And what is that upon your cheek?
A... ERR... PIMPLE.
LEAD ME WHERE YOU WILL.
You recollect the way?
REMEMBER IT! I COULD WALK IT BLINDFOLD.
Strange to have forgotten it for so many years!
Let us go on.
THEY WALKED ALONG THE ROAD; SCROOGE RECOGNISING EVERY GATE, AND POST, AND TREE...

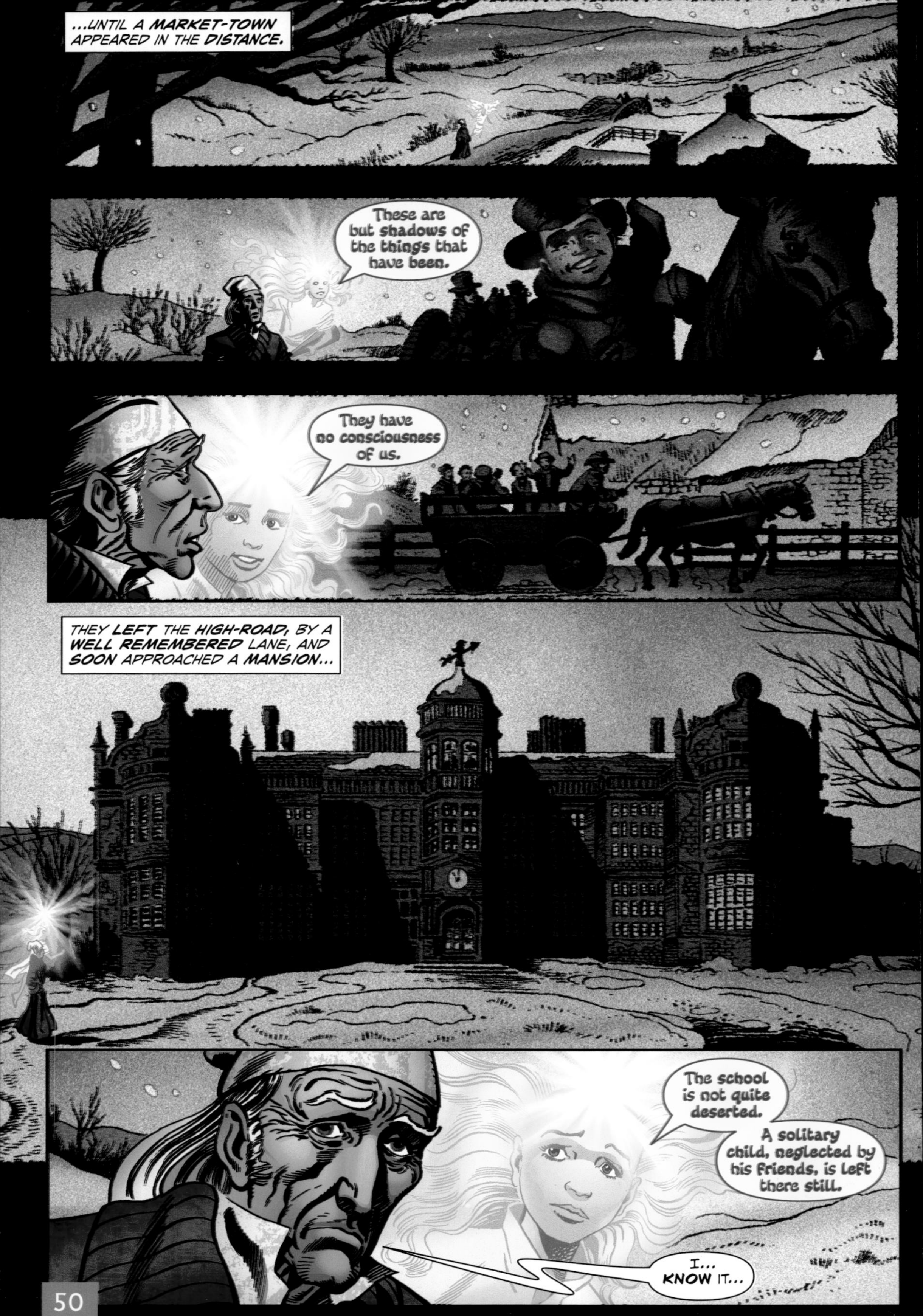
...UNTIL A MARKET-TOWN APPEARED IN THE DISTANCE.
These are but shadows of the things that have been.
They have no consciousness of us.
THEY LEFT THE HIGH-ROAD, BY A WELL REMEMBERED LANE, AND SOON APPROACHED A MANSION...
The school is not quite deserted.
A solitary child, neglected by his friends, is left there still.
I... KNOW IT...

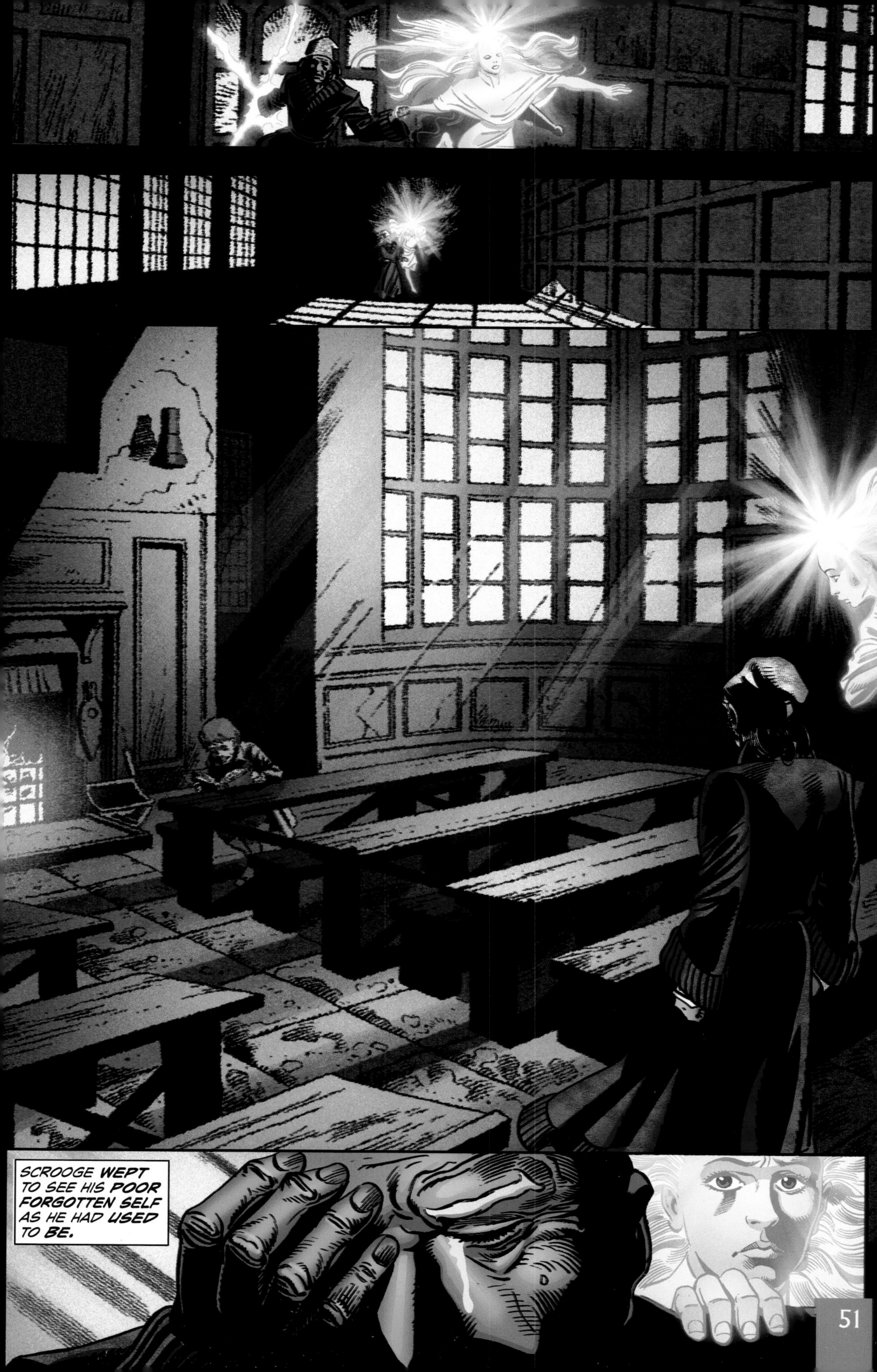
SCROOGE WEPT TO SEE HIS POOR FORGOTTEN SELF AS HE HAD USED TO BE.

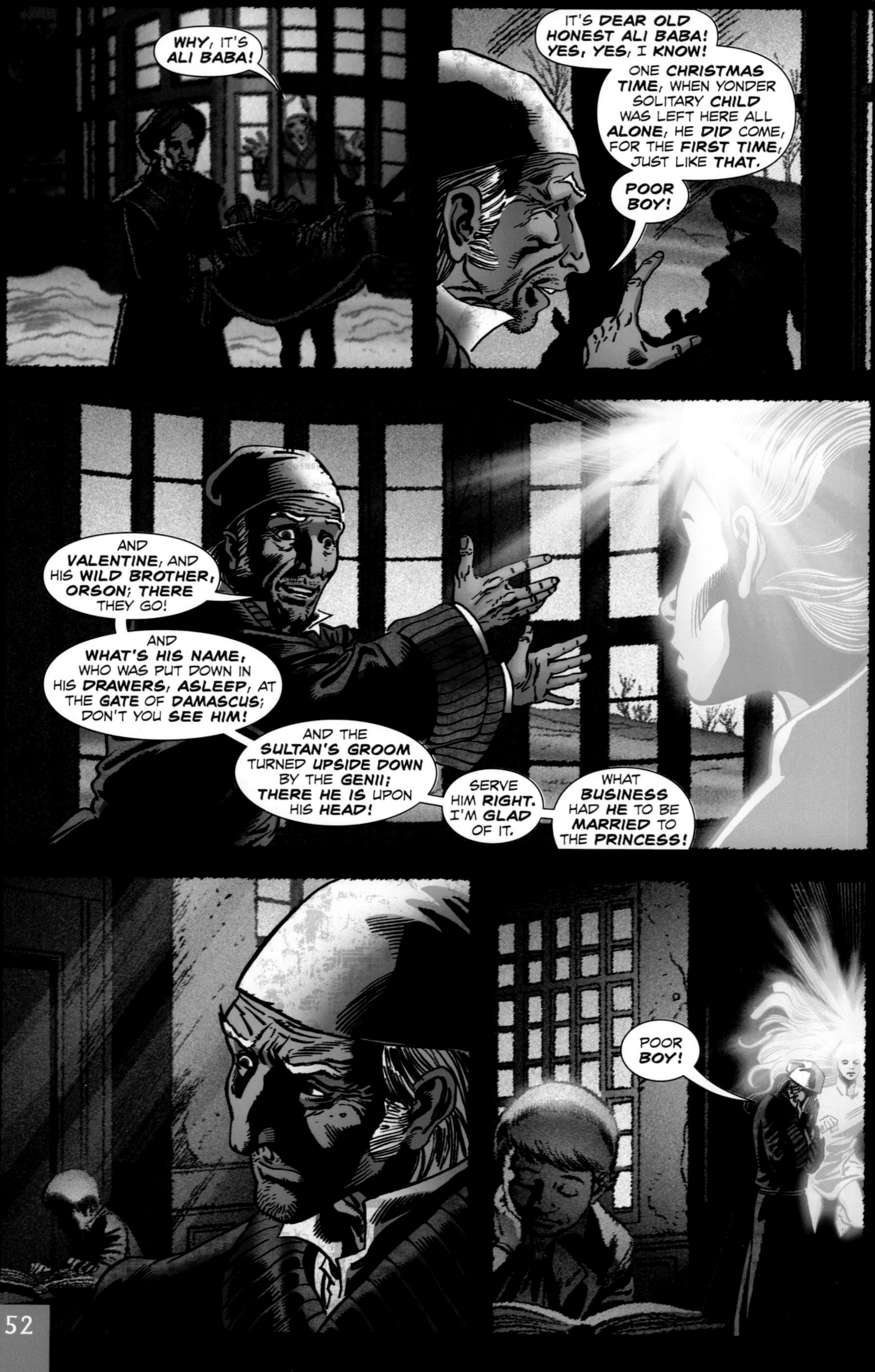
WHY, IT'S ALI BABA!
IT'S DEAR OLD HONEST ALI BABA! YES, YES, I KNOW!
ONE CHRISTMAS TIME, WHEN YONDER SOLITARY CHILD WAS LEFT HERE ALL ALONE, HE DID COME, FOR THE FIRST TIME, JUST LIKE THAT.
POOR BOY!
AND VALENTINE, AND HIS WILD BROTHER, ORSON; THERE THEY GO!
AND WHAT'S HIS NAME, WHO WAS PUT DOWN IN HIS DRAWERS, ASLEEP, AT THE GATE OF DAMASCUS; DON'T YOU SEE HIM!
AND THE SULTAN'S GROOM TURNED UPSIDE DOWN BY THE GENII; THERE HE IS UPON HIS HEAD!
SERVE HIM RIGHT. I'M GLAD OF IT.
WHAT BUSINESS HAD HE TO BE MARRIED TO THE PRINCESS!
POOR BOY!

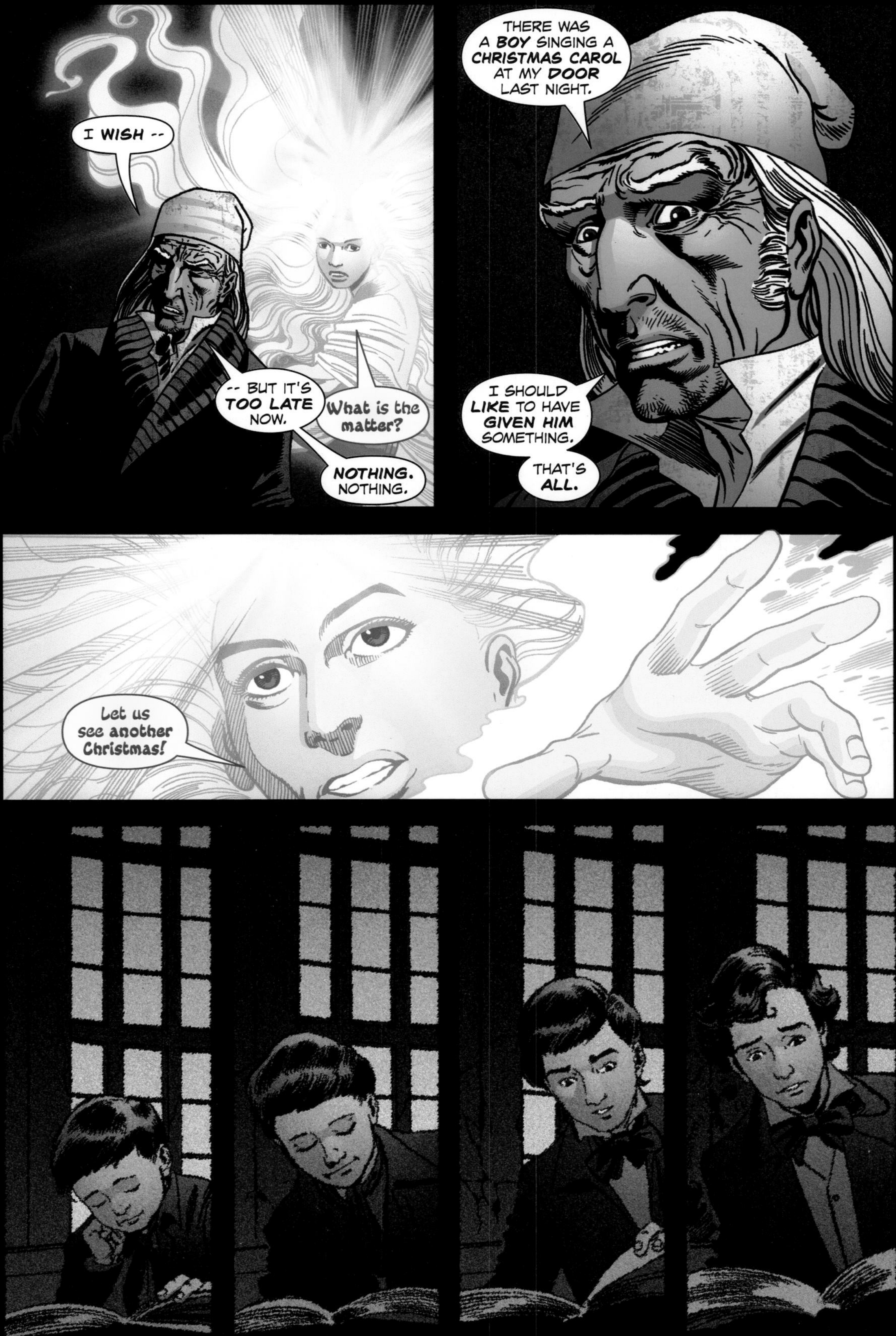
I WISH --
-- BUT IT'S TOO LATE NOW.
What is the matter?
NOTHING. NOTHING.
THERE WAS A BOY SINGING A CHRISTMAS CAROL AT MY DOOR LAST NIGHT.
I SHOULD LIKE TO HAVE GIVEN HIM SOMETHING.
THAT'S ALL.
Let us see another Christmas!

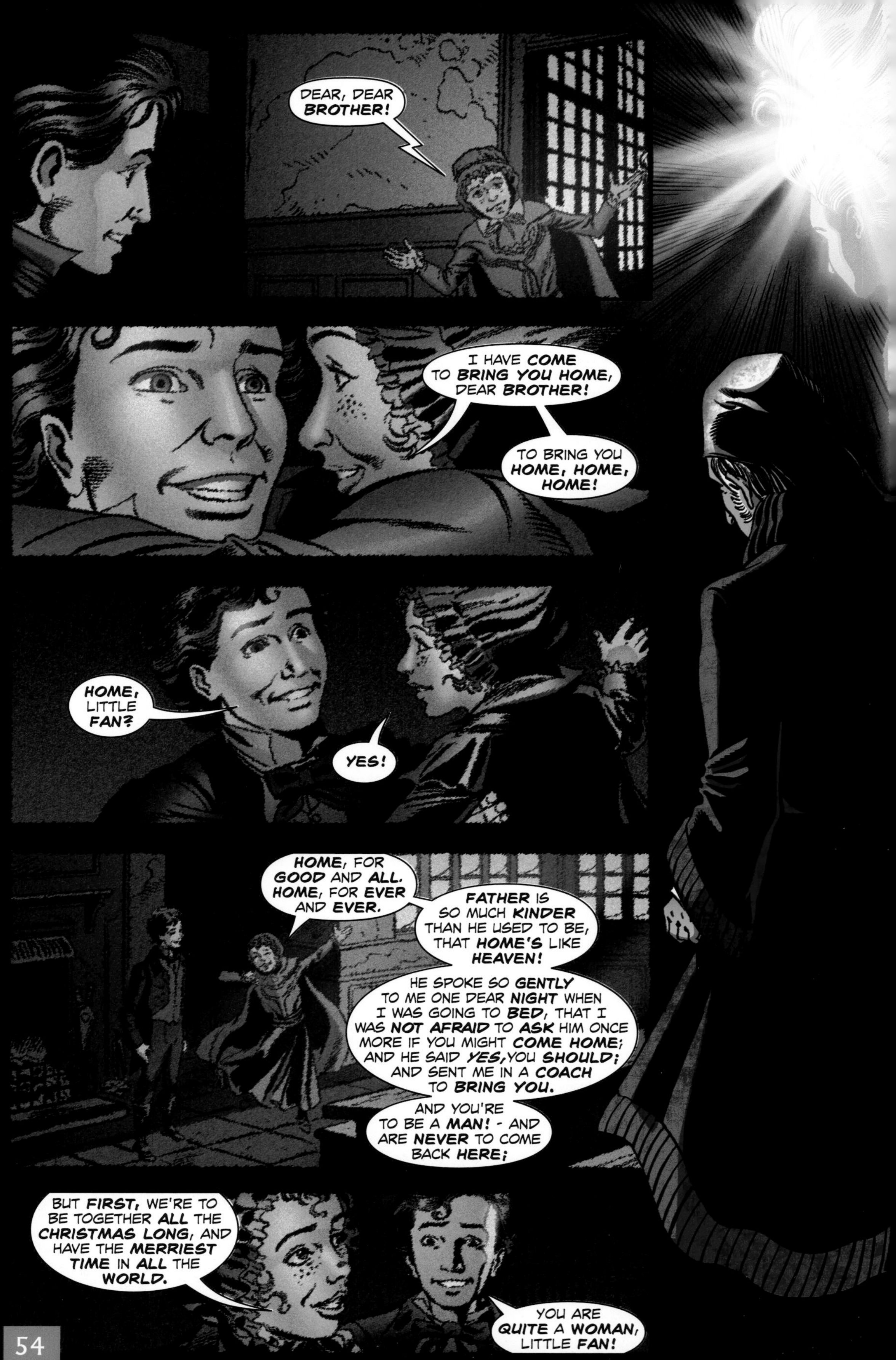
DEAR, DEAR BROTHER!
I HAVE COME TO BRING YOU HOME, DEAR BROTHER!
TO BRING YOU HOME, HOME, HOME!
HOME, LITTLE FAN?
YES!
HOME, FOR GOOD AND ALL. HOME, FOR EVER AND EVER.
FATHER IS SO MUCH KINDER THAN HE USED TO BE, THAT HOME'S LIKE HEAVEN!
HE SPOKE SO GENTLY TO ME ONE DEAR NIGHT WHEN I WAS GOING TO BED, THAT I WAS NOT AFRAID TO ASK HIM ONCE MORE IF YOU MIGHT COME HOME; AND HE SAID YES, YOU SHOULD; AND SENT ME IN A COACH TO BRING YOU.
AND YOU'RE TO BE A MAN! - AND ARE NEVER TO COME BACK HERE;
BUT FIRST, WE'RE TO BE TOGETHER ALL THE CHRISTMAS LONG, AND HAVE THE MERRIEST TIME IN ALL THE WORLD.
YOU ARE QUITE A WOMAN, LITTLE FAN!

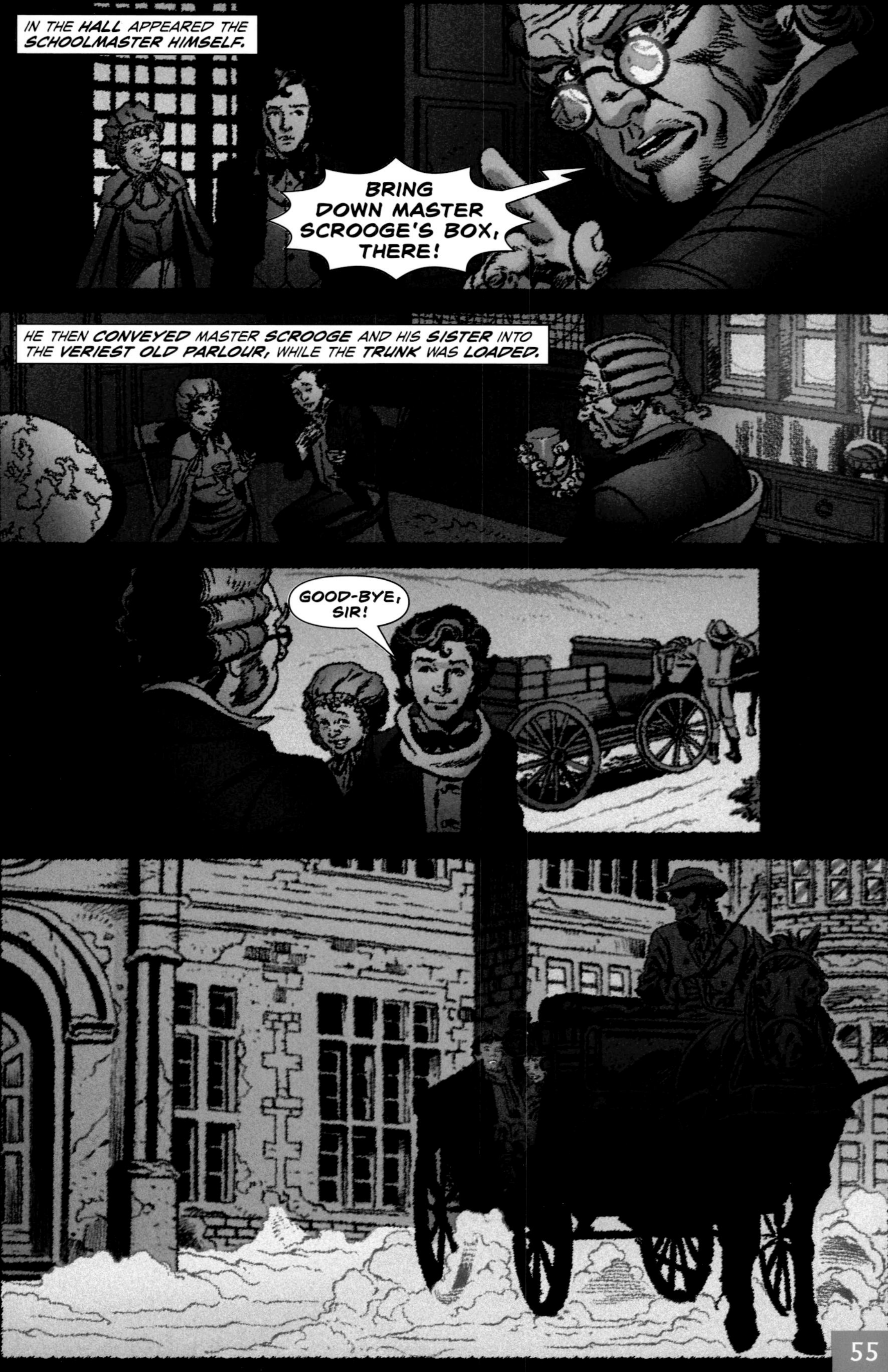
IN THE HALL APPEARED THE SCHOOLMASTER HIMSELF.
BRING DOWN MASTER SCROOGE'S BOX, THERE!
HE THEN CONVEYED MASTER SCROOGE AND HIS SISTER INTO THE VERIEST OLD PARLOUR, WHILE THE TRUNK WAS LOADED.
GOOD-BYE, SIR!

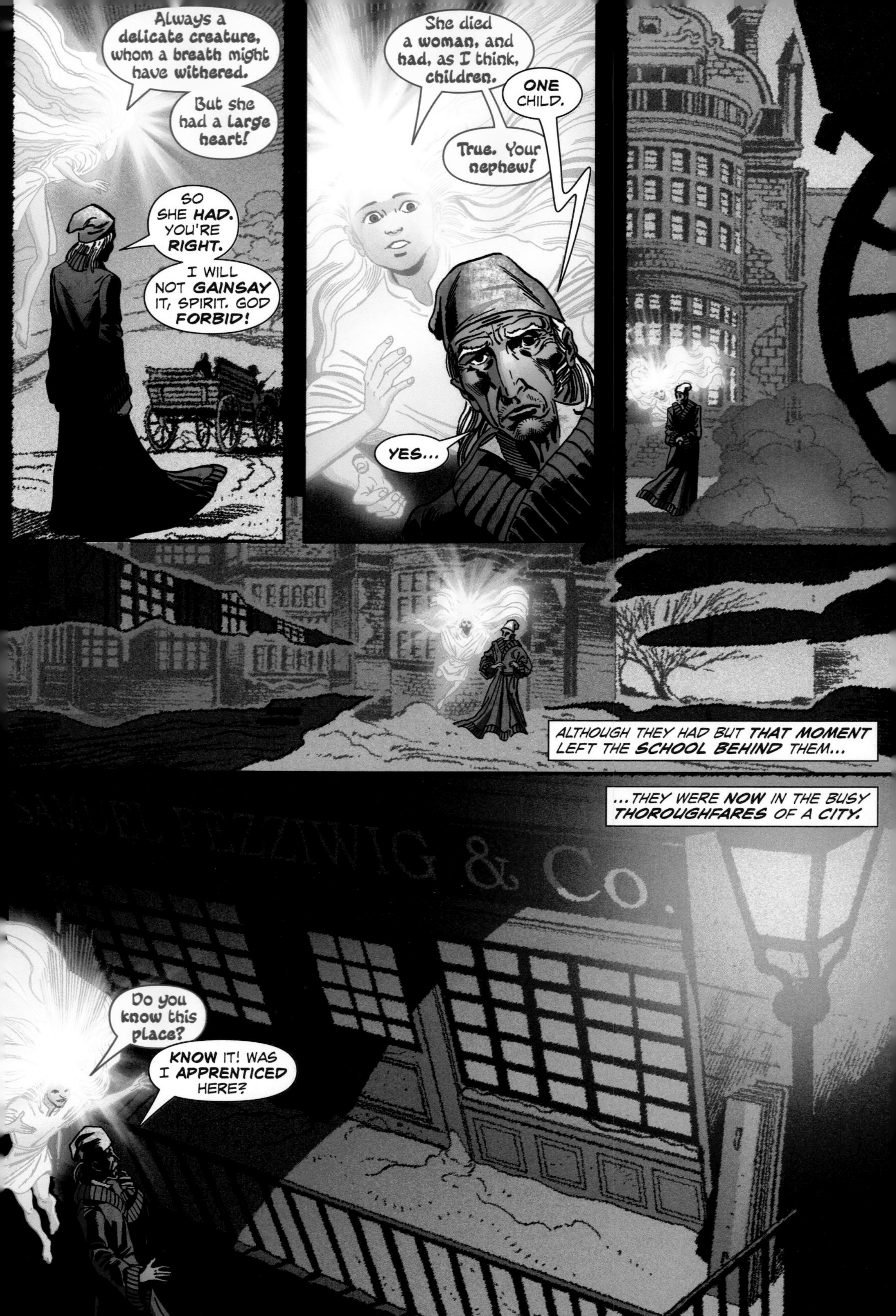
Always a delicate creature, whom a breath might have withered.
But she had a large heart!
SO SHE HAD. YOU'RE RIGHT.
I WILL NOT GAINSAY IT, SPIRIT. GOD FORBID!
She died a woman, and had, as I think, children.
ONE CHILD.
True. Your nephew!
YES...
ALTHOUGH THEY HAD BUT THAT MOMENT LEFT THE SCHOOL BEHIND THEM...
...THEY WERE NOW IN THE BUSY THOROUGHFARES OF A CITY.
SAMUEL FEZZIWIG & Co.
Do you know this place?
KNOW IT! WAS I APPRENTICED HERE?

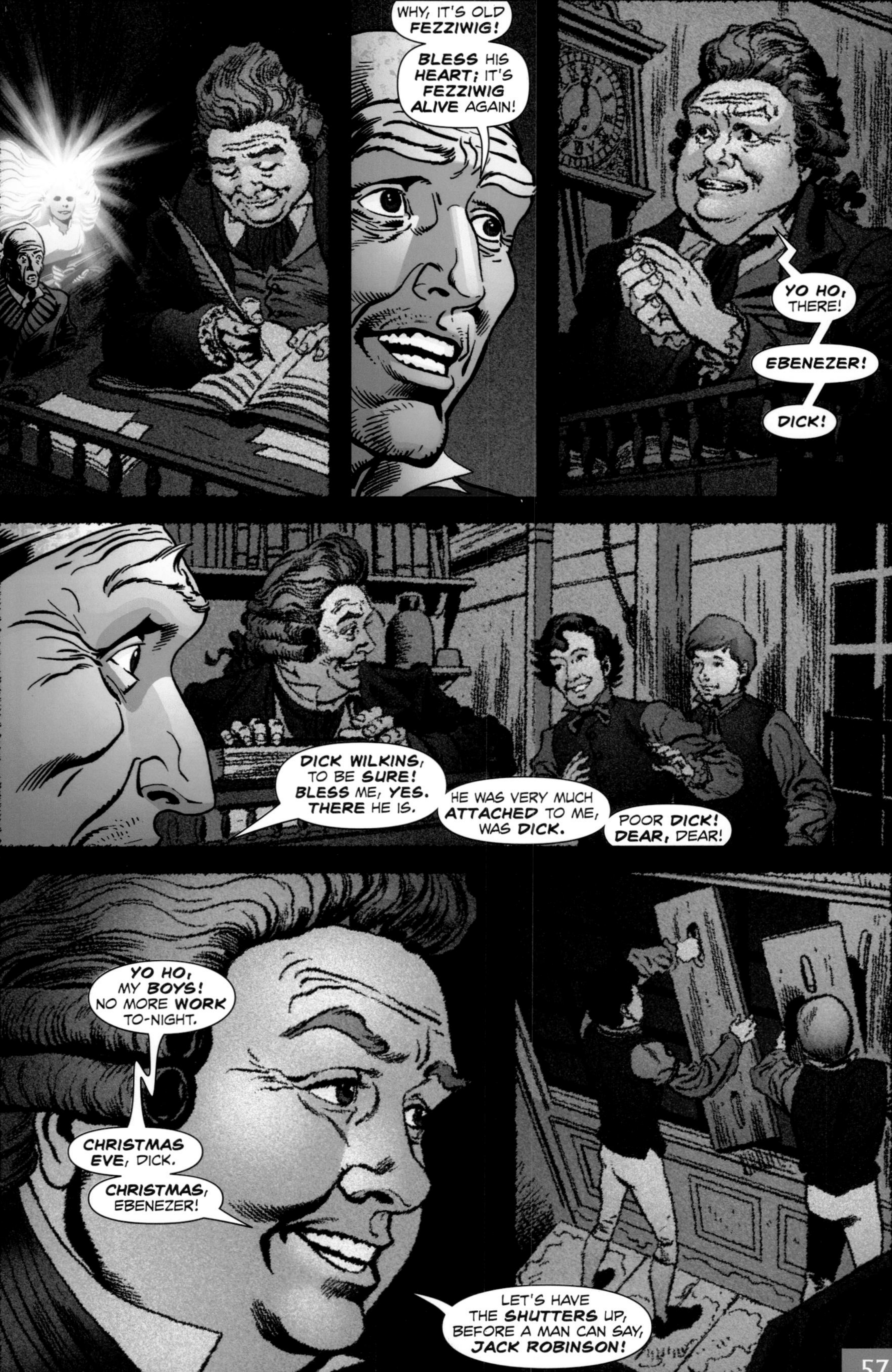
WHY, IT'S OLD FEZZIWIG!
BLESS HIS HEART; IT'S FEZZIWIG ALIVE AGAIN!
YO HO, THERE!
EBENEZER!
DICK!
DICK WILKINS, TO BE SURE! BLESS ME, YES. THERE HE IS.
HE WAS VERY MUCH ATTACHED TO ME, WAS DICK.
POOR DICK! DEAR, DEAR!
YO HO, MY BOYS! NO MORE WORK TO-NIGHT.
CHRISTMAS EVE, DICK.
CHRISTMAS, EBENEZER!
LET'S HAVE THE SHUTTERS UP, BEFORE A MAN CAN SAY, JACK ROBINSON!

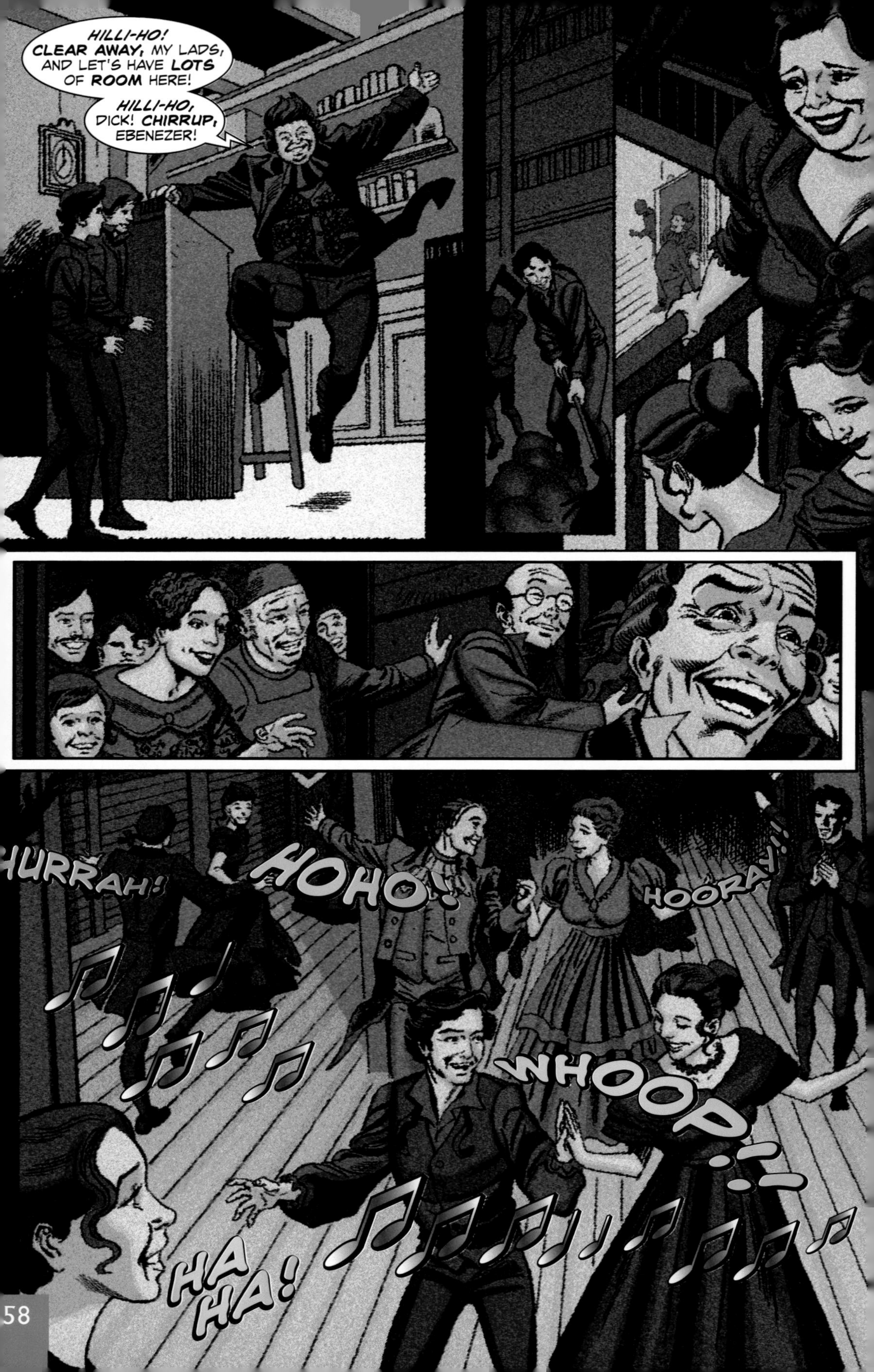
HILLI-HO! CLEAR AWAY, MY LADS, AND LET'S HAVE LOTS OF ROOM HERE!
HILLI-HO, DICK! CHIRRUP, EBENEZER!
HURRAH!
HOHO!
HOORAY!!
WHOOP!!!
HA HA!

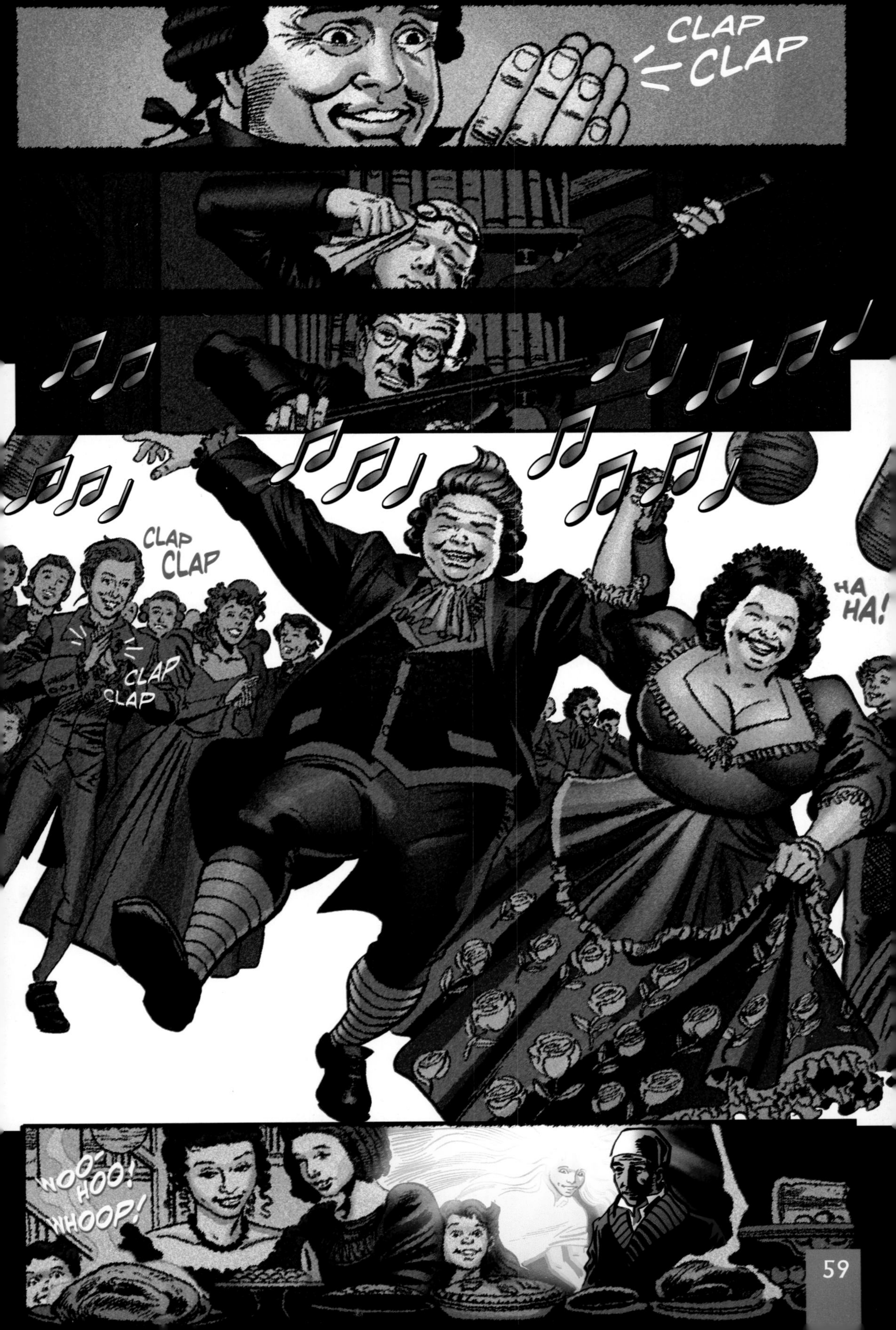
CLAP
CLAP
CLAP
CLAP
CLAP
CLAP
HA
HA!
WOO-
HOO!
WHOOP!

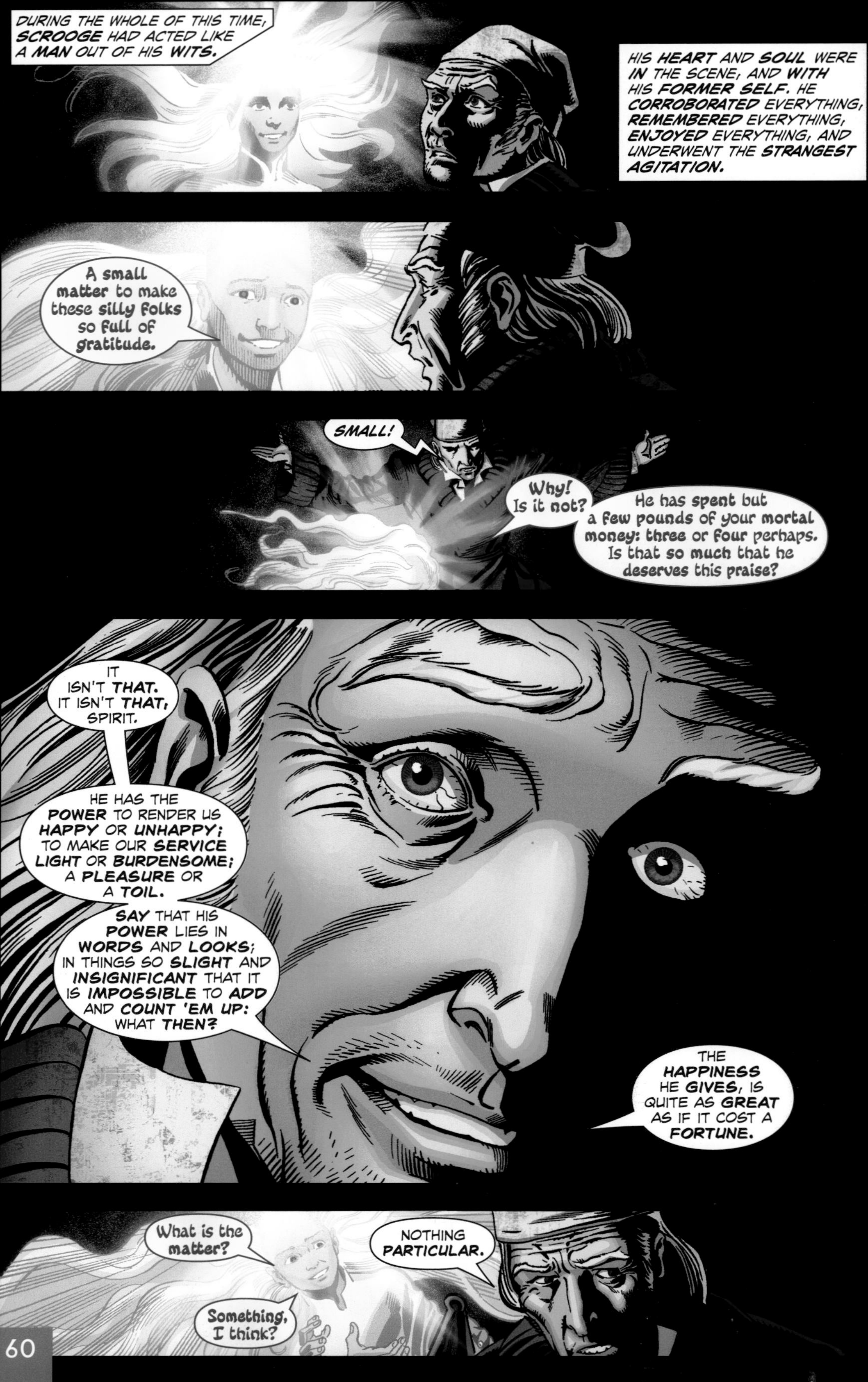
DURING THE WHOLE OF THIS TIME, SCROOGE HAD ACTED LIKE A MAN OUT OF HIS WITS.
HIS HEART AND SOUL WERE IN THE SCENE, AND WITH HIS FORMER SELF. HE CORROBORATED EVERYTHING, REMEMBERED EVERYTHING, ENJOYED EVERYTHING, AND UNDERWENT THE STRANGEST AGITATION.
A small matter to make these silly folks so full of gratitude.
SMALL!
Why! Is it not?
He has spent but a few pounds of your mortal money: three or four perhaps. Is that so much that he deserves this praise?
IT ISN'T THAT. IT ISN'T THAT, SPIRIT.
HE HAS THE POWER TO RENDER US HAPPY OR UNHAPPY; TO MAKE OUR SERVICE LIGHT OR BURDENSOME; A PLEASURE OR A TOIL.
SAY THAT HIS POWER LIES IN WORDS AND LOOKS; IN THINGS SO SLIGHT AND INSIGNIFICANT THAT IT IS IMPOSSIBLE TO ADD AND COUNT 'EM UP: WHAT THEN?
THE HAPPINESS HE GIVES, IS QUITE AS GREAT AS IF IT COST A FORTUNE.
What is the matter?
NOTHING PARTICULAR.
Something, I think?

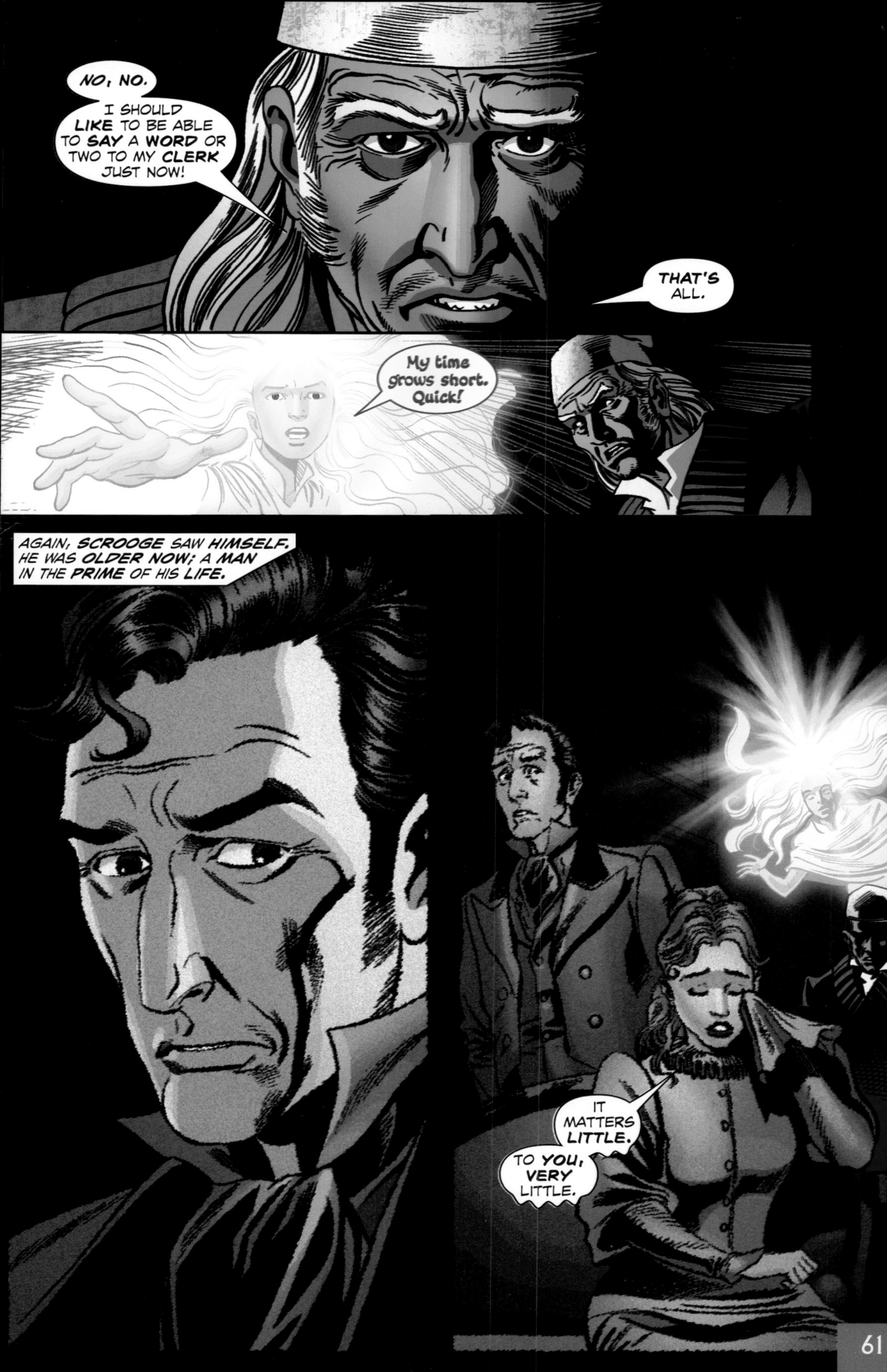
NO, NO.
I SHOULD LIKE TO BE ABLE TO SAY A WORD OR TWO TO MY CLERK JUST NOW!
THAT'S ALL.
My time grows short. Quick!
AGAIN, SCROOGE SAW HIMSELF. HE WAS OLDER NOW; A MAN IN THE PRIME OF HIS LIFE.
IT MATTERS LITTLE.
TO YOU, VERY LITTLE.

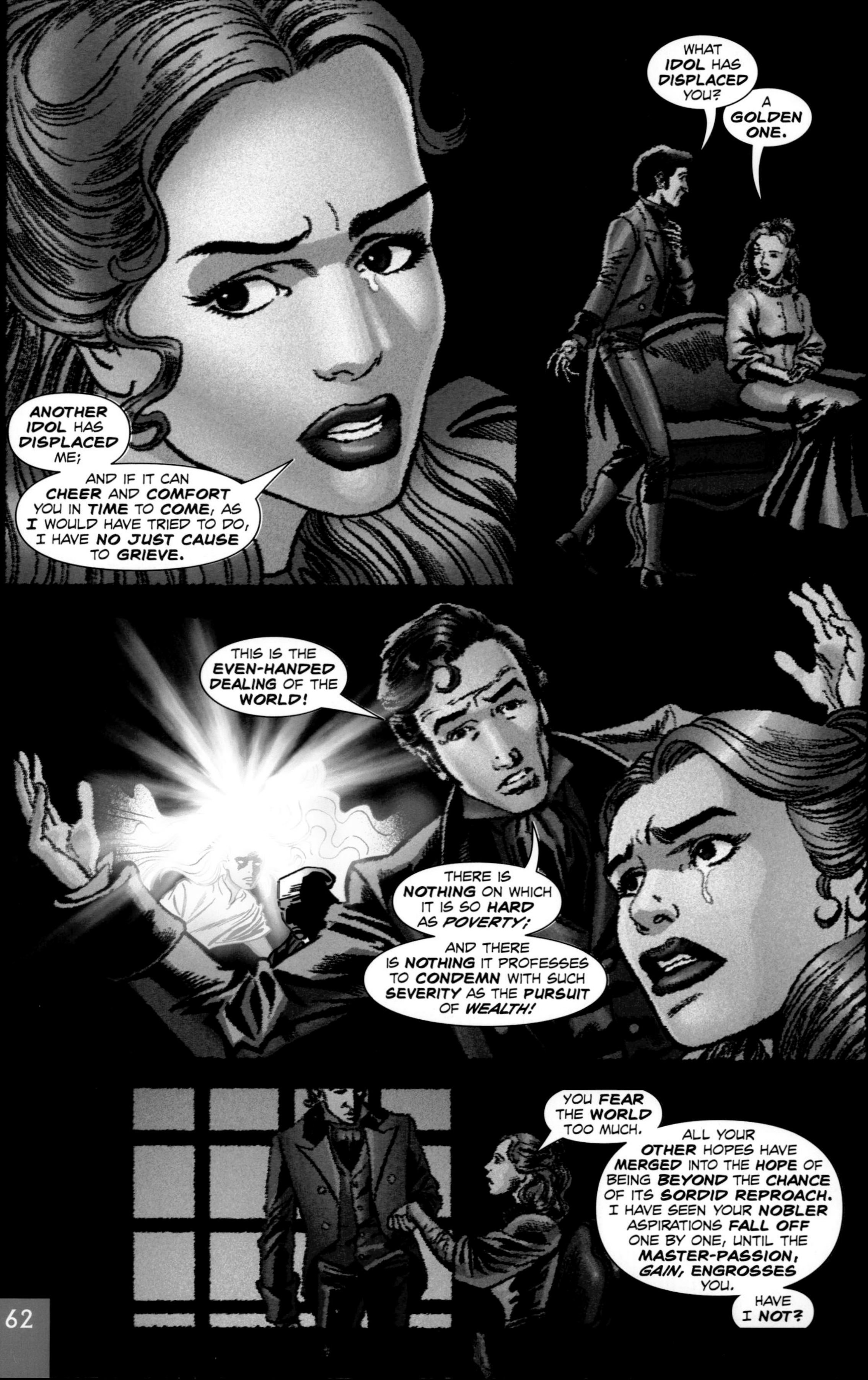
ANOTHER IDOL HAS DISPLACED ME;
AND IF IT CAN CHEER AND COMFORT YOU IN TIME TO COME, AS I WOULD HAVE TRIED TO DO, I HAVE NO JUST CAUSE TO GRIEVE.
WHAT IDOL HAS DISPLACED YOU?
A GOLDEN ONE.
THIS IS THE EVEN-HANDED DEALING OF THE WORLD!
THERE IS NOTHING ON WHICH IT IS SO HARD AS POVERTY;
AND THERE IS NOTHING IT PROFESSES TO CONDEMN WITH SUCH SEVERITY AS THE PURSUIT OF WEALTH!
YOU FEAR THE WORLD TOO MUCH.
ALL YOUR OTHER HOPES HAVE MERGED INTO THE HOPE OF BEING BEYOND THE CHANCE OF ITS SORDID REPROACH. I HAVE SEEN YOUR NOBLER ASPIRATIONS FALL OFF ONE BY ONE, UNTIL THE MASTER-PASSION, GAIN, ENGROSSES YOU.
HAVE I NOT?

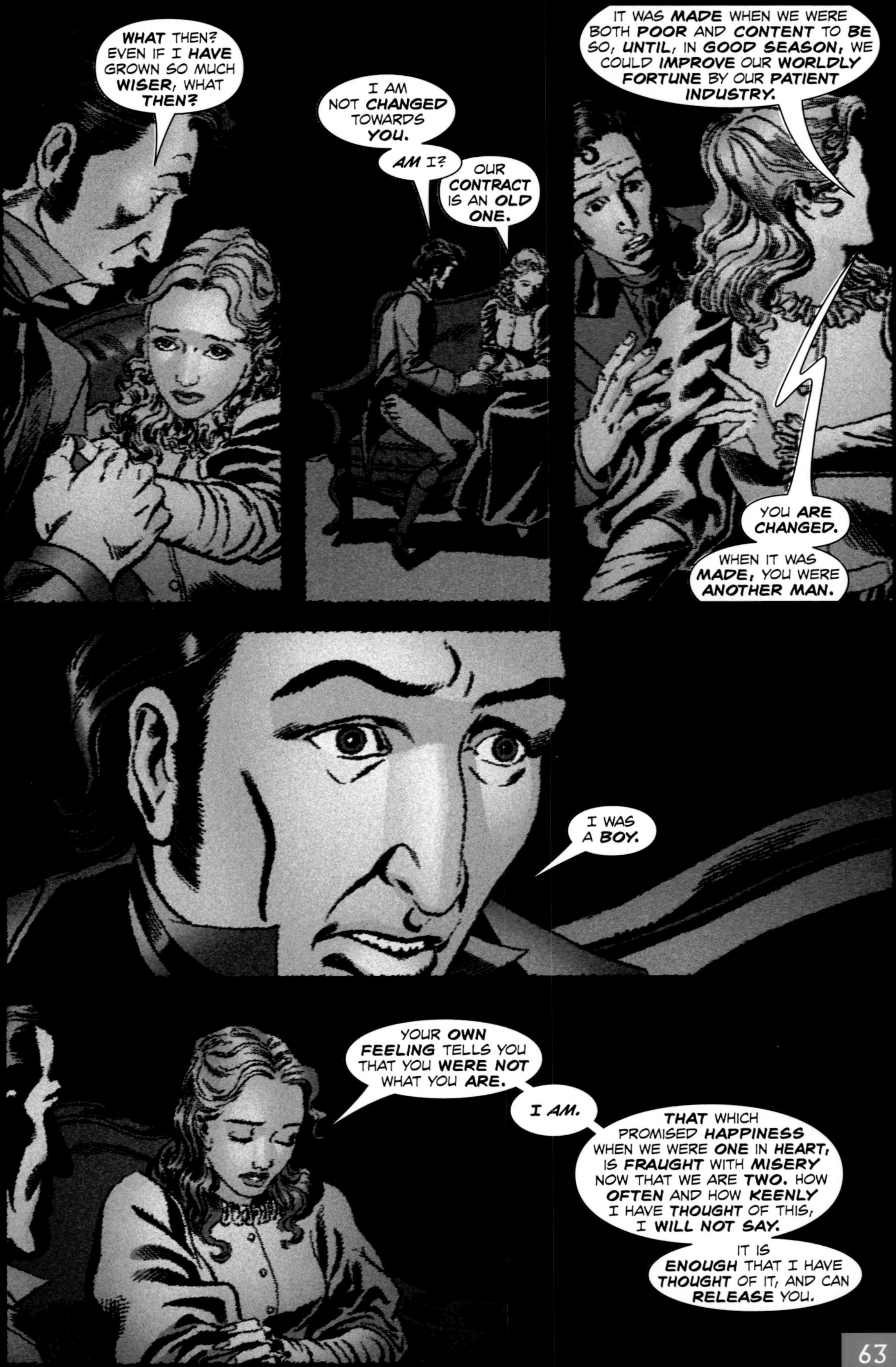
WHAT THEN? EVEN IF I HAVE GROWN SO MUCH WISER, WHAT THEN?
I AM NOT CHANGED TOWARDS YOU.
AM I?
OUR CONTRACT IS AN OLD ONE.
IT WAS MADE WHEN WE WERE BOTH POOR AND CONTENT TO BE SO, UNTIL, IN GOOD SEASON, WE COULD IMPROVE OUR WORLDLY FORTUNE BY OUR PATIENT INDUSTRY.
YOU ARE CHANGED.
WHEN IT WAS MADE, YOU WERE ANOTHER MAN.
I WAS A BOY.
YOUR OWN FEELING TELLS YOU THAT YOU WERE NOT WHAT YOU ARE.
I AM.
THAT WHICH PROMISED HAPPINESS WHEN WE WERE ONE IN HEART, IS FRAUGHT WITH MISERY NOW THAT WE ARE TWO. HOW OFTEN AND HOW KEENLY I HAVE THOUGHT OF THIS, I WILL NOT SAY.
IT IS ENOUGH THAT I HAVE THOUGHT OF IT, AND CAN RELEASE YOU.

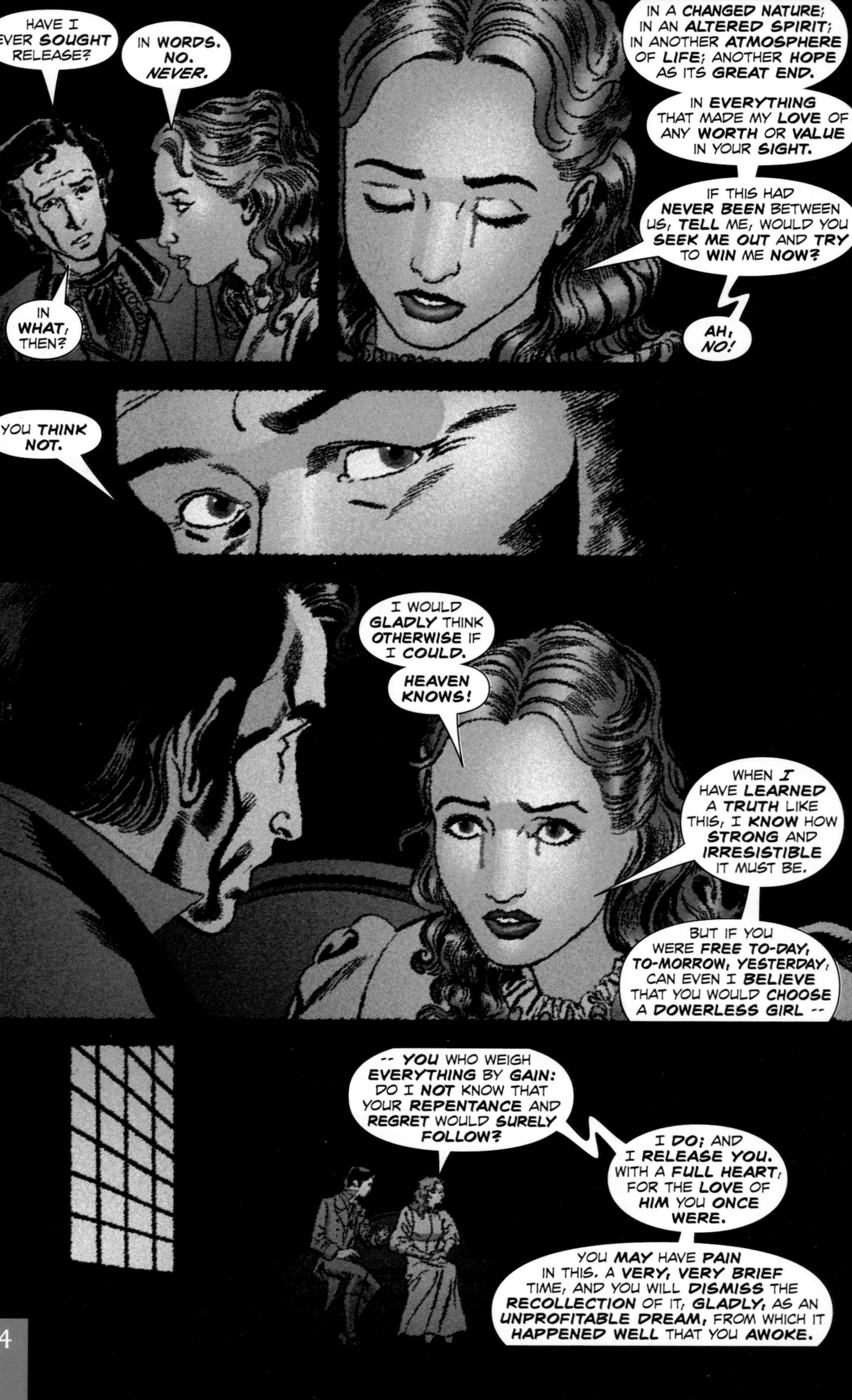
HAVE I EVER SOUGHT RELEASE?
IN WORDS. NO. NEVER.
IN WHAT, THEN?
IN A CHANGED NATURE; IN AN ALTERED SPIRIT; IN ANOTHER ATMOSPHERE OF LIFE; ANOTHER HOPE AS ITS GREAT END.
IN EVERYTHING THAT MADE MY LOVE OF ANY WORTH OR VALUE IN YOUR SIGHT.
IF THIS HAD NEVER BEEN BETWEEN US, TELL ME, WOULD YOU SEEK ME OUT AND TRY TO WIN ME NOW?
AH, NO!
YOU THINK NOT.
I WOULD GLADLY THINK OTHERWISE IF I COULD.
HEAVEN KNOWS!
WHEN I HAVE LEARNED A TRUTH LIKE THIS, I KNOW HOW STRONG AND IRRESISTIBLE IT MUST BE.
BUT IF YOU WERE FREE TO-DAY, TO-MORROW, YESTERDAY, CAN EVEN I BELIEVE THAT YOU WOULD CHOOSE A DOWERLESS GIRL --
-- YOU WHO WEIGH EVERYTHING BY GAIN: DO I NOT KNOW THAT YOUR REPENTANCE AND REGRET WOULD SURELY FOLLOW?
I DO; AND I RELEASE YOU. WITH A FULL HEART, FOR THE LOVE OF HIM YOU ONCE WERE.
YOU MAY HAVE PAIN IN THIS. A VERY, VERY BRIEF TIME, AND YOU WILL DISMISS THE RECOLLECTION OF IT, GLADLY, AS AN UNPROFITABLE DREAM, FROM WHICH IT HAPPENED WELL THAT YOU AWOKE.

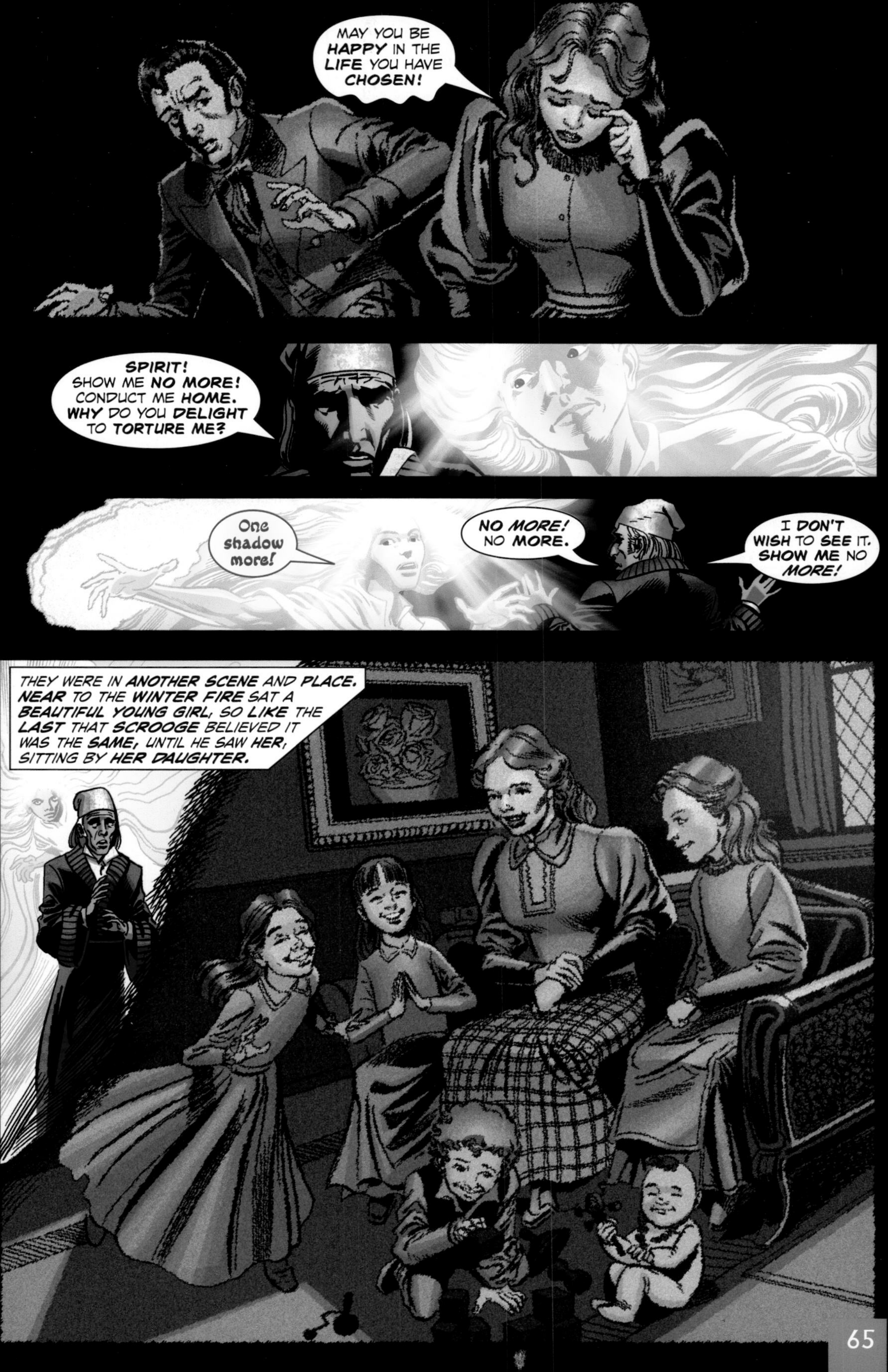
MAY YOU BE HAPPY IN THE LIFE YOU HAVE CHOSEN!
SPIRIT! SHOW ME NO MORE! CONDUCT ME HOME. WHY DO YOU DELIGHT TO TORTURE ME?
One shadow more!
NO MORE! NO MORE.
I DON'T WISH TO SEE IT. SHOW ME NO MORE!
THEY WERE IN ANOTHER SCENE AND PLACE. NEAR TO THE WINTER FIRE SAT A BEAUTIFUL YOUNG GIRL, SO LIKE THE LAST THAT SCROOGE BELIEVED IT WAS THE SAME, UNTIL HE SAW HER, SITTING BY HER DAUGHTER.

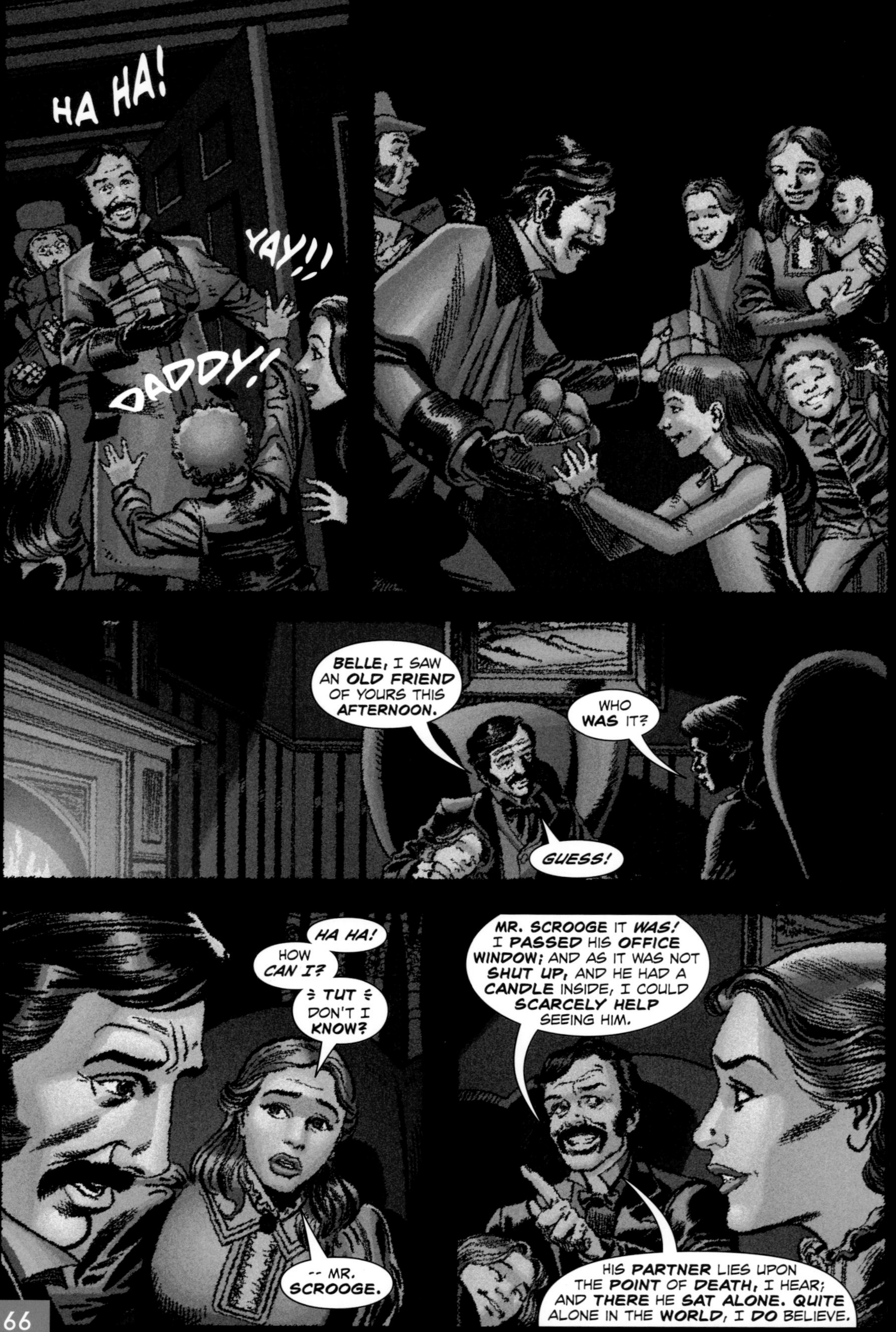
HA HA!
YAY!!
DADDY!
BELLE, I SAW AN OLD FRIEND OF YOURS THIS AFTERNOON.
WHO WAS IT?
GUESS!
HA HA! HOW CAN I?
TUT DON'T I KNOW?
-- MR. SCROOGE.
MR. SCROOGE IT WAS! I PASSED HIS OFFICE WINDOW; AND AS IT WAS NOT SHUT UP, AND HE HAD A CANDLE INSIDE, I COULD SCARCELY HELP SEEING HIM.
HIS PARTNER LIES UPON THE POINT OF DEATH, I HEAR; AND THERE HE SAT ALONE. QUITE ALONE IN THE WORLD, I DO BELIEVE.

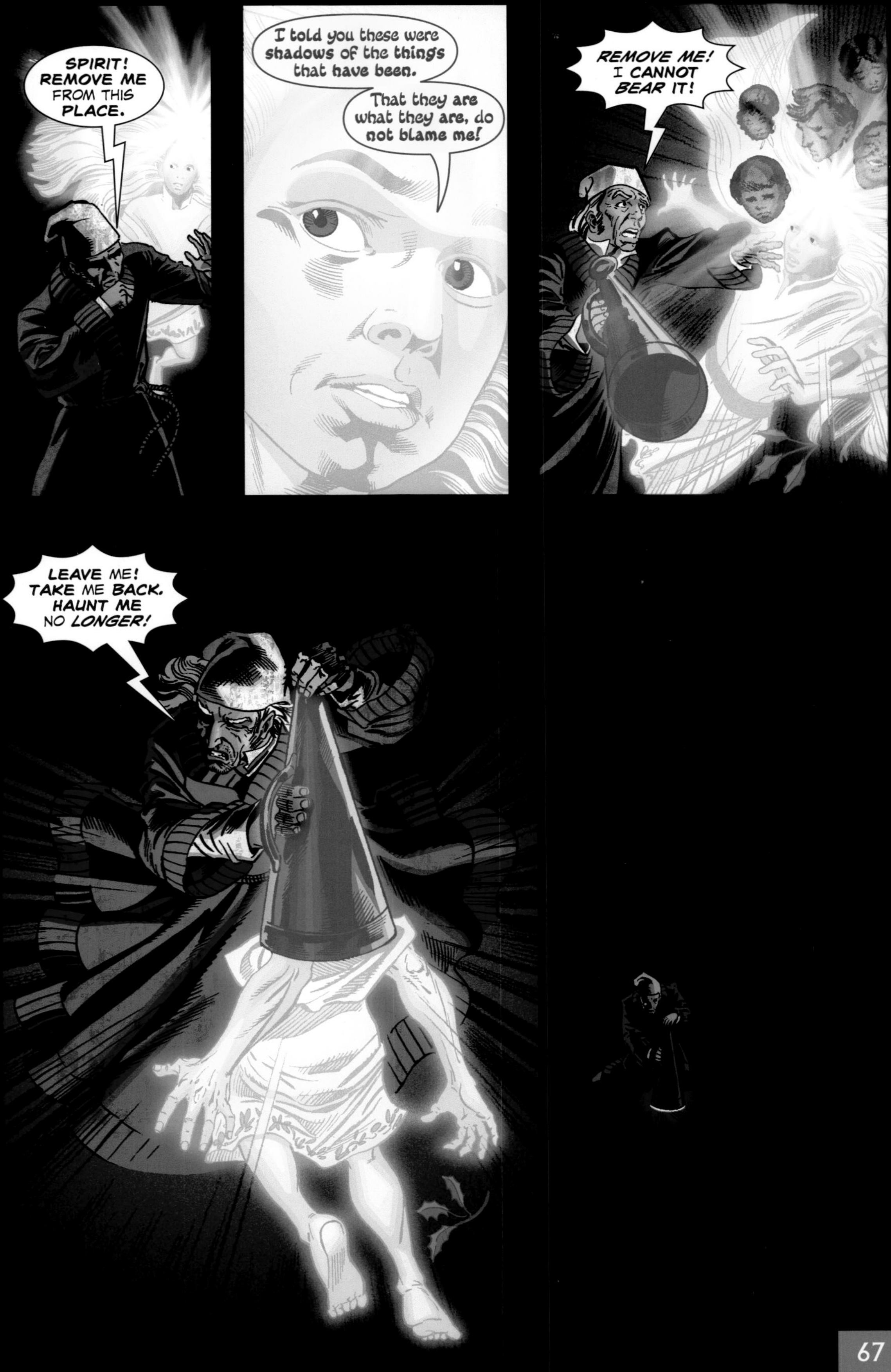
SPIRIT! REMOVE ME FROM THIS PLACE.
I told you these were shadows of the things that have been.
That they are what they are, do not blame me!
REMOVE ME! I CANNOT BEAR IT!
LEAVE ME! TAKE ME BACK. HAUNT ME NO LONGER!

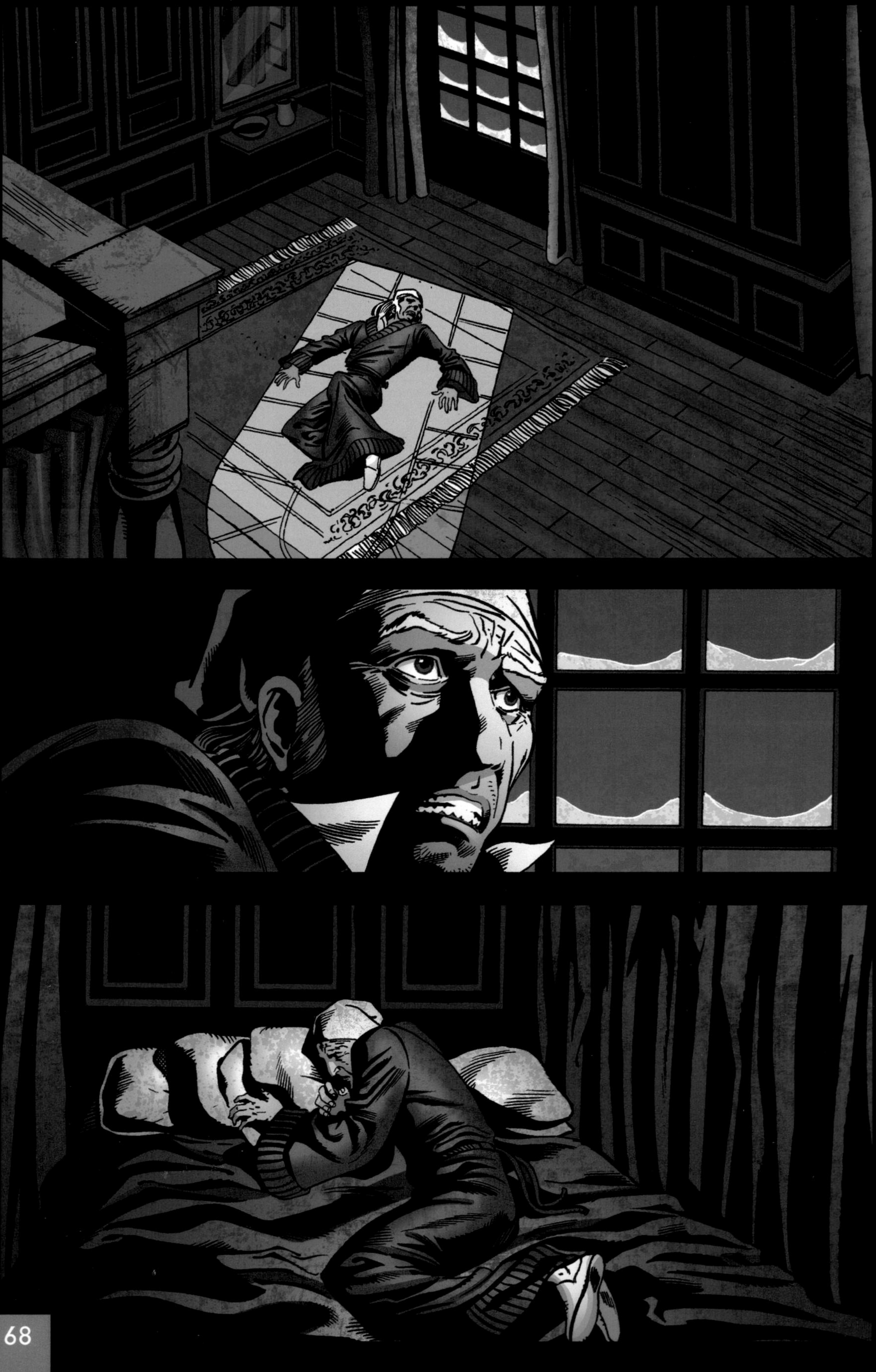

Stave Three: The Second of the Three Spirits

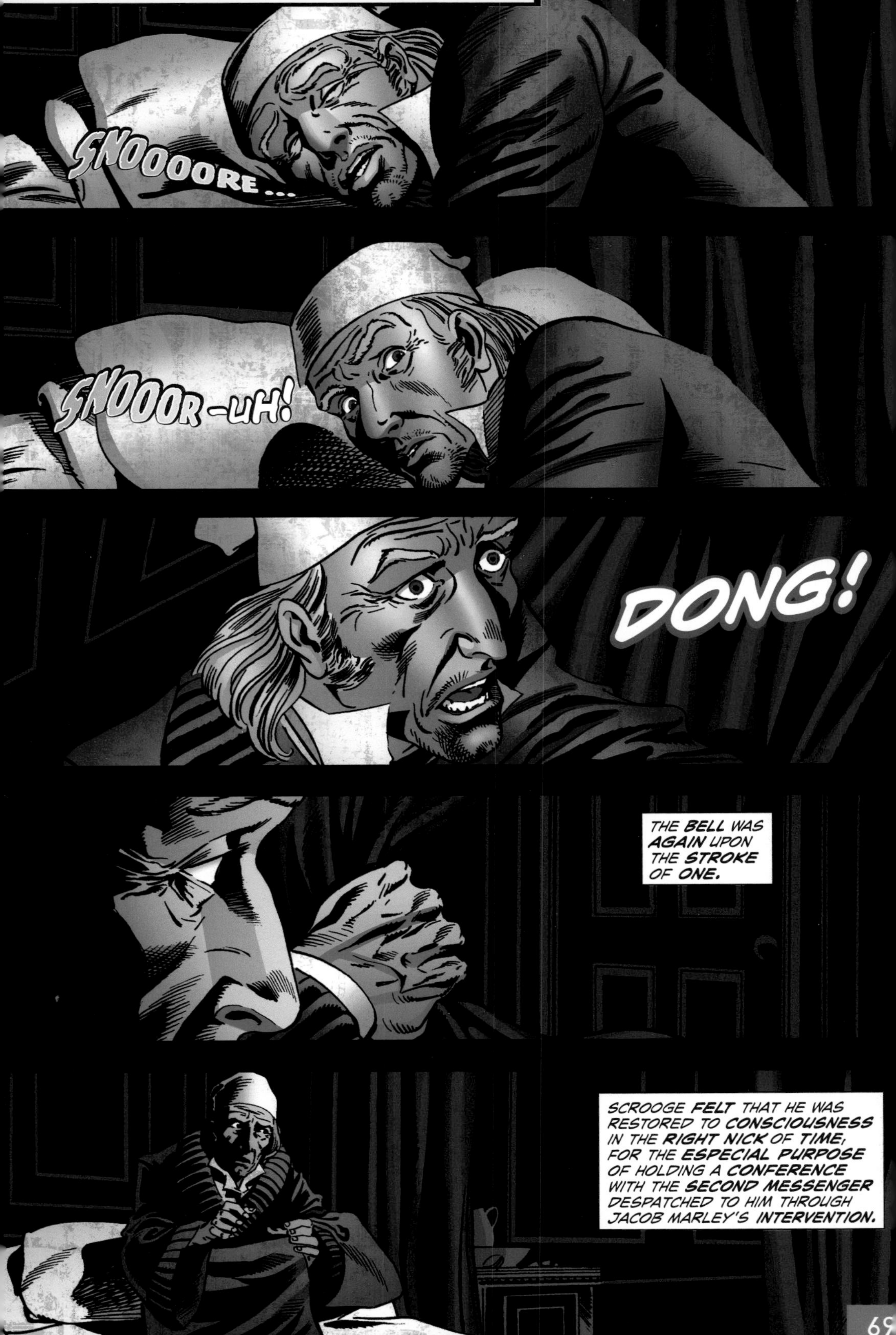
SNOOOORE...
SNOOOR-UH!
DONG!
THE BELL WAS AGAIN UPON THE STROKE OF ONE.
SCROOGE FELT THAT HE WAS RESTORED TO CONSCIOUSNESS IN THE RIGHT NICK OF TIME, FOR THE ESPECIAL PURPOSE OF HOLDING A CONFERENCE WITH THE SECOND MESSENGER DESPATCHED TO HIM THROUGH JACOB MARLEY'S INTERVENTION.

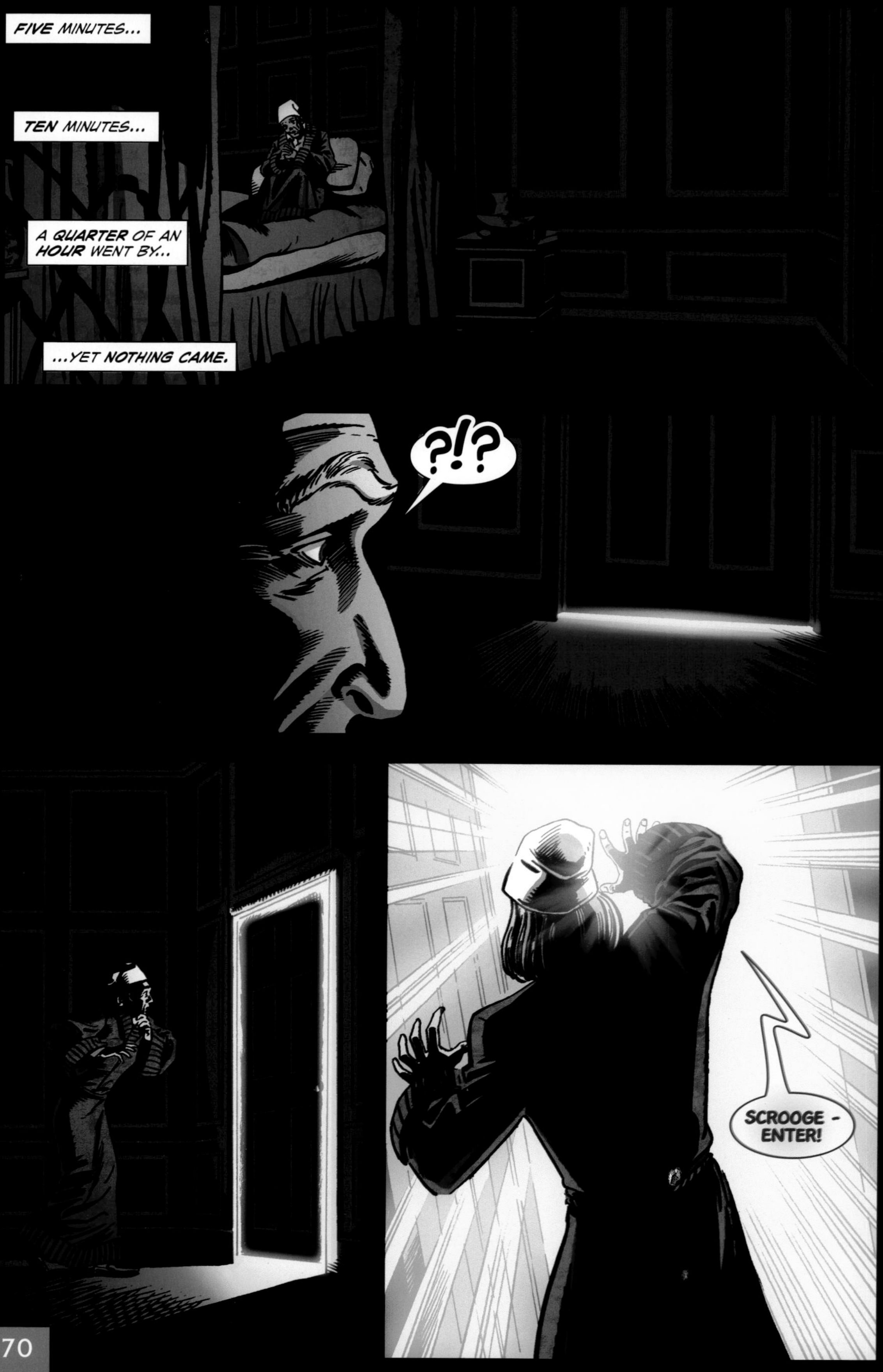
FIVE MINUTES...
TEN MINUTES...
A QUARTER OF AN HOUR WENT BY...
...YET NOTHING CAME.
?!?
SCROOGE - ENTER!

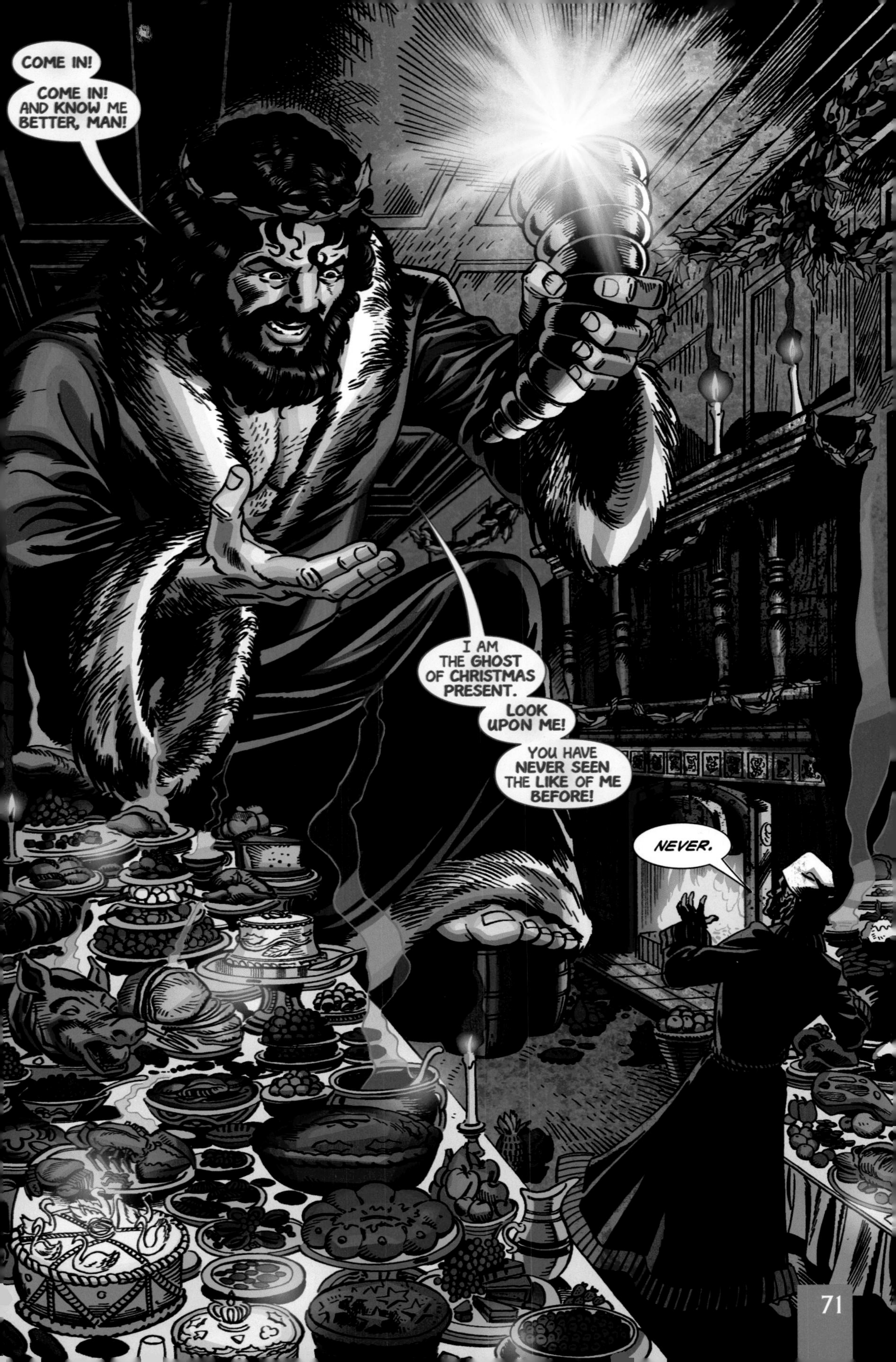
COME IN!
COME IN! AND KNOW ME BETTER, MAN!
I AM THE GHOST OF CHRISTMAS PRESENT.
LOOK UPON ME!
YOU HAVE NEVER SEEN THE LIKE OF ME BEFORE!
NEVER.

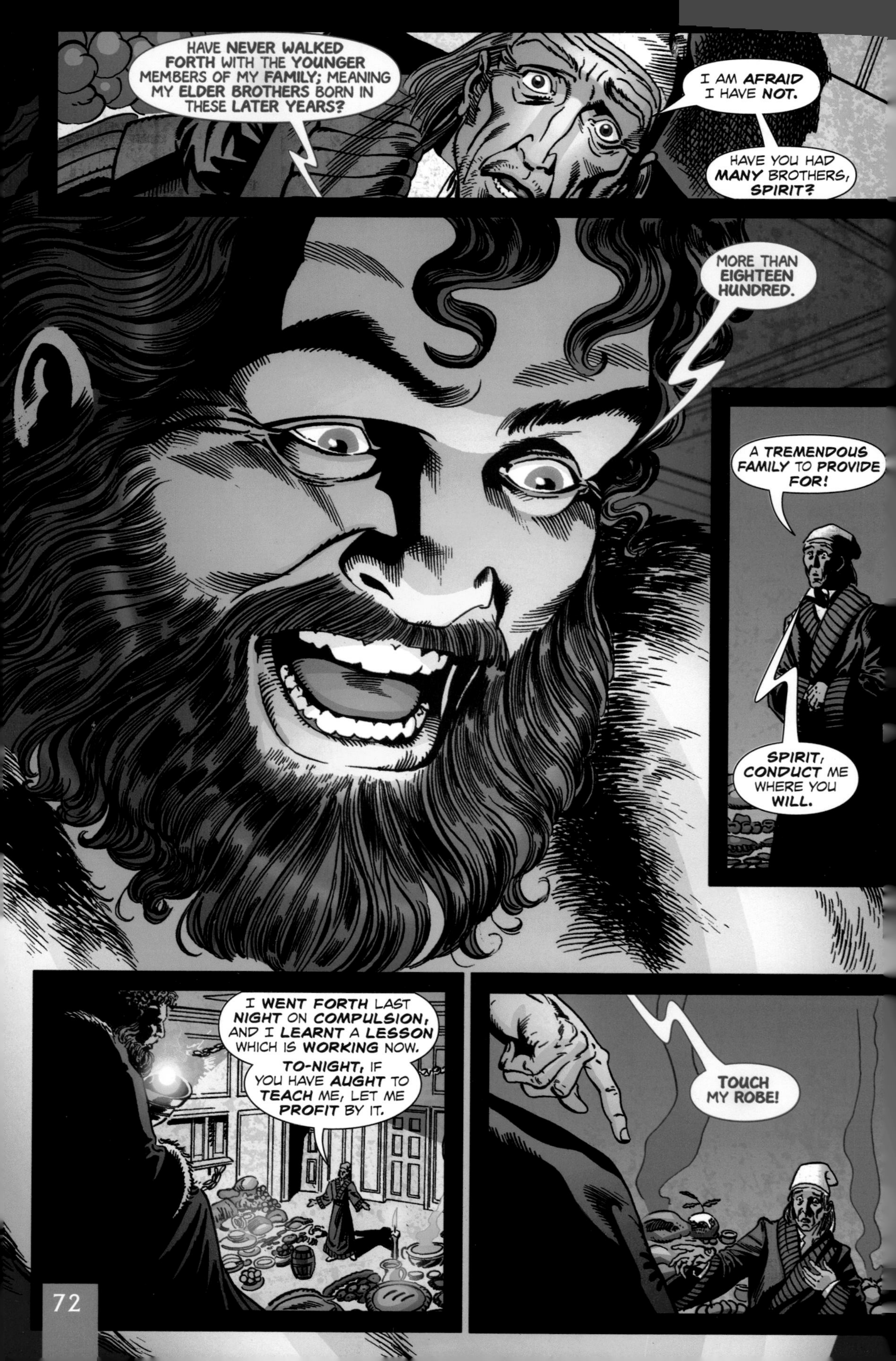

HAVE NEVER WALKED FORTH WITH THE YOUNGER MEMBERS OF MY FAMILY; MEANING MY ELDER BROTHERS BORN IN THESE LATER YEARS?
I AM AFRAID I HAVE NOT.
HAVE YOU HAD MANY BROTHERS, SPIRIT?
MORE THAN EIGHTEEN HUNDRED.
A TREMENDOUS FAMILY TO PROVIDE FOR!
SPIRIT, CONDUCT ME WHERE YOU WILL.
I WENT FORTH LAST NIGHT ON COMPULSION, AND I LEARNT A LESSON WHICH IS WORKING NOW.
TO-NIGHT, IF YOU HAVE AUGHT TO TEACH ME, LET ME PROFIT BY IT.
TOUCH MY ROBE!

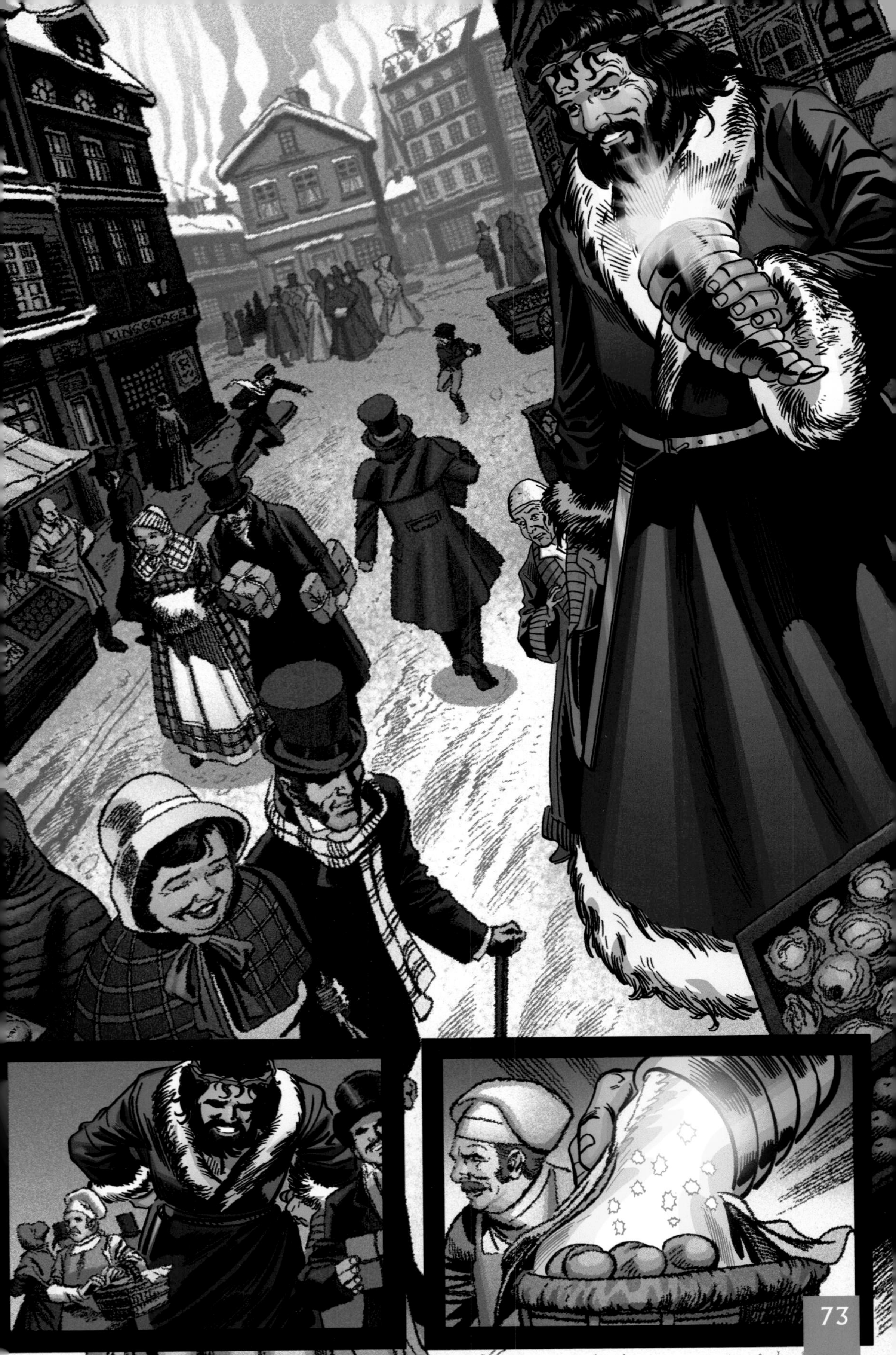

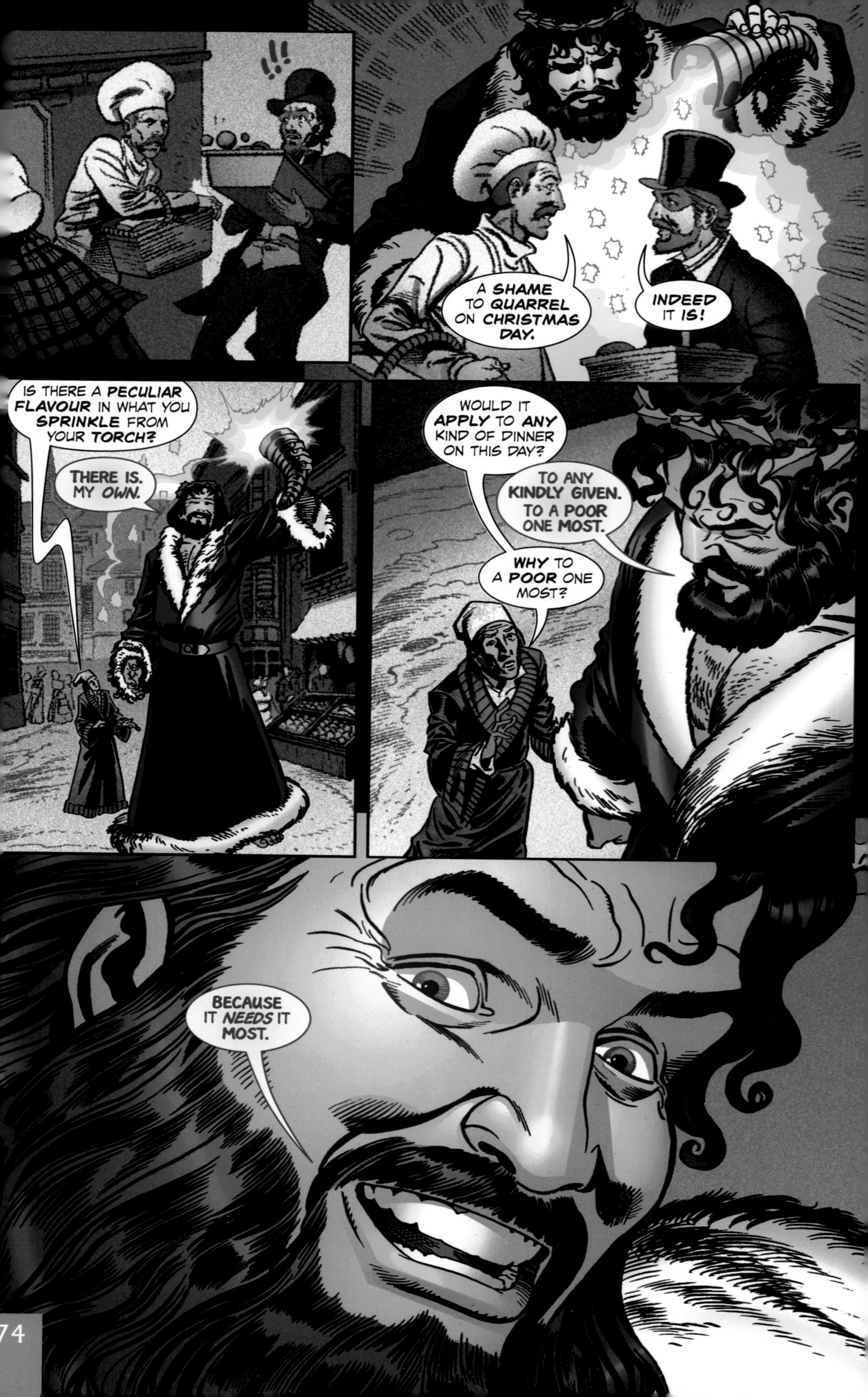
!!
A SHAME TO QUARREL ON CHRISTMAS DAY.
INDEED IT IS!
IS THERE A PECULIAR FLAVOUR IN WHAT YOU SPRINKLE FROM YOUR TORCH?
THERE IS. MY OWN.
WOULD IT APPLY TO ANY KIND OF DINNER ON THIS DAY?
TO ANY KINDLY GIVEN. TO A POOR ONE MOST.
WHY TO A POOR ONE MOST?
BECAUSE IT NEEDS IT MOST.

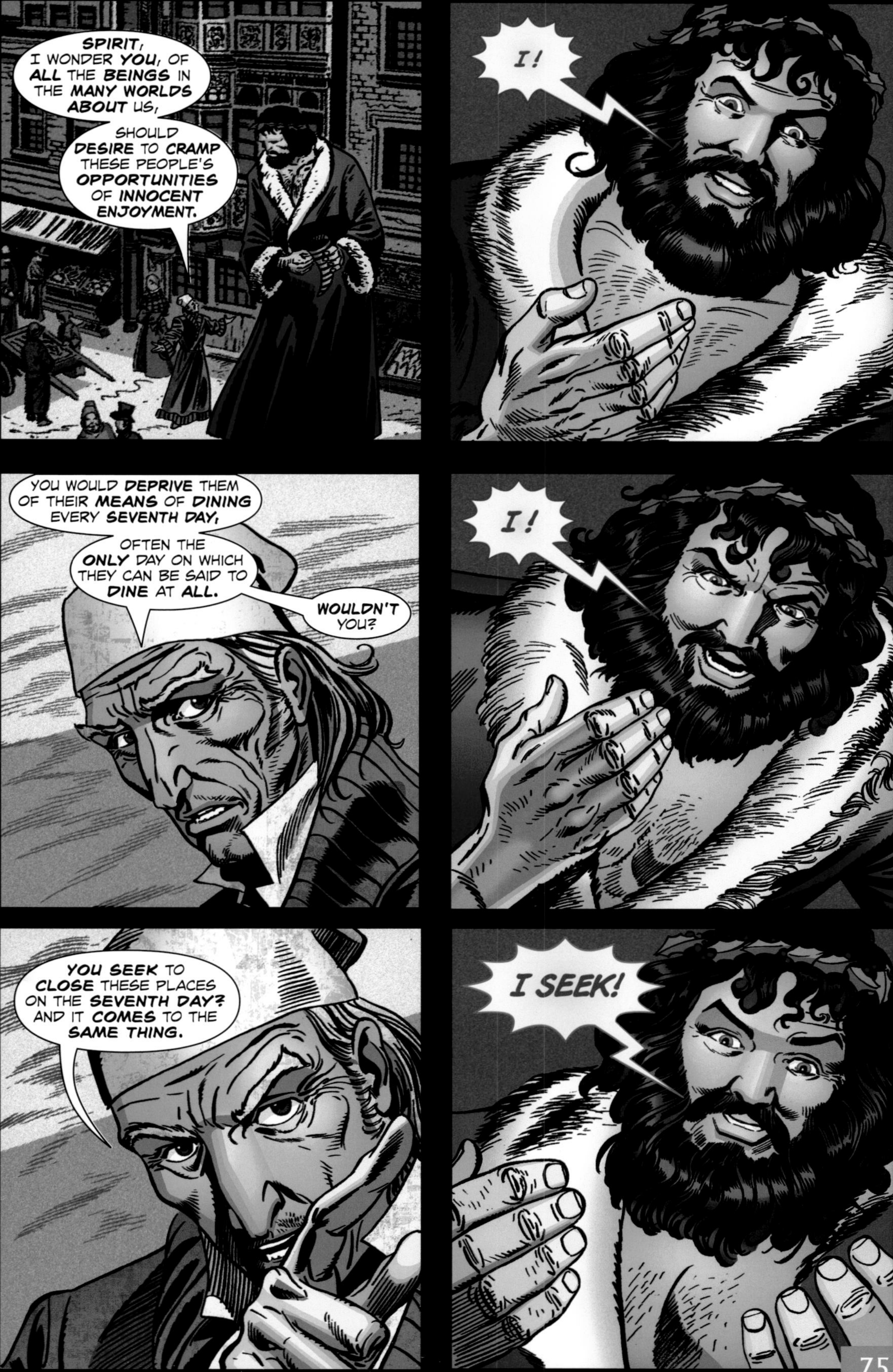
SPIRIT, I WONDER YOU, OF ALL THE BEINGS IN THE MANY WORLDS ABOUT US,
SHOULD DESIRE TO CRAMP THESE PEOPLE'S OPPORTUNITIES OF INNOCENT ENJOYMENT.
I!
YOU WOULD DEPRIVE THEM OF THEIR MEANS OF DINING EVERY SEVENTH DAY,
OFTEN THE ONLY DAY ON WHICH THEY CAN BE SAID TO DINE AT ALL.
WOULDN'T YOU?
I!
YOU SEEK TO CLOSE THESE PLACES ON THE SEVENTH DAY? AND IT COMES TO THE SAME THING.
I SEEK!

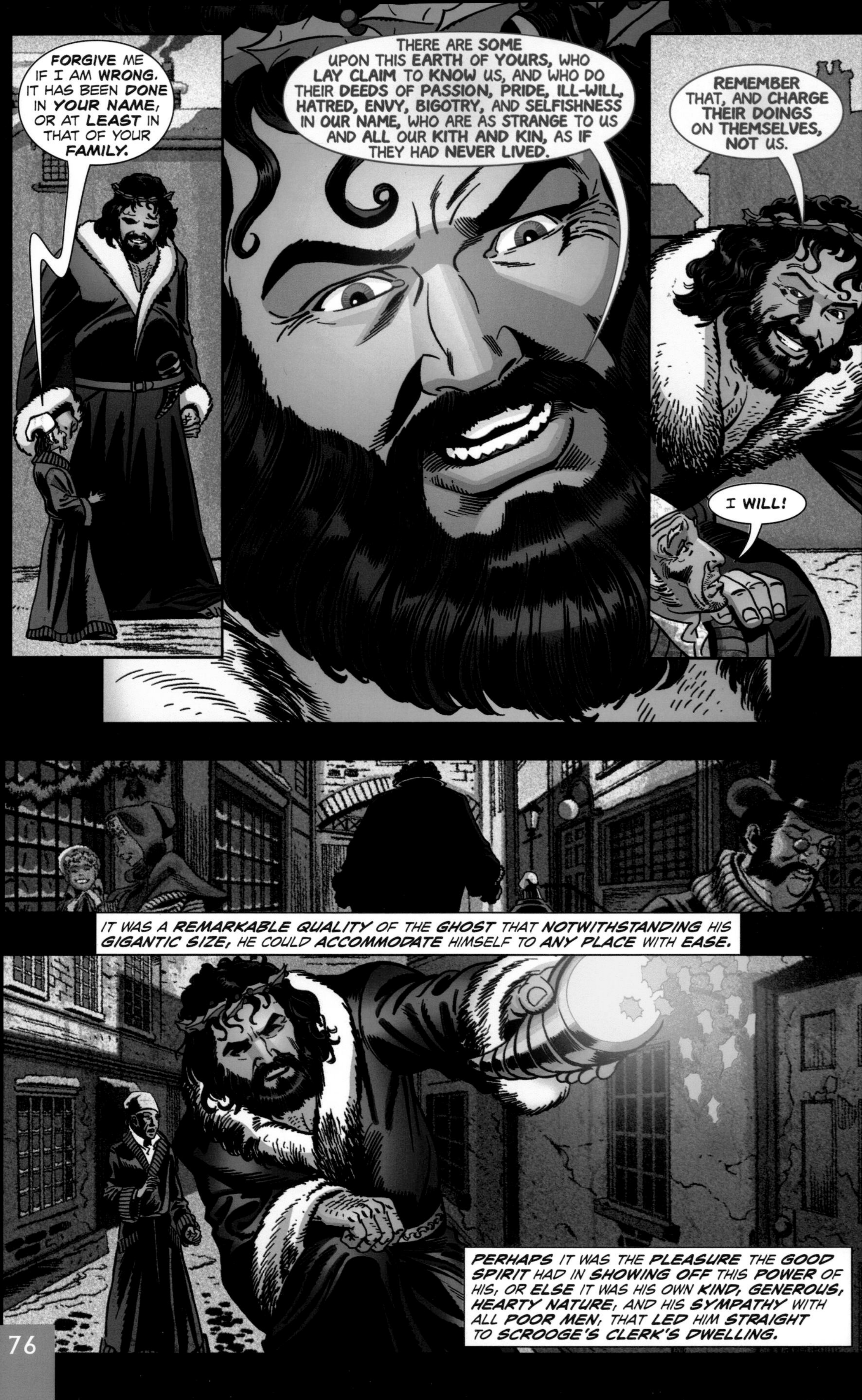
FORGIVE ME IF I AM WRONG. IT HAS BEEN DONE IN YOUR NAME, OR AT LEAST IN THAT OF YOUR FAMILY.
THERE ARE SOME UPON THIS EARTH OF YOURS, WHO LAY CLAIM TO KNOW US, AND WHO DO THEIR DEEDS OF PASSION, PRIDE, ILL-WILL, HATRED, ENVY, BIGOTRY, AND SELFISHNESS IN OUR NAME, WHO ARE AS STRANGE TO US AND ALL OUR KITH AND KIN, AS IF THEY HAD NEVER LIVED.
REMEMBER THAT, AND CHARGE THEIR DOINGS ON THEMSELVES, NOT US.
I WILL!
IT WAS A REMARKABLE QUALITY OF THE GHOST THAT NOTWITHSTANDING HIS GIGANTIC SIZE, HE COULD ACCOMMODATE HIMSELF TO ANY PLACE WITH EASE.
PERHAPS IT WAS THE PLEASURE THE GOOD SPIRIT HAD IN SHOWING OFF THIS POWER OF HIS, OR ELSE IT WAS HIS OWN KIND, GENEROUS, HEARTY NATURE, AND HIS SYMPATHY WITH ALL POOR MEN, THAT LED HIM STRAIGHT TO SCROOGE'S CLERK'S DWELLING.

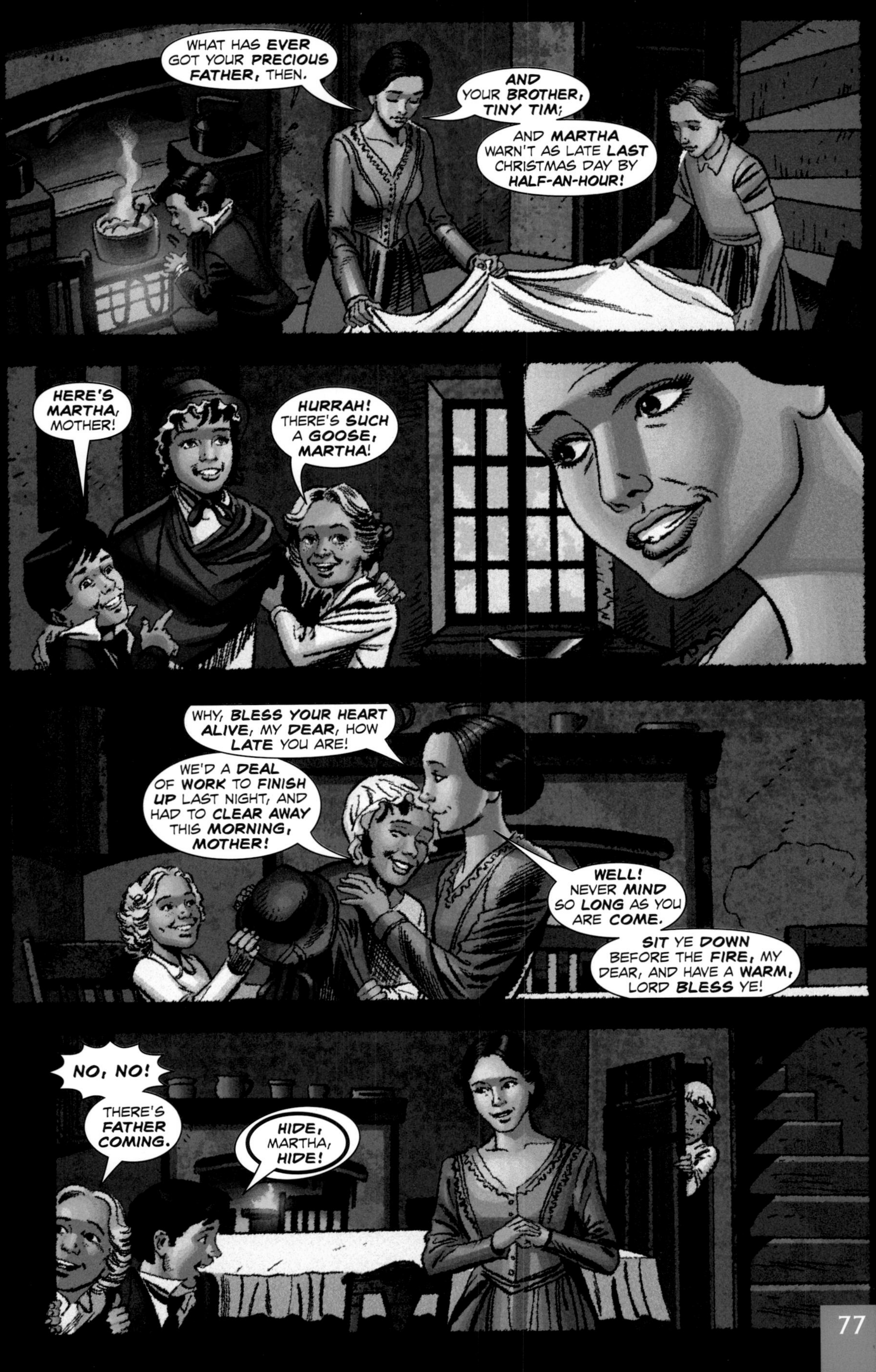
WHAT HAS EVER GOT YOUR PRECIOUS FATHER, THEN.
AND YOUR BROTHER, TINY TIM;
AND MARTHA WARN'T AS LATE LAST CHRISTMAS DAY BY HALF-AN-HOUR!
HERE'S MARTHA, MOTHER!
HURRAH! THERE'S SUCH A GOOSE, MARTHA!
WHY, BLESS YOUR HEART ALIVE, MY DEAR, HOW LATE YOU ARE!
WE'D A DEAL OF WORK TO FINISH UP LAST NIGHT, AND HAD TO CLEAR AWAY THIS MORNING, MOTHER!
WELL! NEVER MIND SO LONG AS YOU ARE COME.
SIT YE DOWN BEFORE THE FIRE, MY DEAR, AND HAVE A WARM, LORD BLESS YE!
NO, NO!
THERE'S FATHER COMING.
HIDE, MARTHA, HIDE!

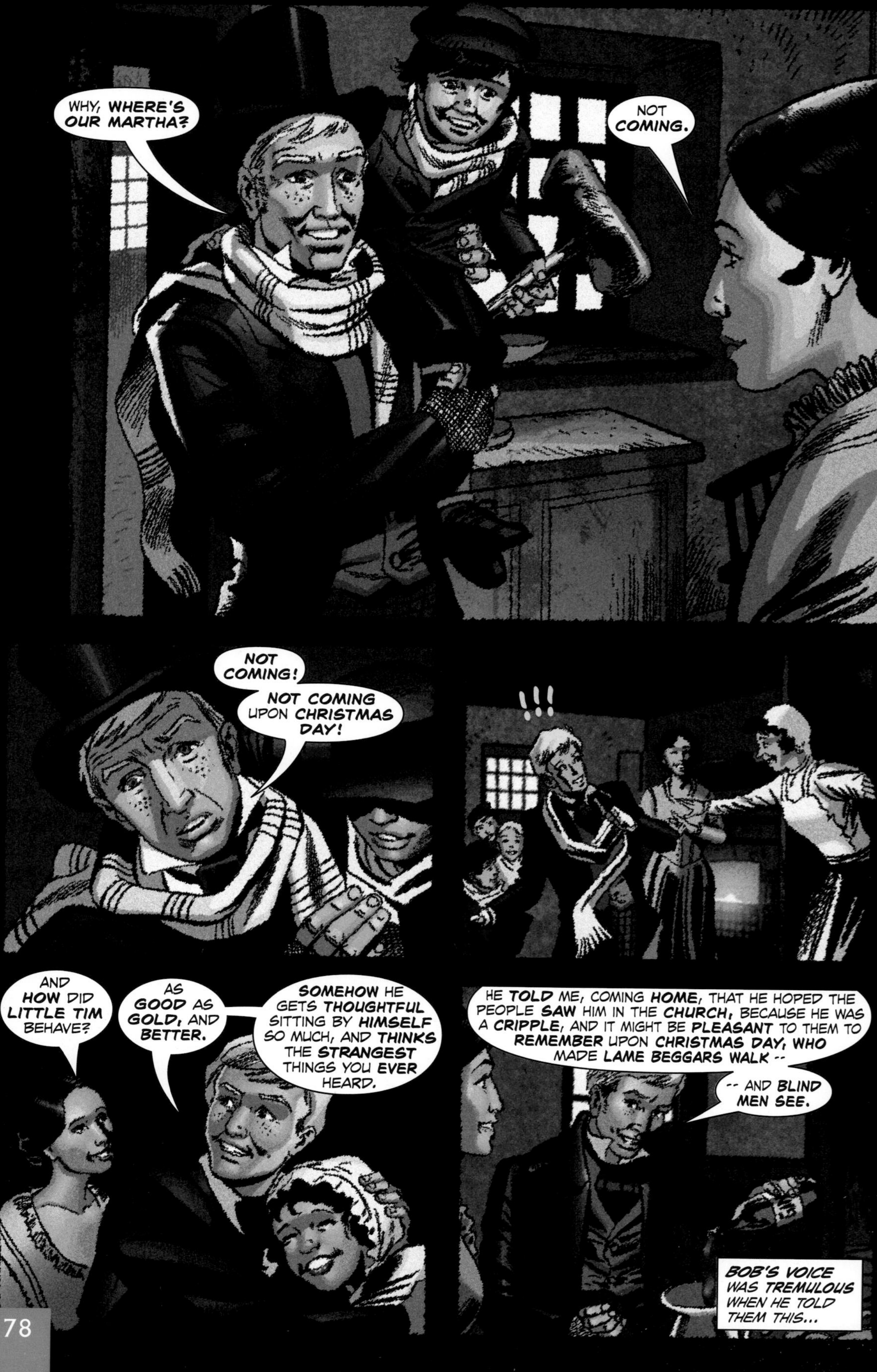
WHY, WHERE'S OUR MARTHA?
NOT COMING.
NOT COMING! NOT COMING UPON CHRISTMAS DAY!
!!!
AND HOW DID LITTLE TIM BEHAVE?
AS GOOD AS GOLD, AND BETTER.
SOMEHOW HE GETS THOUGHTFUL SITTING BY HIMSELF SO MUCH, AND THINKS THE STRANGEST THINGS YOU EVER HEARD.
HE TOLD ME, COMING HOME, THAT HE HOPED THE PEOPLE SAW HIM IN THE CHURCH, BECAUSE HE WAS A CRIPPLE, AND IT MIGHT BE PLEASANT TO THEM TO REMEMBER UPON CHRISTMAS DAY, WHO MADE LAME BEGGARS WALK --
-- AND BLIND MEN SEE.
BOB'S VOICE WAS TREMULOUS WHEN HE TOLD THEM THIS...

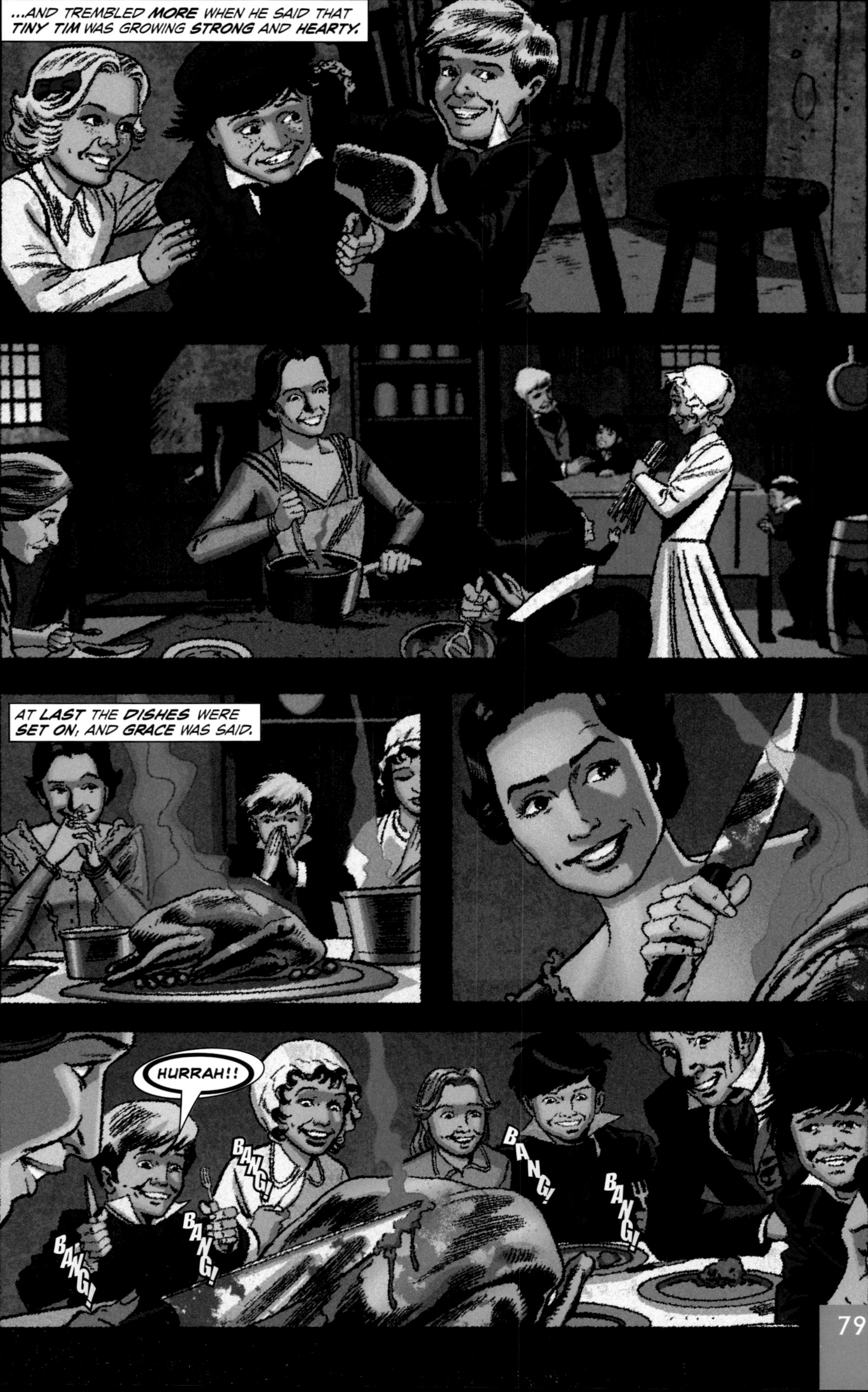
...AND TREMBLED MORE WHEN HE SAID THAT TINY TIM WAS GROWING STRONG AND HEARTY.
AT LAST THE DISHES WERE SET ON, AND GRACE WAS SAID.
HURRAH!!
BANG!
BANG!
BANG!
BANG!
BANG!

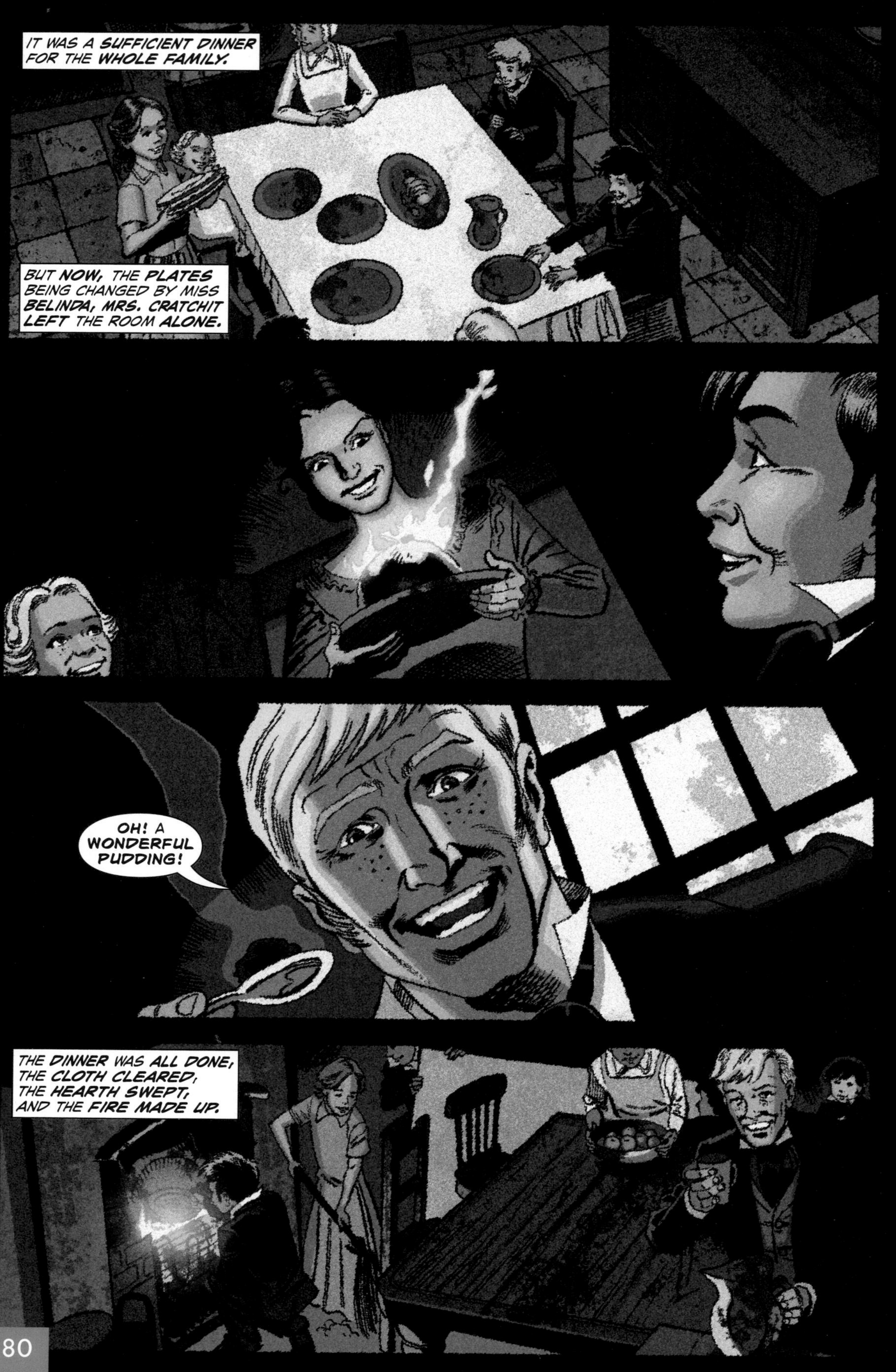
IT WAS A SUFFICIENT DINNER FOR THE WHOLE FAMILY.
BUT NOW, THE PLATES BEING CHANGED BY MISS BELINDA, MRS. CRATCHIT LEFT THE ROOM ALONE.
OH! A WONDERFUL PUDDING!
THE DINNER WAS ALL DONE, THE CLOTH CLEARED, THE HEARTH SWEPT, AND THE FIRE MADE UP.

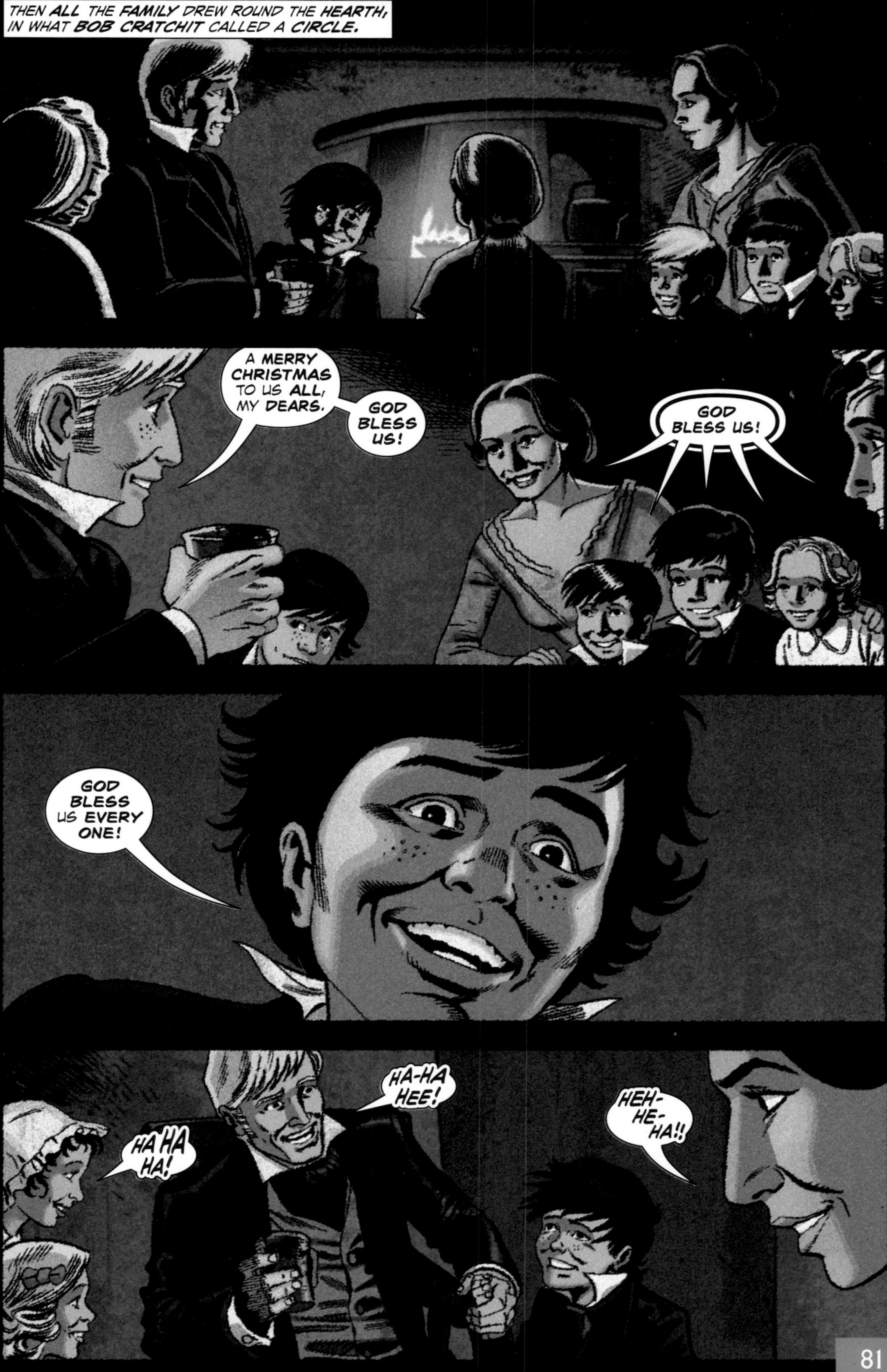
THEN ALL THE FAMILY DREW ROUND THE HEARTH, IN WHAT BOB CRATCHIT CALLED A CIRCLE.
A MERRY CHRISTMAS TO US ALL, MY DEARS.
GOD BLESS US!
GOD BLESS US!
GOD BLESS US EVERY ONE!
HA-HA HEE!
HEH-HE-HA!!
HA HA HA!

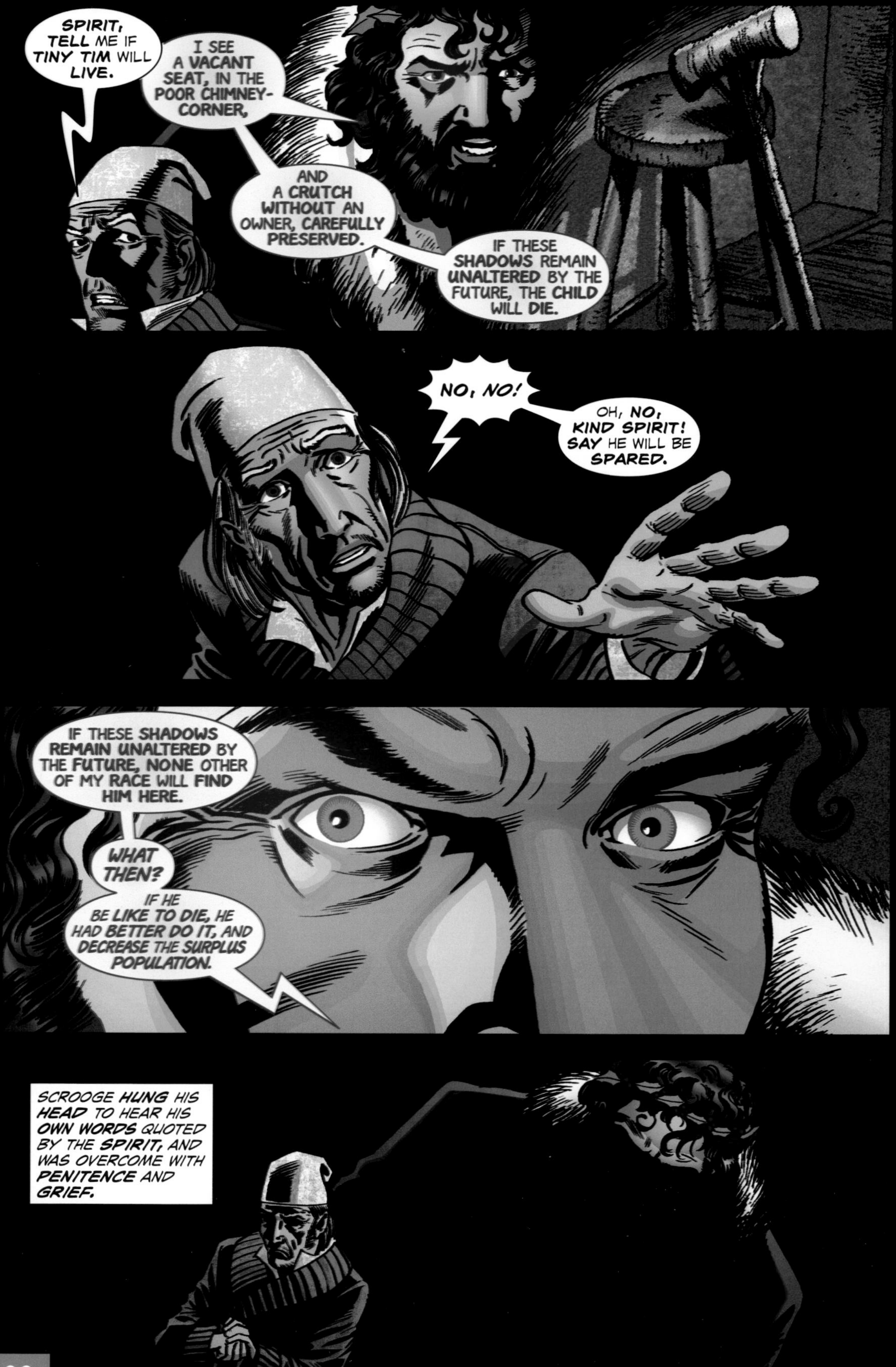
SPIRIT, TELL ME IF TINY TIM WILL LIVE.
I SEE A VACANT SEAT, IN THE POOR CHIMNEY-CORNER,
AND A CRUTCH WITHOUT AN OWNER, CAREFULLY PRESERVED.
IF THESE SHADOWS REMAIN UNALTERED BY THE FUTURE, THE CHILD WILL DIE.
NO, NO!
OH, NO, KIND SPIRIT! SAY HE WILL BE SPARED.
IF THESE SHADOWS REMAIN UNALTERED BY THE FUTURE, NONE OTHER OF MY RACE WILL FIND HIM HERE.
WHAT THEN?
IF HE BE LIKE TO DIE, HE HAD BETTER DO IT, AND DECREASE THE SURPLUS POPULATION.
SCROOGE HUNG HIS HEAD TO HEAR HIS OWN WORDS QUOTED BY THE SPIRIT, AND WAS OVERCOME WITH PENITENCE AND GRIEF.

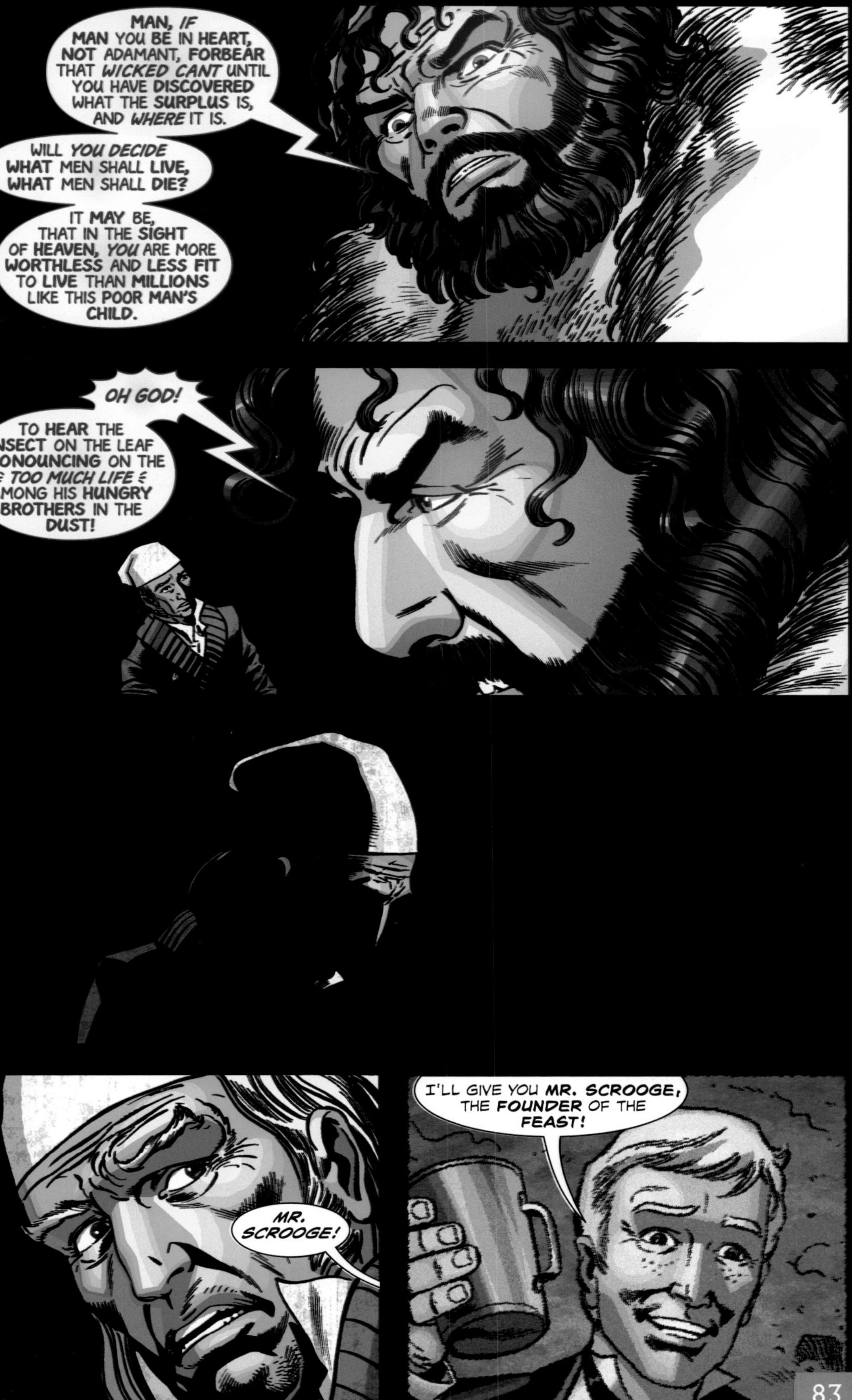
MAN, IF MAN YOU BE IN HEART, NOT ADAMANT, FORBEAR THAT WICKED CANT UNTIL YOU HAVE DISCOVERED WHAT THE SURPLUS IS, AND WHERE IT IS.
WILL YOU DECIDE WHAT MEN SHALL LIVE, WHAT MEN SHALL DIE?
IT MAY BE, THAT IN THE SIGHT OF HEAVEN, YOU ARE MORE WORTHLESS AND LESS FIT TO LIVE THAN MILLIONS LIKE THIS POOR MAN'S CHILD.
OH GOD!
TO HEAR THE INSECT ON THE LEAF PRONOUNCING ON THE TOO MUCH LIFE AMONG HIS HUNGRY BROTHERS IN THE DUST!
MR. SCROOGE!
I'LL GIVE YOU MR. SCROOGE, THE FOUNDER OF THE FEAST!

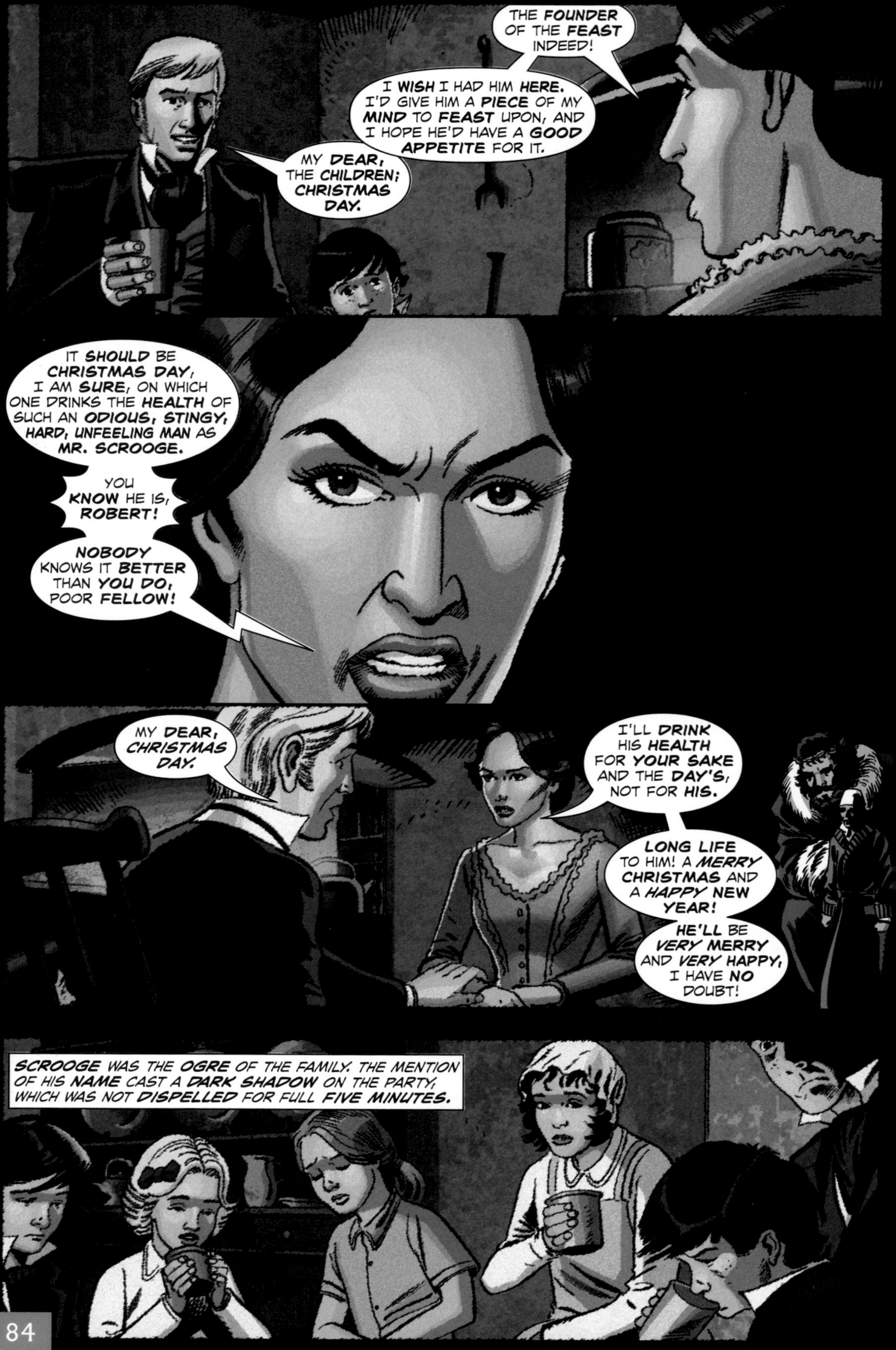
THE FOUNDER OF THE FEAST INDEED!
I WISH I HAD HIM HERE. I'D GIVE HIM A PIECE OF MY MIND TO FEAST UPON, AND I HOPE HE'D HAVE A GOOD APPETITE FOR IT.
MY DEAR, THE CHILDREN; CHRISTMAS DAY.
IT SHOULD BE CHRISTMAS DAY, I AM SURE, ON WHICH ONE DRINKS THE HEALTH OF SUCH AN ODIOUS, STINGY, HARD, UNFEELING MAN AS MR. SCROOGE.
YOU KNOW HE IS, ROBERT!
NOBODY KNOWS IT BETTER THAN YOU DO, POOR FELLOW!
MY DEAR, CHRISTMAS DAY.
I'LL DRINK HIS HEALTH FOR YOUR SAKE AND THE DAY'S, NOT FOR HIS.
LONG LIFE TO HIM! A MERRY CHRISTMAS AND A HAPPY NEW YEAR!
HE'LL BE VERY MERRY AND VERY HAPPY, I HAVE NO DOUBT!
SCROOGE WAS THE OGRE OF THE FAMILY. THE MENTION OF HIS NAME CAST A DARK SHADOW ON THE PARTY, WHICH WAS NOT DISPELLED FOR FULL FIVE MINUTES.

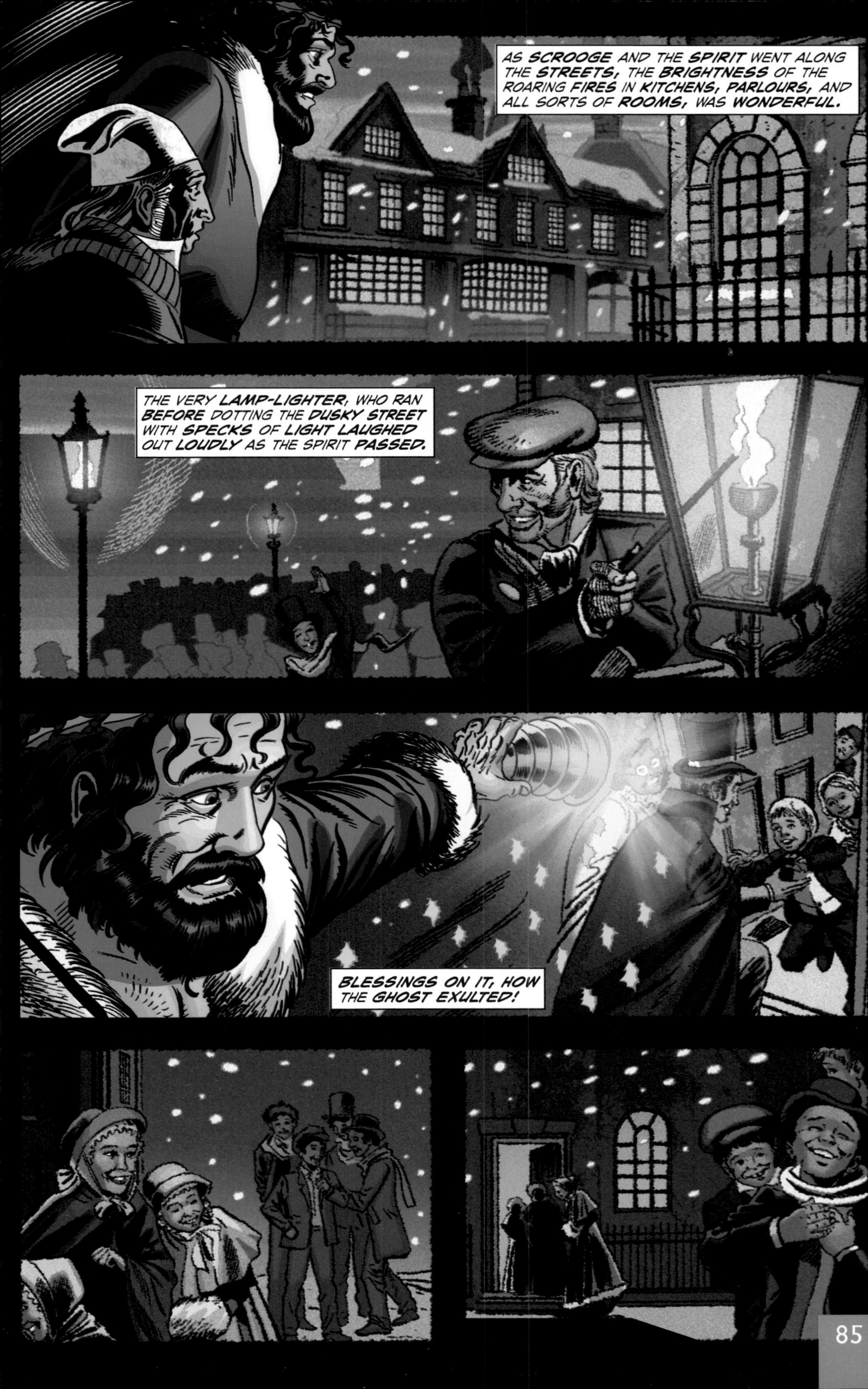
AS SCROOGE AND THE SPIRIT WENT ALONG THE STREETS, THE BRIGHTNESS OF THE ROARING FIRES IN KITCHENS, PARLOURS, AND ALL SORTS OF ROOMS, WAS WONDERFUL.
THE VERY LAMP-LIGHTER, WHO RAN BEFORE DOTTING THE DUSKY STREET WITH SPECKS OF LIGHT LAUGHED OUT LOUDLY AS THE SPIRIT PASSED.
BLESSINGS ON IT, HOW THE GHOST EXULTED!

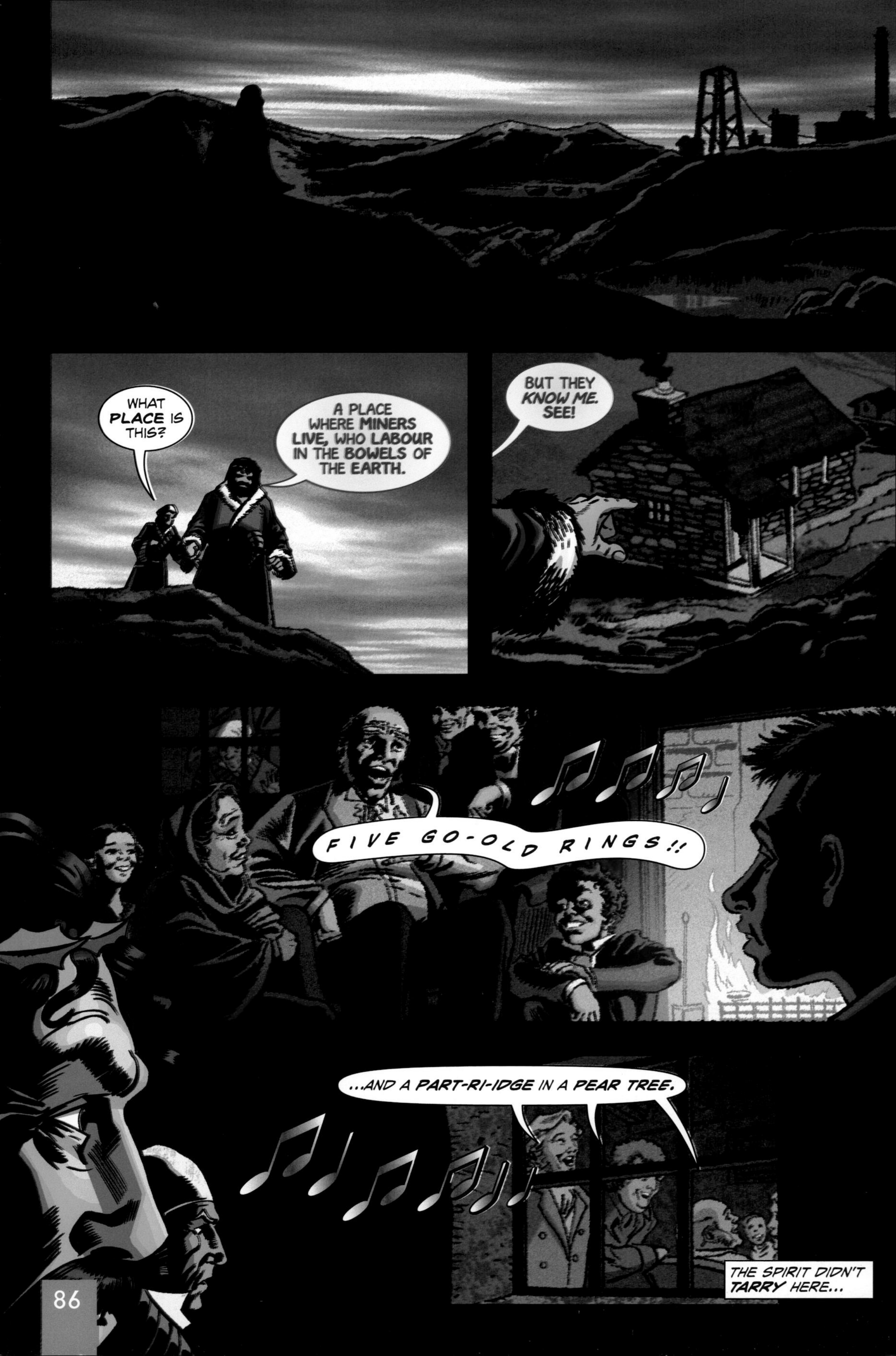
WHAT PLACE IS THIS?
A PLACE WHERE MINERS LIVE, WHO LABOUR IN THE BOWELS OF THE EARTH.
BUT THEY KNOW ME. SEE!
FIVE GO-OLD RINGS!!
...AND A PART-RI-IDGE IN A PEAR TREE.
THE SPIRIT DIDN'T TARRY HERE...

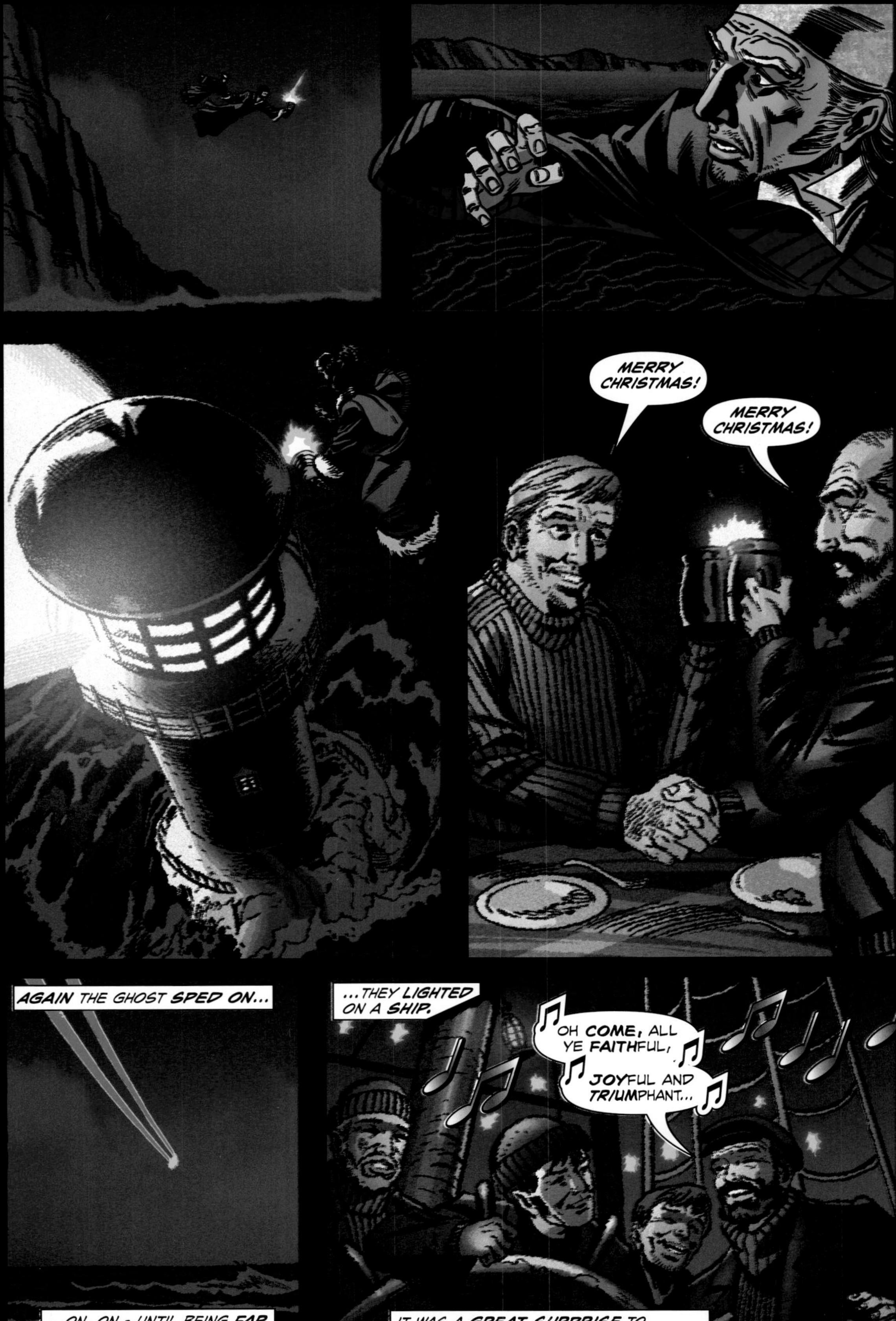
MERRY CHRISTMAS!
MERRY CHRISTMAS!
AGAIN THE GHOST SPED ON...
...ON, ON - UNTIL BEING FAR AWAY FROM ANY SHORE...
...THEY LIGHTED ON A SHIP.
OH COME, ALL YE FAITHFUL, JOYFUL AND TRIUMPHANT...
IT WAS A GREAT SURPRISE TO SCROOGE TO HEAR A HEARTY LAUGH...

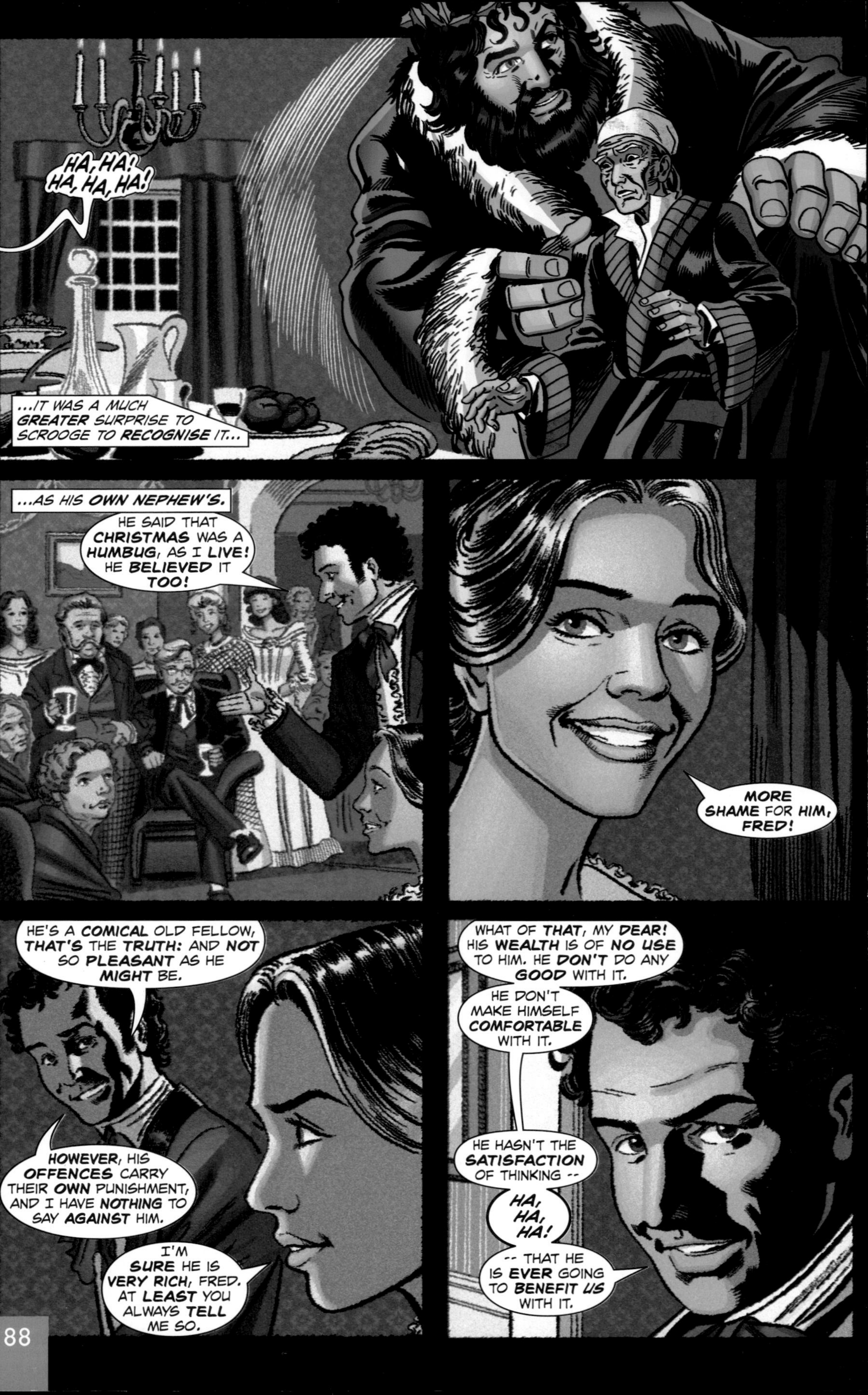
HA, HA! HA, HA, HA!
...IT WAS A MUCH GREATER SURPRISE TO SCROOGE TO RECOGNISE IT...
...AS HIS OWN NEPHEW'S.
HE SAID THAT CHRISTMAS WAS A HUMBUG, AS I LIVE! HE BELIEVED IT TOO!
MORE SHAME FOR HIM, FRED!
HE'S A COMICAL OLD FELLOW, THAT'S THE TRUTH: AND NOT SO PLEASANT AS HE MIGHT BE.
HOWEVER, HIS OFFENCES CARRY THEIR OWN PUNISHMENT, AND I HAVE NOTHING TO SAY AGAINST HIM.
I'M SURE HE IS VERY RICH, FRED. AT LEAST YOU ALWAYS TELL ME SO.
WHAT OF THAT, MY DEAR! HIS WEALTH IS OF NO USE TO HIM. HE DON'T DO ANY GOOD WITH IT.
HE DON'T MAKE HIMSELF COMFORTABLE WITH IT.
HE HASN'T THE SATISFACTION OF THINKING --
HA, HA, HA!
-- THAT HE IS EVER GOING TO BENEFIT US WITH IT.

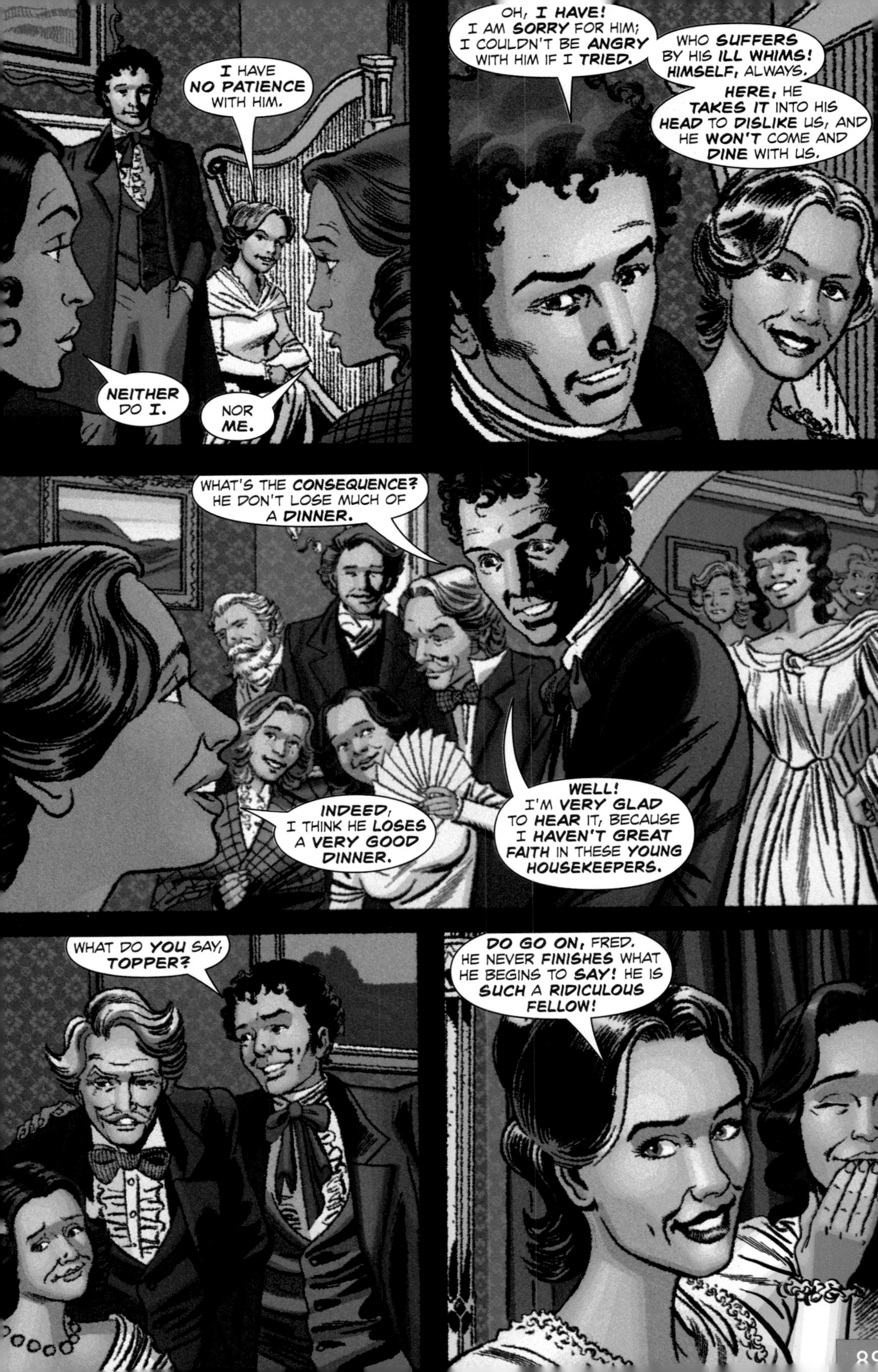
I HAVE NO PATIENCE WITH HIM.
NEITHER DO I.
NOR ME.
OH, I HAVE! I AM SORRY FOR HIM; I COULDN'T BE ANGRY WITH HIM IF I TRIED.
WHO SUFFERS BY HIS ILL WHIMS! HIMSELF, ALWAYS.
HERE, HE TAKES IT INTO HIS HEAD TO DISLIKE US, AND HE WON'T COME AND DINE WITH US.
WHAT'S THE CONSEQUENCE? HE DON'T LOSE MUCH OF A DINNER.
INDEED, I THINK HE LOSES A VERY GOOD DINNER.
WELL! I'M VERY GLAD TO HEAR IT, BECAUSE I HAVEN'T GREAT FAITH IN THESE YOUNG HOUSEKEEPERS.
WHAT DO YOU SAY, TOPPER?
DO GO ON, FRED. HE NEVER FINISHES WHAT HE BEGINS TO SAY! HE IS SUCH A RIDICULOUS FELLOW!

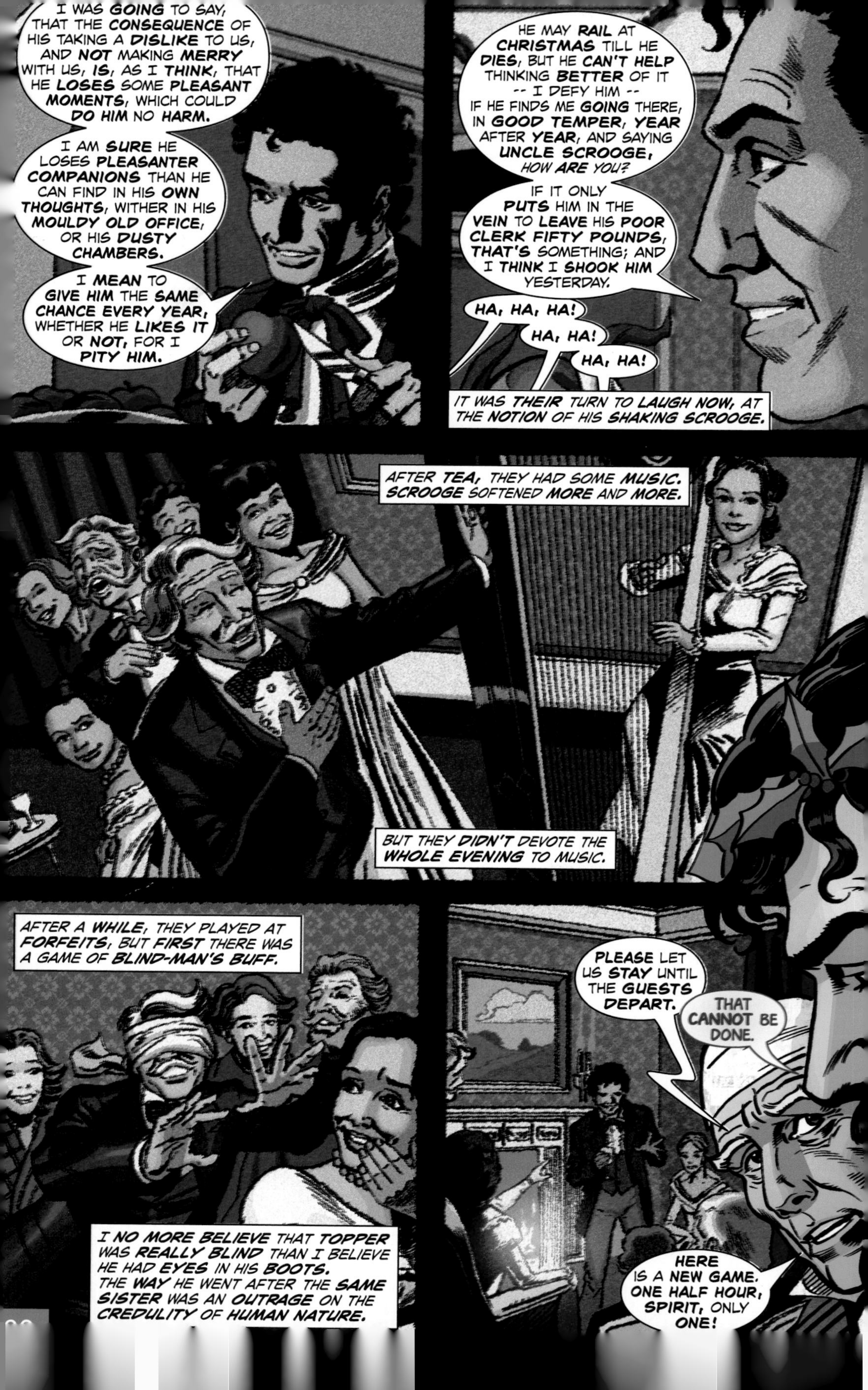
I WAS GOING TO SAY, THAT THE CONSEQUENCE OF HIS TAKING A DISLIKE TO US, AND NOT MAKING MERRY WITH US, IS, AS I THINK, THAT HE LOSES SOME PLEASANT MOMENTS, WHICH COULD DO HIM NO HARM.
I AM SURE HE LOSES PLEASANTER COMPANIONS THAN HE CAN FIND IN HIS OWN THOUGHTS, WITHER IN HIS MOULDY OLD OFFICE, OR HIS DUSTY CHAMBERS.
I MEAN TO GIVE HIM THE SAME CHANCE EVERY YEAR, WHETHER HE LIKES IT OR NOT, FOR I PITY HIM.
HE MAY RAIL AT CHRISTMAS TILL HE DIES, BUT HE CAN'T HELP THINKING BETTER OF IT -- I DEFY HIM -- IF HE FINDS ME GOING THERE, IN GOOD TEMPER, YEAR AFTER YEAR, AND SAYING UNCLE SCROOGE, HOW ARE YOU?
IF IT ONLY PUTS HIM IN THE VEIN TO LEAVE HIS POOR CLERK FIFTY POUNDS, THAT'S SOMETHING; AND I THINK I SHOOK HIM YESTERDAY.
HA, HA, HA!
HA, HA!
HA, HA!
IT WAS THEIR TURN TO LAUGH NOW, AT THE NOTION OF HIS SHAKING SCROOGE.
AFTER TEA, THEY HAD SOME MUSIC. SCROOGE SOFTENED MORE AND MORE.
BUT THEY DIDN'T DEVOTE THE WHOLE EVENING TO MUSIC.
AFTER A WHILE, THEY PLAYED AT FORFEITS, BUT FIRST THERE WAS A GAME OF BLIND-MAN'S BUFF.
I NO MORE BELIEVE THAT TOPPER WAS REALLY BLIND THAN I BELIEVE HE HAD EYES IN HIS BOOTS. THE WAY HE WENT AFTER THE SAME SISTER WAS AN OUTRAGE ON THE CREDULITY OF HUMAN NATURE.
PLEASE LET US STAY UNTIL THE GUESTS DEPART.
THAT CANNOT BE DONE.
HERE IS A NEW GAME. ONE HALF HOUR, SPIRIT, ONLY ONE!

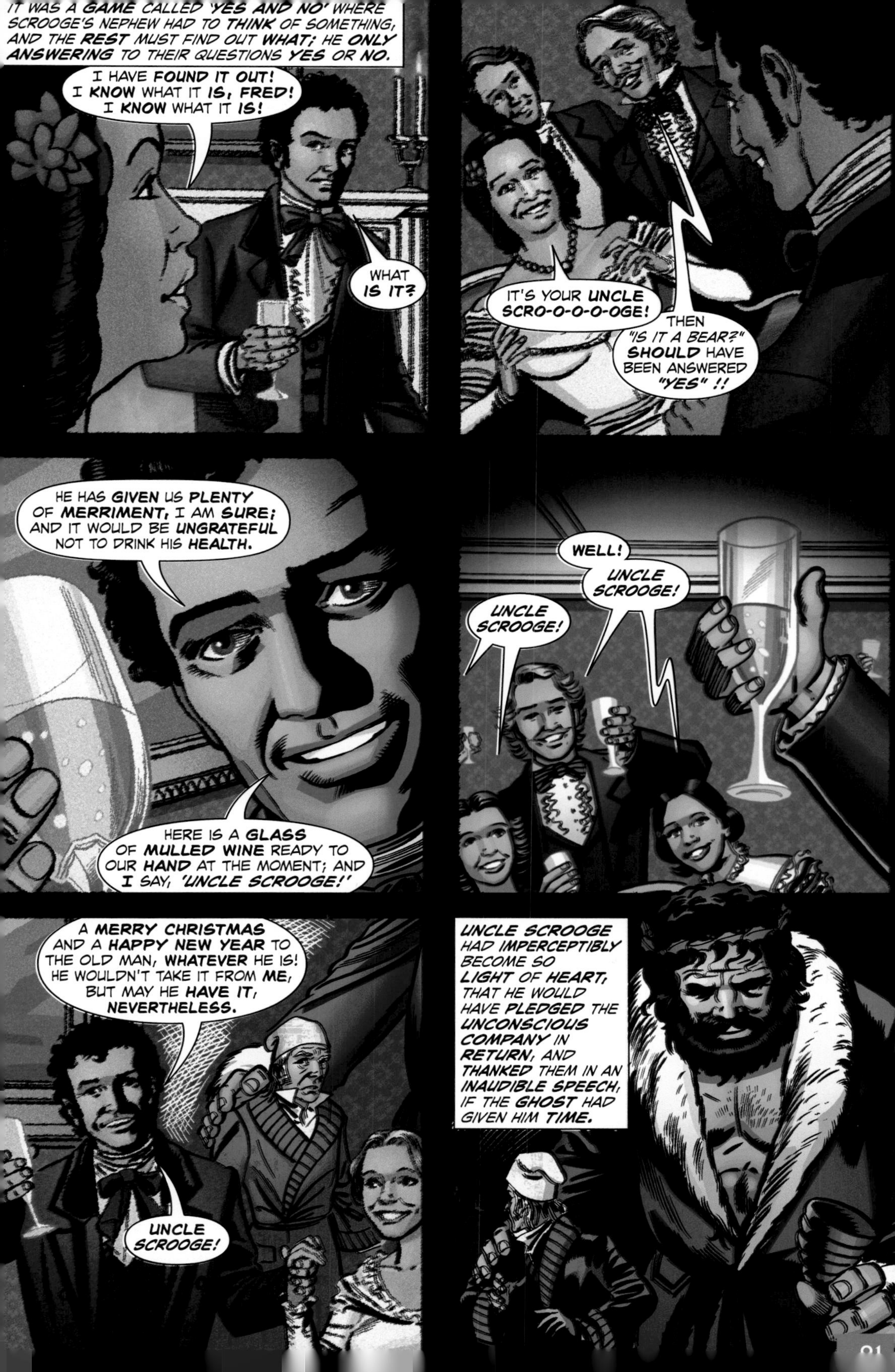
IT WAS A GAME CALLED 'YES AND NO' WHERE SCROOGE'S NEPHEW HAD TO THINK OF SOMETHING, AND THE REST MUST FIND OUT WHAT; HE ONLY ANSWERING TO THEIR QUESTIONS YES OR NO.
I HAVE FOUND IT OUT! I KNOW WHAT IT IS, FRED! I KNOW WHAT IT IS!
WHAT IS IT?
IT'S YOUR UNCLE SCRO-O-O-O-OGE!
THEN "IS IT A BEAR?" SHOULD HAVE BEEN ANSWERED "YES" !!
HE HAS GIVEN US PLENTY OF MERRIMENT, I AM SURE; AND IT WOULD BE UNGRATEFUL NOT TO DRINK HIS HEALTH.
HERE IS A GLASS OF MULLED WINE READY TO OUR HAND AT THE MOMENT; AND I SAY, 'UNCLE SCROOGE!'
WELL!
UNCLE SCROOGE!
UNCLE SCROOGE!
A MERRY CHRISTMAS AND A HAPPY NEW YEAR TO THE OLD MAN, WHATEVER HE IS! HE WOULDN'T TAKE IT FROM ME, BUT MAY HE HAVE IT, NEVERTHELESS.
UNCLE SCROOGE!
UNCLE SCROOGE HAD IMPERCEPTIBLY BECOME SO LIGHT OF HEART, THAT HE WOULD HAVE PLEDGED THE UNCONSCIOUS COMPANY IN RETURN, AND THANKED THEM IN AN INAUDIBLE SPEECH, IF THE GHOST HAD GIVEN HIM TIME.

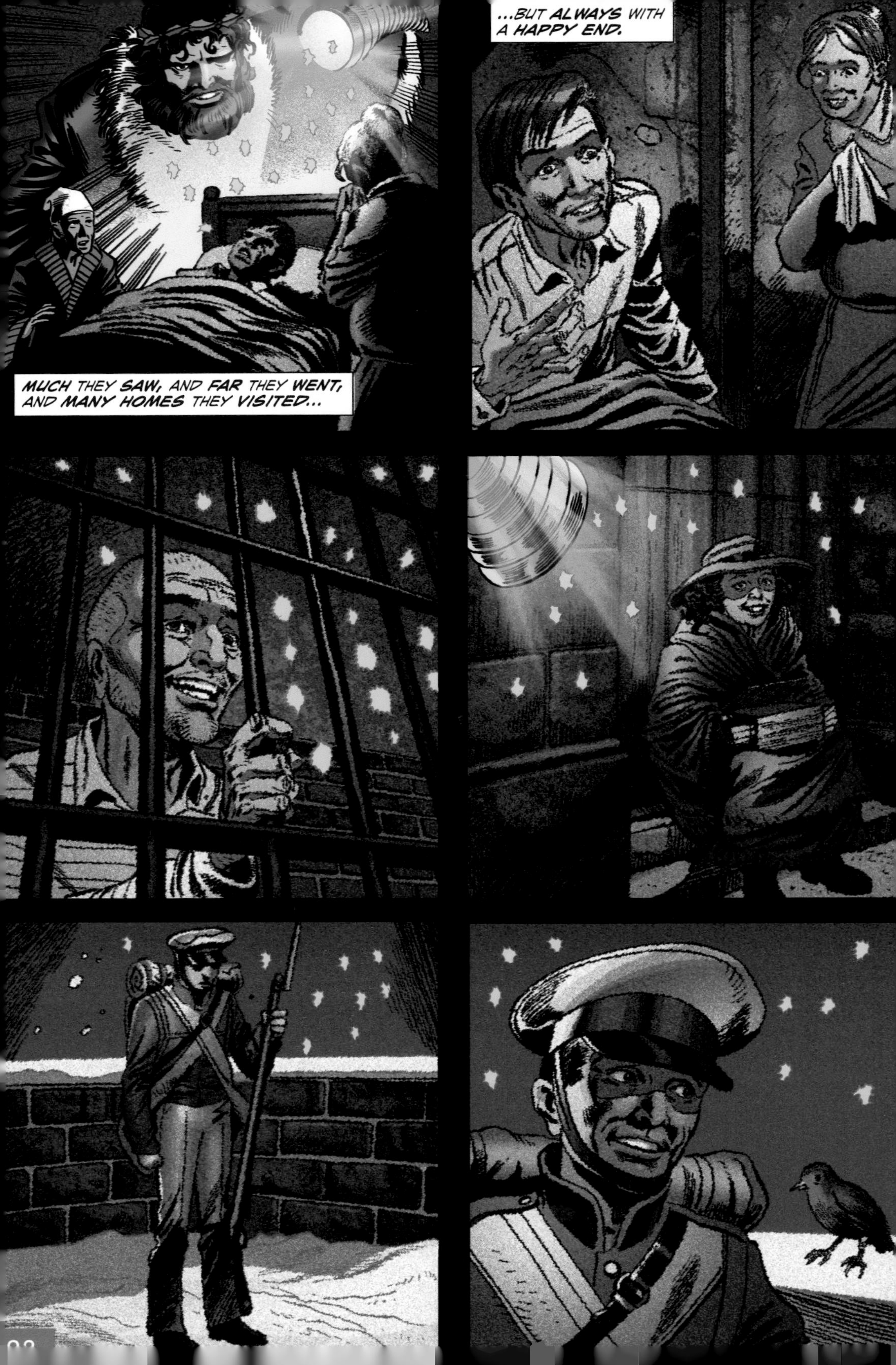
MUCH THEY SAW, AND FAR THEY WENT, AND MANY HOMES THEY VISITED...
...BUT ALWAYS WITH A HAPPY END.

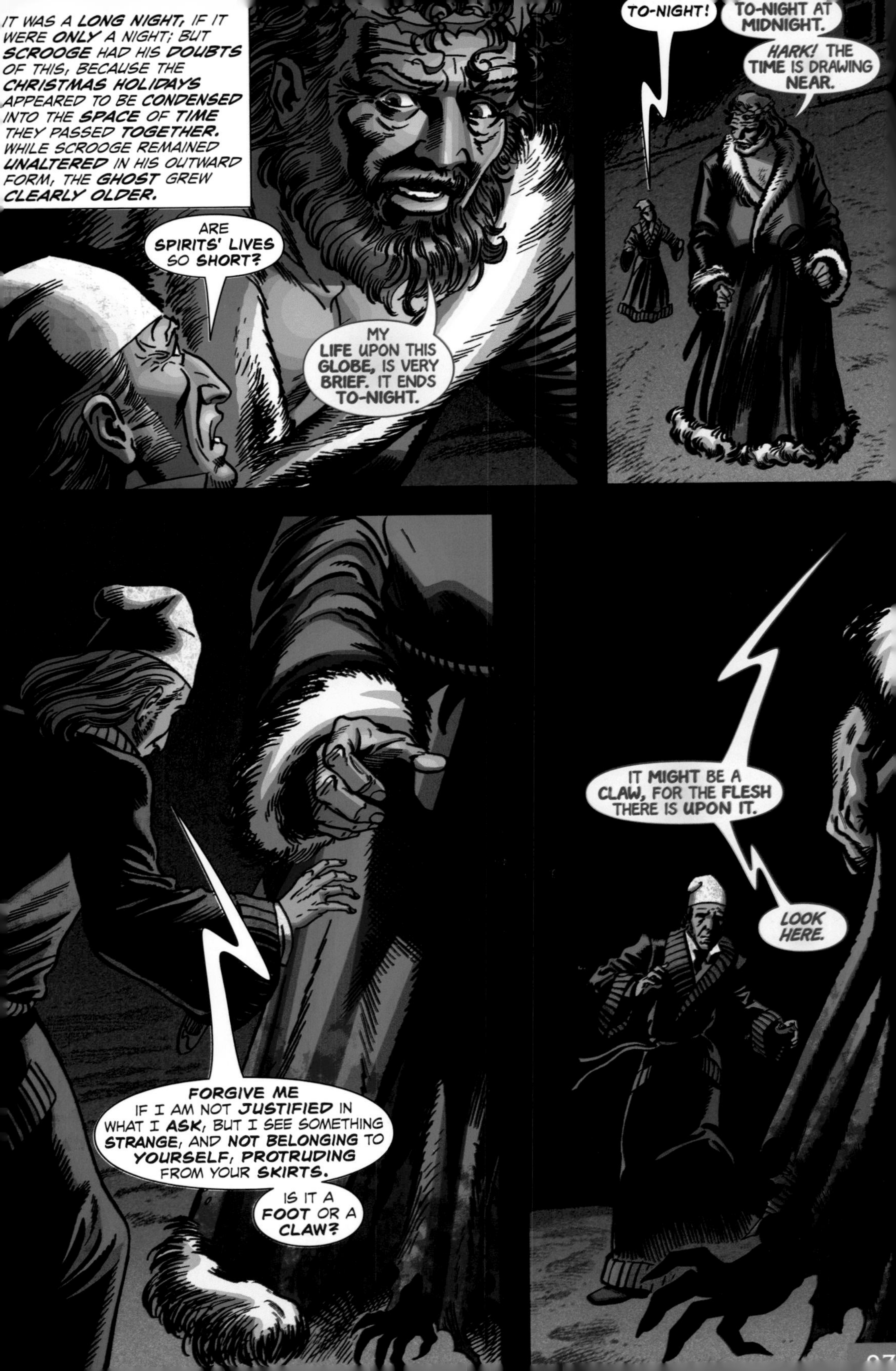
IT WAS A LONG NIGHT, IF IT WERE ONLY A NIGHT; BUT SCROOGE HAD HIS DOUBTS OF THIS, BECAUSE THE CHRISTMAS HOLIDAYS APPEARED TO BE CONDENSED INTO THE SPACE OF TIME THEY PASSED TOGETHER. WHILE SCROOGE REMAINED UNALTERED IN HIS OUTWARD FORM, THE GHOST GREW CLEARLY OLDER.
ARE SPIRITS' LIVES SO SHORT?
MY LIFE UPON THIS GLOBE, IS VERY BRIEF. IT ENDS TO-NIGHT.
TO-NIGHT!
TO-NIGHT AT MIDNIGHT.
HARK! THE TIME IS DRAWING NEAR.
FORGIVE ME IF I AM NOT JUSTIFIED IN WHAT I ASK, BUT I SEE SOMETHING STRANGE, AND NOT BELONGING TO YOURSELF, PROTRUDING FROM YOUR SKIRTS.
IS IT A FOOT OR A CLAW?
IT MIGHT BE A CLAW, FOR THE FLESH THERE IS UPON IT.
LOOK HERE.

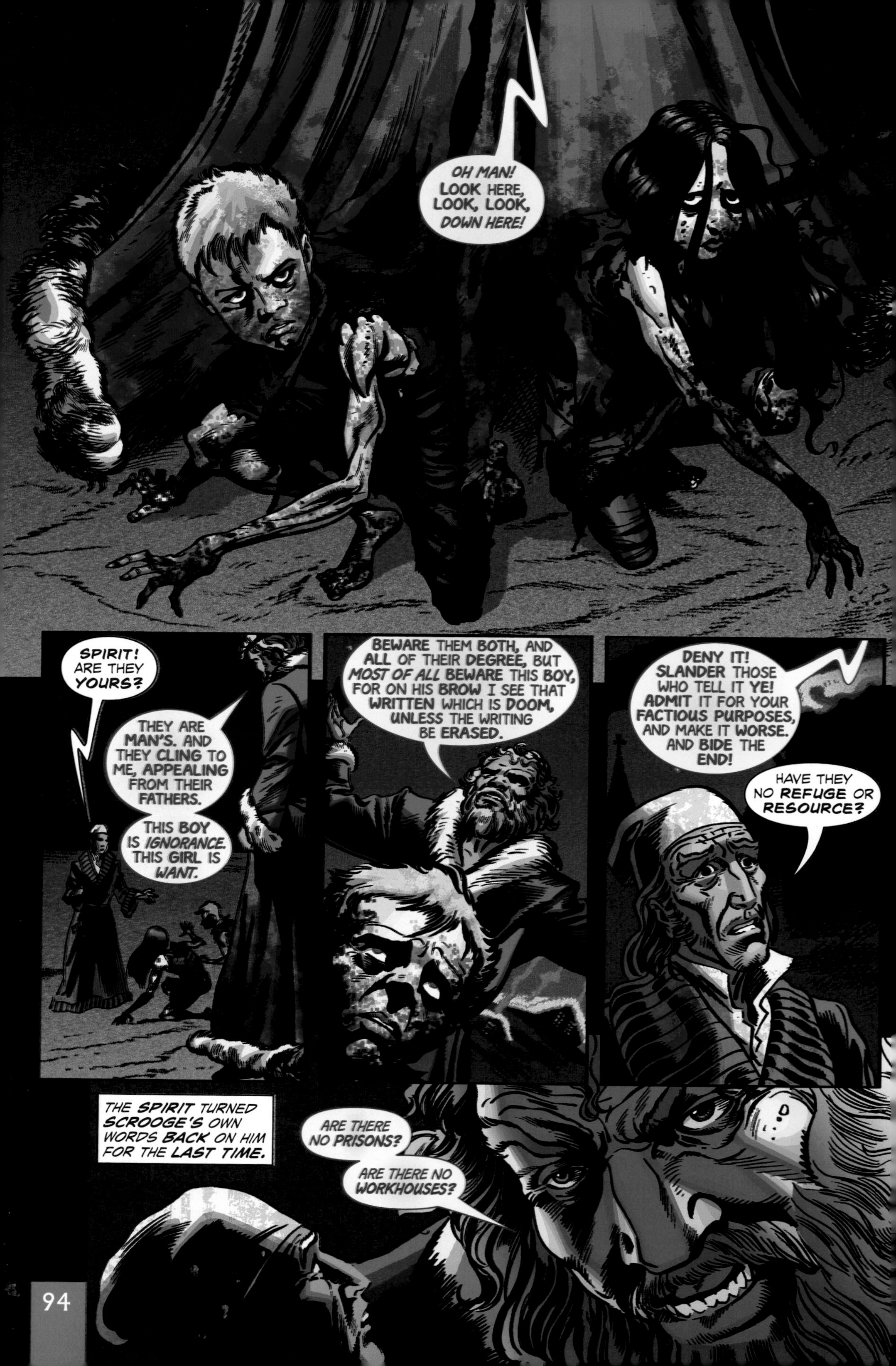
OH MAN! LOOK HERE, LOOK, LOOK, DOWN HERE!
SPIRIT! ARE THEY YOURS?
THEY ARE MAN'S. AND THEY CLING TO ME, APPEALING FROM THEIR FATHERS.
THIS BOY IS IGNORANCE. THIS GIRL IS WANT.
BEWARE THEM BOTH, AND ALL OF THEIR DEGREE, BUT MOST OF ALL BEWARE THIS BOY, FOR ON HIS BROW I SEE THAT WRITTEN WHICH IS DOOM, UNLESS THE WRITING BE ERASED.
DENY IT! SLANDER THOSE WHO TELL IT YE! ADMIT IT FOR YOUR FACTIOUS PURPOSES, AND MAKE IT WORSE. AND BIDE THE END!
HAVE THEY NO REFUGE OR RESOURCE?
THE SPIRIT TURNED SCROOGE'S OWN WORDS BACK ON HIM FOR THE LAST TIME.
ARE THERE NO PRISONS?
ARE THERE NO WORKHOUSES?

DONG!
DONG!
DONG!
DONG!
DONG!
DONG!
DONG!

THE BELL STRUCK TWELVE.

GHOST, AND SAW IT NOT.

AS THE LAST *STROKE* CEASED TO *VIBRATE*, HE *REMEMBERED* THE *PREDICTION* OF OLD *JACOB MARLEY*, AND *LIFTING* UP HIS *EYES*, BEHELD...

Stave Four: The Last of the Spirits

I AM IN THE *PRESENCE* OF THE *GHOST* OF *CHRISTMAS YET* TO *COME*?

THE *SPIRIT DID* NOT *ANSWER.*

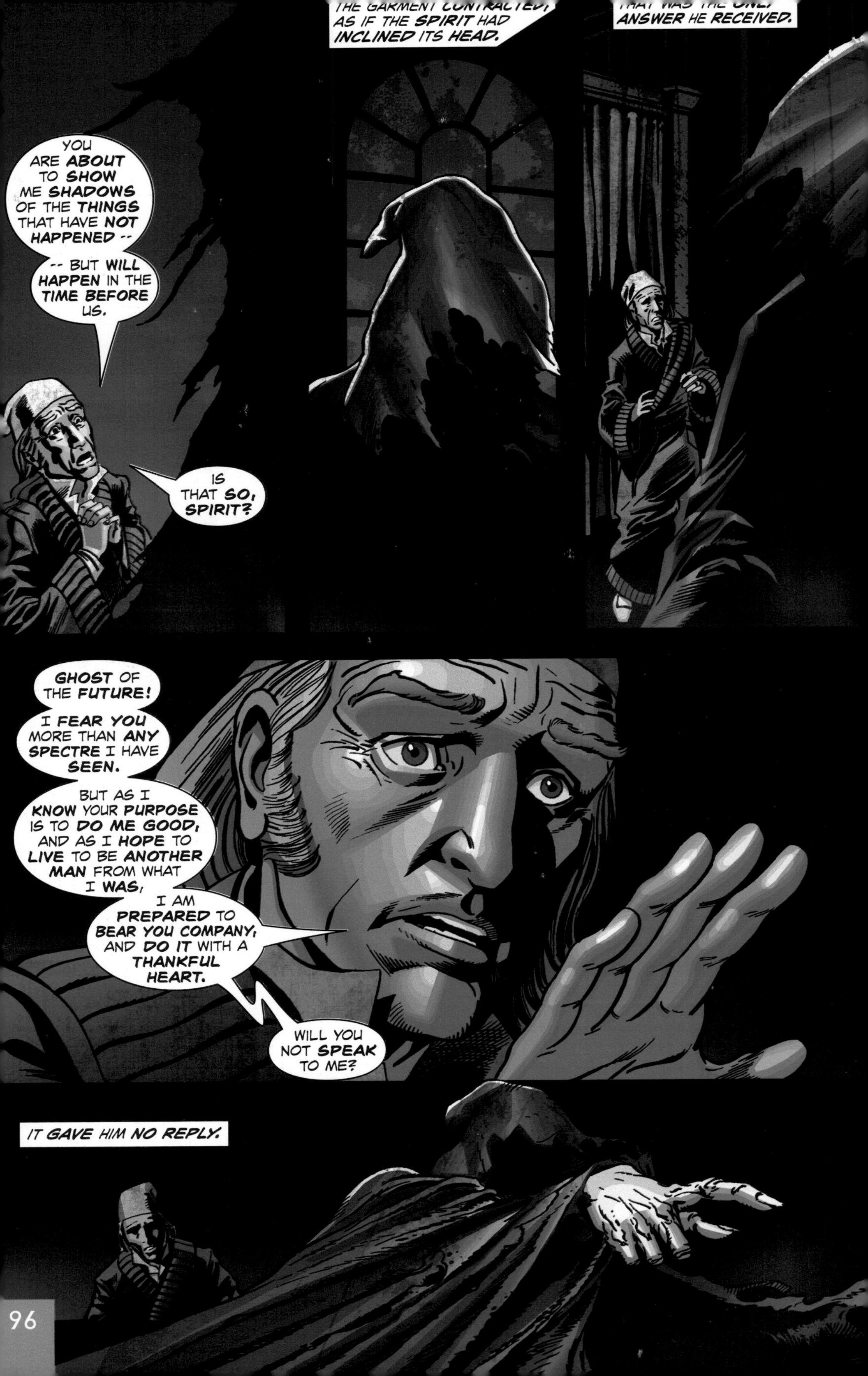

YOU ARE ABOUT TO SHOW ME SHADOWS OF THE THINGS THAT HAVE NOT HAPPENED --
-- BUT WILL HAPPEN IN THE TIME BEFORE US.
IS THAT SO, SPIRIT?
THE GARMENT CONTRACTED, AS IF THE SPIRIT HAD INCLINED ITS HEAD.
ANSWER HE RECEIVED.
GHOST OF THE FUTURE!
I FEAR YOU MORE THAN ANY SPECTRE I HAVE SEEN.
BUT AS I KNOW YOUR PURPOSE IS TO DO ME GOOD, AND AS I HOPE TO LIVE TO BE ANOTHER MAN FROM WHAT I WAS,
I AM PREPARED TO BEAR YOU COMPANY, AND DO IT WITH A THANKFUL HEART.
WILL YOU NOT SPEAK TO ME?
IT GAVE HIM NO REPLY.

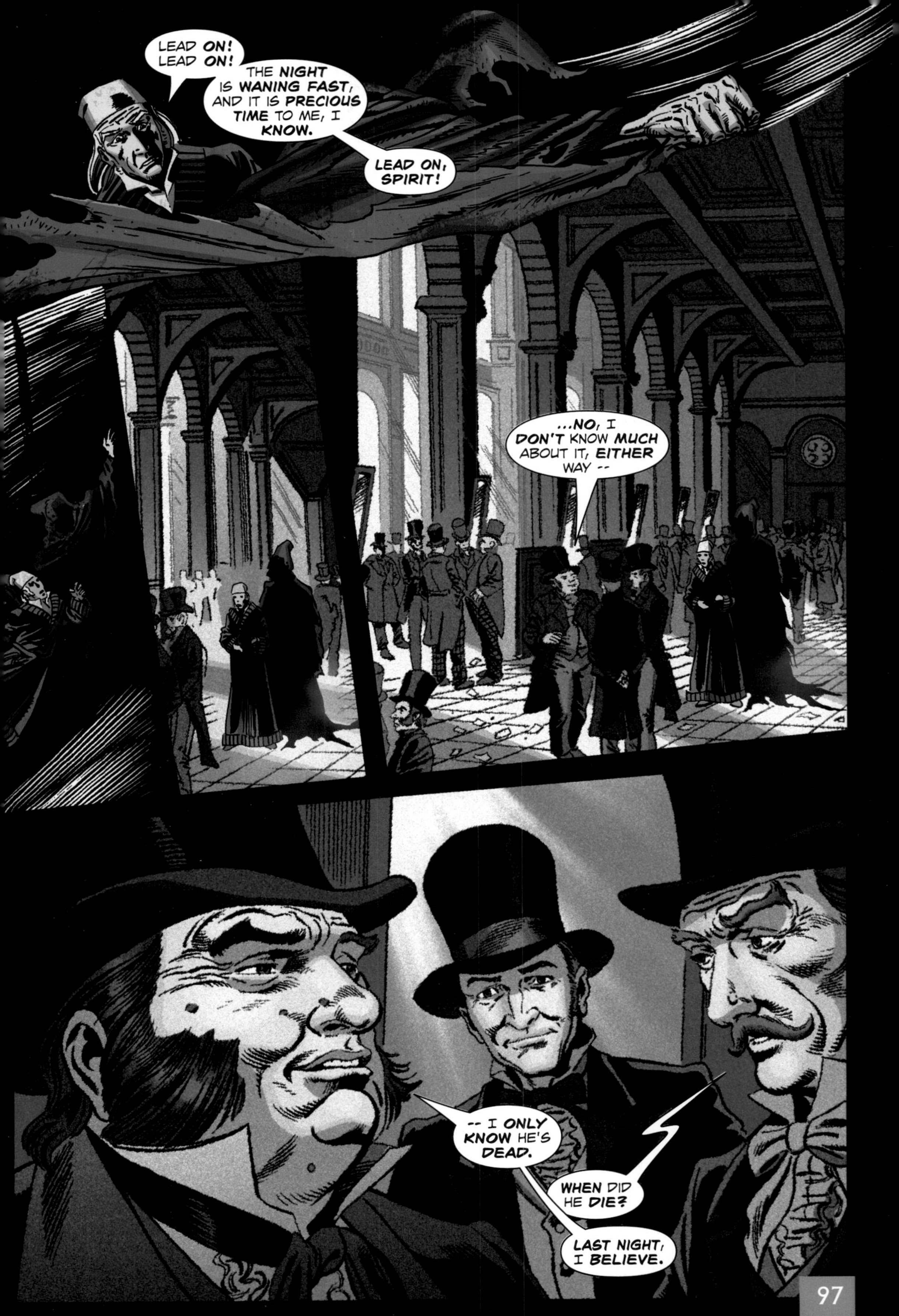

LEAD ON! LEAD ON!
THE NIGHT IS WANING FAST, AND IT IS PRECIOUS TIME TO ME, I KNOW.
LEAD ON, SPIRIT!
...NO, I DON'T KNOW MUCH ABOUT IT, EITHER WAY --
-- I ONLY KNOW HE'S DEAD.
WHEN DID HE DIE?
LAST NIGHT, I BELIEVE.

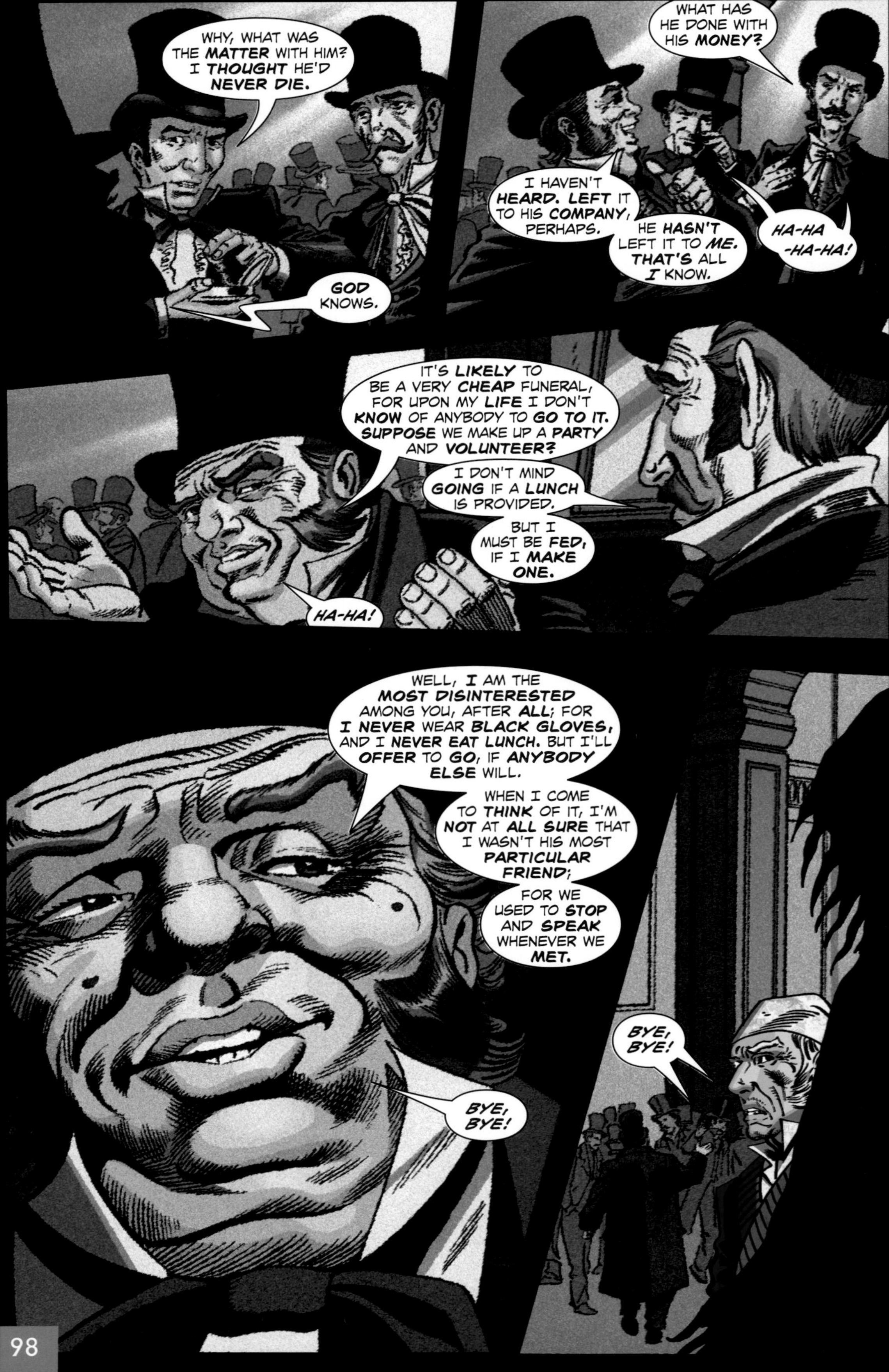
WHY, WHAT WAS THE MATTER WITH HIM? I THOUGHT HE'D NEVER DIE.
GOD KNOWS.
WHAT HAS HE DONE WITH HIS MONEY?
I HAVEN'T HEARD. LEFT IT TO HIS COMPANY, PERHAPS.
HE HASN'T LEFT IT TO ME. THAT'S ALL I KNOW.
HA-HA -HA-HA!
IT'S LIKELY TO BE A VERY CHEAP FUNERAL, FOR UPON MY LIFE I DON'T KNOW OF ANYBODY TO GO TO IT. SUPPOSE WE MAKE UP A PARTY AND VOLUNTEER?
I DON'T MIND GOING IF A LUNCH IS PROVIDED.
BUT I MUST BE FED, IF I MAKE ONE.
HA-HA!
WELL, I AM THE MOST DISINTERESTED AMONG YOU, AFTER ALL; FOR I NEVER WEAR BLACK GLOVES, AND I NEVER EAT LUNCH. BUT I'LL OFFER TO GO, IF ANYBODY ELSE WILL.
WHEN I COME TO THINK OF IT, I'M NOT AT ALL SURE THAT I WASN'T HIS MOST PARTICULAR FRIEND;
FOR WE USED TO STOP AND SPEAK WHENEVER WE MET.
BYE, BYE!
BYE, BYE!

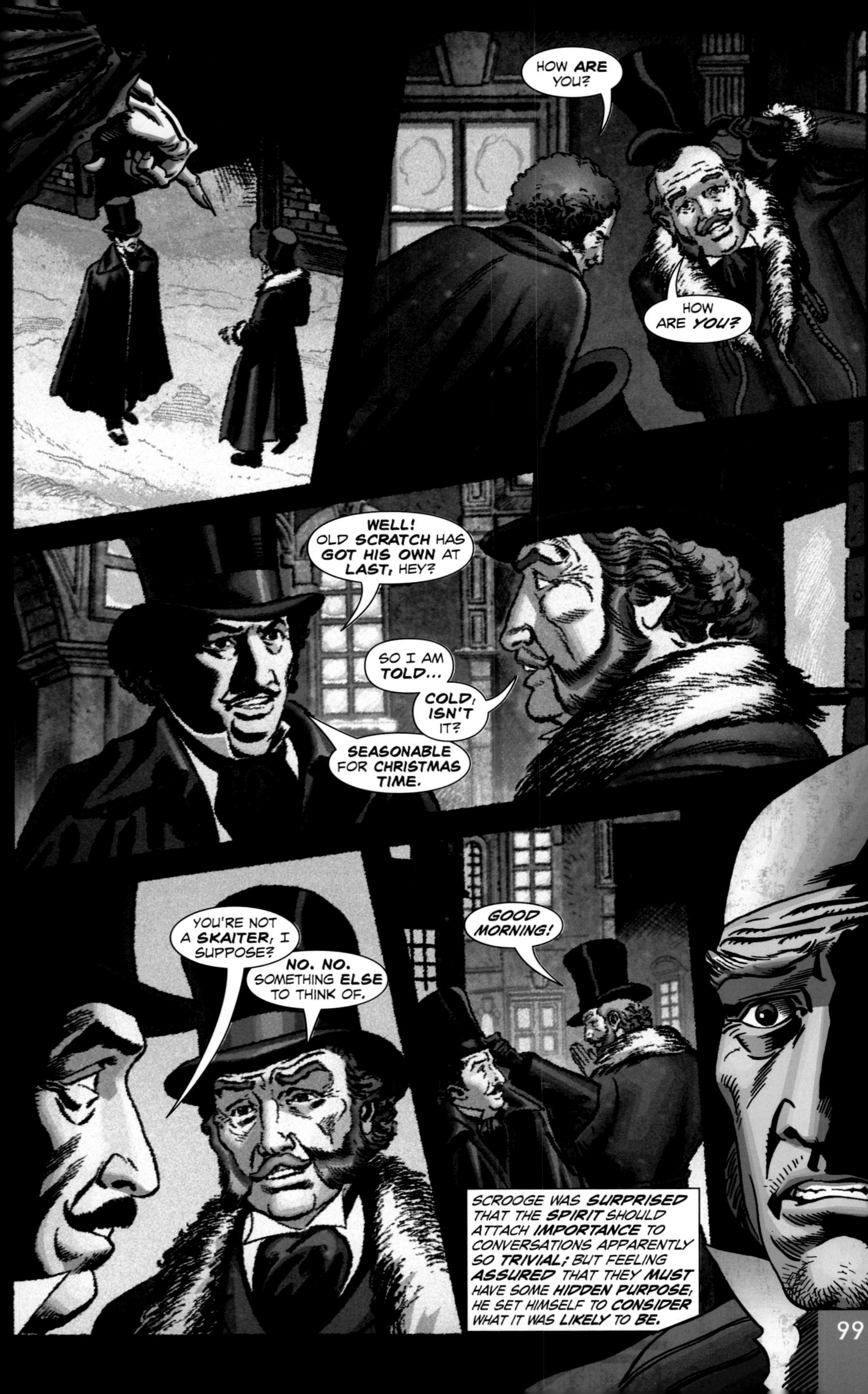
HOW ARE YOU?
HOW ARE YOU?
WELL! OLD SCRATCH HAS GOT HIS OWN AT LAST, HEY?
SO I AM TOLD...
COLD, ISN'T IT?
SEASONABLE FOR CHRISTMAS TIME.
YOU'RE NOT A SKAITER, I SUPPOSE?
NO. NO. SOMETHING ELSE TO THINK OF.
GOOD MORNING!
SCROOGE WAS SURPRISED THAT THE SPIRIT SHOULD ATTACH IMPORTANCE TO CONVERSATIONS APPARENTLY SO TRIVIAL; BUT FEELING ASSURED THAT THEY MUST HAVE SOME HIDDEN PURPOSE, HE SET HIMSELF TO CONSIDER WHAT IT WAS LIKELY TO BE.

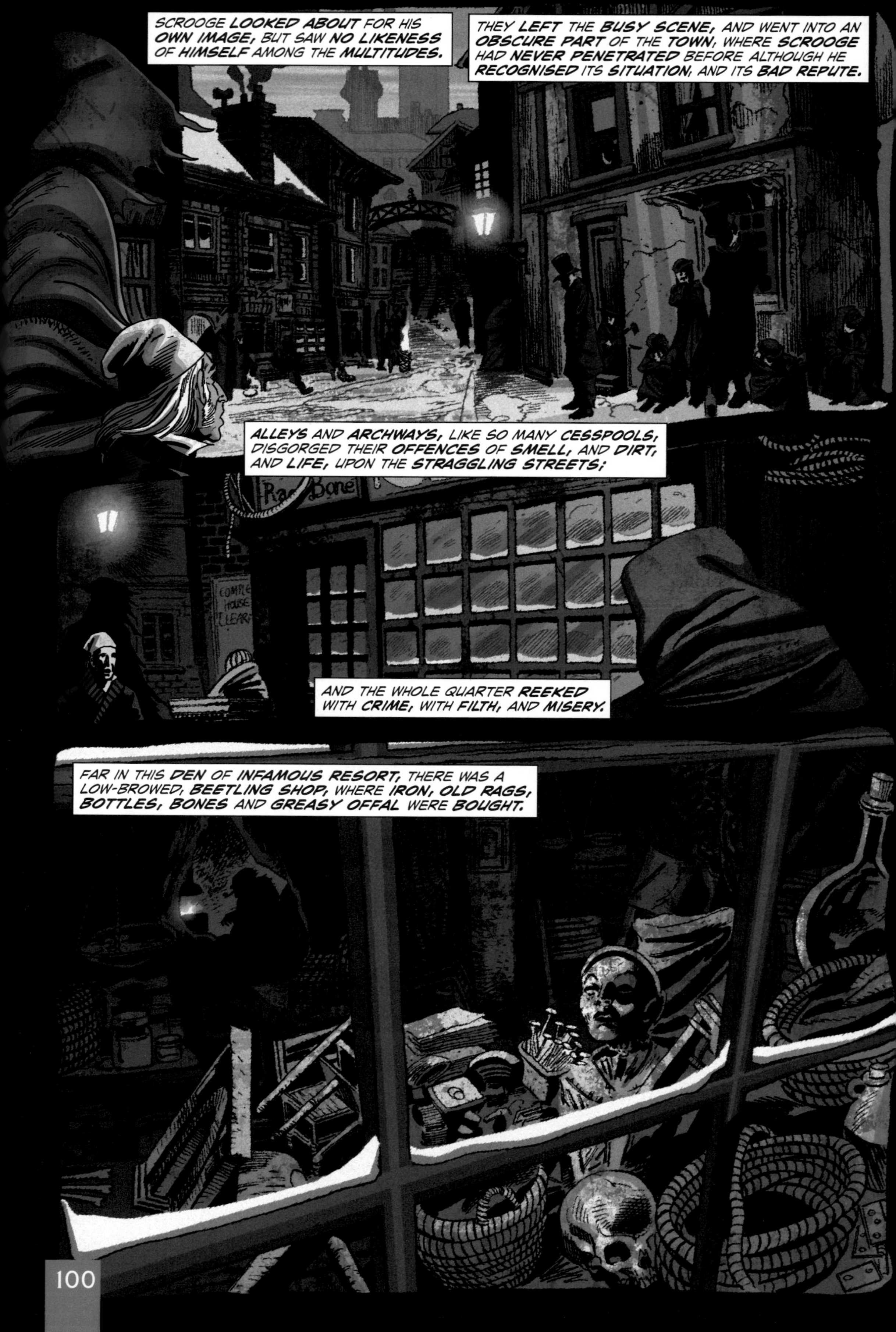
SCROOGE LOOKED ABOUT FOR HIS OWN IMAGE; BUT SAW NO LIKENESS OF HIMSELF AMONG THE MULTITUDES.
THEY LEFT THE BUSY SCENE, AND WENT INTO AN OBSCURE PART OF THE TOWN, WHERE SCROOGE HAD NEVER PENETRATED BEFORE ALTHOUGH HE RECOGNISED ITS SITUATION, AND ITS BAD REPUTE.
ALLEYS AND ARCHWAYS, LIKE SO MANY CESSPOOLS, DISGORGED THEIR OFFENCES OF SMELL, AND DIRT, AND LIFE, UPON THE STRAGGLING STREETS;
AND THE WHOLE QUARTER REEKED WITH CRIME, WITH FILTH, AND MISERY.
FAR IN THIS DEN OF INFAMOUS RESORT, THERE WAS A LOW-BROWED, BEETLING SHOP, WHERE IRON, OLD RAGS, BOTTLES, BONES AND GREASY OFFAL WERE BOUGHT.

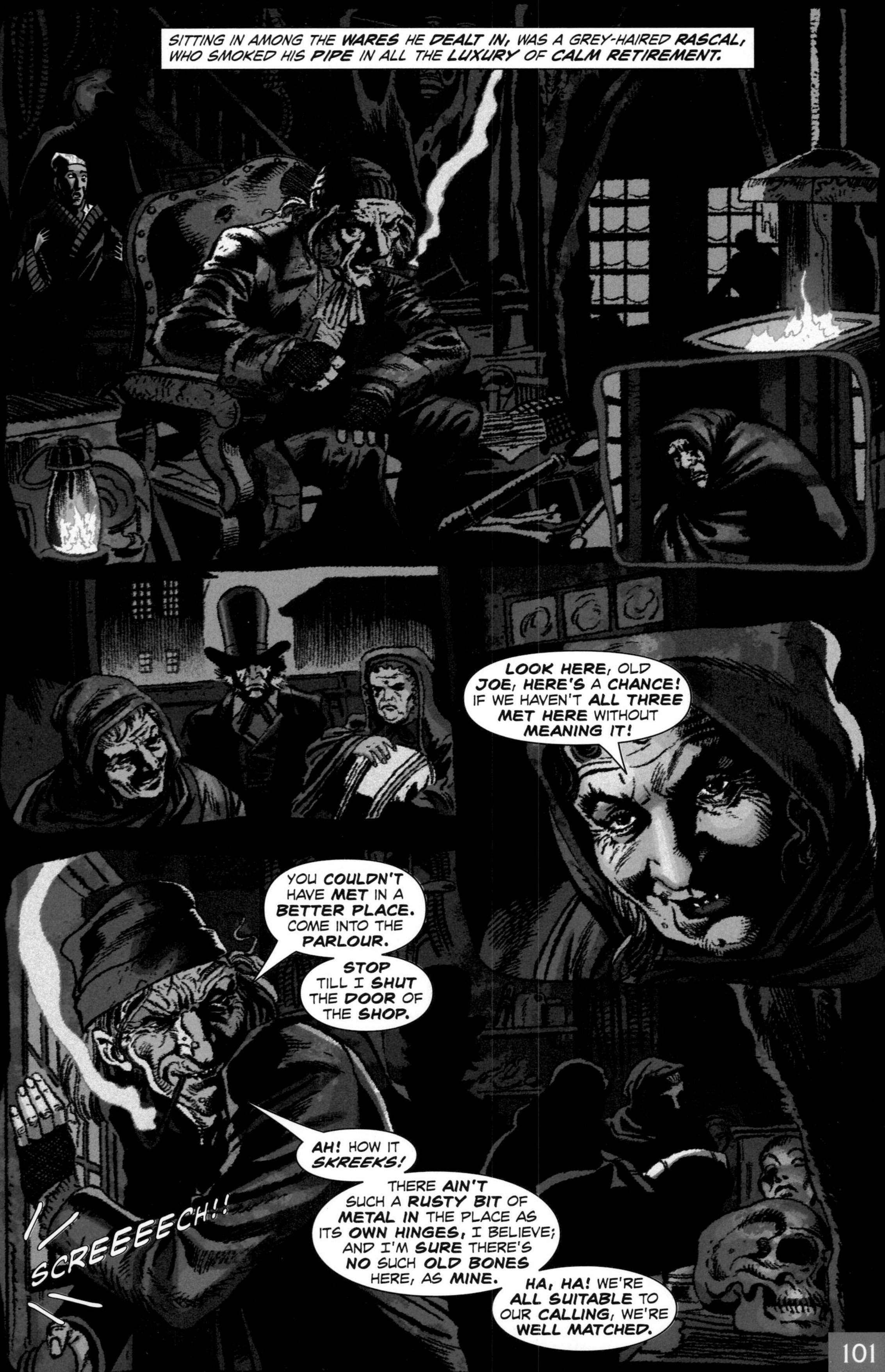
SITTING IN AMONG THE WARES HE DEALT IN, WAS A GREY-HAIRED RASCAL, WHO SMOKED HIS PIPE IN ALL THE LUXURY OF CALM RETIREMENT.
LOOK HERE, OLD JOE, HERE'S A CHANCE! IF WE HAVEN'T ALL THREE MET HERE WITHOUT MEANING IT!
YOU COULDN'T HAVE MET IN A BETTER PLACE. COME INTO THE PARLOUR.
STOP TILL I SHUT THE DOOR OF THE SHOP.
SCREEEEECH!!
AH! HOW IT SKREEKS!
THERE AIN'T SUCH A RUSTY BIT OF METAL IN THE PLACE AS ITS OWN HINGES, I BELIEVE; AND I'M SURE THERE'S NO SUCH OLD BONES HERE, AS MINE.
HA, HA! WE'RE ALL SUITABLE TO OUR CALLING, WE'RE WELL MATCHED.

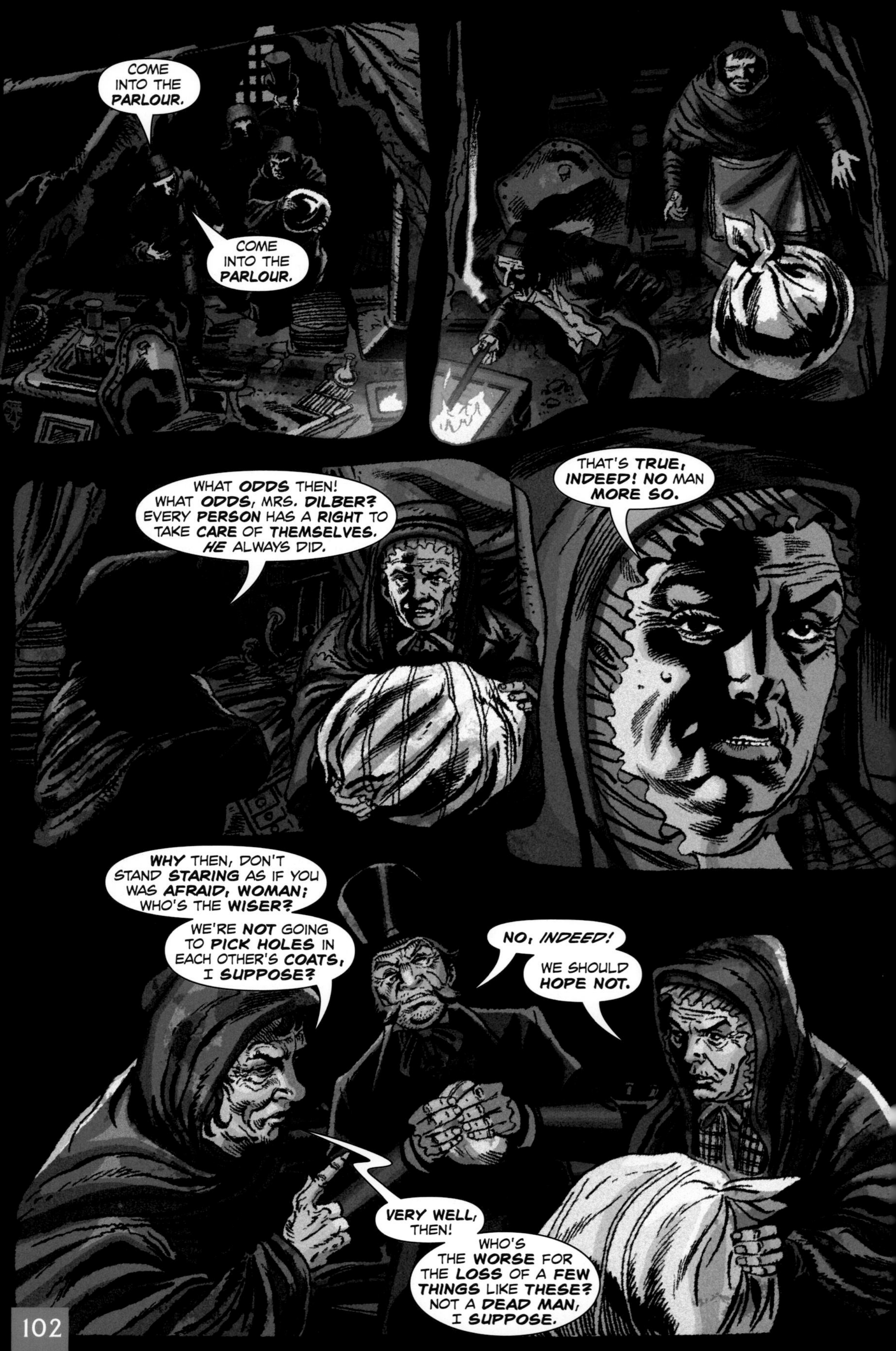
COME INTO THE PARLOUR.
COME INTO THE PARLOUR.
WHAT ODDS THEN! WHAT ODDS, MRS. DILBER? EVERY PERSON HAS A RIGHT TO TAKE CARE OF THEMSELVES. HE ALWAYS DID.
THAT'S TRUE, INDEED! NO MAN MORE SO.
WHY THEN, DON'T STAND STARING AS IF YOU WAS AFRAID, WOMAN; WHO'S THE WISER?
WE'RE NOT GOING TO PICK HOLES IN EACH OTHER'S COATS, I SUPPOSE?
NO, INDEED!
WE SHOULD HOPE NOT.
VERY WELL, THEN!
WHO'S THE WORSE FOR THE LOSS OF A FEW THINGS LIKE THESE? NOT A DEAD MAN, I SUPPOSE.

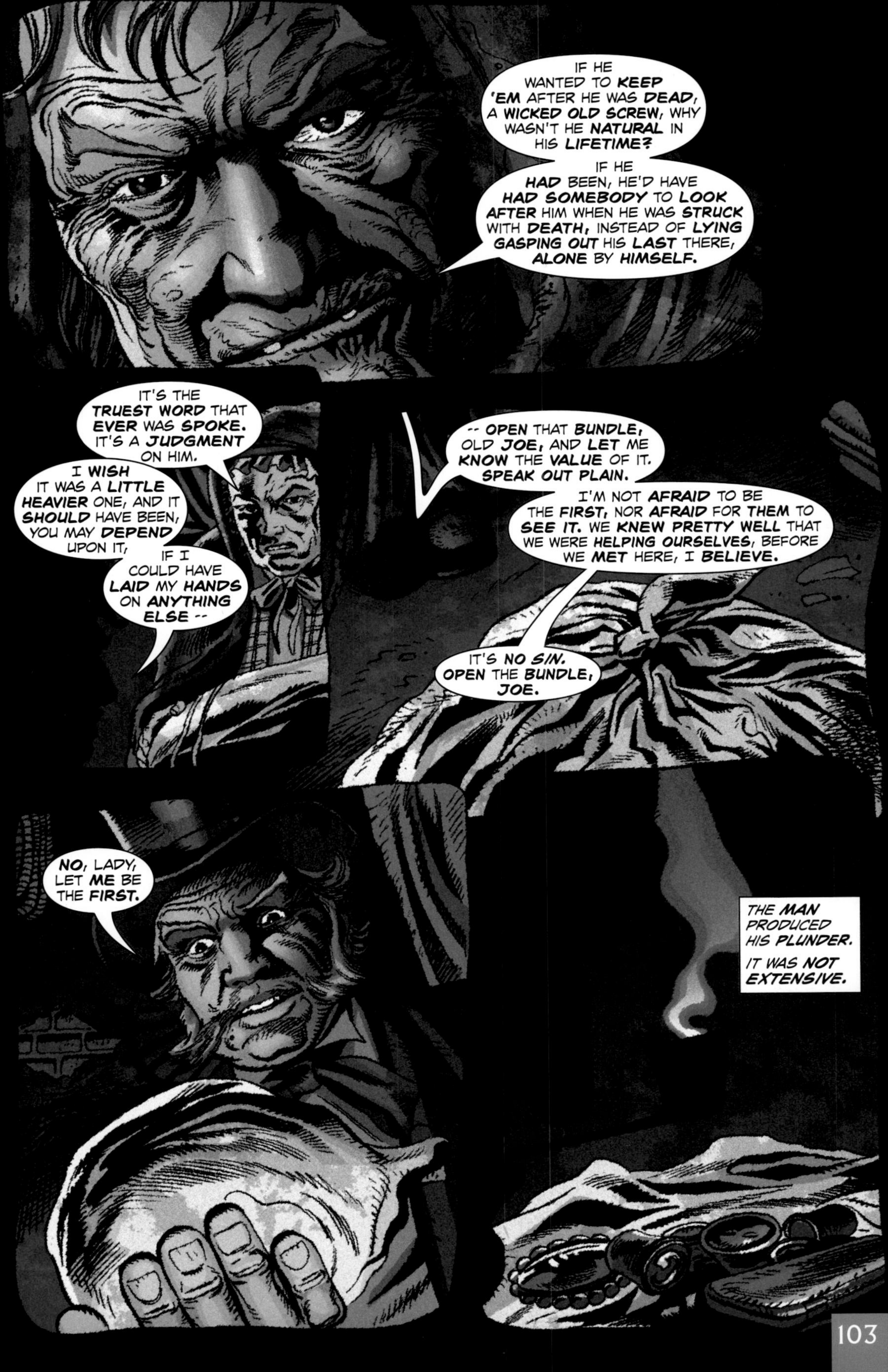
IF HE WANTED TO KEEP 'EM AFTER HE WAS DEAD, A WICKED OLD SCREW, WHY WASN'T HE NATURAL IN HIS LIFETIME?
IF HE HAD BEEN, HE'D HAVE HAD SOMEBODY TO LOOK AFTER HIM WHEN HE WAS STRUCK WITH DEATH, INSTEAD OF LYING GASPING OUT HIS LAST THERE, ALONE BY HIMSELF.
IT'S THE TRUEST WORD THAT EVER WAS SPOKE. IT'S A JUDGMENT ON HIM.
I WISH IT WAS A LITTLE HEAVIER ONE, AND IT SHOULD HAVE BEEN, YOU MAY DEPEND UPON IT,
IF I COULD HAVE LAID MY HANDS ON ANYTHING ELSE --
-- OPEN THAT BUNDLE, OLD JOE, AND LET ME KNOW THE VALUE OF IT. SPEAK OUT PLAIN.
I'M NOT AFRAID TO BE THE FIRST, NOR AFRAID FOR THEM TO SEE IT. WE KNEW PRETTY WELL THAT WE WERE HELPING OURSELVES, BEFORE WE MET HERE, I BELIEVE.
IT'S NO SIN. OPEN THE BUNDLE, JOE.
NO, LADY, LET ME BE THE FIRST.
THE MAN PRODUCED HIS PLUNDER.
IT WAS NOT EXTENSIVE.

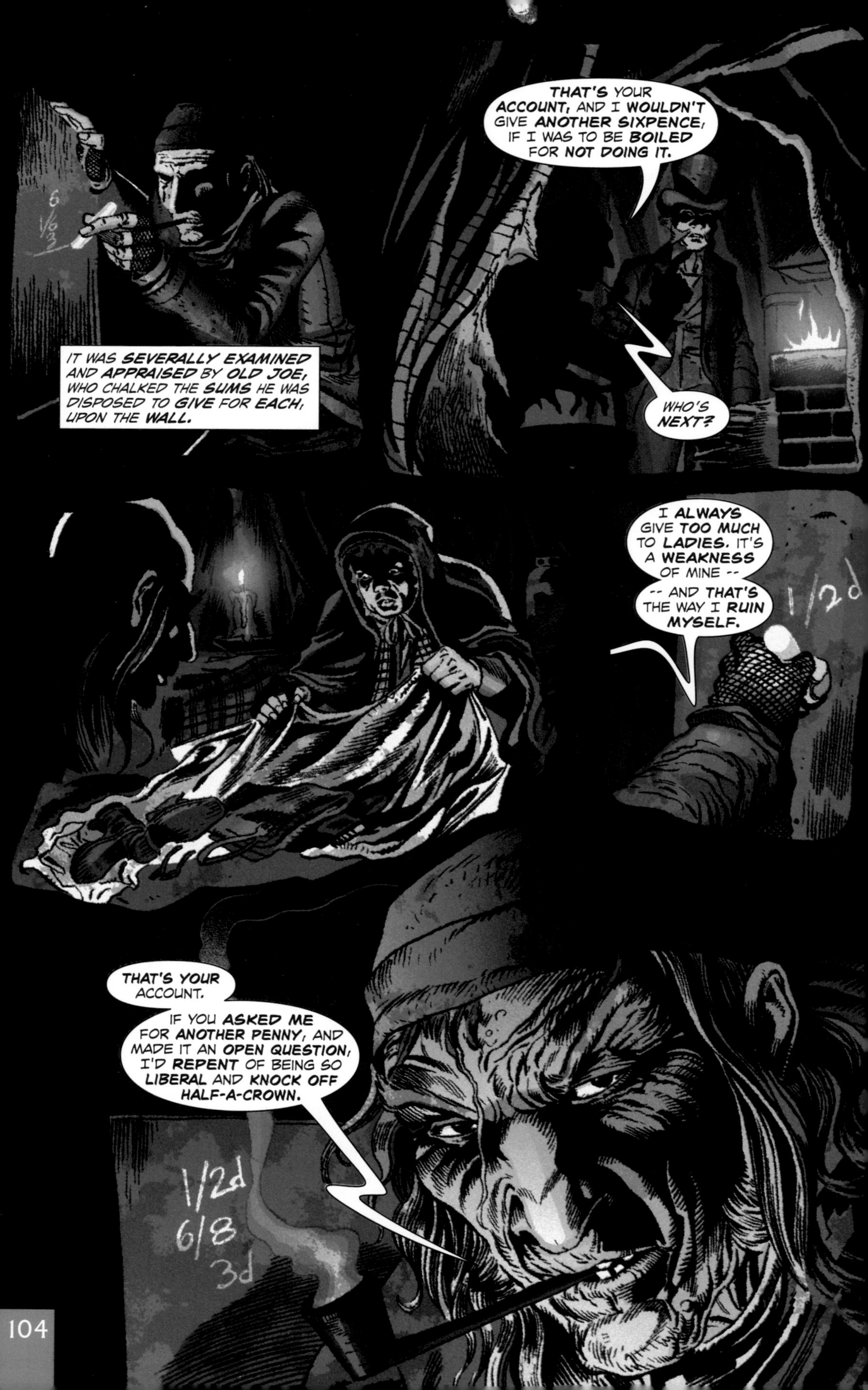
IT WAS SEVERALLY EXAMINED AND APPRAISED BY OLD JOE, WHO CHALKED THE SUMS HE WAS DISPOSED TO GIVE FOR EACH, UPON THE WALL.
THAT'S YOUR ACCOUNT, AND I WOULDN'T GIVE ANOTHER SIXPENCE, IF I WAS TO BE BOILED FOR NOT DOING IT.
WHO'S NEXT?
I ALWAYS GIVE TOO MUCH TO LADIES. IT'S A WEAKNESS OF MINE --
-- AND THAT'S THE WAY I RUIN MYSELF.
1/2d
THAT'S YOUR ACCOUNT.
IF YOU ASKED ME FOR ANOTHER PENNY, AND MADE IT AN OPEN QUESTION, I'D REPENT OF BEING SO LIBERAL AND KNOCK OFF HALF-A-CROWN.
1/2d
6/8
3d

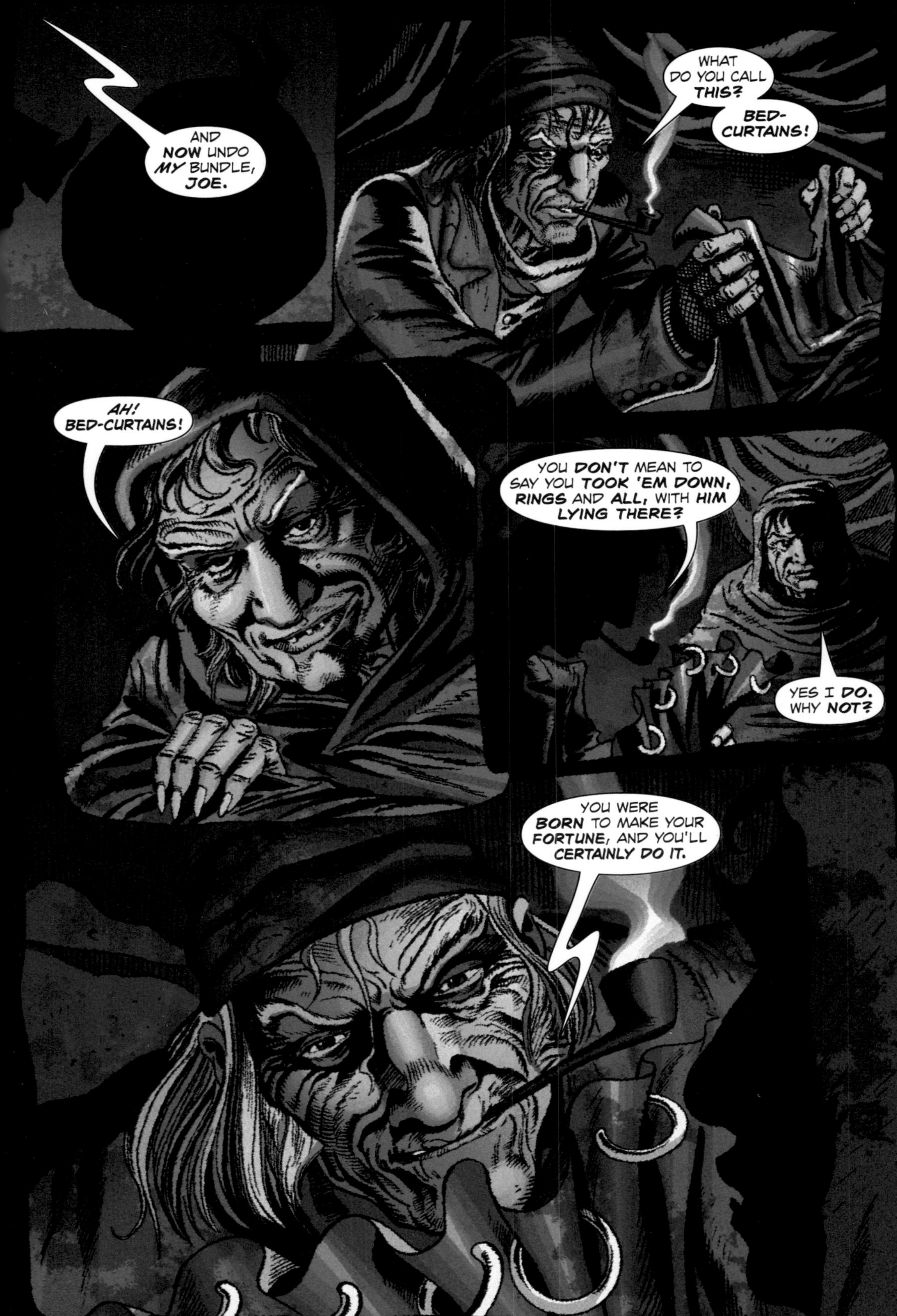
AND NOW UNDO MY BUNDLE, JOE.
WHAT DO YOU CALL THIS?
BED-CURTAINS!
AH! BED-CURTAINS!
YOU DON'T MEAN TO SAY YOU TOOK 'EM DOWN, RINGS AND ALL, WITH HIM LYING THERE?
YES I DO. WHY NOT?
YOU WERE BORN TO MAKE YOUR FORTUNE, AND YOU'LL CERTAINLY DO IT.

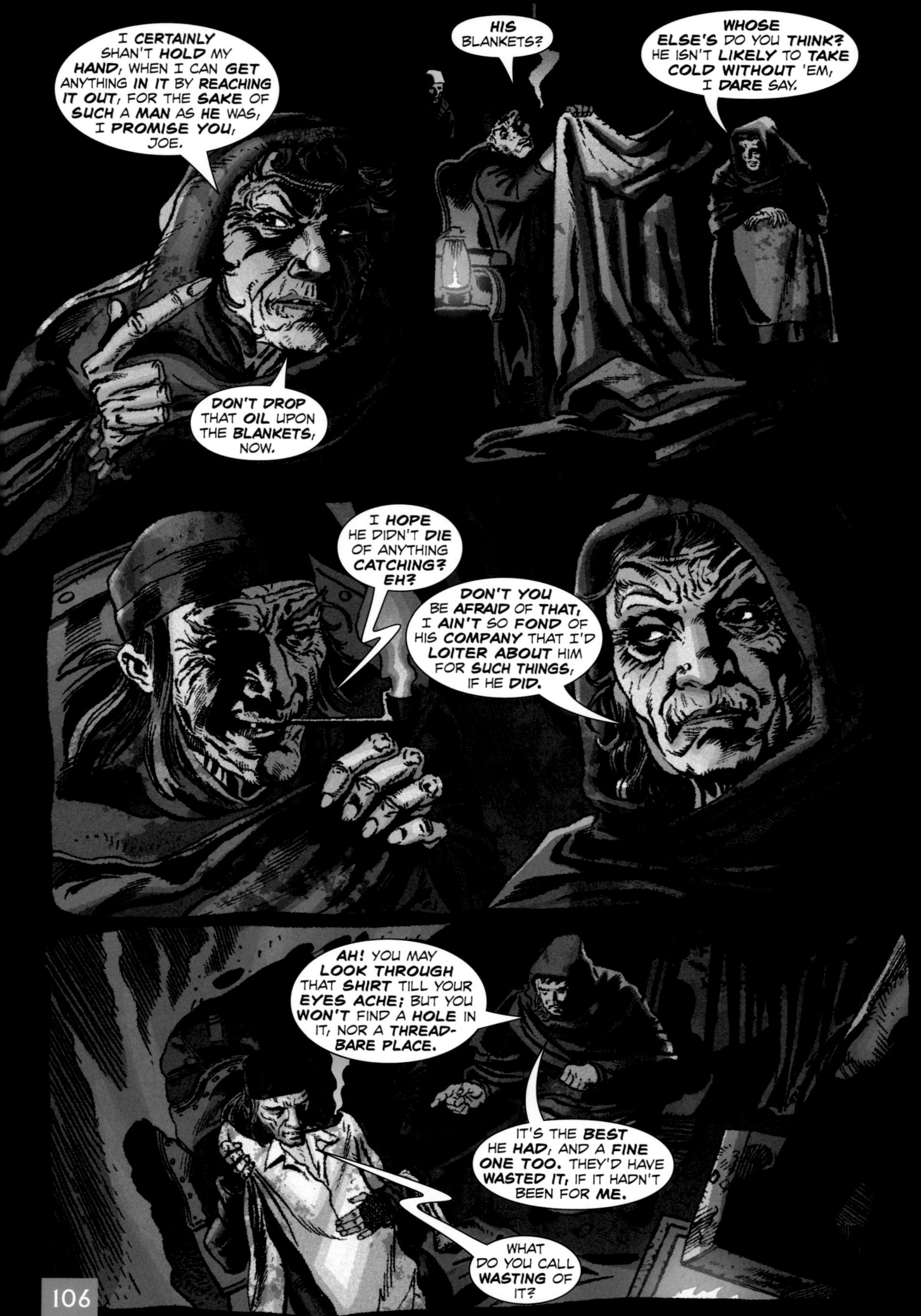
I CERTAINLY SHAN'T HOLD MY HAND, WHEN I CAN GET ANYTHING IN IT BY REACHING IT OUT, FOR THE SAKE OF SUCH A MAN AS HE WAS, I PROMISE YOU, JOE.
DON'T DROP THAT OIL UPON THE BLANKETS, NOW.
HIS BLANKETS?
WHOSE ELSE'S DO YOU THINK? HE ISN'T LIKELY TO TAKE COLD WITHOUT 'EM, I DARE SAY.
I HOPE HE DIDN'T DIE OF ANYTHING CATCHING? EH?
DON'T YOU BE AFRAID OF THAT, I AIN'T SO FOND OF HIS COMPANY THAT I'D LOITER ABOUT HIM FOR SUCH THINGS, IF HE DID.
AH! YOU MAY LOOK THROUGH THAT SHIRT TILL YOUR EYES ACHE; BUT YOU WON'T FIND A HOLE IN IT, NOR A THREAD-BARE PLACE.
IT'S THE BEST HE HAD, AND A FINE ONE TOO. THEY'D HAVE WASTED IT, IF IT HADN'T BEEN FOR ME.
WHAT DO YOU CALL WASTING OF IT?

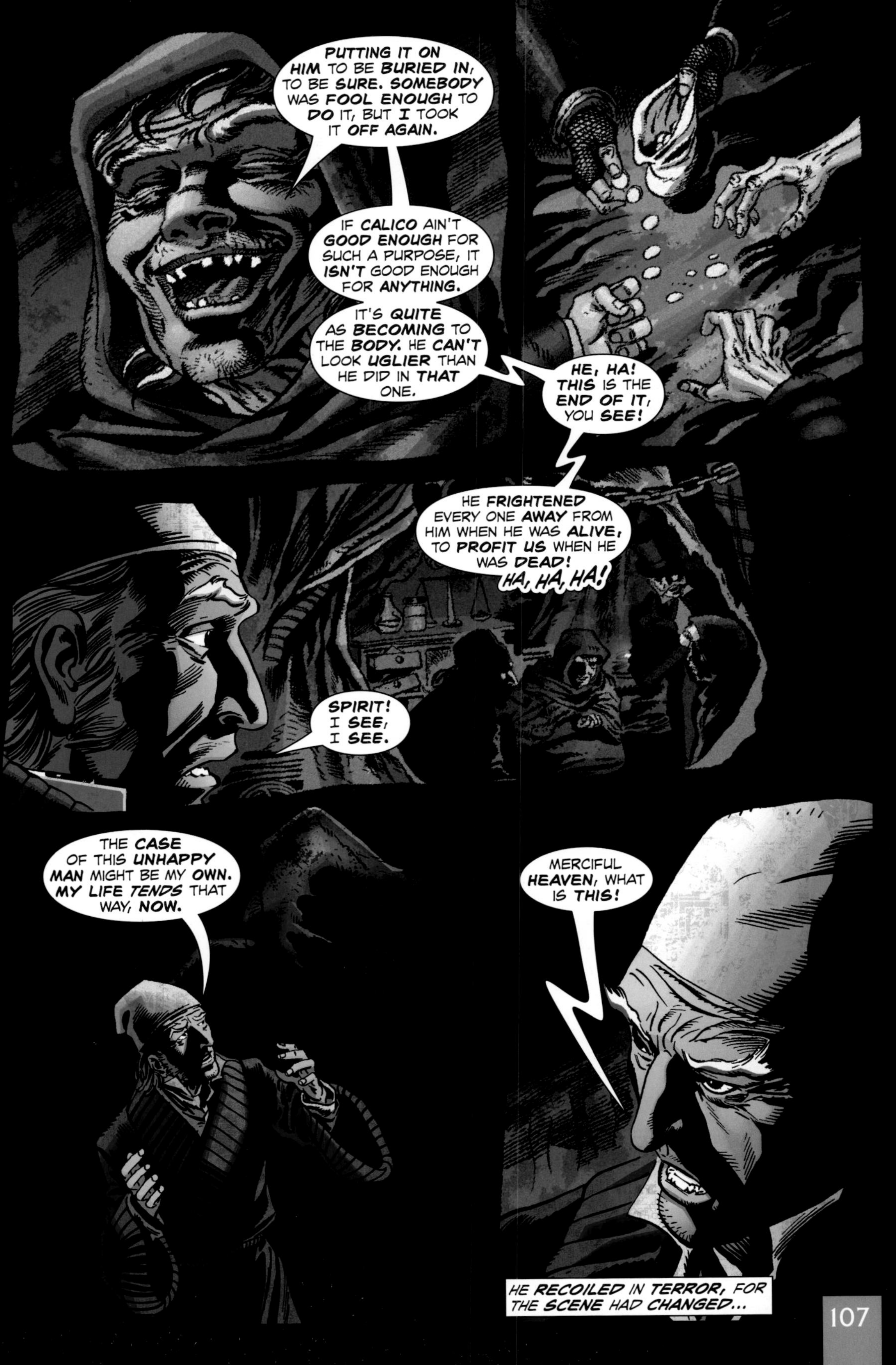
PUTTING IT ON HIM TO BE BURIED IN, TO BE SURE. SOMEBODY WAS FOOL ENOUGH TO DO IT, BUT I TOOK IT OFF AGAIN.
IF CALICO AIN'T GOOD ENOUGH FOR SUCH A PURPOSE, IT ISN'T GOOD ENOUGH FOR ANYTHING.
IT'S QUITE AS BECOMING TO THE BODY. HE CAN'T LOOK UGLIER THAN HE DID IN THAT ONE.
HE, HA! THIS IS THE END OF IT, YOU SEE!
HE FRIGHTENED EVERY ONE AWAY FROM HIM WHEN HE WAS ALIVE, TO PROFIT US WHEN HE WAS DEAD!
HA, HA, HA!
SPIRIT! I SEE, I SEE.
THE CASE OF THIS UNHAPPY MAN MIGHT BE MY OWN. MY LIFE TENDS THAT WAY, NOW.
MERCIFUL HEAVEN, WHAT IS THIS!
HE RECOILED IN TERROR, FOR THE SCENE HAD CHANGED...

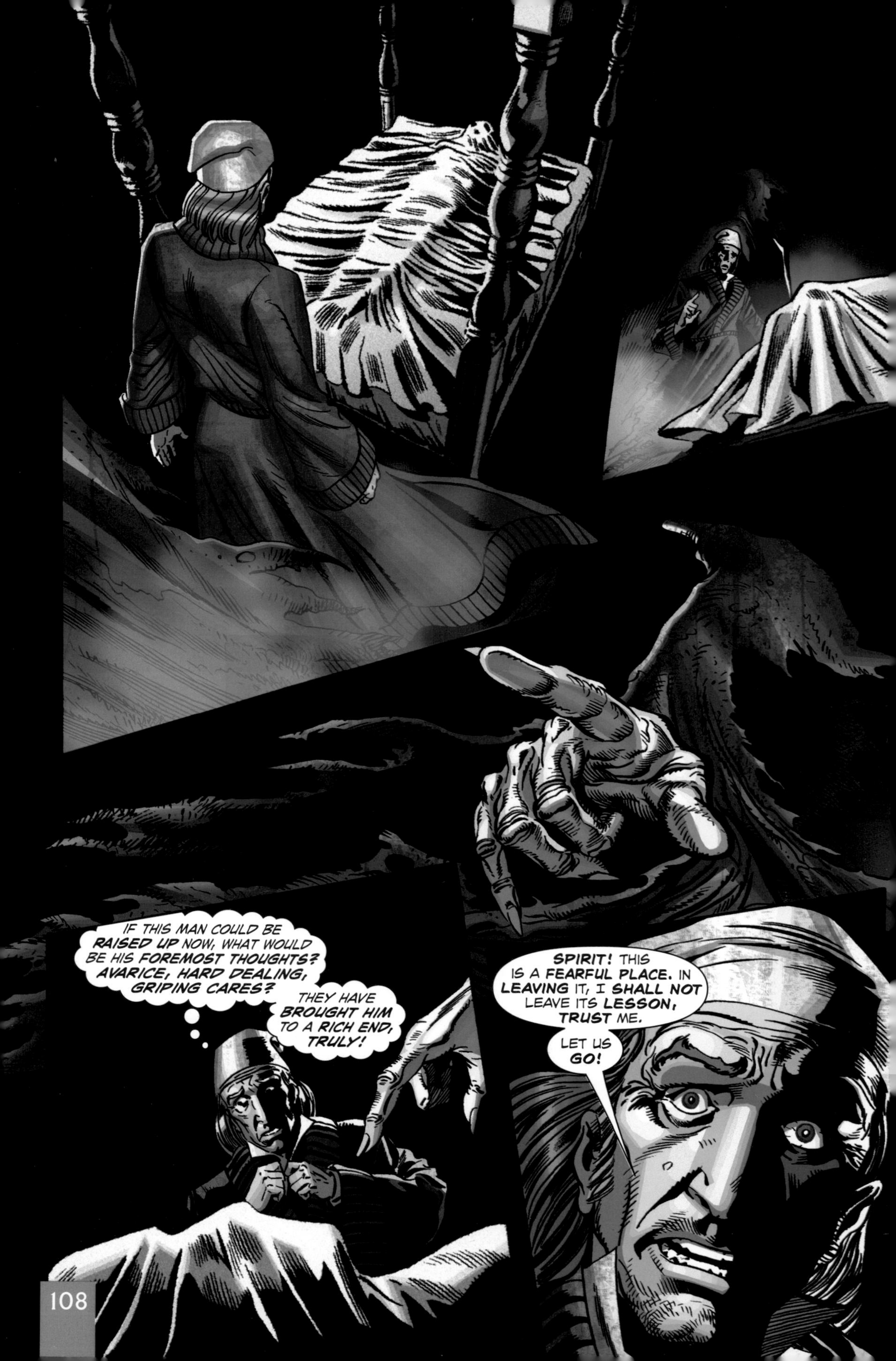
IF THIS MAN COULD BE RAISED UP NOW, WHAT WOULD BE HIS FOREMOST THOUGHTS? AVARICE, HARD DEALING, GRIPING CARES?
THEY HAVE BROUGHT HIM TO A RICH END, TRULY!
SPIRIT! THIS IS A FEARFUL PLACE. IN LEAVING IT, I SHALL NOT LEAVE ITS LESSON, TRUST ME.
LET US GO!

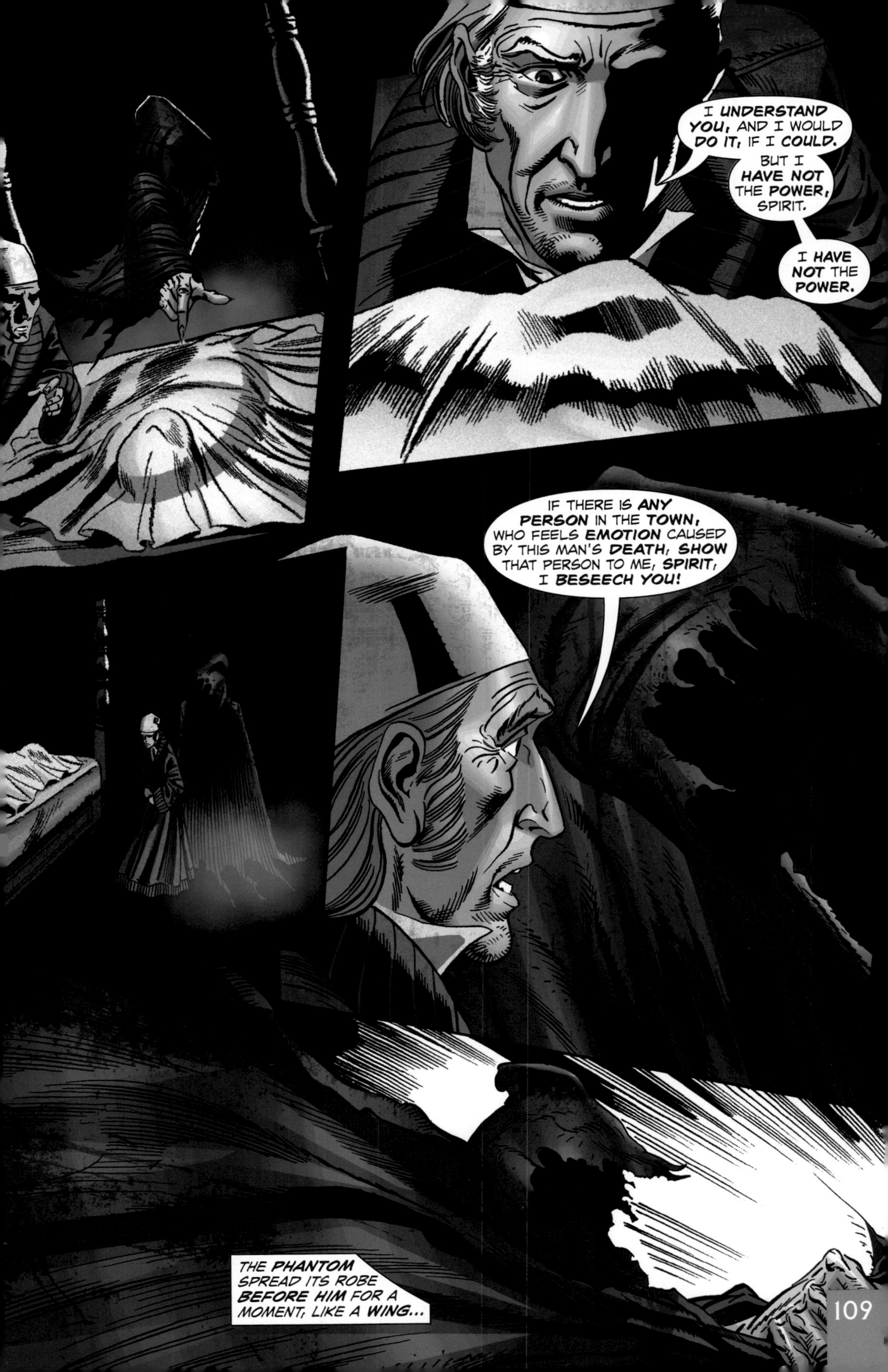
I UNDERSTAND YOU, AND I WOULD DO IT, IF I COULD.
BUT I HAVE NOT THE POWER, SPIRIT.
I HAVE NOT THE POWER.
IF THERE IS ANY PERSON IN THE TOWN, WHO FEELS EMOTION CAUSED BY THIS MAN'S DEATH, SHOW THAT PERSON TO ME, SPIRIT, I BESEECH YOU!
THE PHANTOM SPREAD ITS ROBE BEFORE HIM FOR A MOMENT, LIKE A WING...

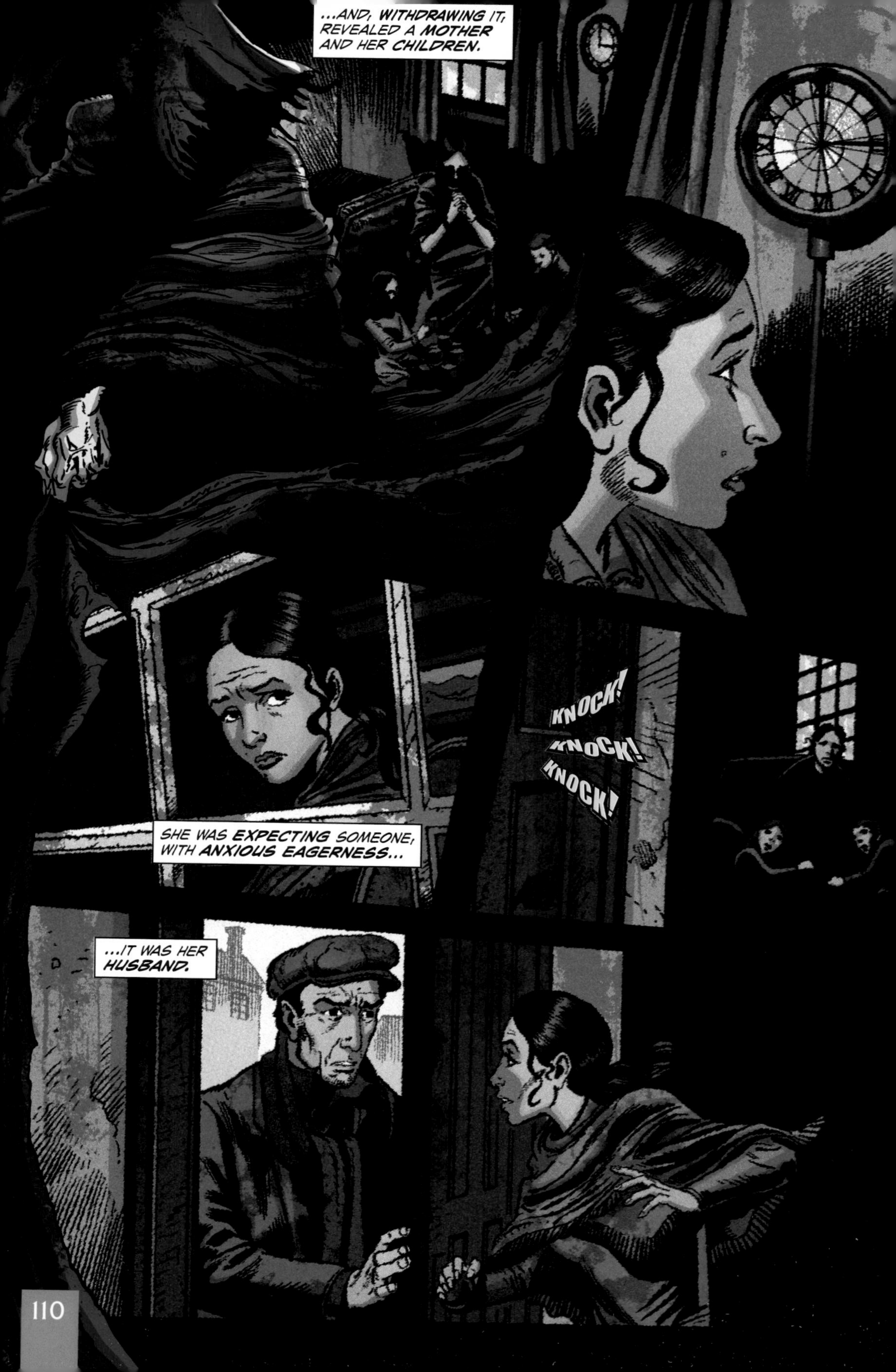
...AND, WITHDRAWING IT, REVEALED A MOTHER AND HER CHILDREN.
SHE WAS EXPECTING SOMEONE, WITH ANXIOUS EAGERNESS...
KNOCK!
KNOCK!
KNOCK!
...IT WAS HER HUSBAND.

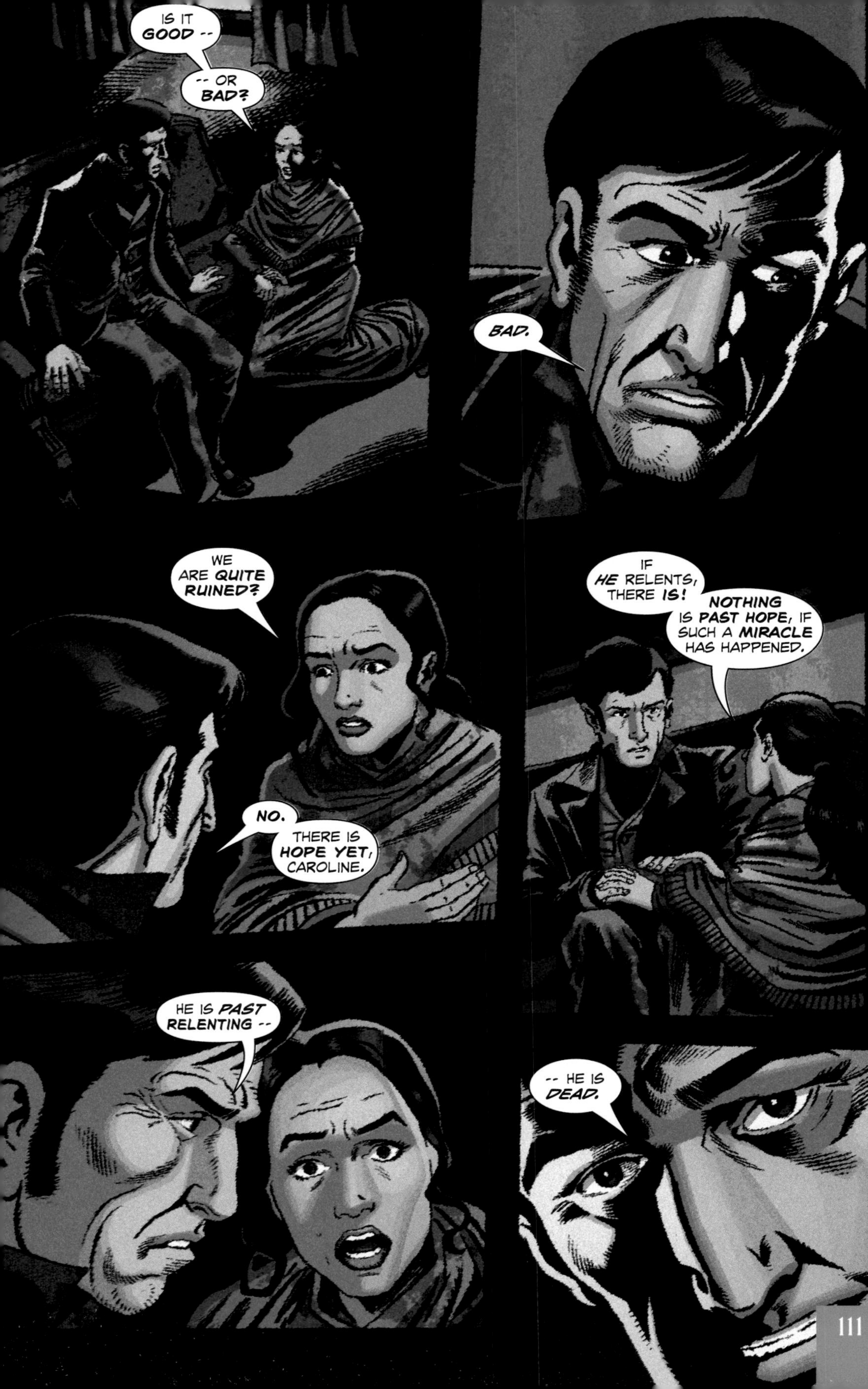
IS IT GOOD --
-- OR BAD?
BAD.
WE ARE QUITE RUINED?
NO.
THERE IS HOPE YET, CAROLINE.
IF HE RELENTS, THERE IS!
NOTHING IS PAST HOPE, IF SUCH A MIRACLE HAS HAPPENED.
HE IS PAST RELENTING --
-- HE IS DEAD.

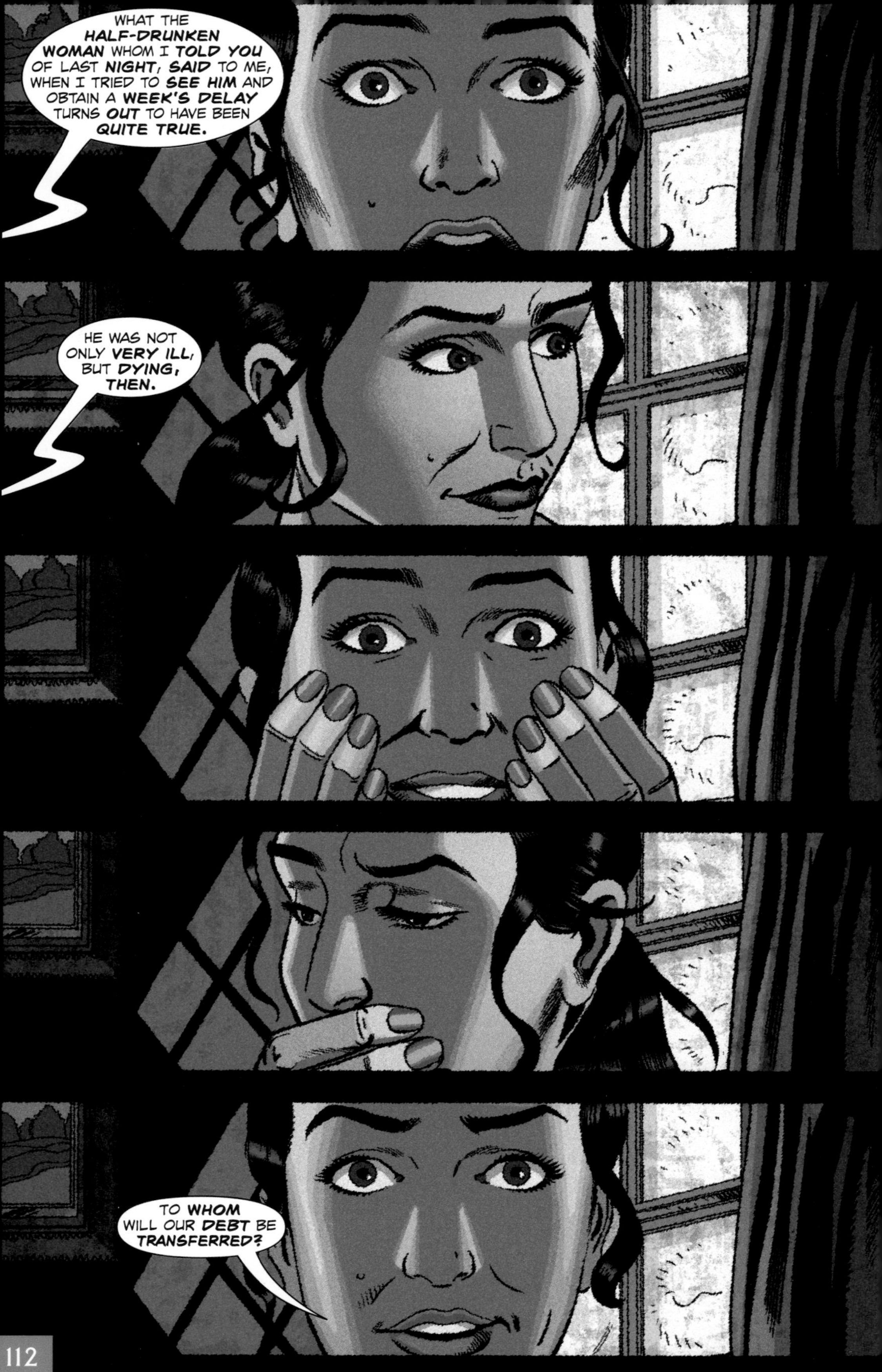
WHAT THE HALF-DRUNKEN WOMAN WHOM I TOLD YOU OF LAST NIGHT, SAID TO ME, WHEN I TRIED TO SEE HIM AND OBTAIN A WEEK'S DELAY TURNS OUT TO HAVE BEEN QUITE TRUE.
HE WAS NOT ONLY VERY ILL, BUT DYING, THEN.
TO WHOM WILL OUR DEBT BE TRANSFERRED?

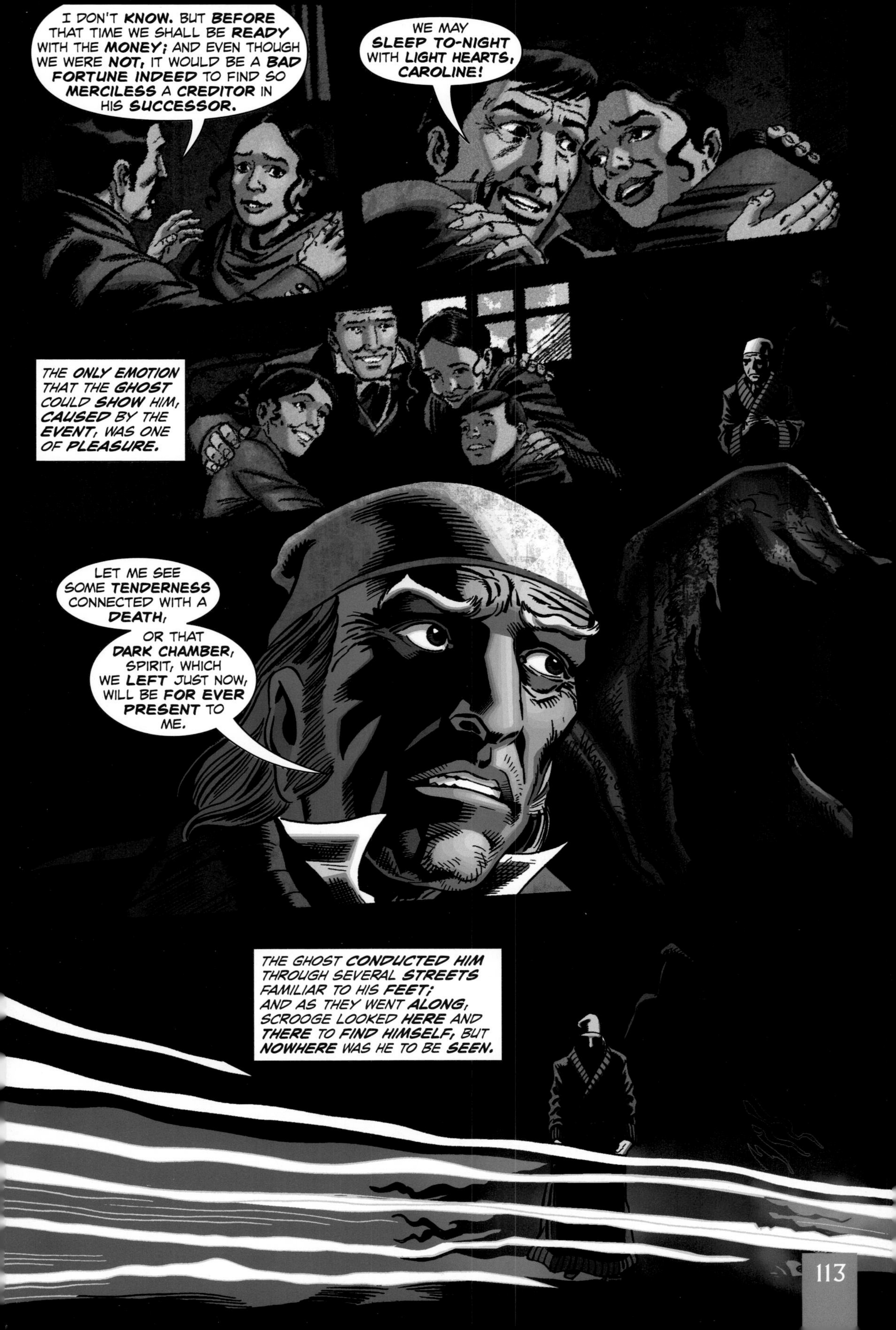
I DON'T KNOW. BUT BEFORE THAT TIME WE SHALL BE READY WITH THE MONEY; AND EVEN THOUGH WE WERE NOT, IT WOULD BE A BAD FORTUNE INDEED TO FIND SO MERCILESS A CREDITOR IN HIS SUCCESSOR.
WE MAY SLEEP TO-NIGHT WITH LIGHT HEARTS, CAROLINE!
THE ONLY EMOTION THAT THE GHOST COULD SHOW HIM, CAUSED BY THE EVENT, WAS ONE OF PLEASURE.
LET ME SEE SOME TENDERNESS CONNECTED WITH A DEATH,
OR THAT DARK CHAMBER, SPIRIT, WHICH WE LEFT JUST NOW, WILL BE FOR EVER PRESENT TO ME.
THE GHOST CONDUCTED HIM THROUGH SEVERAL STREETS FAMILIAR TO HIS FEET; AND AS THEY WENT ALONG, SCROOGE LOOKED HERE AND THERE TO FIND HIMSELF, BUT NOWHERE WAS HE TO BE SEEN.

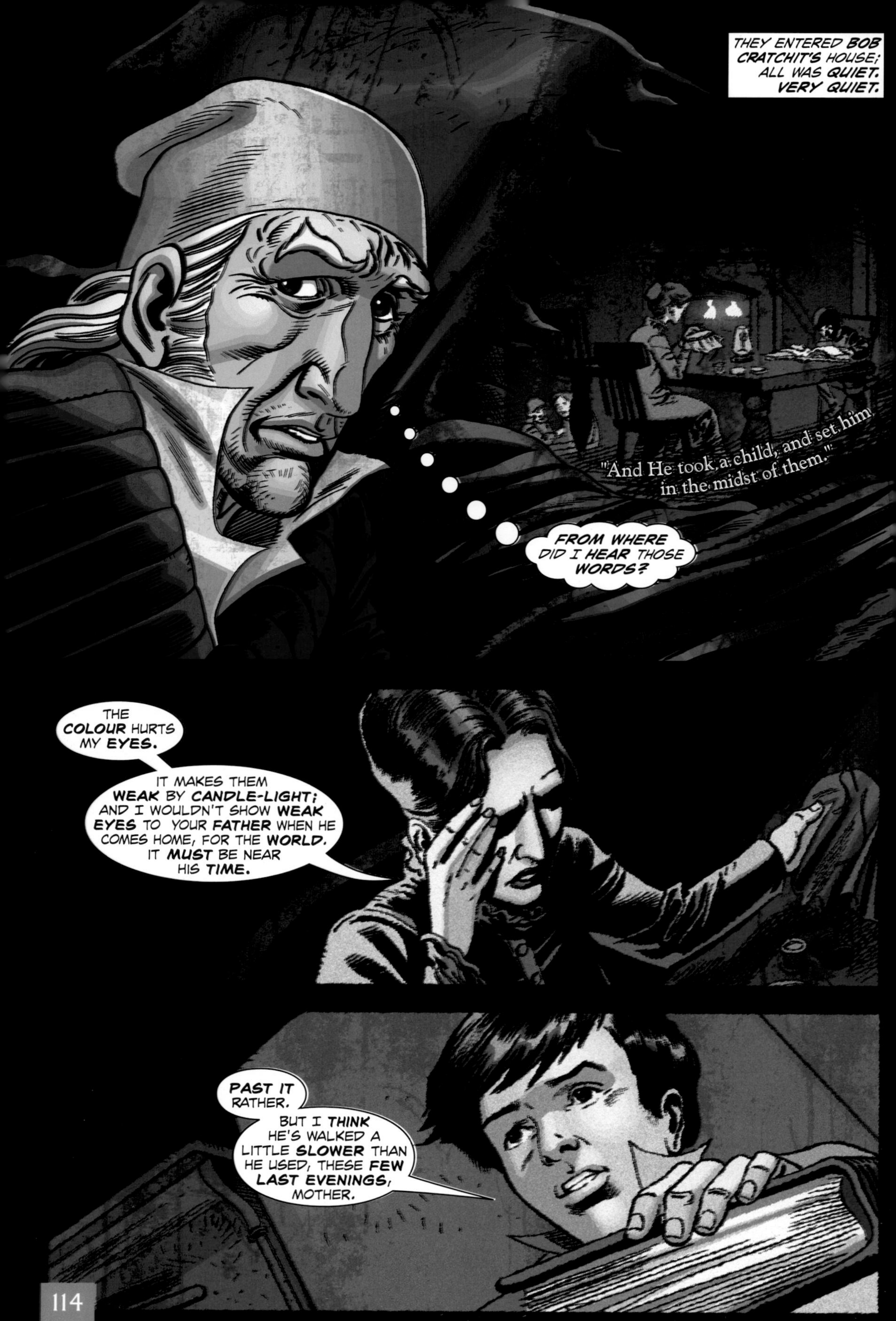
THEY ENTERED BOB CRATCHIT'S HOUSE; ALL WAS QUIET. VERY QUIET.
"And He took a child, and set him in the midst of them."
FROM WHERE DID I HEAR THOSE WORDS?
THE COLOUR HURTS MY EYES.
IT MAKES THEM WEAK BY CANDLE-LIGHT; AND I WOULDN'T SHOW WEAK EYES TO YOUR FATHER WHEN HE COMES HOME, FOR THE WORLD. IT MUST BE NEAR HIS TIME.
PAST IT RATHER.
BUT I THINK HE'S WALKED A LITTLE SLOWER THAN HE USED, THESE FEW LAST EVENINGS, MOTHER.

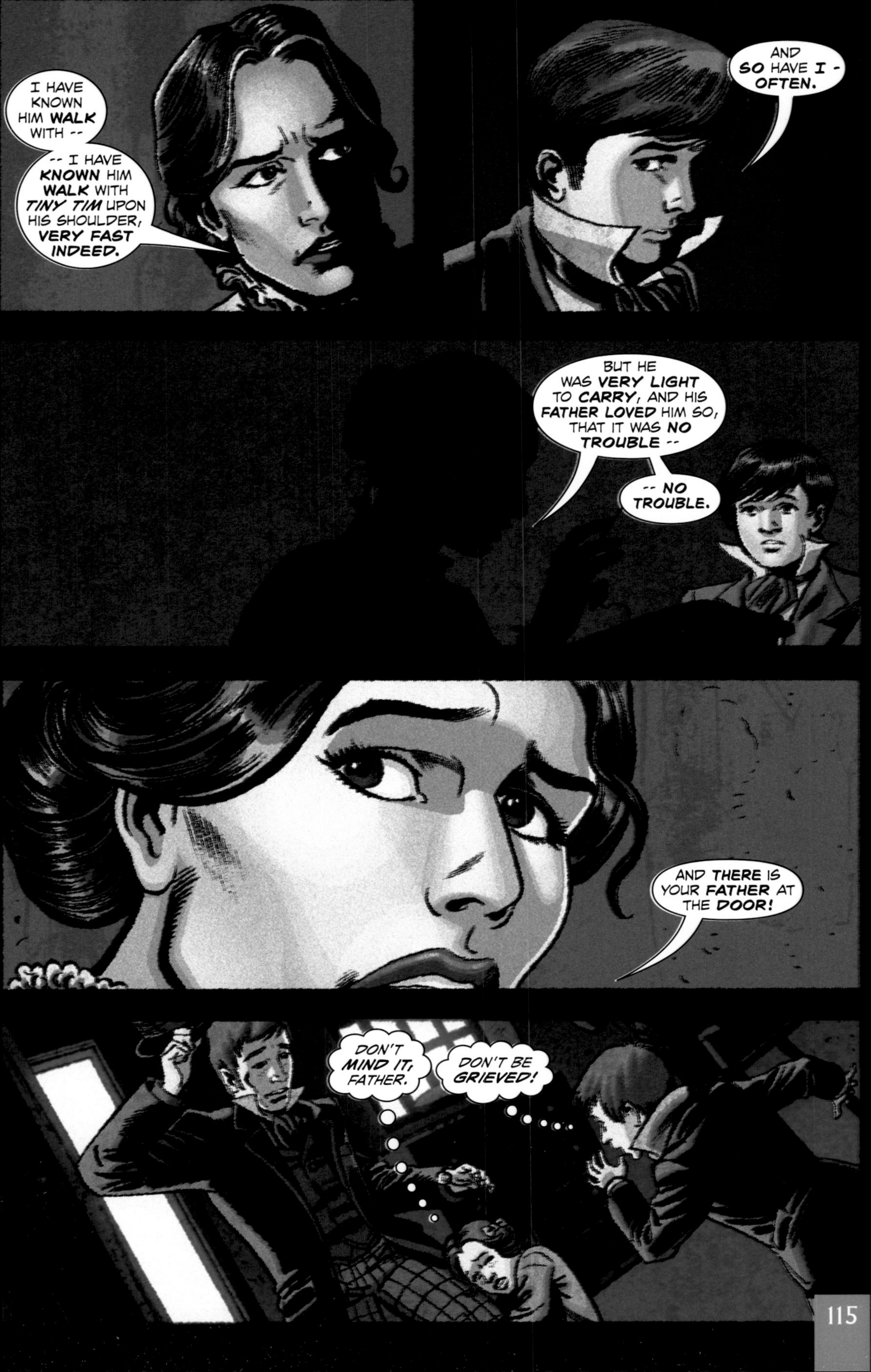
I HAVE KNOWN HIM WALK WITH --
-- I HAVE KNOWN HIM WALK WITH TINY TIM UPON HIS SHOULDER, VERY FAST INDEED.
AND SO HAVE I - OFTEN.
BUT HE WAS VERY LIGHT TO CARRY, AND HIS FATHER LOVED HIM SO, THAT IT WAS NO TROUBLE --
-- NO TROUBLE.
AND THERE IS YOUR FATHER AT THE DOOR!
DON'T MIND IT, FATHER.
DON'T BE GRIEVED!

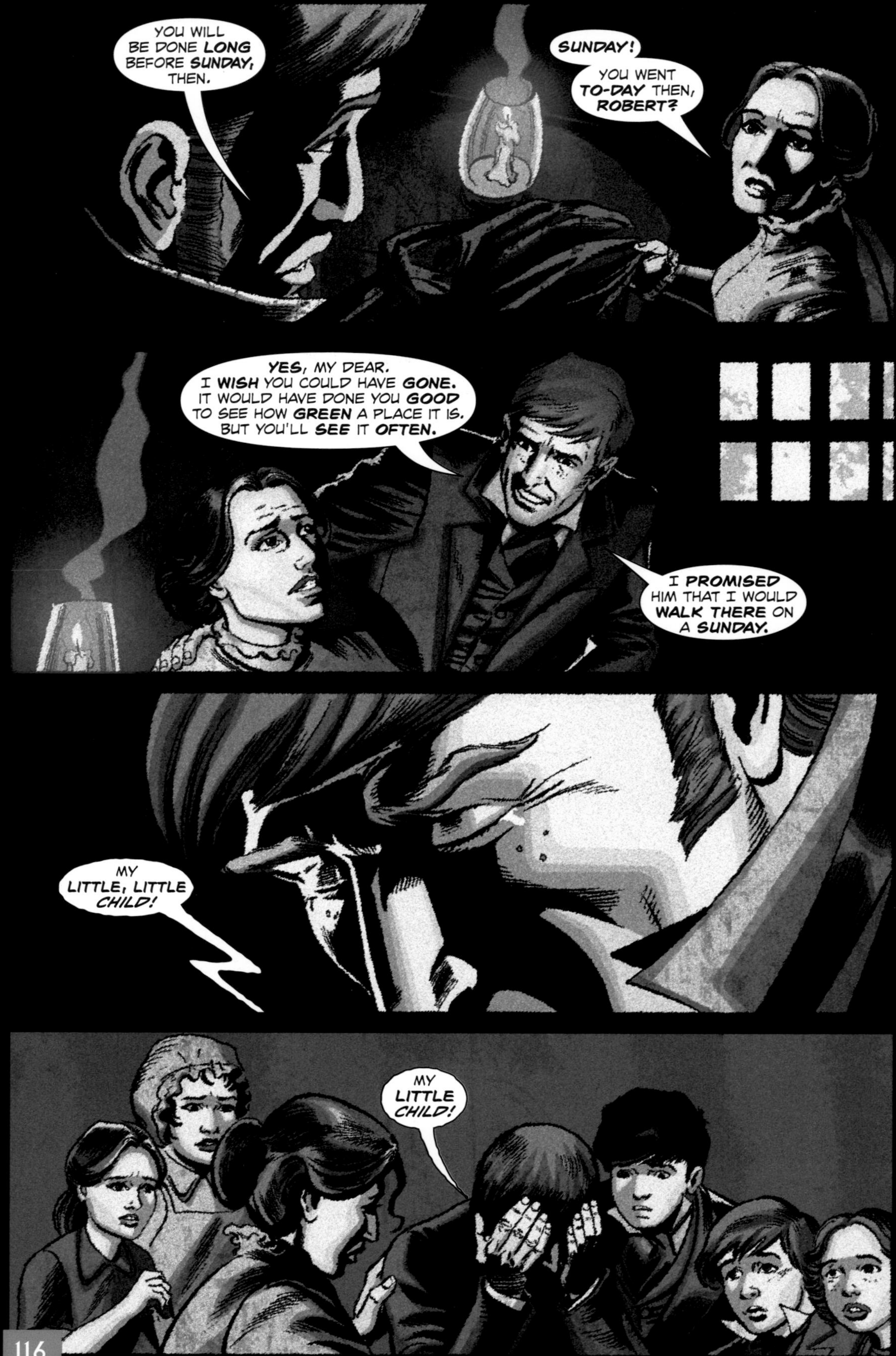
YOU WILL BE DONE LONG BEFORE SUNDAY, THEN.
SUNDAY!
YOU WENT TO-DAY THEN, ROBERT?
YES, MY DEAR. I WISH YOU COULD HAVE GONE. IT WOULD HAVE DONE YOU GOOD TO SEE HOW GREEN A PLACE IT IS. BUT YOU'LL SEE IT OFTEN.
I PROMISED HIM THAT I WOULD WALK THERE ON A SUNDAY.
MY LITTLE, LITTLE CHILD!
MY LITTLE CHILD!

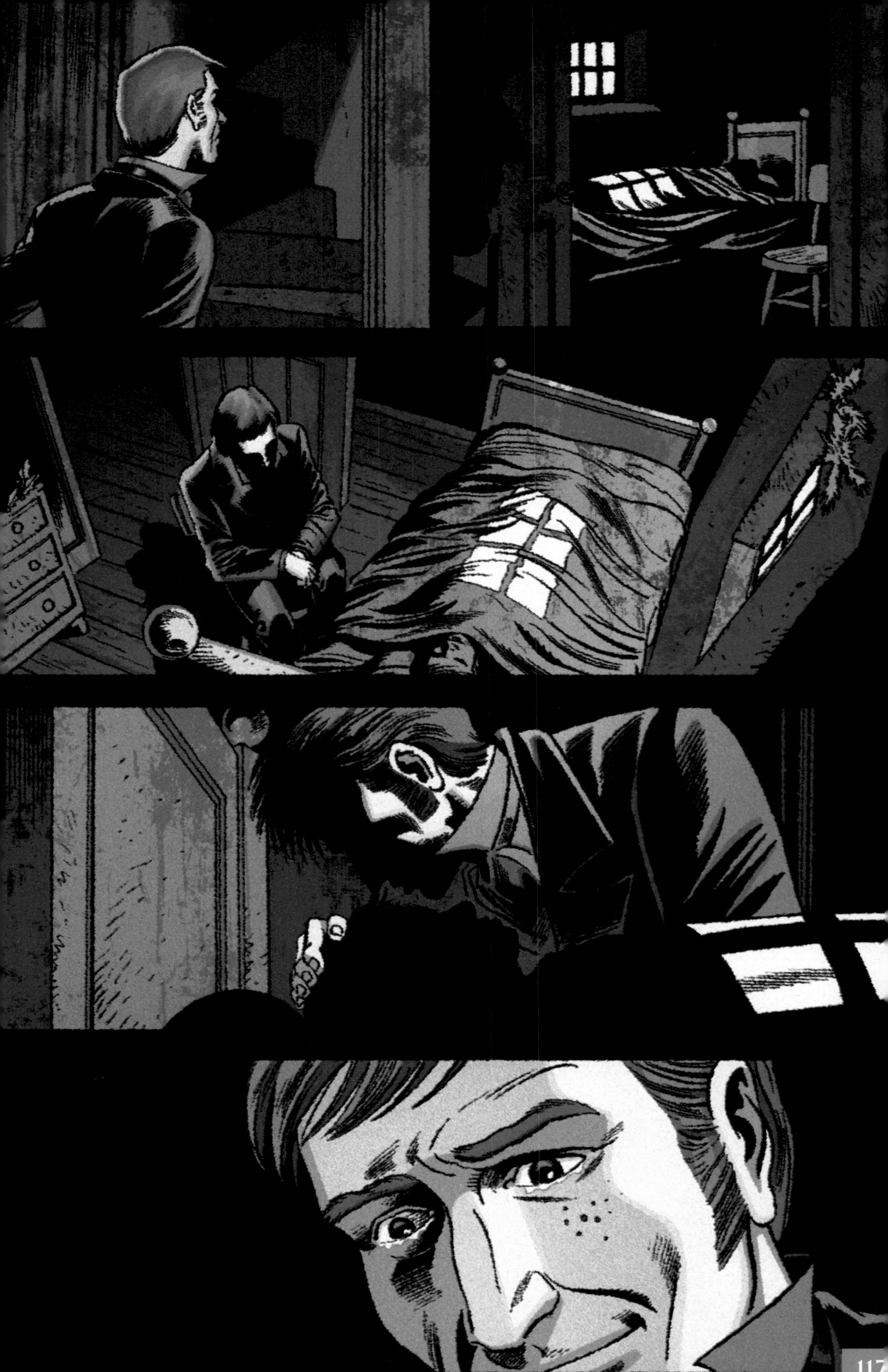

I MET **SCROOGE'S NEPHEW** TODAY; AND HE **NOTICED** THAT I LOOKED A LITTLE --

YOU **LOOK** JUST A LITTLE **DOWN**, YOU **KNOW**.

WHAT HAS **HAPPENED** TO DISTRESS YOU?

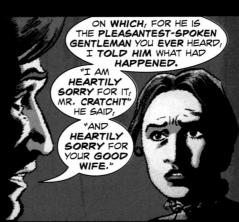

ON **WHICH**, FOR HE IS THE **PLEASANTEST-SPOKEN GENTLEMAN** YOU EVER HEARD, I **TOLD HIM** WHAT HAD HAPPENED.

"I AM **HEARTILY SORRY** FOR IT, MR. **CRATCHIT**" HE SAID,

"AND **HEARTILY SORRY** FOR YOUR **GOOD WIFE**."

BY THE **BYE**, HOW HE EVER **KNEW THAT**, I **DON'T** KNOW.

KNEW **WHAT**, MY **DEAR**?

WHY, THAT YOU WERE A **GOOD WIFE**.

EVERYBODY KNOWS **THAT**!

VERY WELL OBSERVED, MY BOY!

I HOPE THEY **DO**.

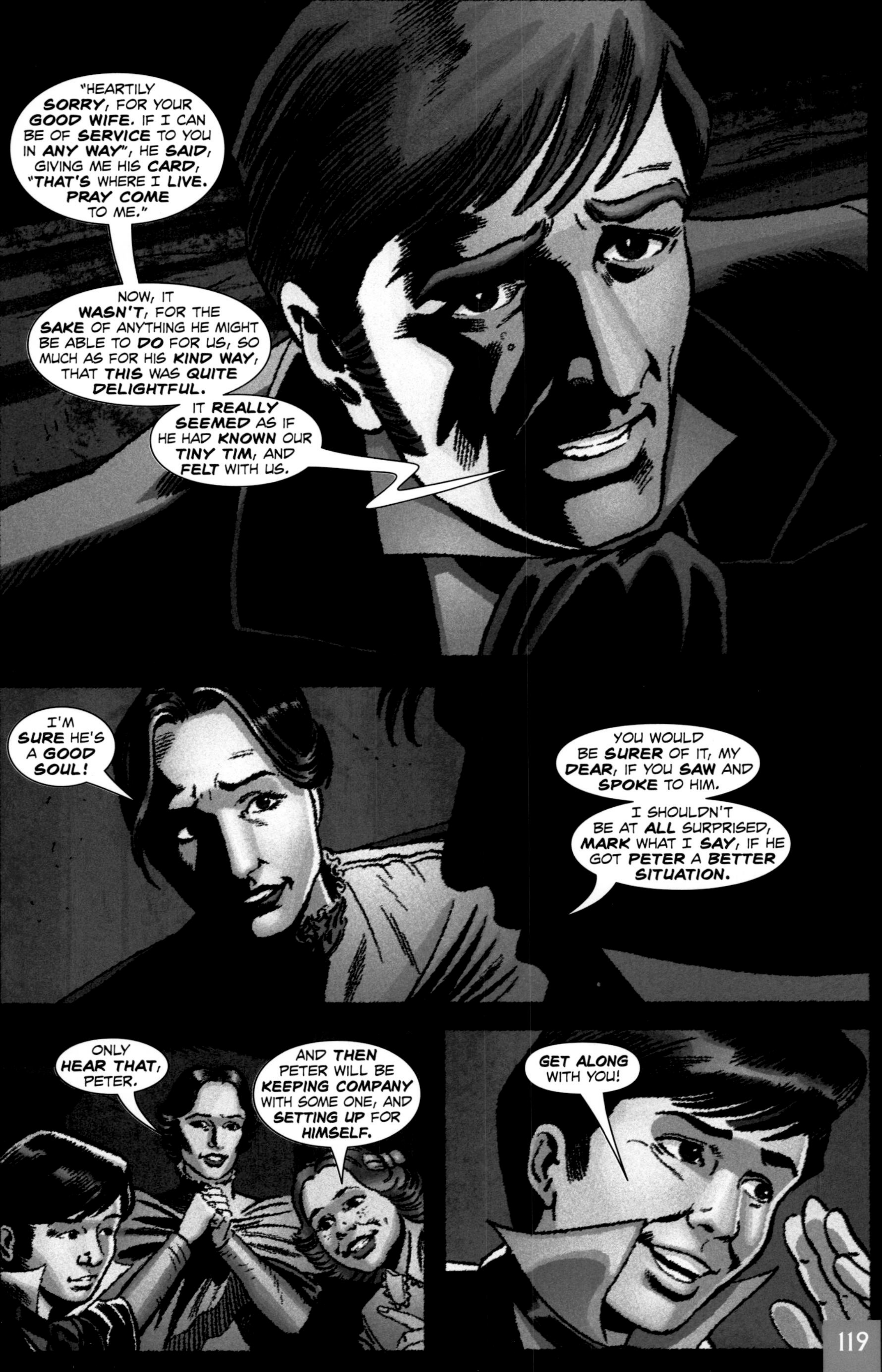
"HEARTILY SORRY, FOR YOUR GOOD WIFE. IF I CAN BE OF SERVICE TO YOU IN ANY WAY", HE SAID, GIVING ME HIS CARD, "THAT'S WHERE I LIVE. PRAY COME TO ME."
NOW, IT WASN'T, FOR THE SAKE OF ANYTHING HE MIGHT BE ABLE TO DO FOR US, SO MUCH AS FOR HIS KIND WAY, THAT THIS WAS QUITE DELIGHTFUL.
IT REALLY SEEMED AS IF HE HAD KNOWN OUR TINY TIM, AND FELT WITH US.
I'M SURE HE'S A GOOD SOUL!
YOU WOULD BE SURER OF IT, MY DEAR, IF YOU SAW AND SPOKE TO HIM.
I SHOULDN'T BE AT ALL SURPRISED, MARK WHAT I SAY, IF HE GOT PETER A BETTER SITUATION.
ONLY HEAR THAT, PETER.
AND THEN PETER WILL BE KEEPING COMPANY WITH SOME ONE, AND SETTING UP FOR HIMSELF.
GET ALONG WITH YOU!

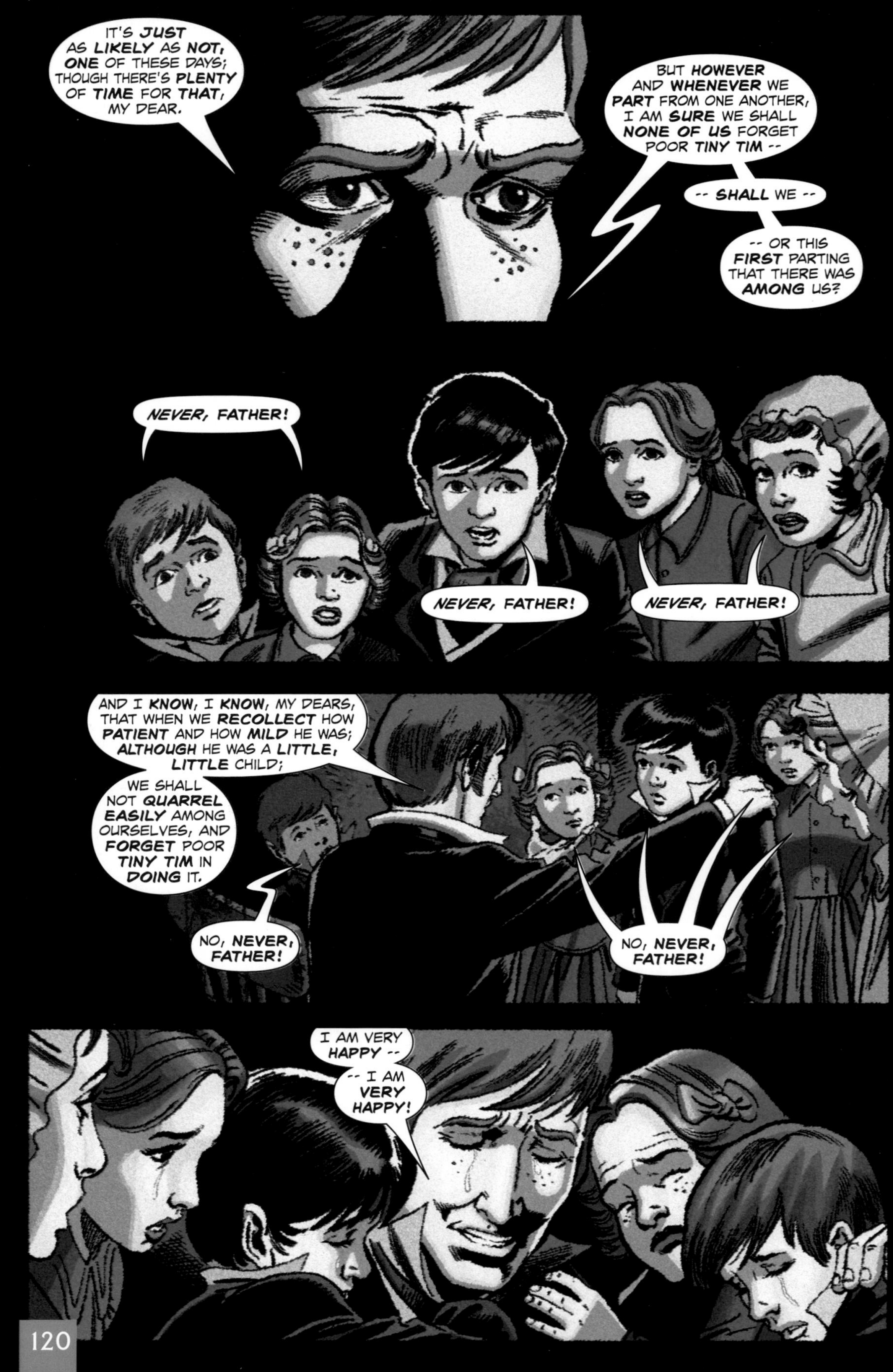
IT'S JUST AS LIKELY AS NOT, ONE OF THESE DAYS; THOUGH THERE'S PLENTY OF TIME FOR THAT, MY DEAR.
BUT HOWEVER AND WHENEVER WE PART FROM ONE ANOTHER, I AM SURE WE SHALL NONE OF US FORGET POOR TINY TIM --
-- SHALL WE --
-- OR THIS FIRST PARTING THAT THERE WAS AMONG US?
NEVER, FATHER!
NEVER, FATHER!
NEVER, FATHER!
AND I KNOW, I KNOW, MY DEARS, THAT WHEN WE RECOLLECT HOW PATIENT AND HOW MILD HE WAS; ALTHOUGH HE WAS A LITTLE, LITTLE CHILD;
WE SHALL NOT QUARREL EASILY AMONG OURSELVES, AND FORGET POOR TINY TIM IN DOING IT.
NO, NEVER, FATHER!
NO, NEVER, FATHER!
I AM VERY HAPPY --
-- I AM VERY HAPPY!

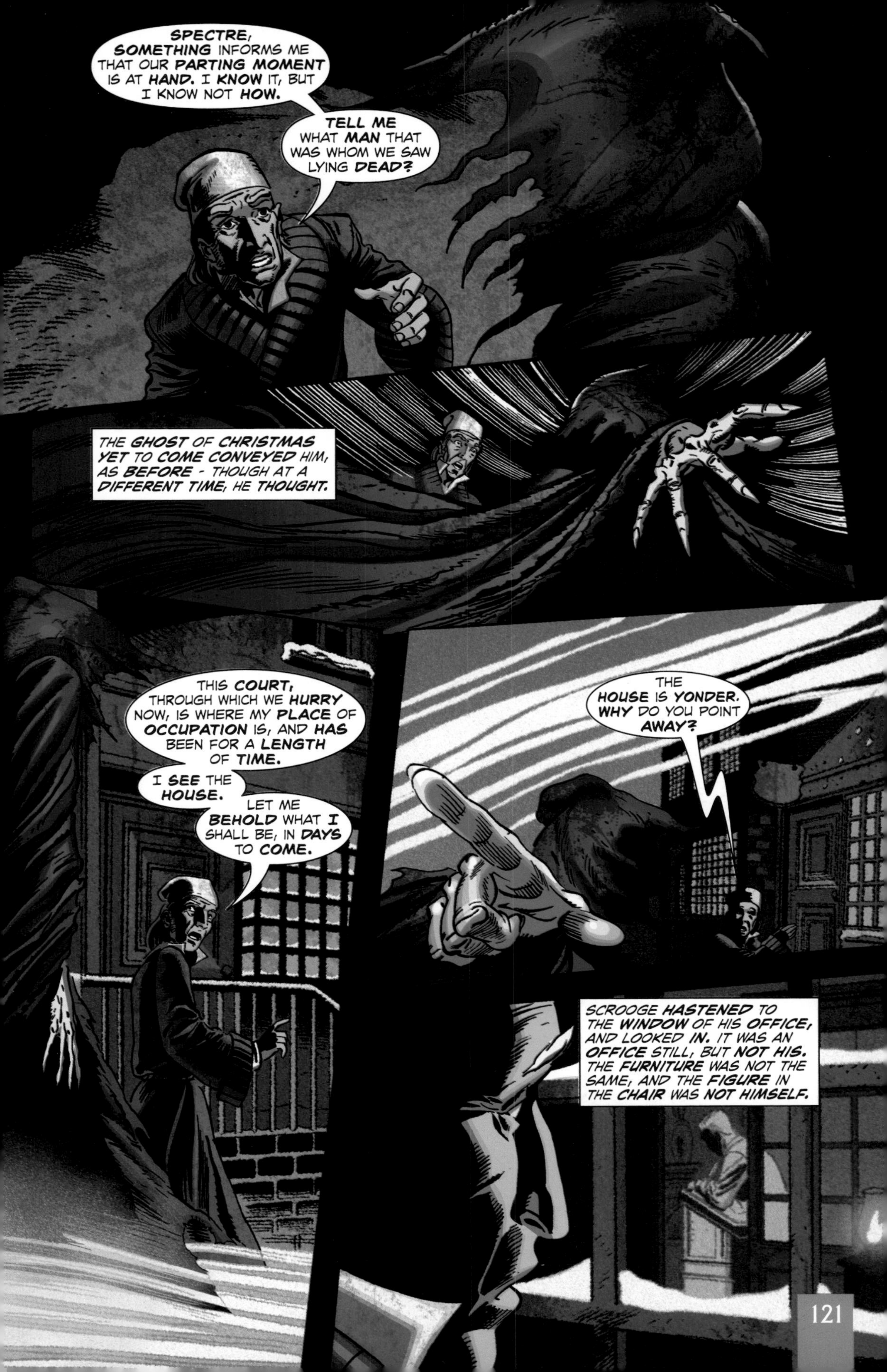
SPECTRE, SOMETHING INFORMS ME THAT OUR PARTING MOMENT IS AT HAND. I KNOW IT, BUT I KNOW NOT HOW.
TELL ME WHAT MAN THAT WAS WHOM WE SAW LYING DEAD?
THE GHOST OF CHRISTMAS YET TO COME CONVEYED HIM, AS BEFORE - THOUGH AT A DIFFERENT TIME, HE THOUGHT.
THIS COURT, THROUGH WHICH WE HURRY NOW, IS WHERE MY PLACE OF OCCUPATION IS, AND HAS BEEN FOR A LENGTH OF TIME.
I SEE THE HOUSE.
LET ME BEHOLD WHAT I SHALL BE, IN DAYS TO COME.
THE HOUSE IS YONDER. WHY DO YOU POINT AWAY?
SCROOGE HASTENED TO THE WINDOW OF HIS OFFICE, AND LOOKED IN. IT WAS AN OFFICE STILL; BUT NOT HIS. THE FURNITURE WAS NOT THE SAME, AND THE FIGURE IN THE CHAIR WAS NOT HIMSELF.

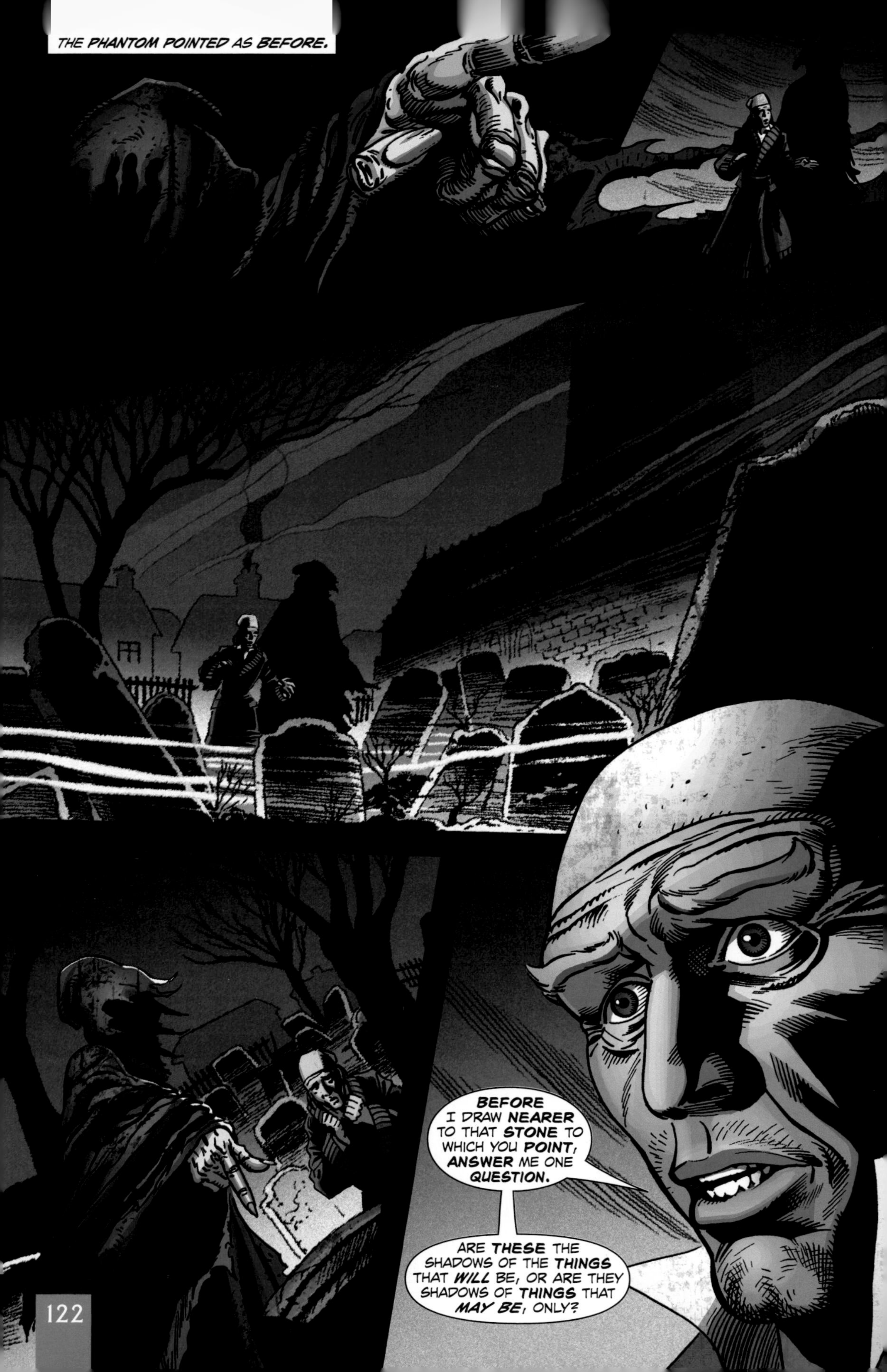
THE PHANTOM POINTED AS BEFORE.
BEFORE I DRAW NEARER TO THAT STONE TO WHICH YOU POINT, ANSWER ME ONE QUESTION.
ARE THESE THE SHADOWS OF THE THINGS THAT WILL BE, OR ARE THEY SHADOWS OF THINGS THAT MAY BE, ONLY?

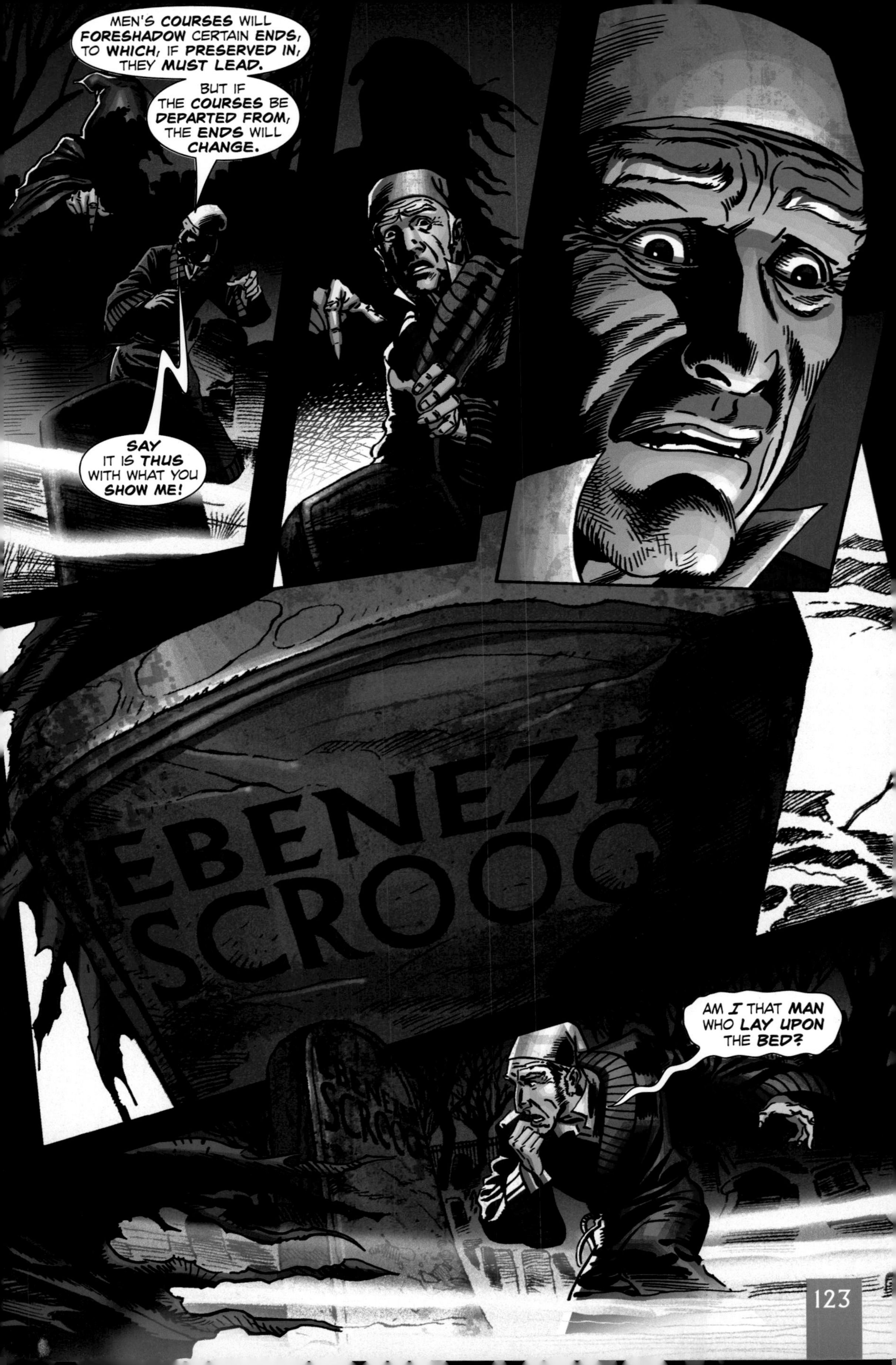
MEN'S COURSES WILL FORESHADOW CERTAIN ENDS, TO WHICH, IF PRESERVED IN, THEY MUST LEAD.
BUT IF THE COURSES BE DEPARTED FROM, THE ENDS WILL CHANGE.
SAY IT IS THUS WITH WHAT YOU SHOW ME!
EBENEZE SCROOG
AM I THAT MAN WHO LAY UPON THE BED?

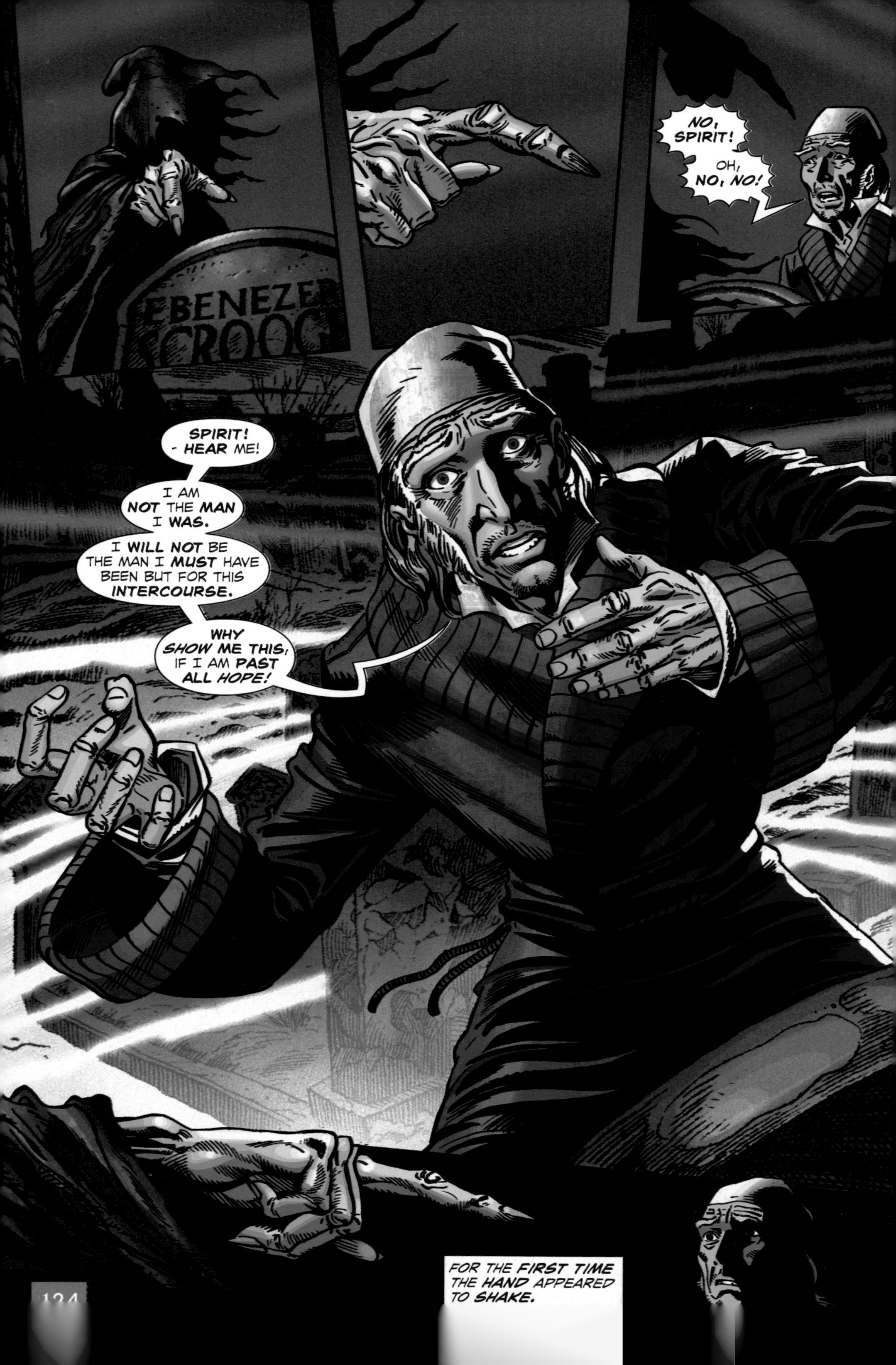

EBENEZER SCROOG
NO, SPIRIT!
OH, NO, NO!
SPIRIT! - HEAR ME!
I AM NOT THE MAN I WAS.
I WILL NOT BE THE MAN I MUST HAVE BEEN BUT FOR THIS INTERCOURSE.
WHY SHOW ME THIS, IF I AM PAST ALL HOPE!
FOR THE FIRST TIME THE HAND APPEARED TO SHAKE.

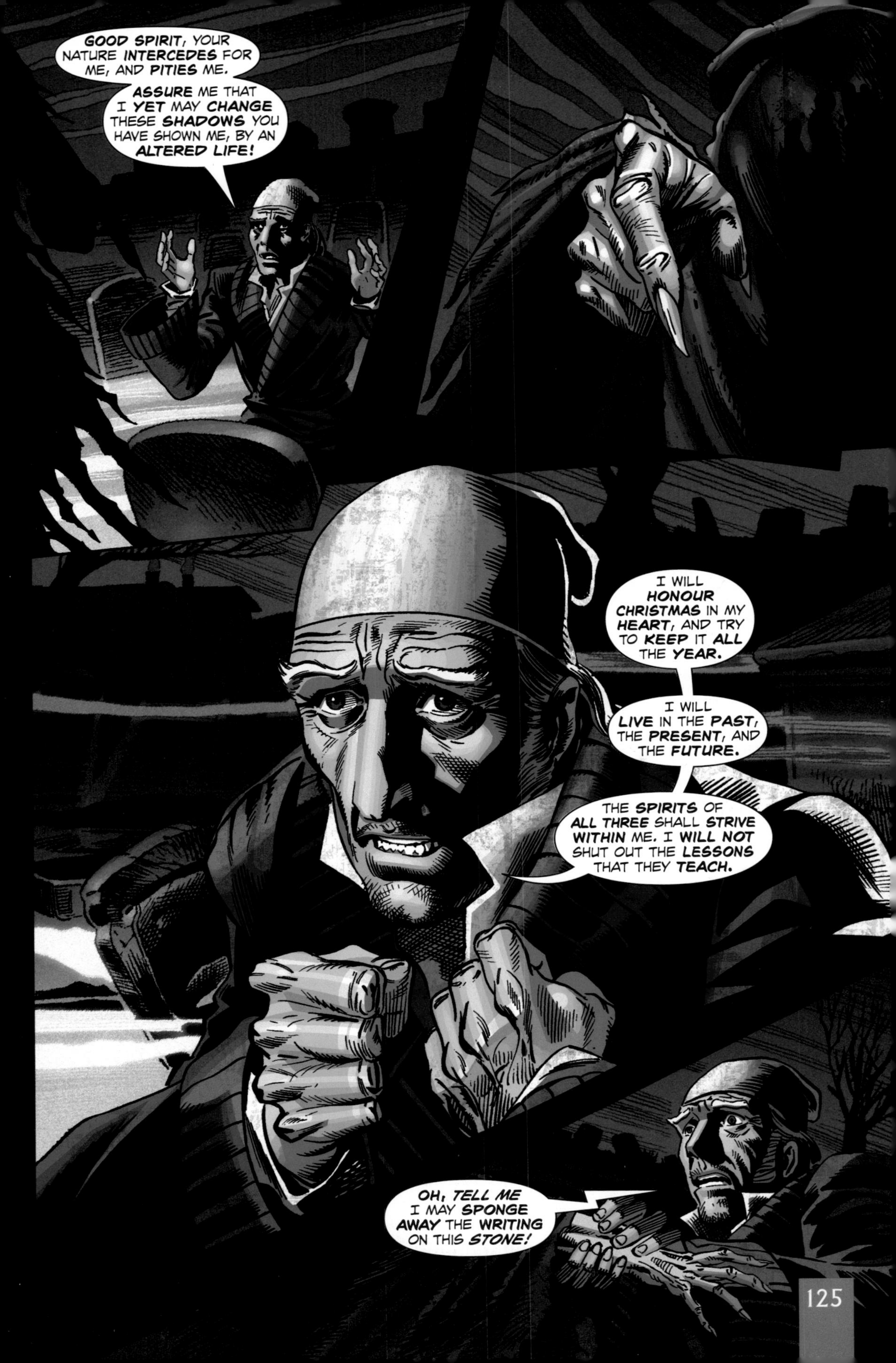
GOOD SPIRIT, YOUR NATURE INTERCEDES FOR ME, AND PITIES ME.
ASSURE ME THAT I YET MAY CHANGE THESE SHADOWS YOU HAVE SHOWN ME, BY AN ALTERED LIFE!
I WILL HONOUR CHRISTMAS IN MY HEART, AND TRY TO KEEP IT ALL THE YEAR.
I WILL LIVE IN THE PAST, THE PRESENT, AND THE FUTURE.
THE SPIRITS OF ALL THREE SHALL STRIVE WITHIN ME. I WILL NOT SHUT OUT THE LESSONS THAT THEY TEACH.
OH, TELL ME I MAY SPONGE AWAY THE WRITING ON THIS STONE!

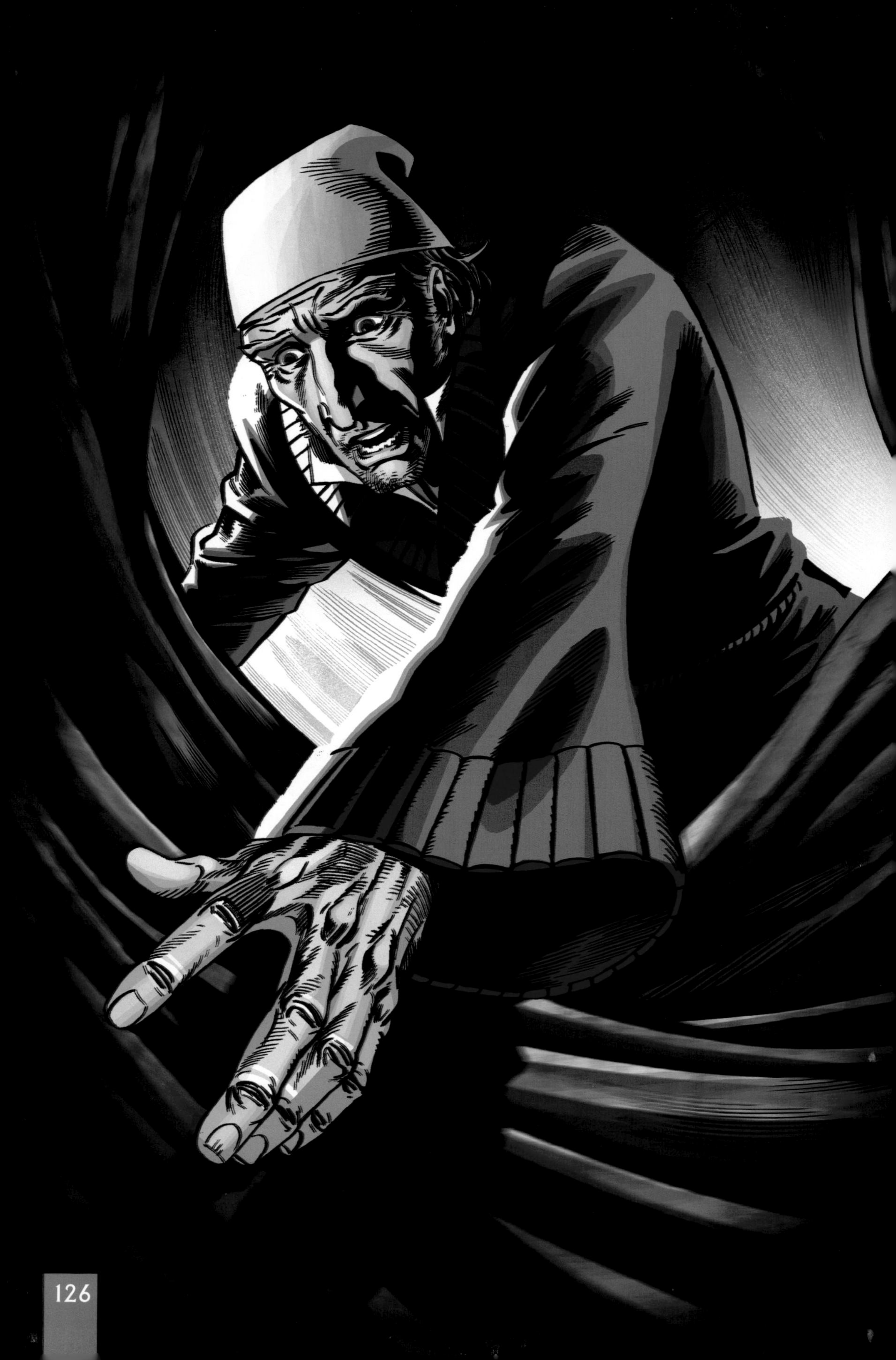

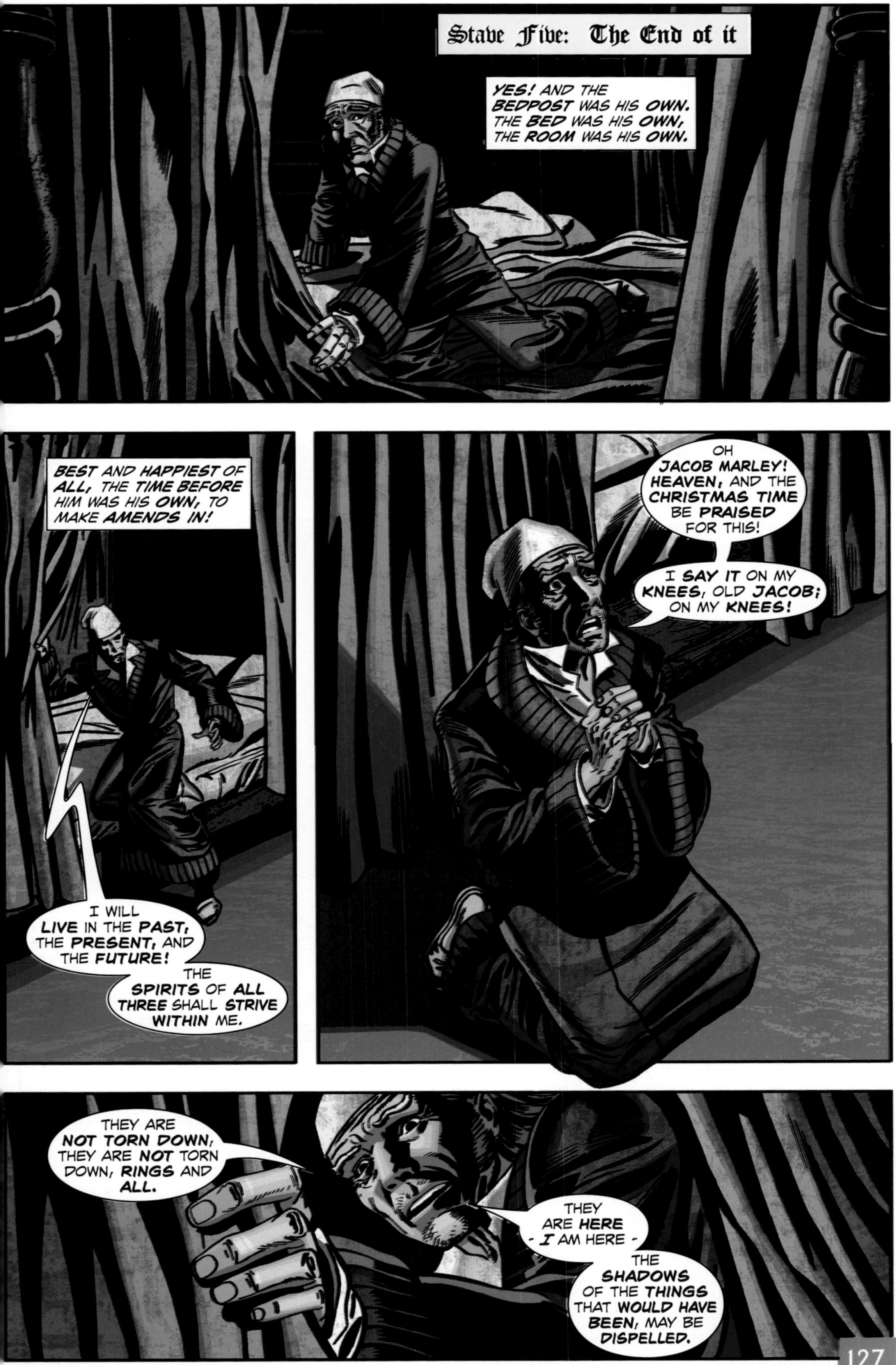
Stave Five: The End of it
YES! AND THE BEDPOST WAS HIS OWN. THE BED WAS HIS OWN, THE ROOM WAS HIS OWN.
BEST AND HAPPIEST OF ALL, THE TIME BEFORE HIM WAS HIS OWN, TO MAKE AMENDS IN!
I WILL LIVE IN THE PAST, THE PRESENT, AND THE FUTURE!
THE SPIRITS OF ALL THREE SHALL STRIVE WITHIN ME.
OH JACOB MARLEY! HEAVEN, AND THE CHRISTMAS TIME BE PRAISED FOR THIS!
I SAY IT ON MY KNEES, OLD JACOB; ON MY KNEES!
THEY ARE NOT TORN DOWN, THEY ARE NOT TORN DOWN, RINGS AND ALL.
THEY ARE HERE - I AM HERE -
THE SHADOWS OF THE THINGS THAT WOULD HAVE BEEN, MAY BE DISPELLED.

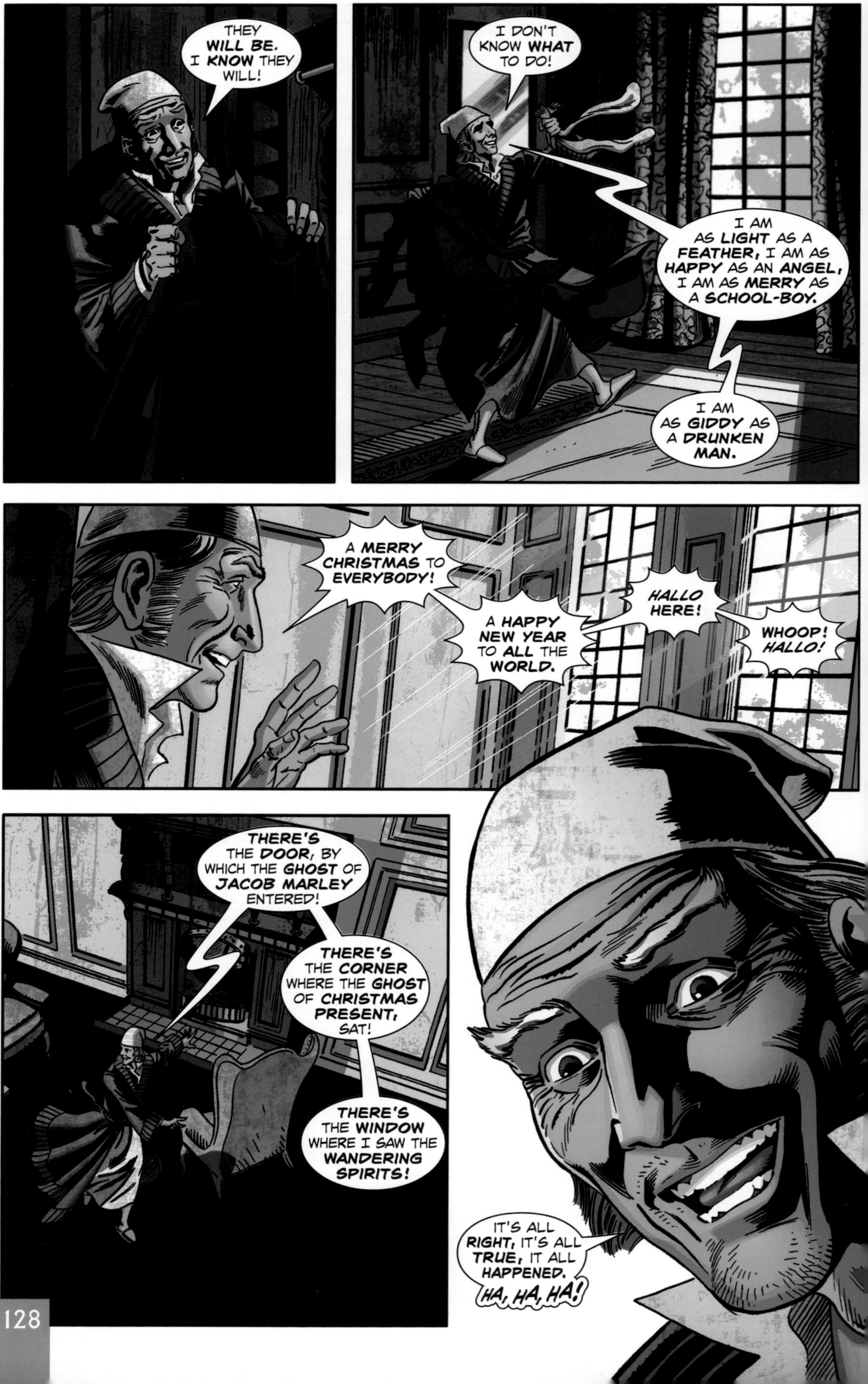
THEY WILL BE. I KNOW THEY WILL!
I DON'T KNOW WHAT TO DO!
I AM AS LIGHT AS A FEATHER, I AM AS HAPPY AS AN ANGEL, I AM AS MERRY AS A SCHOOL-BOY.
I AM AS GIDDY AS A DRUNKEN MAN.
A MERRY CHRISTMAS TO EVERYBODY!
A HAPPY NEW YEAR TO ALL THE WORLD.
HALLO HERE!
WHOOP! HALLO!
THERE'S THE DOOR, BY WHICH THE GHOST OF JACOB MARLEY ENTERED!
THERE'S THE CORNER WHERE THE GHOST OF CHRISTMAS PRESENT, SAT!
THERE'S THE WINDOW WHERE I SAW THE WANDERING SPIRITS!
IT'S ALL RIGHT, IT'S ALL TRUE, IT ALL HAPPENED.
HA, HA, HA!

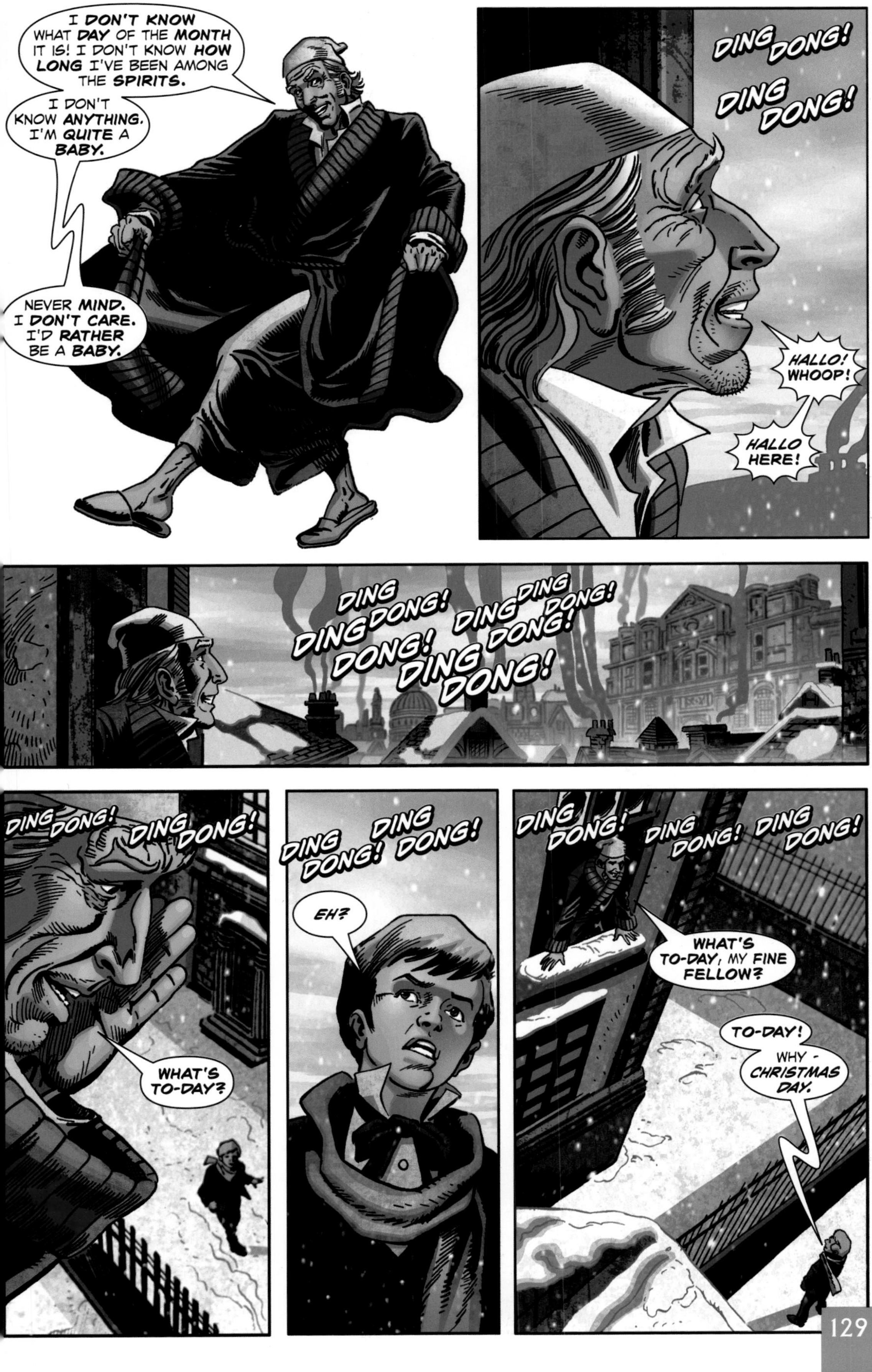
I DON'T KNOW WHAT DAY OF THE MONTH IT IS! I DON'T KNOW HOW LONG I'VE BEEN AMONG THE SPIRITS.
I DON'T KNOW ANYTHING. I'M QUITE A BABY.
NEVER MIND. I DON'T CARE. I'D RATHER BE A BABY.
DING DONG!
DING DONG!
HALLO! WHOOP!
HALLO HERE!
DING DING DONG! DONG! DING DING DONG! DING DONG! DING DONG!
DING DONG! DING DONG!
WHAT'S TO-DAY?
DING DONG! DING DONG!
EH?
DING DONG! DING DONG! DING DONG!
WHAT'S TO-DAY, MY FINE FELLOW?
TO-DAY! WHY - CHRISTMAS DAY.

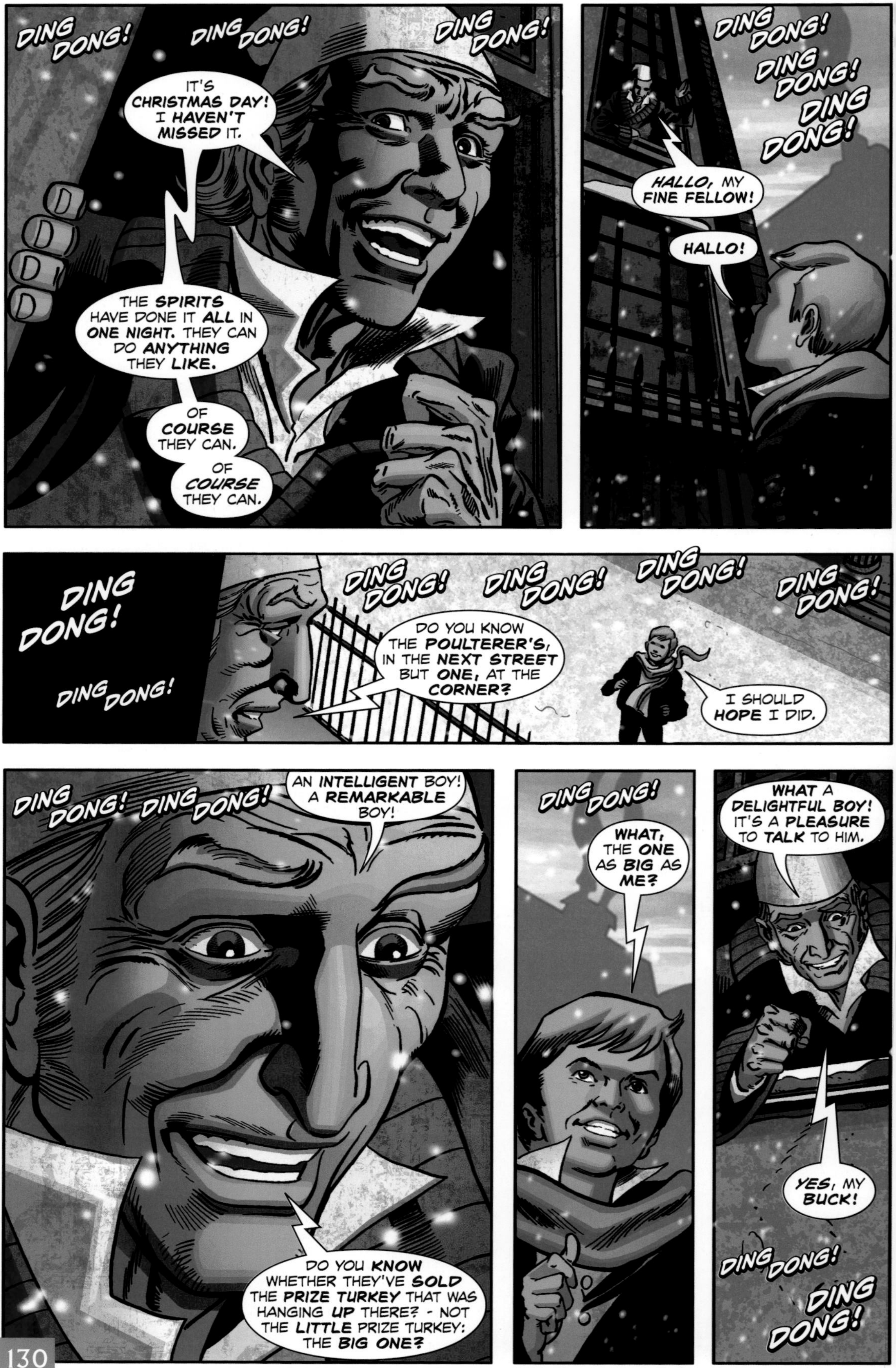
DING DONG! DING DONG! DING DONG!
IT'S CHRISTMAS DAY! I HAVEN'T MISSED IT.
THE SPIRITS HAVE DONE IT ALL IN ONE NIGHT. THEY CAN DO ANYTHING THEY LIKE.
OF COURSE THEY CAN.
OF COURSE THEY CAN.
DING DONG! DING DONG! DING DONG!
HALLO, MY FINE FELLOW!
HALLO!
DING DONG! DING DONG!
DING DONG! DING DONG! DING DONG!
DO YOU KNOW THE POULTERER'S, IN THE NEXT STREET BUT ONE, AT THE CORNER?
DING DONG!
I SHOULD HOPE I DID.
DING DONG! DING DONG!
AN INTELLIGENT BOY! A REMARKABLE BOY!
DO YOU KNOW WHETHER THEY'VE SOLD THE PRIZE TURKEY THAT WAS HANGING UP THERE? - NOT THE LITTLE PRIZE TURKEY: THE BIG ONE?
DING DONG!
WHAT, THE ONE AS BIG AS ME?
WHAT A DELIGHTFUL BOY! IT'S A PLEASURE TO TALK TO HIM.
YES, MY BUCK!
DING DONG! DING DONG!

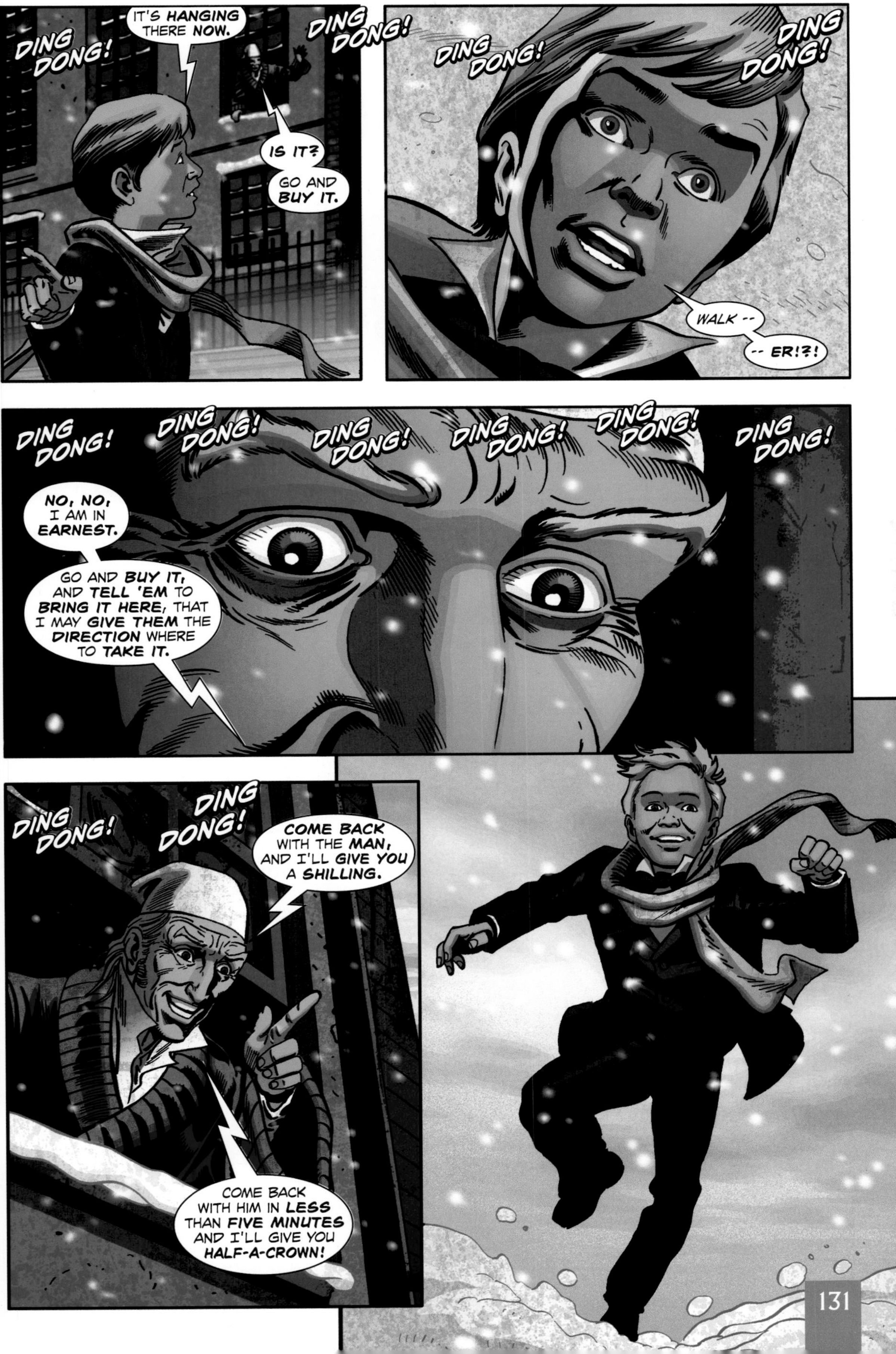
DING DONG!
IT'S HANGING THERE NOW.
DING DONG!
IS IT?
GO AND BUY IT.
DING DONG!
DING DONG!
WALK --
-- ER!?!
DING DONG!
DING DONG!
DING DONG!
DING DONG!
DING DONG!
DING DONG!
NO, NO, I AM IN EARNEST.
GO AND BUY IT, AND TELL 'EM TO BRING IT HERE, THAT I MAY GIVE THEM THE DIRECTION WHERE TO TAKE IT.
DING DONG!
DING DONG!
COME BACK WITH THE MAN, AND I'LL GIVE YOU A SHILLING.
COME BACK WITH HIM IN LESS THAN FIVE MINUTES AND I'LL GIVE YOU HALF-A-CROWN!

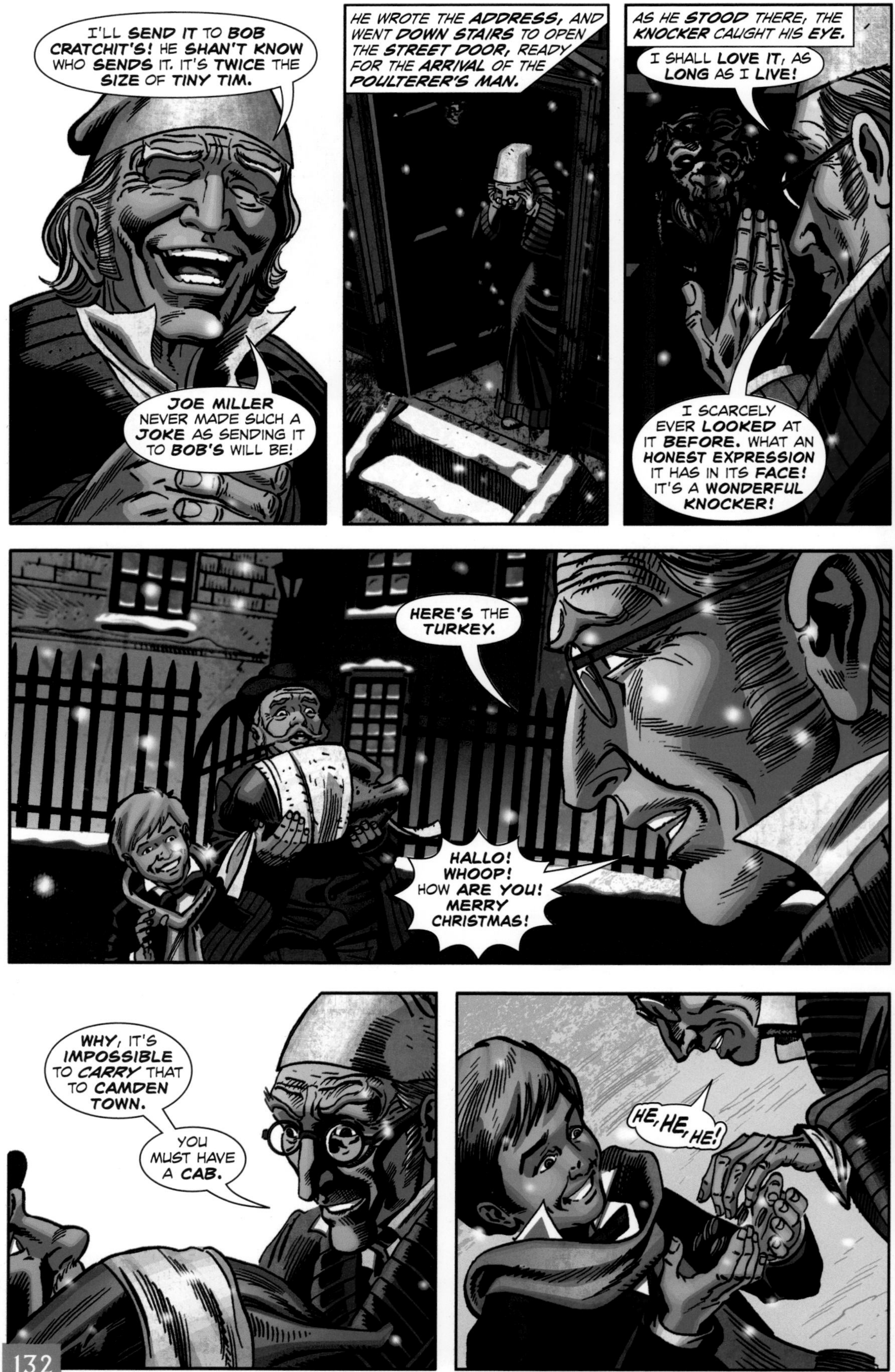
I'LL SEND IT TO BOB CRATCHIT'S! HE SHAN'T KNOW WHO SENDS IT. IT'S TWICE THE SIZE OF TINY TIM.
JOE MILLER NEVER MADE SUCH A JOKE AS SENDING IT TO BOB'S WILL BE!
HE WROTE THE ADDRESS, AND WENT DOWN STAIRS TO OPEN THE STREET DOOR, READY FOR THE ARRIVAL OF THE POULTERER'S MAN.
AS HE STOOD THERE, THE KNOCKER CAUGHT HIS EYE.
I SHALL LOVE IT, AS LONG AS I LIVE!
I SCARCELY EVER LOOKED AT IT BEFORE. WHAT AN HONEST EXPRESSION IT HAS IN ITS FACE! IT'S A WONDERFUL KNOCKER!
HERE'S THE TURKEY.
HALLO! WHOOP! HOW ARE YOU! MERRY CHRISTMAS!
WHY, IT'S IMPOSSIBLE TO CARRY THAT TO CAMDEN TOWN.
YOU MUST HAVE A CAB.
HE, HE, HE!

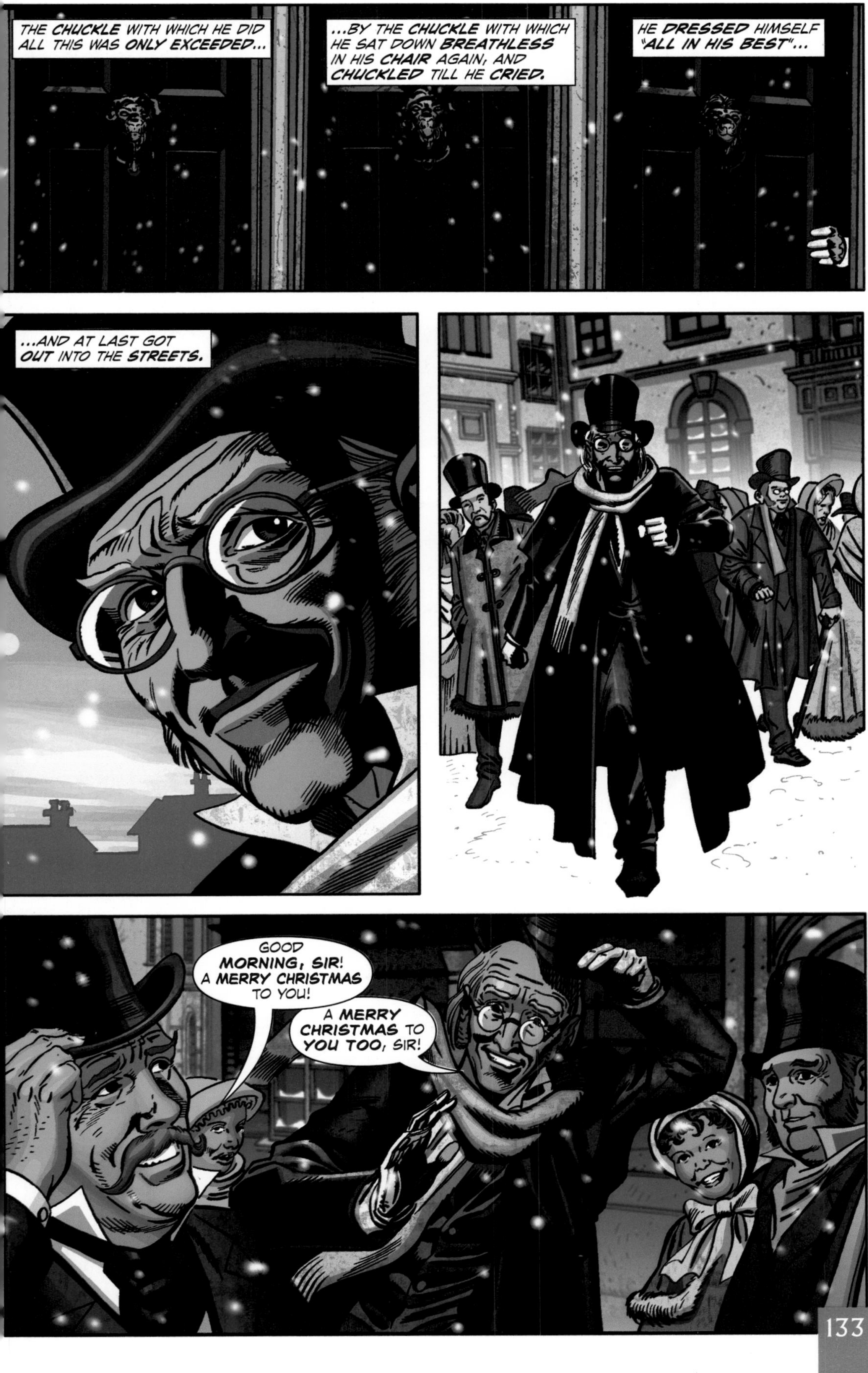
THE CHUCKLE WITH WHICH HE DID ALL THIS WAS ONLY EXCEEDED...
...BY THE CHUCKLE WITH WHICH HE SAT DOWN BREATHLESS IN HIS CHAIR AGAIN, AND CHUCKLED TILL HE CRIED.
HE DRESSED HIMSELF "ALL IN HIS BEST"...
...AND AT LAST GOT OUT INTO THE STREETS.
GOOD MORNING, SIR! A MERRY CHRISTMAS TO YOU!
A MERRY CHRISTMAS TO YOU TOO, SIR!

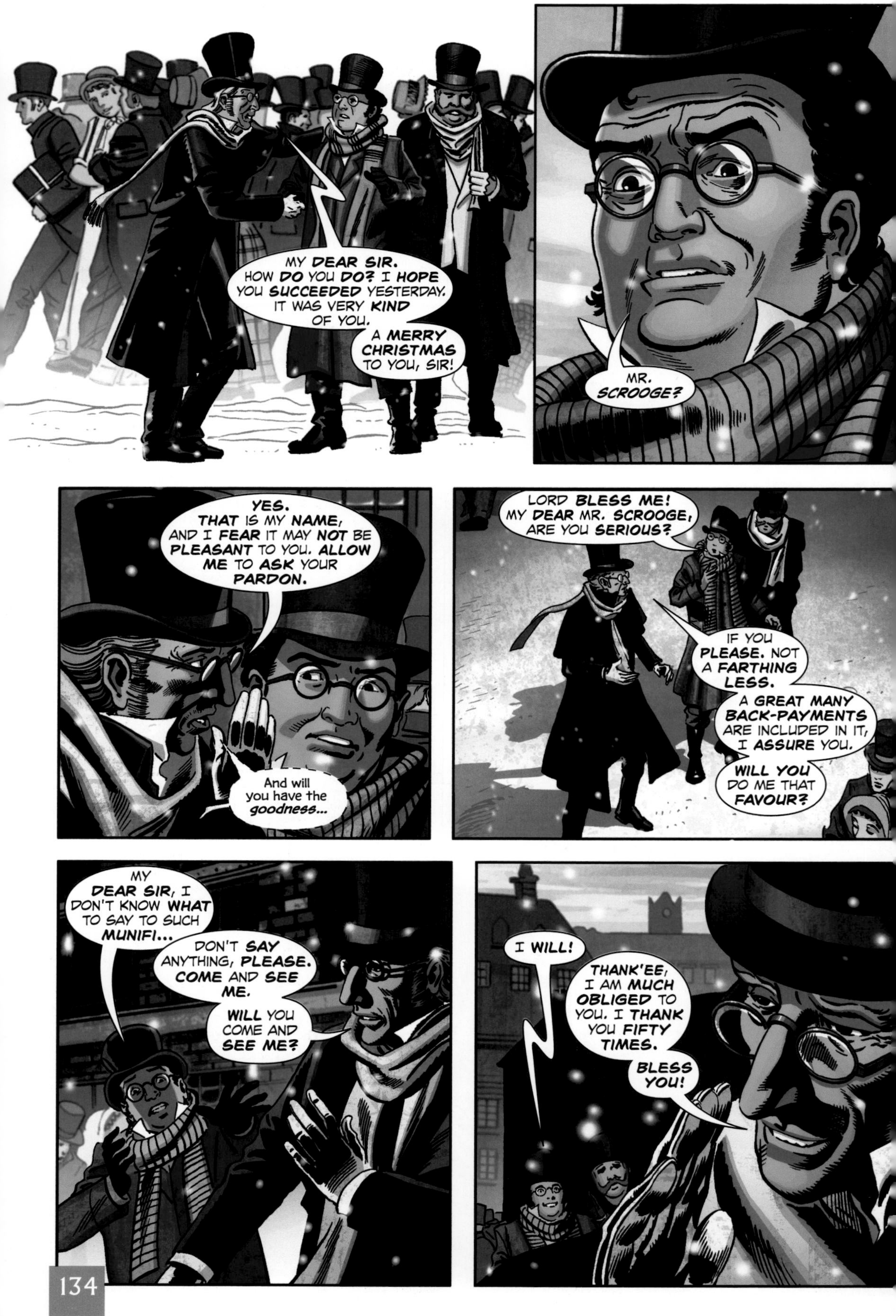
MY DEAR SIR. HOW DO YOU DO? I HOPE YOU SUCCEEDED YESTERDAY. IT WAS VERY KIND OF YOU.
A MERRY CHRISTMAS TO YOU, SIR!
MR. SCROOGE?
YES. THAT IS MY NAME, AND I FEAR IT MAY NOT BE PLEASANT TO YOU. ALLOW ME TO ASK YOUR PARDON.
And will you have the goodness...
LORD BLESS ME! MY DEAR MR. SCROOGE, ARE YOU SERIOUS?
IF YOU PLEASE. NOT A FARTHING LESS.
A GREAT MANY BACK-PAYMENTS ARE INCLUDED IN IT, I ASSURE YOU.
WILL YOU DO ME THAT FAVOUR?
MY DEAR SIR, I DON'T KNOW WHAT TO SAY TO SUCH MUNIFI...
DON'T SAY ANYTHING, PLEASE. COME AND SEE ME.
WILL YOU COME AND SEE ME?
I WILL!
THANK'EE, I AM MUCH OBLIGED TO YOU. I THANK YOU FIFTY TIMES.
BLESS YOU!

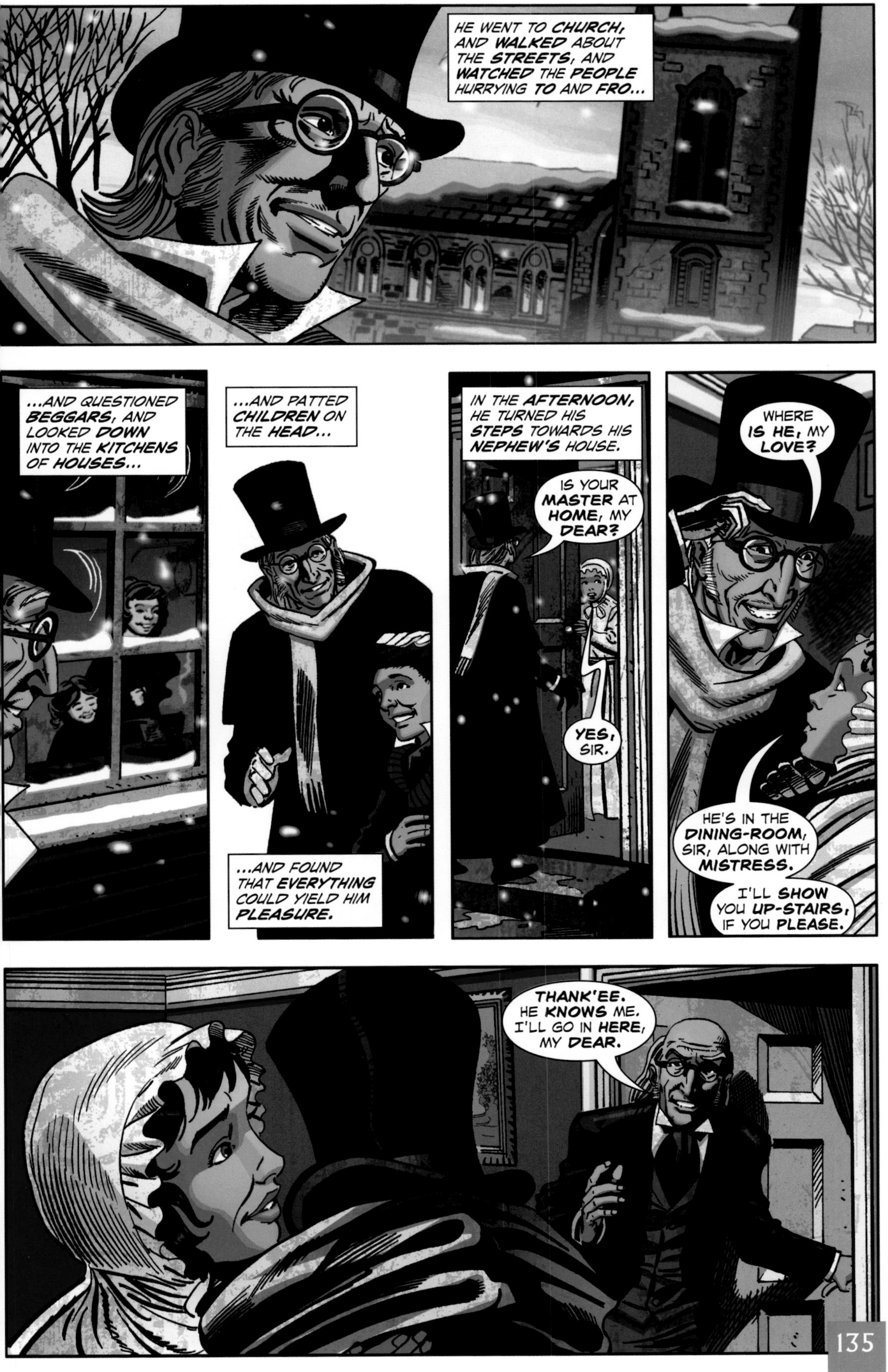
HE WENT TO CHURCH, AND WALKED ABOUT THE STREETS, AND WATCHED THE PEOPLE HURRYING TO AND FRO...
...AND QUESTIONED BEGGARS, AND LOOKED DOWN INTO THE KITCHENS OF HOUSES...
...AND PATTED CHILDREN ON THE HEAD...
...AND FOUND THAT EVERYTHING COULD YIELD HIM PLEASURE.
IN THE AFTERNOON, HE TURNED HIS STEPS TOWARDS HIS NEPHEW'S HOUSE.
IS YOUR MASTER AT HOME, MY DEAR?
YES, SIR.
WHERE IS HE, MY LOVE?
HE'S IN THE DINING-ROOM, SIR, ALONG WITH MISTRESS.
I'LL SHOW YOU UP-STAIRS, IF YOU PLEASE.
THANK'EE. HE KNOWS ME. I'LL GO IN HERE, MY DEAR.

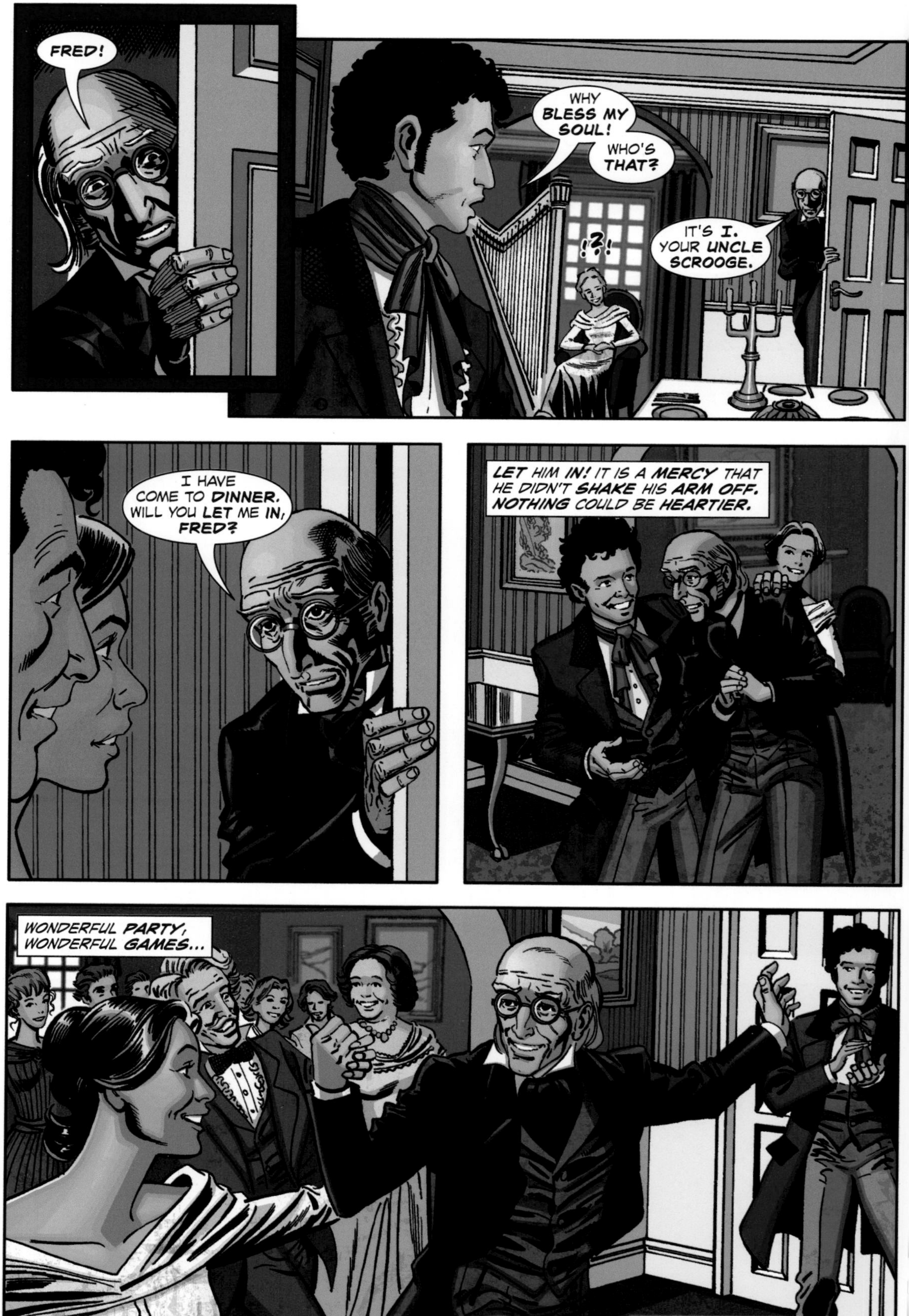
FRED!
WHY BLESS MY SOUL!
WHO'S THAT?
!?!
IT'S I. YOUR UNCLE SCROOGE.
I HAVE COME TO DINNER. WILL YOU LET ME IN, FRED?
LET HIM IN! IT IS A MERCY THAT HE DIDN'T SHAKE HIS ARM OFF. NOTHING COULD BE HEARTIER.
WONDERFUL PARTY, WONDERFUL GAMES...
...WONDERFUL UNANIMITY, WON-DER-FUL HAPPINESS!

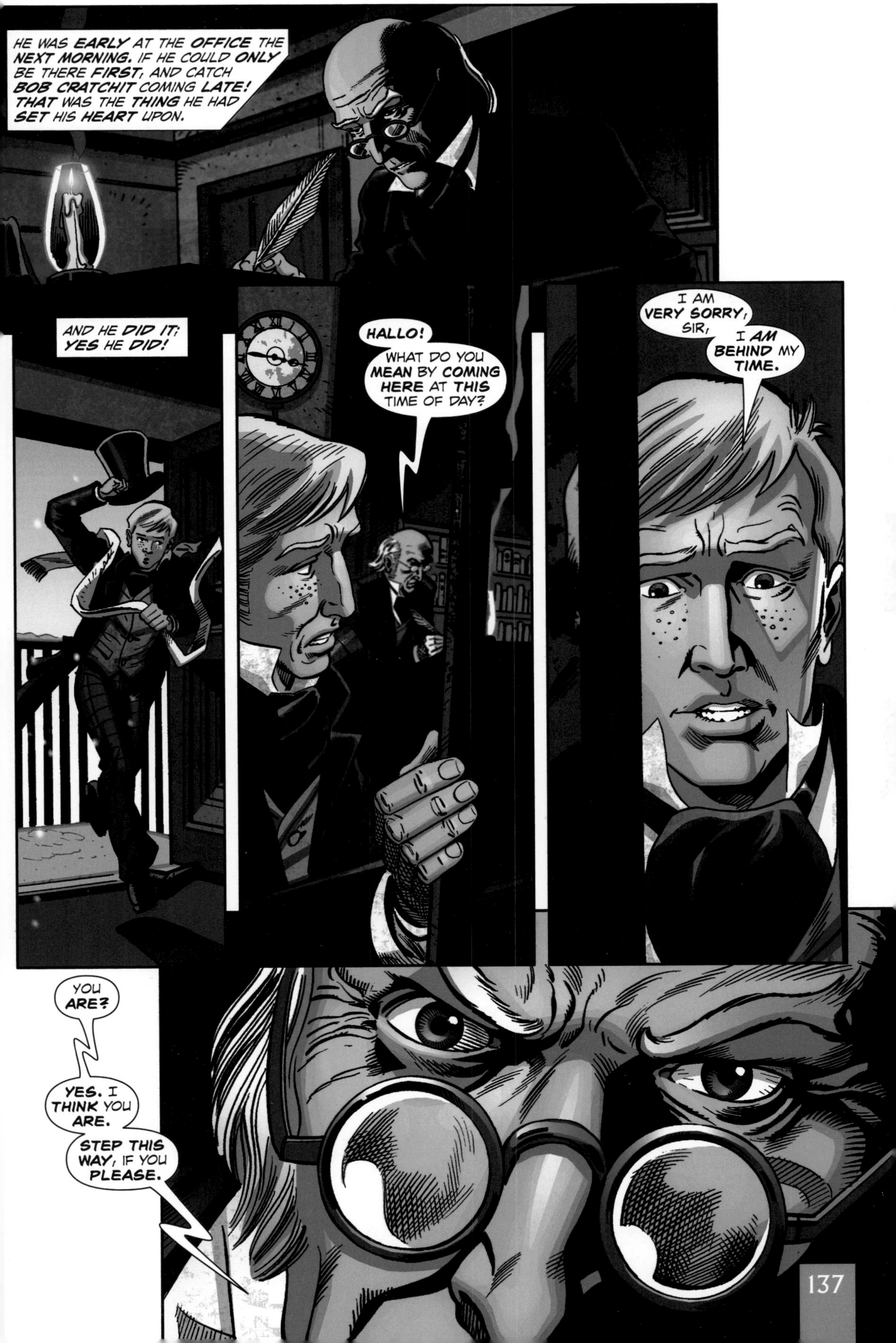
HE WAS EARLY AT THE OFFICE THE NEXT MORNING. IF HE COULD ONLY BE THERE FIRST, AND CATCH BOB CRATCHIT COMING LATE! THAT WAS THE THING HE HAD SET HIS HEART UPON.
AND HE DID IT; YES HE DID!
HALLO!
WHAT DO YOU MEAN BY COMING HERE AT THIS TIME OF DAY?
I AM VERY SORRY, SIR,
I AM BEHIND MY TIME.
YOU ARE?
YES. I THINK YOU ARE.
STEP THIS WAY, IF YOU PLEASE.

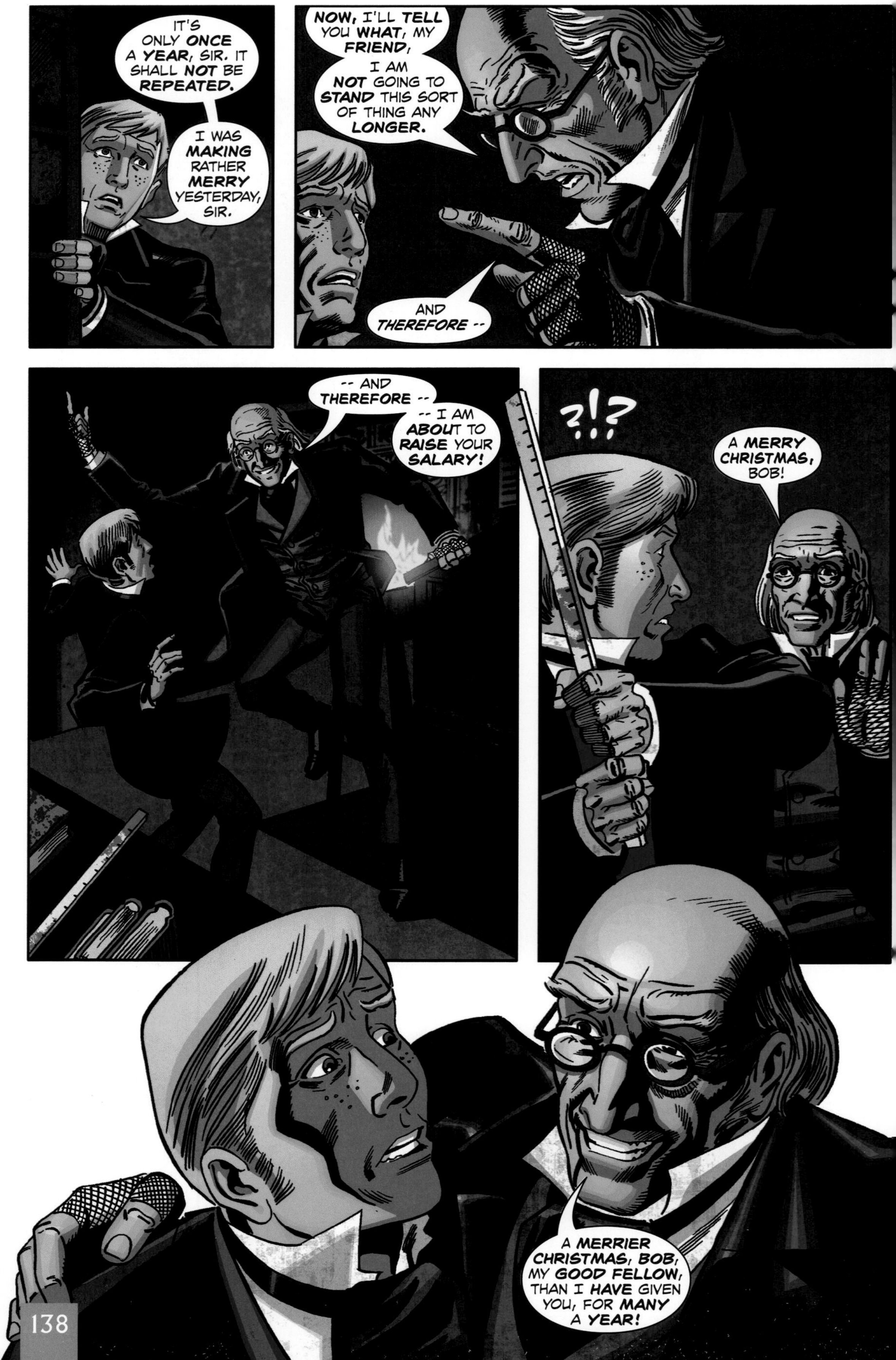

IT'S ONLY ONCE A YEAR, SIR. IT SHALL NOT BE REPEATED.
I WAS MAKING RATHER MERRY YESTERDAY, SIR.
NOW, I'LL TELL YOU WHAT, MY FRIEND,
I AM NOT GOING TO STAND THIS SORT OF THING ANY LONGER.
AND THEREFORE --
-- AND THEREFORE --
-- I AM ABOUT TO RAISE YOUR SALARY!
?!?
A MERRY CHRISTMAS, BOB!
A MERRIER CHRISTMAS, BOB, MY GOOD FELLOW, THAN I HAVE GIVEN YOU, FOR MANY A YEAR!

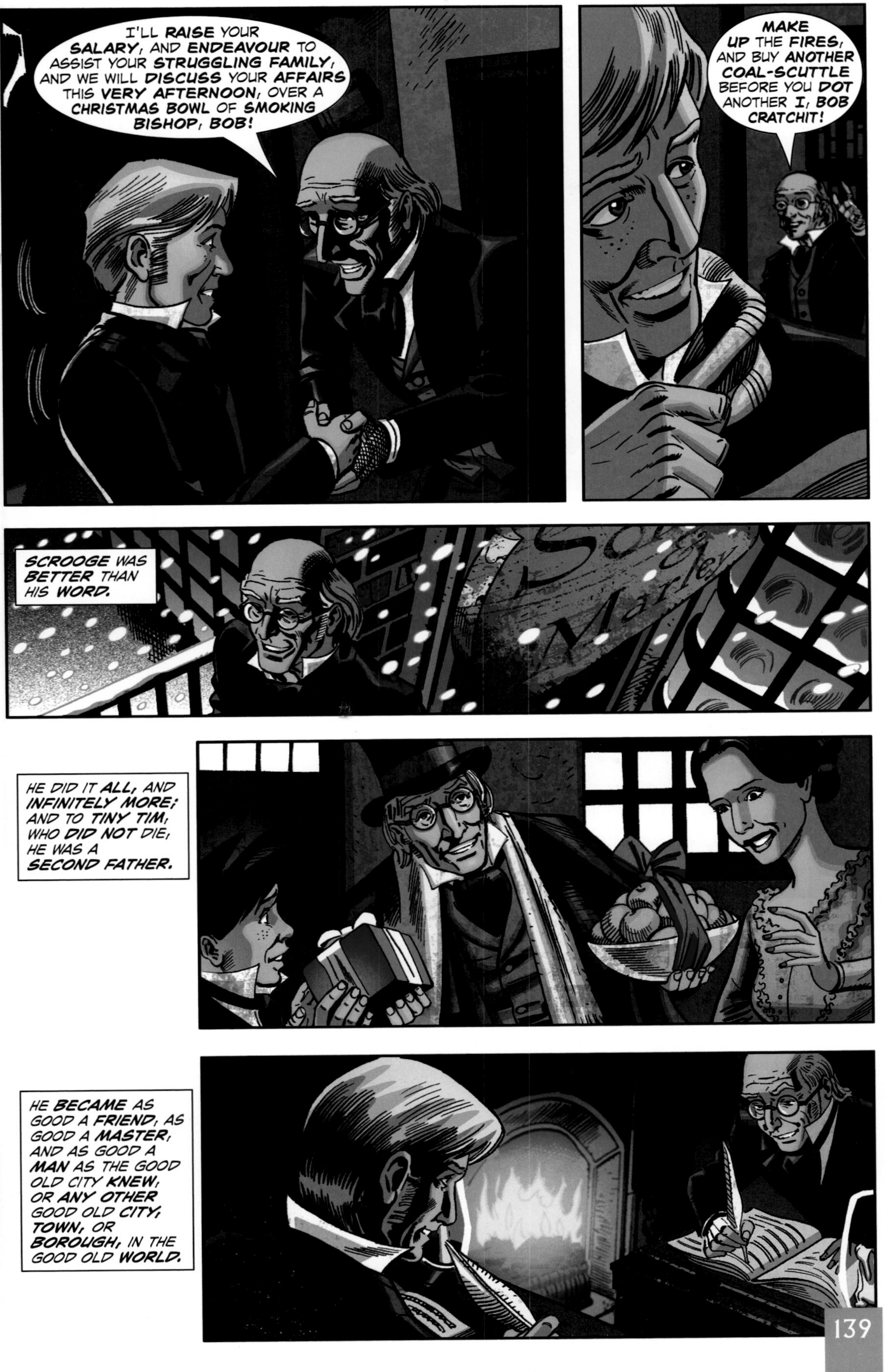
I'LL RAISE YOUR SALARY, AND ENDEAVOUR TO ASSIST YOUR STRUGGLING FAMILY, AND WE WILL DISCUSS YOUR AFFAIRS THIS VERY AFTERNOON, OVER A CHRISTMAS BOWL OF SMOKING BISHOP, BOB!
MAKE UP THE FIRES, AND BUY ANOTHER COAL-SCUTTLE BEFORE YOU DOT ANOTHER I, BOB CRATCHIT!
SCROOGE WAS BETTER THAN HIS WORD.
HE DID IT ALL, AND INFINITELY MORE; AND TO TINY TIM, WHO DID NOT DIE, HE WAS A SECOND FATHER.
HE BECAME AS GOOD A FRIEND, AS GOOD A MASTER, AND AS GOOD A MAN AS THE GOOD OLD CITY KNEW, OR ANY OTHER GOOD OLD CITY, TOWN, OR BOROUGH, IN THE GOOD OLD WORLD.

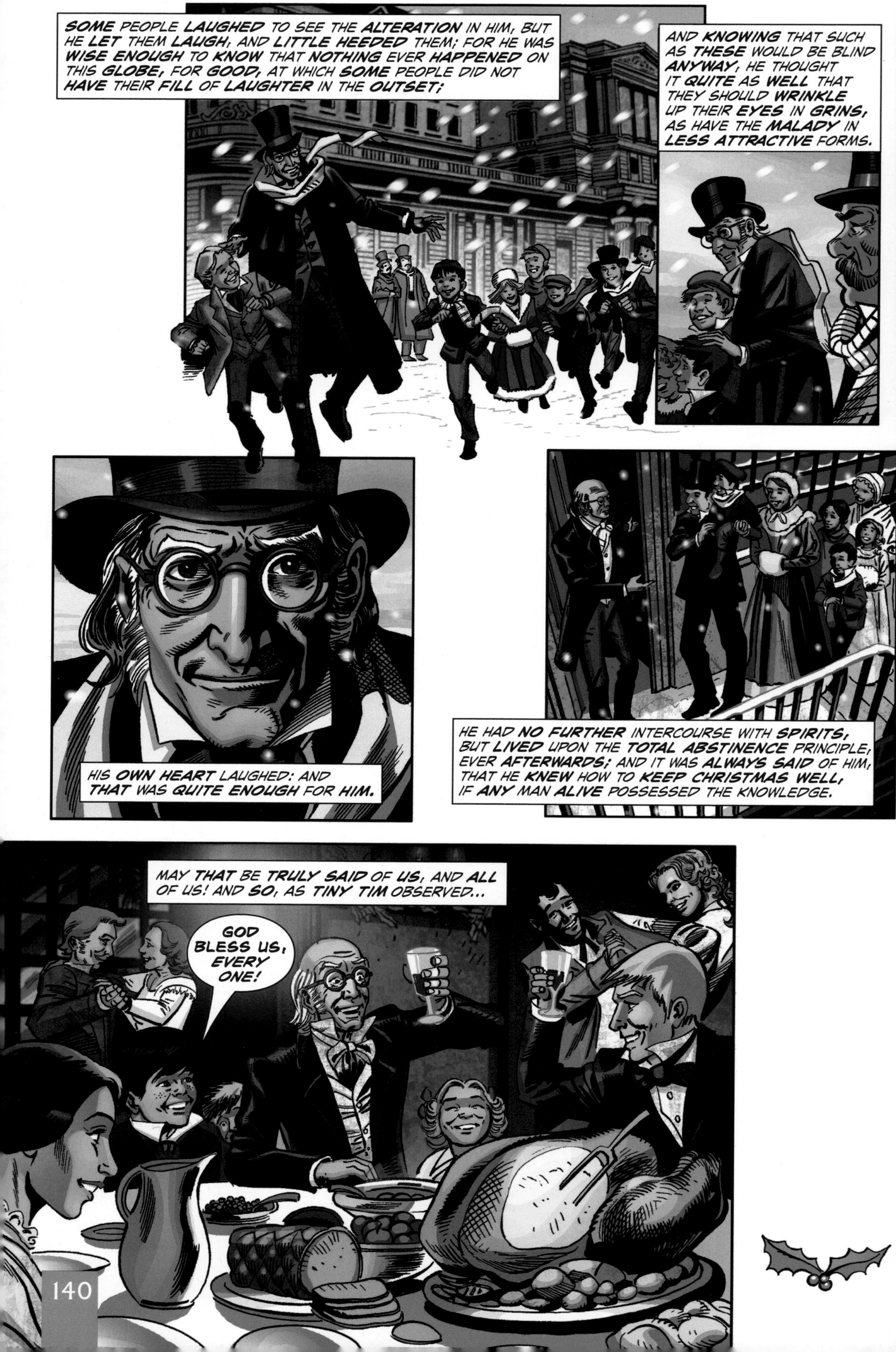
SOME PEOPLE LAUGHED TO SEE THE ALTERATION IN HIM, BUT HE LET THEM LAUGH, AND LITTLE HEEDED THEM; FOR HE WAS WISE ENOUGH TO KNOW THAT NOTHING EVER HAPPENED ON THIS GLOBE, FOR GOOD, AT WHICH SOME PEOPLE DID NOT HAVE THEIR FILL OF LAUGHTER IN THE OUTSET;
AND KNOWING THAT SUCH AS THESE WOULD BE BLIND ANYWAY, HE THOUGHT IT QUITE AS WELL THAT THEY SHOULD WRINKLE UP THEIR EYES IN GRINS, AS HAVE THE MALADY IN LESS ATTRACTIVE FORMS.
HIS OWN HEART LAUGHED: AND THAT WAS QUITE ENOUGH FOR HIM.
HE HAD NO FURTHER INTERCOURSE WITH SPIRITS, BUT LIVED UPON THE TOTAL ABSTINENCE PRINCIPLE, EVER AFTERWARDS; AND IT WAS ALWAYS SAID OF HIM, THAT HE KNEW HOW TO KEEP CHRISTMAS WELL, IF ANY MAN ALIVE POSSESSED THE KNOWLEDGE.
MAY THAT BE TRULY SAID OF US, AND ALL OF US! AND SO, AS TINY TIM OBSERVED...
GOD BLESS US, EVERY ONE!

A Christmas Carol

The End

"It was the best of times, it was the worst of times, it was the age of wisdom, it was the age of foolishness, it was the epoch of belief, it was the epoch of incredulity, it was the season of Light, it was the season of Darkness, it was the spring of hope, it was the winter of despair, we had everything before us, we had nothing before us, we were all going direct to Heaven, we were all going direct the other way – in short, the period was so far like the present period, that some of its noisiest authorities insisted on its being received, for good or for evil, in the superlative degree of comparison only."

Excerpt from *A Tale of Two Cities* by Charles Dickens

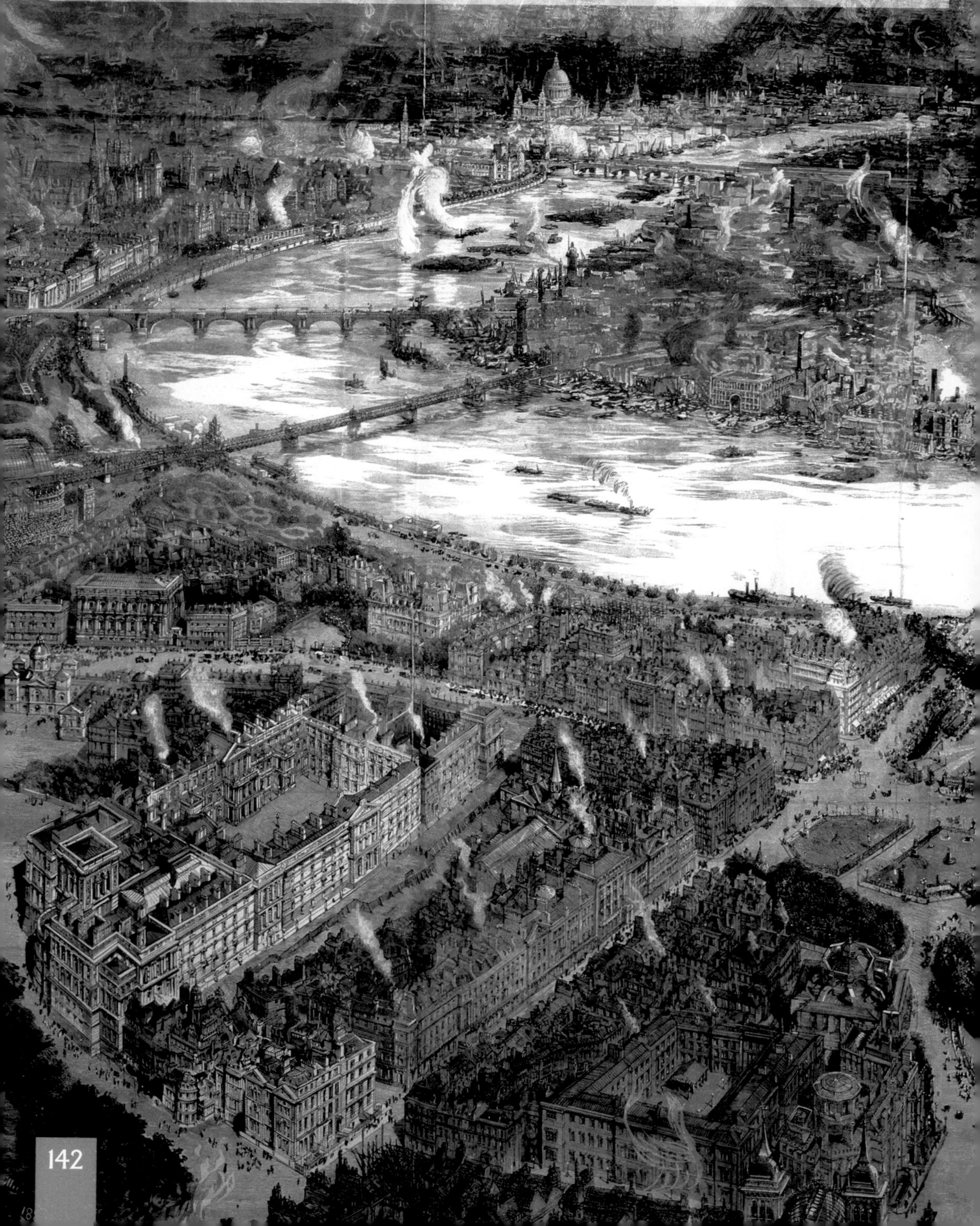

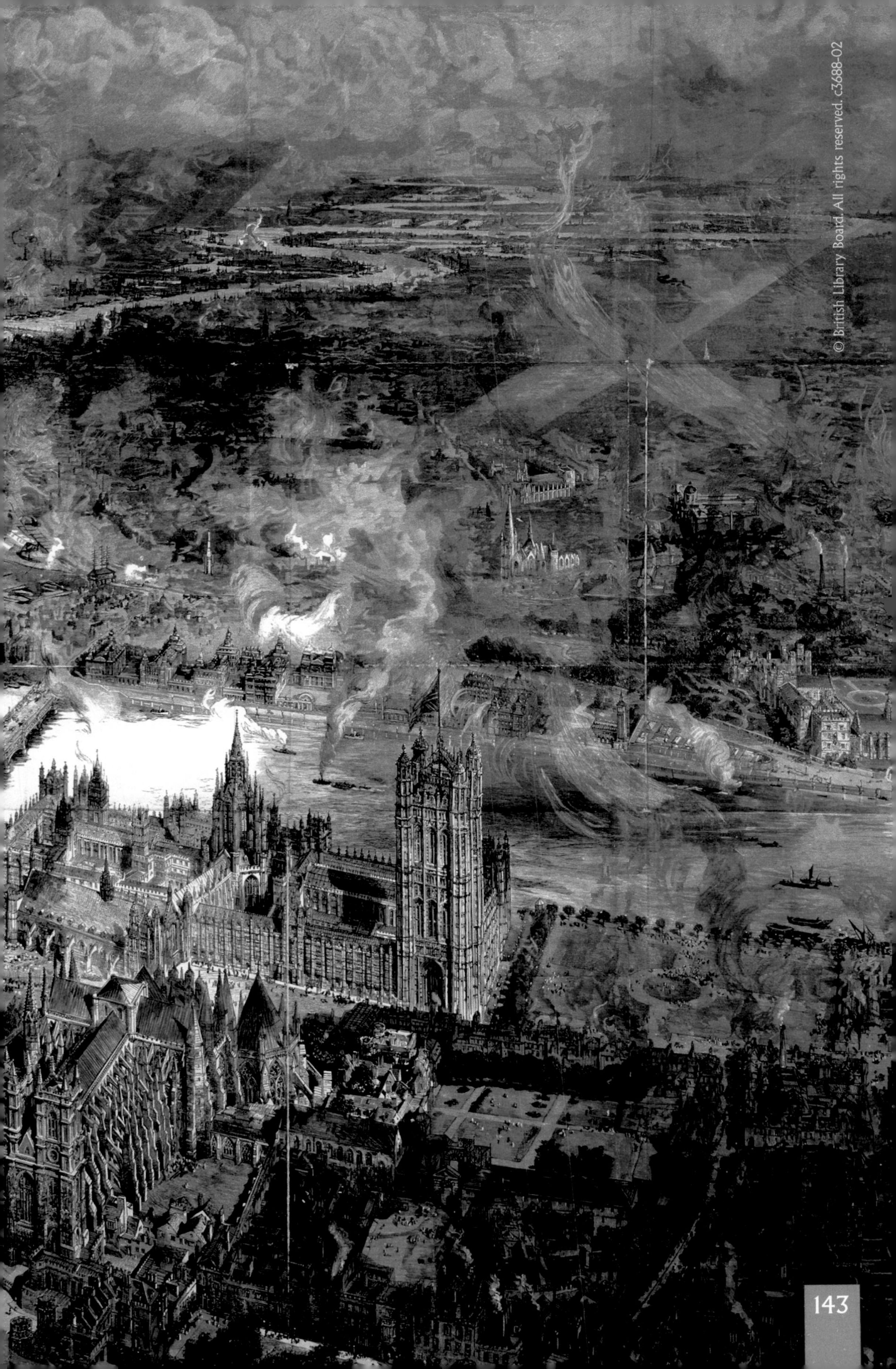

What the Dickens?

(1812 - 1870 AD)

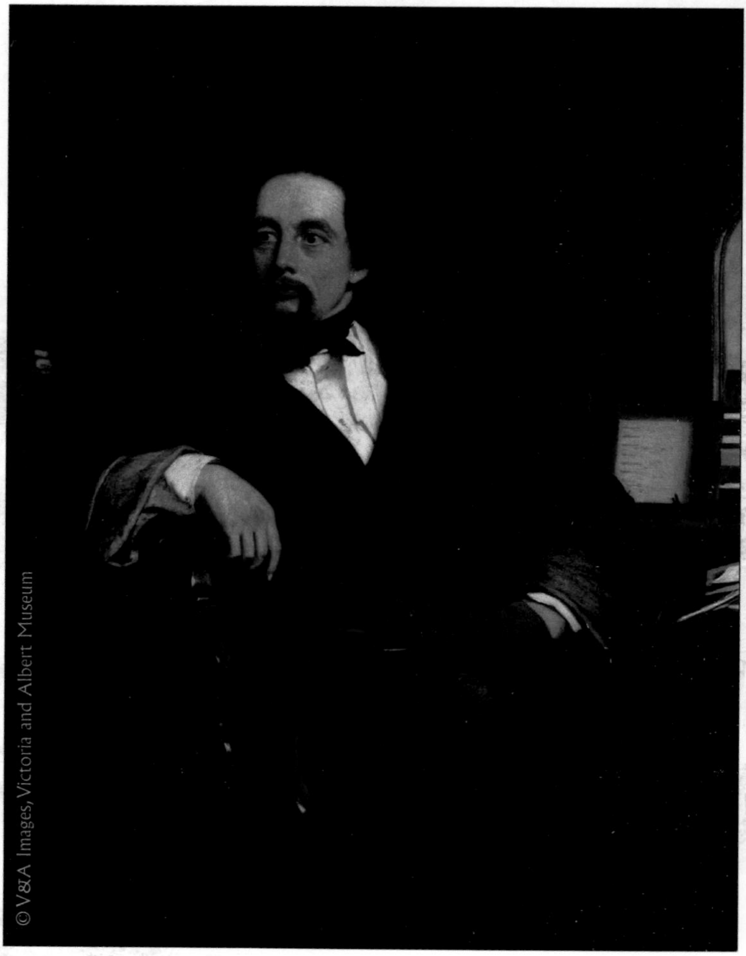
© V&A Images, Victoria and Albert Museum

Charles Dickens

Charles John Huffam Dickens was born in Landport, Portsmouth (on the south coast of England) on February 7, 1812. He was the second of eight children born to John and Elizabeth Dickens, and described himself as a "very small and not-over-particularly-taken-care-of boy." Although not wealthy, the Dickens family was not poor. They moved to Chatham, Kent in 1817 and sent Charles to the fee paying William Giles' school in the area. Despite his youth, he was a frequent visitor to the theater. He enjoyed Shakespeare, and claimed to have learned many things from watching plays.

By the time he was ten, the family had moved again; this time to London following the career of his father, John, who was a clerk in the Naval Pay Office. John had a poor head for money, but liked to impress people. As a result, he got into debt and was sent to Marshalsea Prison in 1824. His wife and most of the children joined him there (a common occurrence in those days before the Bankruptcy Act of 1869 abolished debtors' prisons). Charles, however, was put to work at Warren's Blacking Factory, where he labeled jars of boot polish.

Later in 1824, John's mother died and left enough money to her son to pay off his debts and get him released. John Dickens retired from the Navy Pay Office later that year and worked as a reporter for ***The Mirror of Parliament***, where his brother-in-law was editor. He allowed Charles to leave Warren's Blacking Factory, and go back to school. Charles's brief time at the factory continued to haunt him for the rest of his life. He later wrote:

> "For many years, when I came near to Robert Warren's, in the Strand, I crossed over to the opposite side of the way, to avoid a certain smell of the cement they put upon the blacking corks, which reminded me of what I once was. My old way home by the borough made me cry, after my oldest child could speak."

Dickens Fact

"Dicken" or "Dickens" was used as another name for the Devil. The first recorded use appears to have been by William Shakespeare in *The Merry Wives of Windsor*.

FORD:
Where had you this pretty weathercock?

MRS PAGE:
I cannot tell what the dickens his name is my husband had him of.

Charles left school at fifteen and worked as an office boy with a Mr. Molloy of Lincoln's Inn. Here, he decided to be a journalist. He studied shorthand at night, and went on to spend two years as a shorthand reporter at the Doctors' Commons Courts. Many thought that the institution of Doctors' Commons (a society of lawyers in London) was old-fashioned and ridiculous - including Dickens: his satirical description of his time there can be found in both *Sketches by Boz* and in *David Copperfield*.

Charles's first love was Maria Beadnell – a banker's daughter whom he met in 1830. Their relationship came to an end after three years, probably through the wishes of Maria's parents who thought that Charles was not good enough for their daughter.

Around this time, Dickens started to achieve recognition for his own written work. He wrote for a number of newspapers: *True Sun* (1830-32), *Mirror of Parliament* (1832-34), and *The Morning Chronicle* (1834-36). He was later to recognize how important these

years were to him, when he wrote,
"To the wholesome training of severe newspaper work, when I was a very young man, I constantly refer my first successes."

December 1833 saw his first published (but unpaid for) work appear in *The Old Monthly* magazine: a story entitled *A Dinner at Poplar Walk*. On seeing his first work in print, Dickens wrote,
"On which occasion I walked down to Westminster-hall, and turned into it for half an hour, because my eyes were so dimmed with joy and pride, that they could not bear the street, and were not fit to be seen there".

He wrote further stories for *The Old Monthly*, but when the magazine could not pay for them, Dickens began to write his "series" for *The Chronicle* at the request of

the editor, George Hogarth. In 1835, Charles got engaged to George Hogarth's eldest daughter, Catherine. They married on April 2, 1836 and went on to have ten children (seven boys and three girls). Biographers have long suspected that Dickens preferred Catherine's sister, Mary, who lived with the Dickens family and died in his arms in 1837 at the age of seventeen. Dickens had asked to be buried next to her; but when her brother died in 1841, Dickens's "place" was taken. He wrote to his great friend and biographer John Forster,
"It is a great trial for me to give up Mary's grave... the desire to be buried next to her is as strong upon me now, as it was five years ago... And I know...that it will never diminish...I cannot bear the thought of being excluded from her dust."

Not only did Dickens wear her ring for the rest of his life, he also wrote the epitaph which appears on her gravestone:
"Young, beautiful, and good, God numbered her among his angels at the early age of seventeen."

In 1844, another of Catherine's sisters, Georgina, moved in to the Dickens household; some say that the novelist fell in love with her too.

The first series of ***Sketches by Boz*** was published in 1836. "Boz" was an early pen name used by Dickens. It came from

> **"the nickname of a pet child, a younger brother, whom I had dubbed Moses, in honour of The Vicar of Wakefield, which, being pronounced Bozes, got shortened into Boz."**

Shortly afterwards, with the success of ***Pickwick Papers*** in 1837, Dickens was at last a full-time novelist. He produced works at an incredible rate; and at the start of his writing career, also continued his work as a journalist and editor. He began his next book, ***Oliver Twist***, in 1837 and continued it in monthly parts until April 1839.

Dickens visited Canada and the United States in 1842, taking Catherine and her maid with him. During that visit he talked on the need for international copyright, because some American publishers were printing his books without his permission and without any payment; he also talked about the need to end slavery. His visit and his opinions were recorded and published as ***American Notes*** in October of that year, causing quite a stir.

December 17, 1843 saw the publication of ***A Christmas Carol.*** It was the first of Dickens's enormously successful series of Christmas books which ran until 1848. It was so popular that it sold five-thousand copies by Christmas Eve – and has never been out of print since.

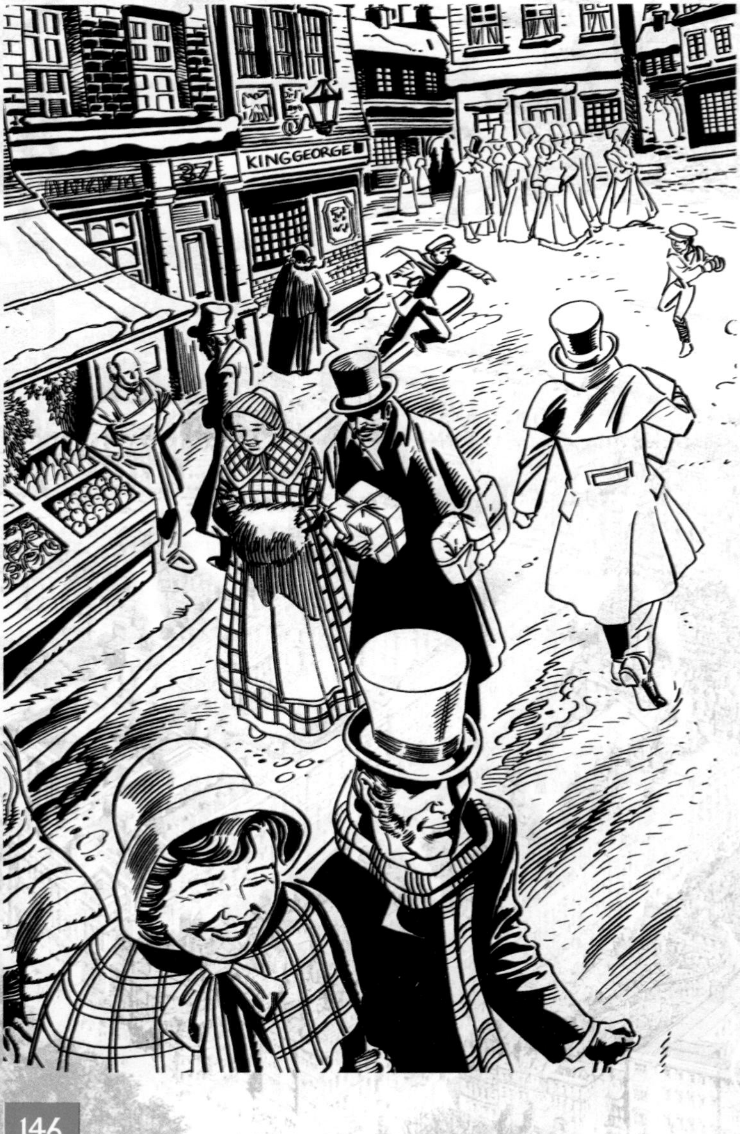
27
KINGGEORGE

Dickens became something of an international celebrity. In 1853 he toured Italy with his friends Augustus Egg (the artist), and Wilkie Collins (the author and playwright). On his return to England, he gave the first of many public readings from his own works: at first he did these for charity, but before long he demanded payment.

From childhood, Dickens had loved the stage and enjoyed the attention and applause he received. He performed in amateur theater throughout the 1840s and 50s, and formed his own amateur theatrical company in 1845, which occupied much of his time.

By 1856, Dickens had made enough money to purchase a fine country house: Gads Hill in Kent. He had admired this place ever since his arrival to the area as a child, and it must have felt a huge achievement to finally own it. However, Gads Hill was not a happy family home. A year later, Charles met a young actress called Ellen Lawless Ternan who

went on to join his theater company; and they began a relationship that was to last until his death.

Charles separated from his wife Catherine in 1858. The event was talked about in the newspapers, and Dickens publicly denied rumors of an affair. He was morally trapped — he was deeply in love with Ellen, but his writing career was based on promoting family values and being a good person; he felt that if he admitted his relationship with Ellen, it would put an end to his writing career.

Catherine moved to a house in London with their eldest son Charles, and Dickens remained at Gads Hill with the rest of the children and Catherine's sister, Georgina (there were rumors of Charles and Georgina having a relationship too). On her deathbed in 1879 Catherine gave her collection of Dickens's letters to her daughter Kate, instructing her to

"Give these to the British Museum, that the world may know he loved me once".

The more he tried to hide his personal life, the more it came out in his writing. One of his most popular books, *Great Expectations* (1860) has elements of imprisonment, love that can never be, people living in isolation, and the urge to better oneself — all subjects that were part of Dickens's own life at the time.

He looked after Ellen until his death, renting houses for her to live in, and making regular secret journeys to see her — not easy for the local celebrity that Dickens had become. He went to incredible lengths to keep his secret safe, including renting houses under different names and setting up offices for his business in places that made it easy for him to visit her. On September 4, 1860 he wrote to William Henry Wills, the sub-editor of *Household Words*:

"Yesterday I burnt, in the field at Gads Hill, the accumulated letters and papers of twenty years. They set up a smoke like the genie when he got out of the casket on the seashore; and as it was an exquisite day when I began, and rained very heavily when I finished, I suspect my correspondence of having overcast the face of the heavens."

In 1865, Dickens was involved in the Staplehurst Rail Crash: an incident which disturbed him greatly. He was traveling by train, along with Ellen and her mother: they were most likely returning from a secret holiday in France. The train left the track, resulting in the deaths of ten people, with a further forty being injured. It is reported that Dickens tended to some of the wounded. He wrote to his old friend Thomas Mitton about the crash:

"My dear Mitton,
I should have written to you yesterday or the day before, if I had been quite up to writing. I am a little shaken, not by the beating and dragging of the carriage in which I was, but by the hard work afterwards in getting out the dying and dead, which was most horrible.
Two ladies were my fellow passengers; an old one, and a young one.
I don't want to be examined at the Inquests and I don't want to write about it. It could do no good either way, and I could only

seem to speak about myself, which, of course, I would rather not do".

Even when writing to a friend, Dickens still hid Ellen's name, and he didn't want to be part of the inquest in case his relationship became public knowledge.

By 1867 Dickens's health was getting worse. His doctor advised him to rest, but he carried on with his busy schedule, including another tour of America.

Mark Twain saw him during this second American tour in January 1868 and wrote:

"Promptly at 8pm, unannounced, and without waiting for any stamping or clapping of hands to call him out, a tall, "spry," (if I may say it,) thin-legged old gentleman, gotten up regardless of expense, especially as to shirt-front and diamonds, with a bright red flower in his button-hole, gray beard and moustache, bald head, and with side hair brushed fiercely and tempestuously forward, as if its owner were sweeping down before a gale of wind, the very Dickens came! He did not emerge upon the stage – that is rather too deliberate a word – he strode."

By the end of this tour, it is said that Dickens was so ill that he could hardly eat solid food, surviving on champagne and eggs beaten in sherry. He returned to England and despite his bad health, continued his public reading appearances. In April 1869, he collapsed during a reading in the north of England, and he was again advised to rest. Dickens didn't listen, and continued to give performances in London as well as starting work on a new novel, *The Mystery of Edwin Drood*.

This novel was never finished: Dickens had a stroke and died suddenly at Gads Hill on June 9, 1870. He had asked to be buried "in an inexpensive, unostentatious, and strictly private manner", but public opinion, led by *The Times* newspaper, insisted that he should be buried in keeping with his status as a great writer. He was buried at Westminster Abbey on June 14, 1870.

His funeral was a private affair, attended by just twelve mourners. After the service his grave was left open, and thousands of people from all walks of life came to pay their respects and throw flowers onto the coffin. Today, a small stone with a simple inscription marks his grave:

"CHARLES DICKENS
BORN 7th FEBRUARY 1812
DIED 9th JUNE 1870"

Dickens was so closely associated with Christmas that, shortly after his death, the critic and poet Theodore Watts-Dunton overheard a London barrow girl say, "Dickens dead? Then will Father Christmas die too?"

The Dickens Family Tree

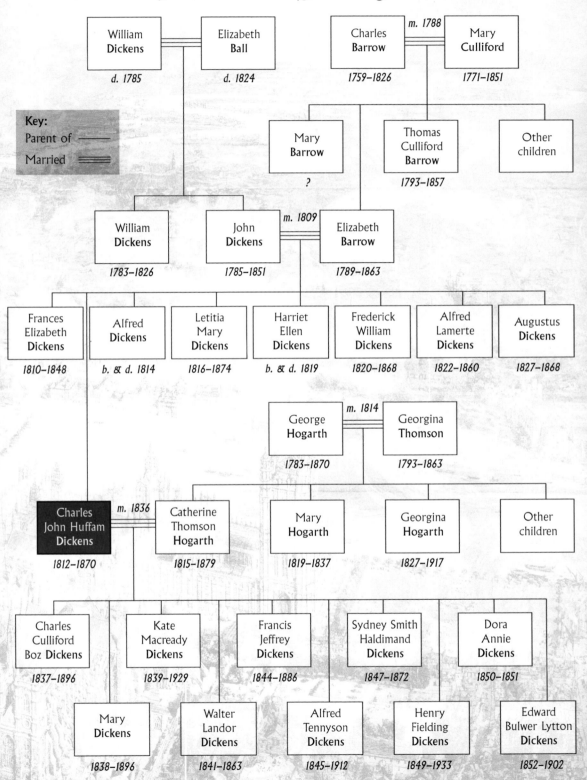

Key:
Parent of ———
Married =====

William **Dickens**
d. 1785

Elizabeth **Ball**
d. 1824

Charles **Barrow** — m. 1788 — Mary **Culliford**
1759–1826   1771–1851

Mary **Barrow**
?

Thomas Culliford **Barrow**
1793–1857

Other children

William **Dickens**
1783–1826

John **Dickens** — m. 1809 — Elizabeth **Barrow**
1785–1851   1789–1863

Frances Elizabeth **Dickens**
1810–1848

Alfred **Dickens**
b. & d. 1814

Letitia Mary **Dickens**
1816–1874

Harriet Ellen **Dickens**
b. & d. 1819

Frederick William **Dickens**
1820–1868

Alfred Lamerte **Dickens**
1822–1860

Augustus **Dickens**
1827–1868

George **Hogarth** — m. 1814 — Georgina **Thomson**
1783–1870   1793–1863

Charles John Huffam **Dickens** — m. 1836 — Catherine Thomson **Hogarth**
1812–1870   1815–1879

Mary **Hogarth**
1819–1837

Georgina **Hogarth**
1827–1917

Other children

Charles Culliford Boz **Dickens**
1837–1896

Kate Macready **Dickens**
1839–1929

Francis Jeffrey **Dickens**
1844–1886

Sydney Smith Haldimand **Dickens**
1847–1872

Dora Annie **Dickens**
1850–1851

Mary **Dickens**
1838–1896

Walter Landor **Dickens**
1841–1863

Alfred Tennyson **Dickens**
1845–1912

Henry Fielding **Dickens**
1849–1933

Edward Bulwer Lytton **Dickens**
1852–1902

Due to the lack of official records of births, deaths and marriages within this period, the above information is derived from extensive research and is as accurate as possible from the limited sources available.

Dickens Timeline

1812

February 7: Charles John Huffam Dickens born at Landport, Portsmouth, England.

1817

April: Family moves to Chatham, Kent.

1821

March: Charles goes to school (William Giles' school, next-door to the family home).

1822

September: Family moves to Camden Town, London.

1824

February: Charles (aged 12) goes to work at Warren's Blacking Factory. Charles's father arrested for debt and sent with his family to Marshalsea Prison.

May: Father and family released from prison.

June: Charles leaves the Blacking Factory and is enrolled in Wellington House Academy.

1827

May: Becomes an office boy for solicitors in Lincoln's Inn, and studies shorthand.

1828

November: Becomes a freelance reporter at Doctors' Commons courts.

1830

Becomes a parliamentary reporter for the *True Sun* newspaper.

1832

March: Moves to the *Mirror of Parliament* newspaper.

1833

December: First published story *A Dinner at Poplar Walk* appears in *The Old Monthly Magazine*.

1834

August: Moves to the *Morning Chronicle* newspaper, and writes under the name of "Boz".

November: Father once again arrested for debt; Charles comes to his aid.

1836

February: His first series of *Sketches by Boz* published.

March: First part of *Pickwick Papers* appears in its serialized form and runs for a year.

April: Marries Catherine Hogarth, daughter of George Hogarth, editor of the *Evening Chronicle*.

December: Becomes editor of *Bentley's Miscellany*, and publishes the second series of *Sketches by Boz*.

1837

February: Begins *Oliver Twist*, which continues in monthly parts in *Bentley's Miscellany* until 1839.

May: Catherine's younger sister Mary, whom he idolizes, dies.

1838

March: Begins serialization of *Nicholas Nickleby*, which continues until 1839.

1839

January: Resigns as editor of *Bentley's Miscellany*.

1840

April: Begins serialization of *The Old Curiosity Shop*, which runs for a year in *Master Humphrey's Clock*.

1842

January: Travels to Canada and United States.

June: Returns to London and declines offer to stand for Parliament

October: Begins *American Notes*.

1843

January: Serialization of *Martin Chuzzlewit* begins.

December: Publishes *A Christmas Carol*, the first of his Christmas books.

1845

September: His amateur theatrical company gives its first performance (*Every Man in his Humour*).

1846

July: Begins *Dombey and Son*, which runs until April 1848.

1848

December: Publishes final Christmas book, *The Haunted Man*.

1849

May: *David Copperfield* serialized in monthly parts until November 1850.

1851

March: His father dies.

April: Death of his infant daughter, Dora.

1852

March: First appearance of *Bleak House*.

1853

December: Gives first public reading, for charity, of *A Christmas Carol* in Birmingham, England.

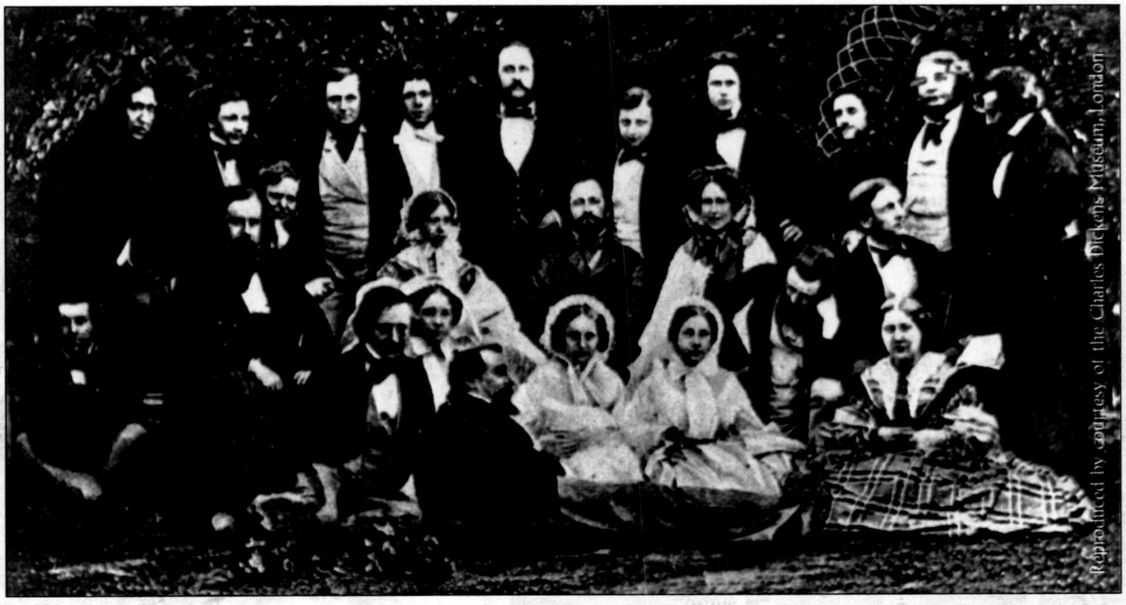
Reproduced by courtesy of the Charles Dickens Museum, London

The Dickens Dramatical Company in 1854 with Charles Dickens at the front.

1854
April-August: ***Hard Times*** appears weekly in ***Household Words.***

1855
December: ***Little Dorrit*** appears in monthly parts until 1857.

1856
March: Purchases Gads Hill, in Rochester, Kent.

1857
July: Performs in front of Queen Victoria.

August: Meets and falls in love with a young actress, Ellen Ternan.

1858
April: Dickens starts series of public readings for profit in London, and continues with a provincial tour.

May: Separates from his wife, Catherine. Her sister Georgina looks after the household.

1860
September: Dickens intentionally burns a large number of his personal letters.

December: Begins writing ***Great Expectations.***

1863
September: His mother, Elizabeth Dickens, dies.

December: His son Walter dies in India.

1864
February: His health begins to fail, probably due to over work.

May: ***Our Mutual Friend*** begins in monthly parts and runs until 1865.

1865
June: Badly shaken after being involved in the Staplehurst Railway Accident, while traveling back from France with Ellen Ternan and her mother.

1867
November: Against doctors' advice, Dickens continues public readings in England and Ireland, and embarks on an American reading tour.

1868
April: Returns to England, and continues his series of readings.

November: His readings now include a sensational version of the death of Nancy in ***Oliver Twist.***

1869
Dickens shows symptoms of having suffered a mild stroke. He cancels his provincial readings.

September: Begins to write ***The Mystery of Edwin Drood,*** and draws up his will.

1870
March: Has a private audience with Queen Victoria. His final public readings take place in London.

June 9: Dies at Gads Hill after suffering a stroke. He is buried on June 14 at Westminster Abbey.

September: Last of his unfinished ***The Mystery of Edwin Drood*** appears.

Hard Times

(Britain in the 1800s)

The Victorian era, 1837-1901, represented the height of the Industrial Revolution - a period of major social, economic, and technological advancement in Great Britain. Queen Victoria's reign also saw a huge expansion of the British Empire, making Britain the most important global power of the age.

It was a time of inventors and inventions; of rapid progress in science, technology and medicine, such as anesthetics and antiseptics. From the steam engine to the steam printer, the skyscraper to the machine-gun, the flush toilet, photography, moving pictures, electricity, the telegraph and telephone — it was as if the Victorian era was a transition from the old traditional world into the new modern age.

Travel was also revolutionized, mainly through the rise of the railway as a method of transporting goods and people. Although the first purpose-built railway in Britain, from Stockton to Darlington, opened in 1825 (twelve years before Victoria became queen) the early years of her reign witnessed the most extraordinary boom — so called, "Railway Fever". In 1850, there were ten thousand miles of railway track in Britain; by 1901, that number had grown to about thirty-five thousand. The railway age changed the way people lived and worked.

The Royal Collection © 2008 Her Majesty Queen Elizabeth II

Queen Victoria

Many important developments, such as the fledgling postal service (the "Penny Post"), could not have happened without railways; and as technology allowed us to travel further and faster, the world was divided into twenty-four time zones — with Greenwich becoming the center of the world's time.

But this new Britain was not a paradise for all: with this rapid progress came massive change in terms of population size, trades and the way in which people lived. The population trebled in Great Britain between 1800 and 1900 and people flocked to the cities to work in the new industries. Accommodation became overcrowded and unsanitary, with London being the area most affected. Much prosperity was generated for the elite through new technology, and on an underpaid workforce consisting of adults and children living in poverty. Millions of workers lived in slums or in old decaying houses. They had no sanitation, no fresh water supply, no paved streets, no schools, no law or order, no decent food and little fuel for fires.

Children were expected to earn wages to help the family; as Dickens himself did in Warren's Blacking Factory. They often worked long hours in dangerous jobs and in appalling conditions for just a few pennies a day.

There were also many homeless children who could only survive by begging and stealing. To the respectable Victorians they must have seemed a real threat to society; and something had to be done about them to preserve law and order.

Many believed that education was the answer, and a number of "Ragged Schools" were started to help meet that need. These were charitable schools dedicated to the free education of destitute children, and they often provided food, clothing and lodging on top of basic education. Charles Dickens's visit to Field Lane Ragged School in 1843 made a lasting impact on him, and it is said to have been a major influence when he wrote *A Christmas Carol*.

In 1870 an act of British parliament allowed "Board Schools" to be paid for out of local rates, which allowed more children to attend school. However, it took another eleven years before schooling up to the age of ten became compulsory (1881), and a further nine years after that until state education became free for everyone (1890).

The government also began to protect the welfare of children in the workplace. The first Factory Act (1819) prohibited children under the age of nine from working in factories and those aged from nine to sixteen from working more than seventy-two hours per week.

In 1833, a second act limited the working hours for nine- to thirteen-year-olds in textile factories to a maximum of forty-eight hours per week. The Mines Act of 1842 stopped women and boys under ten from working underground. Further Factory Acts in 1844 and 1847 established the twelve-hour day for women and the six-and-a-half-hour day for children under thirteen. These laws were enforced by factory inspectors; but they were so poorly paid that they were easily bribed. In addition, many parents were so desperate for money that they lied about the ages of their children so that they could work. Before 1837 births didn't have to be registered, and without a birth certificate, it was impossible for anyone to prove the age of a child.

Life was indeed harsh. As well as appalling working conditions, low wages, slum housing and disease, the majority of the population had no means by which to change their circumstances; and nowhere was this better described than in the writings of Charles Dickens.

Dickens Fact

"Dickensian" = denoting poverty, distress, and exploitation, as depicted in the novels of Charles Dickens.

A Very Victorian Christmas

Prior to the arrival of Christianity in northern Europe, a twelve-day mid-winter "Yule" festival was celebrated, beginning the traditions of using evergreen plants like mistletoe, holly and ivy for decorations, and the burning of the yule log. With the introduction of the Julian calendar, this festival was fixed on December 25 and was combined with Christian celebrations to create the twelve days of what we now call Christmas.

Re-inventing Christmas

The Victorian era saw the re-invention of Christmas in Britain. When Queen Victoria's reign began in 1837, the celebration of Christmas was in decline. Nobody in Britain had heard of Santa Claus; Christmas cards and crackers had not been thought of; and most people were not allowed the time off from work or had the money with which to buy gifts or extra food – but this all began to change.

The wealth generated by the new factories and industries now gave middle class families the opportunity to take time off work and celebrate the festive season over Christmas Day and Boxing Day. The advent of the railways also allowed the country folk, who had moved into the towns and cities in search of work, to return home for a family Christmas.

Children's toys that used to be handmade and expensive were suddenly made more affordable through mass-production in factories. However, they were still too expensive for working families and the poor, whose Christmas stockings, (which first became popular around 1870), would contain only an apple, orange and a few nuts, or maybe a small home-made gift.

Food was a major part of the festivities. In northern England roast beef was the traditional fare for Christmas dinner while in London and the south, goose was favored. Many of the poor had to make do with rabbit. It wasn't until the end of the century that most people had turkey for their Christmas dinner.

The introduction of a national postal service in 1840 (the "Penny Post") paved the way for the sending of Christmas cards. The first Christmas card was created in 1843 by Sir Henry Cole, a wealthy British businessman, who wanted a card that he could send to friends and professional acquaintances to wish them a "Merry Christmas".

In 1846, Tom Smith, a London sweet maker, made the first Christmas cracker. The original idea was to wrap his sweets in a twist of fancy colored paper, but he found that they were more popular when he added mottos, paper hats and small toys; and especially when he devised a way to make the parcel open with a bang!

A Royal Celebration

Queen Victoria loved celebrating Christmas, which she described as a "most dear happy time". With nine children, her Christmases became great family occasions and many of the royal Christmas traditions were described in her personal diaries and in the newspapers of the day. These traditions included decorated trees, the sending of cards, a lavish family meal, and taking gifts to the poor. It was Queen Charlotte (Queen Victoria's grandmother, and wife of George III) who brought the German tradition of Christmas trees to England, and they were a feature of Victoria's Christmas festivities from childhood.

In her journal for Christmas Eve 1832, the thirteen-year-old Princess Victoria wrote:

> "After dinner... we then went into the drawing-room near the dining-room... There were two large round tables on which were placed two trees hung with lights and sugar ornaments. All the presents being placed round the trees..."

And for those less fortunate?

The Victorian era was one of stark contrasts, and Christmas was no exception. For the very poor, the passing of the Christmas season made little difference to their lives.

Following the example set by Queen Victoria, it became fashionable amongst the Victorian middle-classes to give "alms" to the poor (which is what the businessmen are trying to organize with Scrooge on page seventeen). The custom of giving gifts and food to the poor on Boxing Day (December 26) was also revived in this period, when the churches opened their alms boxes and distributed money to the poor.

For those without employment or homes of their own, the workhouse provided the venue for Christmas celebrations. In the era of the parish workhouse, prior to 1834, Christmas Day meant a treat for most of the residents. However, with the advent of union workhouses set up by the 1834 Poor Law Amendment Act, no extra food

was to be allowed on Christmas Day (or any other feast day). Despite that, Christmas Day was one of the special days when the workhouse inmates rested. It took six years for the rules to be revised to allow extra treats — but only if they came from private sources and not from union funds. A change in the ruling seven years later, in 1847, finally allowed the provision of Christmas extras from the workhouse funds.

With the exception of the very poor, Victorian Christmases were a time of celebration, and of families gathering together with the prospect of a feast (however small) and entertainment - all of which is captured in the most famous "Christmas Book" of all time.

A Christmas Carol

Dickens's first "Christmas Book", the best loved and most read of all of his books, began life as seeds planted in Dickens's mind during his travels around England, where he saw children working in

appalling conditions. His belief that education was a remedy for crime and poverty, along with scenes he had recently witnessed at the Field Lane Ragged School, made Dickens resolve to **"strike a sledge hammer blow"** for the poor.

As the idea for the story took shape and the writing began in earnest, Dickens became engrossed in the book. He later wrote that as the tale unfolded, he:

"wept and laughed, and wept again"

and that

> **"thinking whereof he walked about the black streets of London fifteen or twenty miles many a night when all of the sober folks had gone to bed."**

A Christmas Carol took just six weeks to complete, and the book was published on December 17, 1843. It was an overwhelming success, selling over five-thousand copies by Christmas Eve.

It is a book of enduring appeal that, due in no small part to the era of its release, has for many people become part of the festival of Christmas itself, and is one of the best-loved Christmas stories in the world.

Page Creation

1. Script

In order to create two versions of the same book, the story is first adapted into two scripts: Original Text and Quick Text. While the degree of complexity changes for each script, the artwork remains the same for both books.

Panel 1: Wide shot of the room, with Scrooge and ghost small within it, to leave room for the big speech balloons.		
SCROOGE	You travel fast?	You travel fast?
MARLEY'S GHOST	On the wings of the wind.	Very!
SCROOGE	You might have got over a great quantity of ground in seven years.	Then you must have gone far in seven years.
MARLEY'S GHOST	Oh! Captive, bound, and double-ironed, not to know that ages of incessant labour by immortal creatures, for this earth must pass into eternity before the good of which it is susceptible is all developed.	Oh! Chained and bound. I didn't know that life is so short.
MARLEY'S GHOST (2nd Bubble)	Not to know that any Christian spirit working kindly in its little sphere, whatever it may be, will find its mortal life too short for its vast means of usefulness. Not to know that no space of regret can make amends for one life's opportunity misused!	And no amount of regret can make up for a lifetime lost.
Panel 2:		
MARLEY'S GHOST	Yet such was I! Oh! Such was I!	Yet, that was my life.
SCROOGE	But you were always a good man of business, Jacob.	You were good at business, Jacob.
Panel 3: Hand in a downward stroke, a dismissive gesture, as if the very word was dirty!		
MARLEY'S GHOST	Business!	Business!
Panel 4: The Ghost, wringing its hands		
MARLEY'S GHOST	Mankind was my business. The common welfare was my business; charity, mercy, forbearance, and benevolence, were, all, my business. The dealings of my trade were but a drop of water in the comprehensive ocean of my business!	Mankind was my business. My work was nothing compared to the good of mankind.
Panel 5: It holds up its chain at arm's length, and then flings it heavily upon the ground again.		
SFX	CLANK !!! (loud)	CLANK !!! (loud)

A page from the script of *A Christmas Carol* showing the two versions of text.

2. Rough Sketch

The artist first creates a rough sketch from the panel directions provided by the scriptwriter. The artist is considering many things at this stage, including story pacing, emphasis of certain elements to tell the story in the best way, and even lighting of the scene.

The rough sketch created from the above script.

3. Pencils

Once a clear direction is established, the artist creates a pencil drawing of the page.

It is interesting to see the changes made from the rough to the pencil, such as in the last panel, where Marley's Ghost's movement has been increased to heighten the drama.

The pencil drawing of page 36.

4. Inks

From the pencil sketch an inked version of the same page is created. Inking is not simply tracing over the pencil sketch, it is the process of using black ink to fill in the shaded areas and to add clarity and cohesion to the "pencils". The "inks" give us the final linework prior to the coloring stage.

The inked image, ready to be colored.

5. Coloring

Adding color really brings the page and its characters to life.

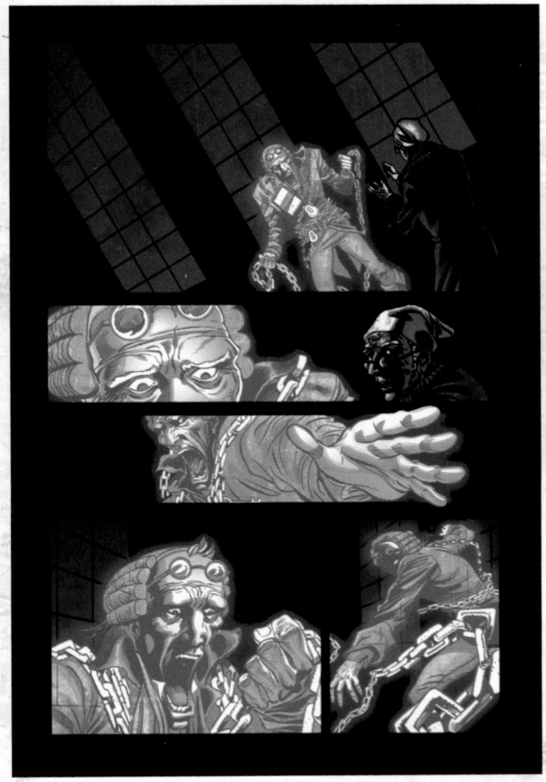

There is far more to the coloring stage than simply replacing the white areas with color. Some of the linework is replaced with color, the light sources are considered for shadows and highlights, and effects added. Finally, the whole page is color-balanced to the other pages of that scene, and to the overall book.

6. Lettering

The final stage is to add the captions, sound effects, and dialogue speech bubbles from the script. These are laid on top of the finished colored pages. Two versions of each page are lettered, one for each of the two versions of the book (Original Text and Quick Text).

These are then saved as final artwork pages and compiled into the finished book.

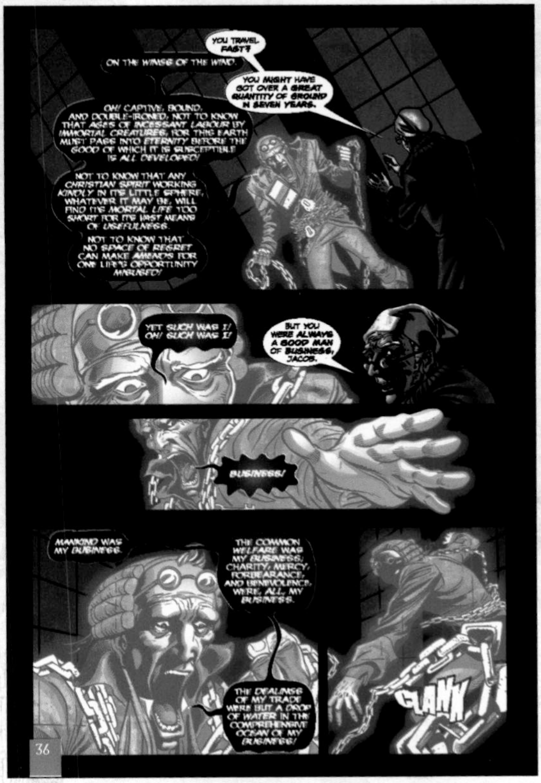
YOU TRAVEL FAST?
ON THE WINGS OF THE WIND.
YOU MIGHT HAVE GOT OVER A GREAT QUANTITY OF GROUND IN SEVEN YEARS.
OH! CAPTIVE, BOUND, AND DOUBLE-IRONED, NOT TO KNOW THAT AGES OF INCESSANT LABOUR BY IMMORTAL CREATURES, FOR THIS EARTH MUST PASS INTO ETERNITY BEFORE THE GOOD OF WHICH IT IS SUSCEPTIBLE IS ALL DEVELOPED!
NOT TO KNOW THAT ANY CHRISTIAN SPIRIT WORKING KINDLY IN ITS LITTLE SPHERE, WHATEVER IT MAY BE, WILL FIND ITS MORTAL LIFE TOO SHORT FOR ITS VAST MEANS OF USEFULNESS.
NOT TO KNOW THAT NO SPACE OF REGRET CAN MAKE AMENDS FOR ONE LIFE'S OPPORTUNITY MISUSED!
YET SUCH WAS I! OH! SUCH WAS I!
BUT YOU WERE ALWAYS A GOOD MAN OF BUSINESS, JACOB.
BUSINESS!
MANKIND WAS MY BUSINESS.
THE COMMON WELFARE WAS MY BUSINESS; CHARITY, MERCY, FORBEARANCE, AND BENEVOLENCE, WERE, ALL, MY BUSINESS.
THE DEALINGS OF MY TRADE WERE BUT A DROP OF WATER IN THE COMPREHENSIVE OCEAN OF MY BUSINESS!
CLANK
36

Original Text

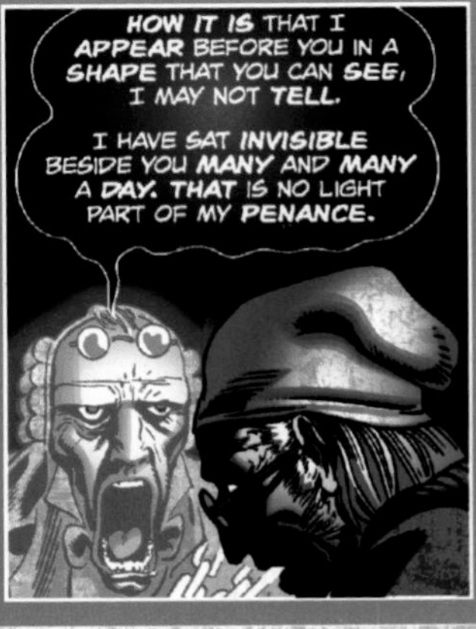
HOW IT IS THAT I APPEAR BEFORE YOU IN A SHAPE THAT YOU CAN SEE, I MAY NOT TELL.
I HAVE SAT INVISIBLE BESIDE YOU MANY AND MANY A DAY. THAT IS NO LIGHT PART OF MY PENANCE.

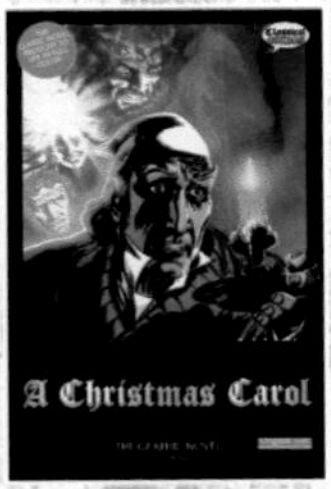
A Christmas Carol

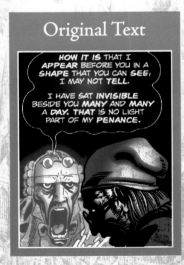

Original Text
(The full story)

ISBN:
978-1-906332-51-8

Quick Text

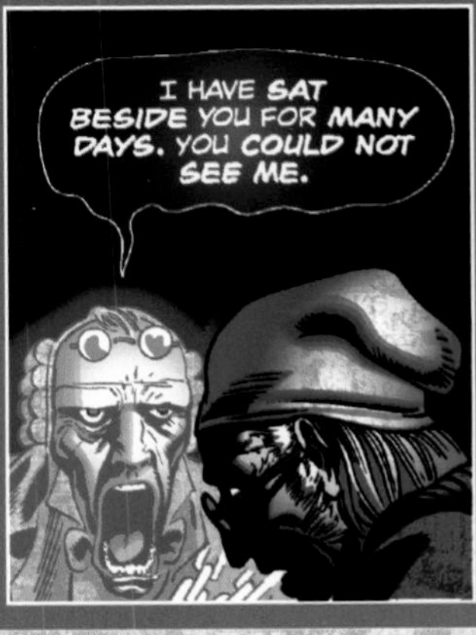
I HAVE SAT BESIDE YOU FOR MANY DAYS. YOU COULD NOT SEE ME.

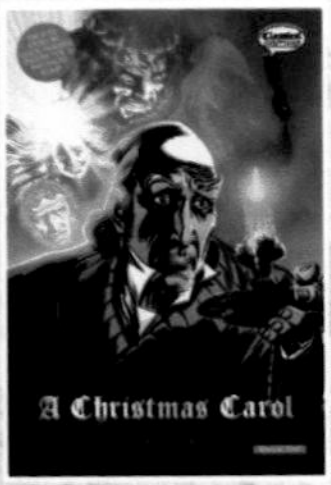
A Christmas Carol

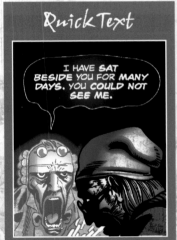

Quick Text
(Fewer words for a fast–paced read)

ISBN:
978-1-906332-52-5

MORE TITLES AVAILABLE FROM

Shakespeare's plays in a choice of 3 text versions. Simply choose the text version to match your reading level.

Original Text	SHAKESPEARE'S ENTIRE PLAY AS A FULL-COLOR GRAPHIC NOVEL
Plain Text	THE ENTIRE PLAY TRANSLATED INTO PLAIN ENGLISH!
Quick Text	THE ENTIRE PLAY IN QUICK MODERN ENGLISH FOR A FAST-PACED READ!

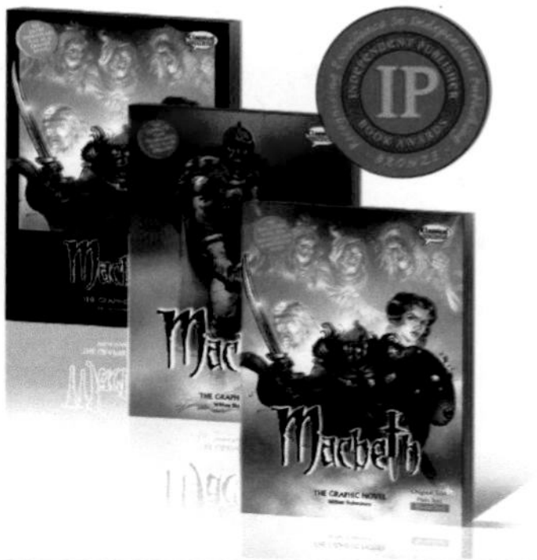

Macbeth: The Graphic Novel (William Shakespeare)

• Script Adaptation: John McDonald • Pencils: & Inks: Jon Haward
• Inking Assistant: Gary Erskine • Colors & Letters: Nigel Dobbyn

144 Pages • $16.95

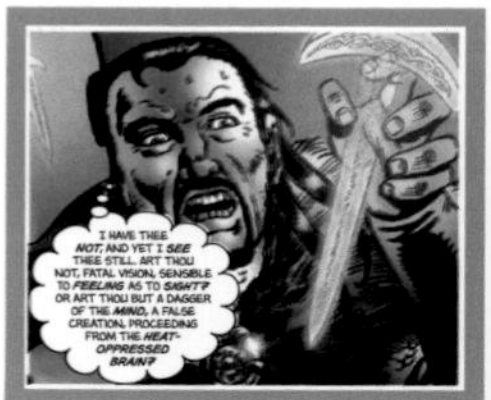

ISBN: 978-1-906332-44-0

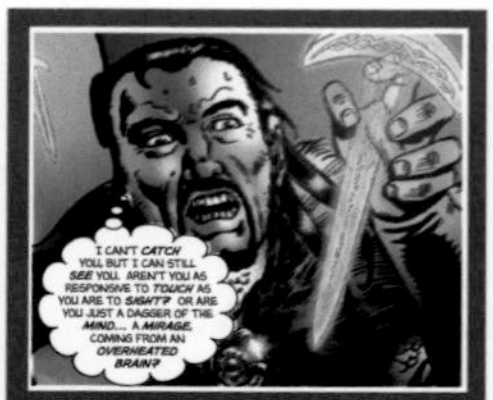

ISBN: 978-1-906332-45-7

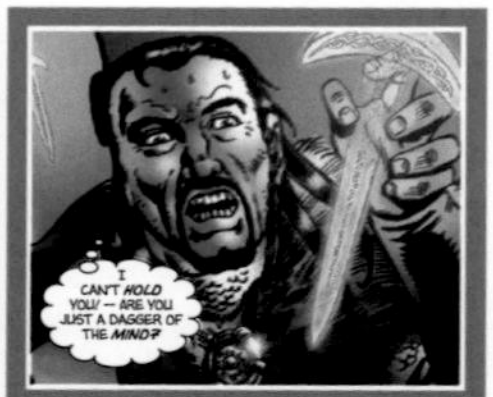

ISBN: 978-1-906332-46-4

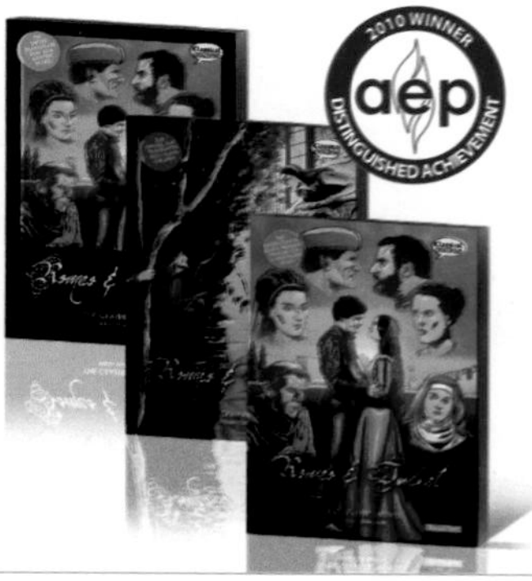

Romeo & Juliet: The Graphic Novel (William Shakespeare)

• Script Adaptation: John McDonald • Linework: Will Volley
• Colors: Jim Devlin • Letters: Jim Campbell

168 Pages • $16.95

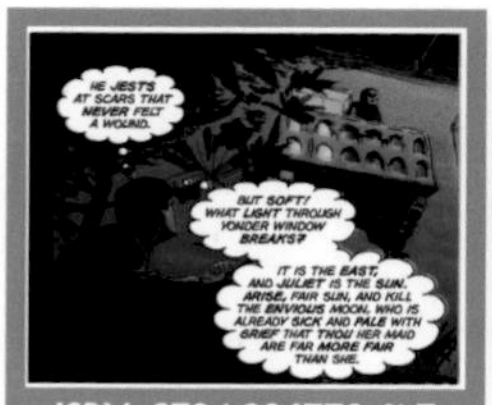

ISBN: 978-1-906332-61-7

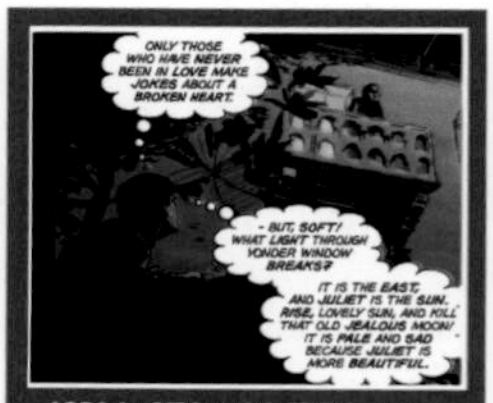

ISBN: 978-1-906332-62-4

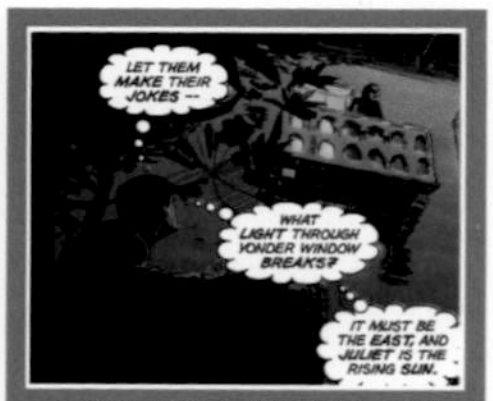

ISBN: 978-1-906332-63-1

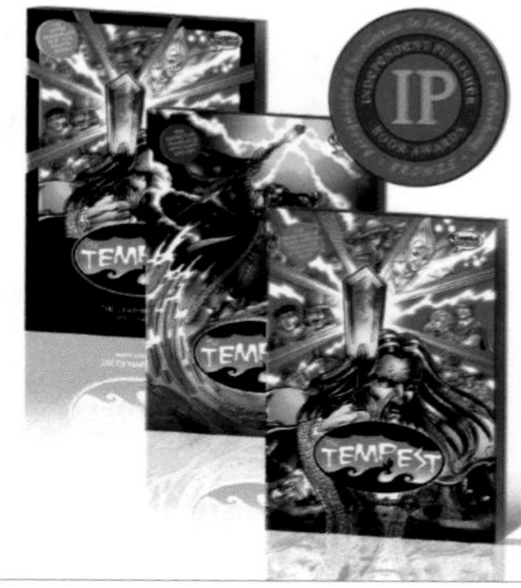

The Tempest: The Graphic Novel (William Shakespeare)

• Script Adaptation: John McDonald • Pencils: Jon Haward
• Inks: Gary Erskine • Colors: & Letters: Nigel Dobbyn

144 Pages • $16.95

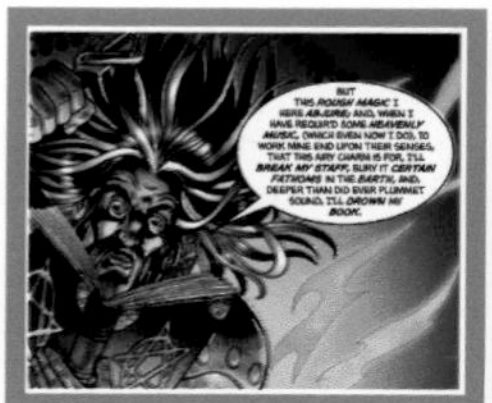

ISBN: 978-1-906332-69-3

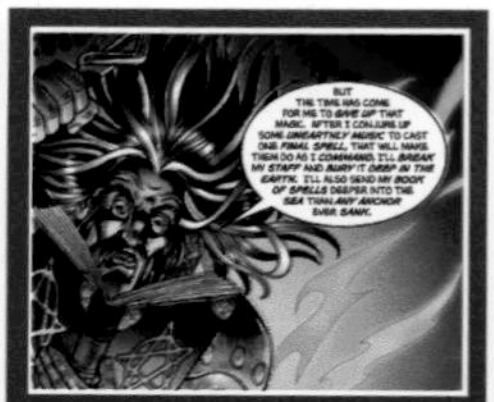

ISBN: 978-1-906332-70-9

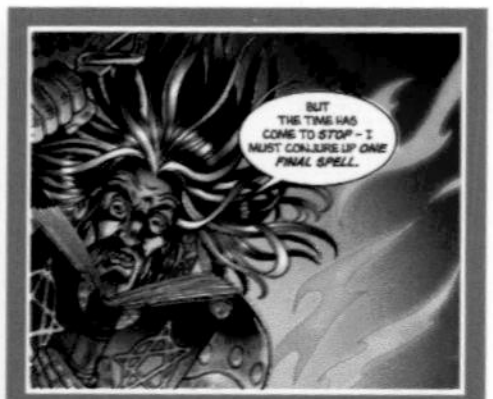

ISBN: 978-1-906332-71-6

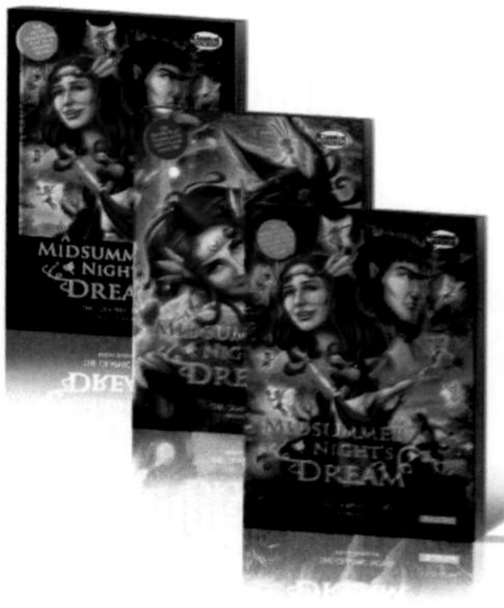

A Midsummer Night's Dream: The Graphic Novel (William Shakespeare)

• Script Adaptation: John McDonald • Characters & Artwork: Kat Nicholson & Jason Cardy
• Letters: Jim Campbell

144 Pages • $16.95

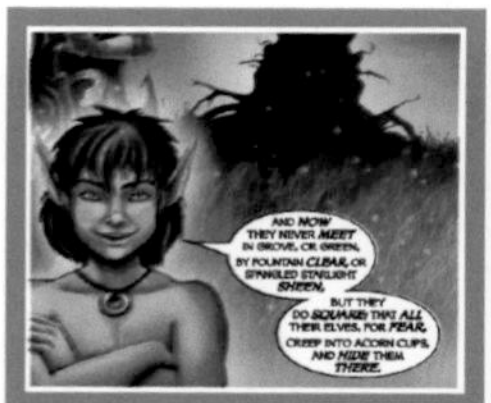

ISBN: 978-1-907127-28-1

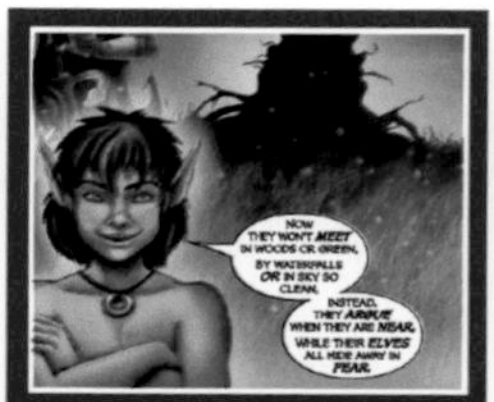

ISBN: 978-1-907127-29-8

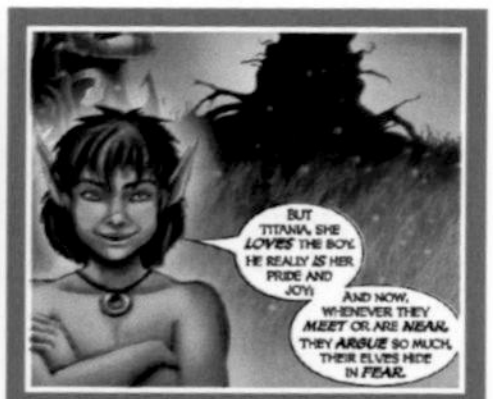

ISBN: 978-1-907127-30-4

OUR AWARD-WINNING RANGE

Classic Literature in a choice of 2 text versions. Simply choose the text version to match your reading level.

Original Text — THE CLASSIC NOVEL BROUGHT TO LIFE IN FULL COLOR!

Quick Text — THE FULL STORY IN QUICK MODERN ENGLISH FOR A FAST-PACED READ!

Frankenstein: The Graphic Novel   [Mary Shelley]

• Script Adaptation: Jason Cobley • Linework: Declan Shalvey • Art Direction: Jon Haward
• Colors: Jason Cardy & Kat Nicholson • Letters: Terry Wiley

ISBN: 978-1-906332-49-5
ISBN: 978-1-906332-50-1

"Cursed be the hands that formed you!"

• 144 Pages • $16.95

Dracula: The Graphic Novel   [Bram Stoker]

• Script Adaptation: Jason Cobley • Linework: Staz Johnson
• Colors: James Offredi • Letters: Jim Campbell

ISBN: 978-1-906332-67-9
ISBN: 978-1-906332-68-6

"I went down into the vaults. There lay the Count! He was either dead or asleep, I could not say which."

• 152 Pages • $16.95

An Inspector Calls: The Graphic Novel   [J. B. Priestley]

• Script Adaptation: Jason Cobley • Linework: Will Volley
• Colors: Alejandro Sanchez • Letters: Jim Campbell

ISBN: 978-1-907127-23-6
ISBN: 978-1-907127-24-3

"But don't you see, if all that's come out tonight is true, then it doesn't much matter who it was who made us confess."

• 144 Pages • $16.95

Wuthering Heights: The Graphic Novel   [Emily Brontë]

• Script Adaptation: Seán Michael Wilson • Artwork: John M. Burns
• Letters: Jim Campbell

ISBN: 978-1-907127-11-3
ISBN: 978-1-907127-12-0

"That minx, Catherine Linton, or Earnshaw, or however she was called – wicked little soul!"

• 160 Pages • $16.95

To see the complete range, and to view samples online, go to www.classicalcomics.com

A Christmas Carol Teaching Resource Pack

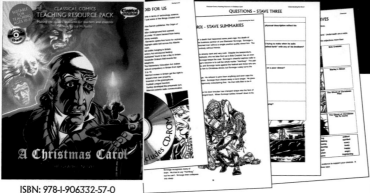

Helping you prepare motivating and stimulating lessons

CLASSICAL COMICS
TEACHING RESOURCE PACK
A Christmas Carol
QUESTIONS – STAVE THREE
ROL - STAVE SUMMARIES
Includes CD-ROM

ISBN: 978-1-906332-57-0

- *Over 100 photocopiable pages.*
- *Cross–curricular topics and activities.*
- *Ideal for differentiated teaching.*
- *CD includes an electronic version of the teaching book for whiteboards, laptops and digital printing.*
- *Only $22.95*

"Thank you! These will be fantastic for all our students. It is a brilliant resource and to have the lesson ideas too are great. Thanks again to all your team who have created these."

"...this is a fantastic way to teach and progress English literature and language!"

To accompany each title in our series of graphic novels and to help with their application in the classroom, we also publish teaching resource packs.

These widely acclaimed 100+ page books are easy to photocopy and include a CD-ROM with the pages in digital format, ideal for whole-class teaching on whiteboards, laptops, etc or for direct printing.

These books are written by teachers, for teachers, helping students to engage in the play or novel.

Suitable for teaching ages 10-17, each book provides exercises that cover structure, listening, understanding, motivation and character as well as key words, themes and literary techniques.

Devised to encompass a broad range of skill levels, they provide many opportunities for differentiated teaching and the tailoring of lessons to meet individual needs.

TEACHING RESOURCE PACKS AVAILABLE TO ACCOMPANY THE SERIES

Macbeth

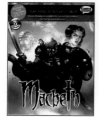

Macbeth
978-1-907127-73-1

Romeo & Juliet

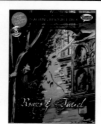

Romeo & Juliet
978-1-907127-74-8

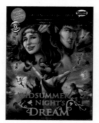

A Midsummer Night's Dream

A Midsummer Night's Dream
978-1-907127-76-2

TEMPEST

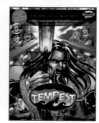

The Tempest
978-1-906332-77-8

Great Expectations

Great Expectations
978-1-906332-58-7

Jane Eyre

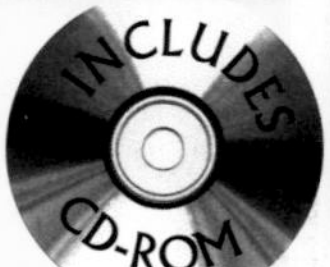

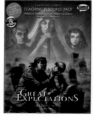

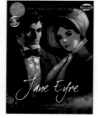

Jane Eyre
978-1-906332-55-6

A Christmas Carol

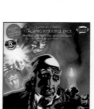

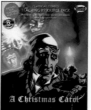

A Christmas Carol
978-1-906332-57-0

Frankenstein

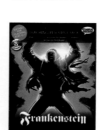

Frankenstein
978-1-907127-77-9

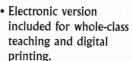

INCLUDES
CD-ROM

- Only $22.95 each.
- 100+ photocopiable pages.
- Electronic version included for whole-class teaching and digital printing.
- Cross-curricular topics and activities.
- Ideal for differentiated teaching.
- Includes CD-ROM with pages in PDF format for direct digital printing.

HELPING YOU PREPARE MOTIVATING AND STIMULATING LESSONS